Kate Abley

Hausa Blue

For Ian

Chapters

Heathland, Outside Stralsund, Stralsund, Germany

The chosen world is different from yours in other ways but it was changed most by Fräulein Greta Roewer on Friday the 13th of April 1917.

Greta and her mother, Frau Hildegard Roewer, were busy on the heathland on the outskirts of Stralsund, a two-hour train ride from their home in Neustrelitz in the Duchy of Mecklenburg-Vorpemmern in Northern Germany. Almost equidistant from the Eastern and Western Fronts of what was already being called the Great War, it was a lonely spot and the salt air from the Baltic blustered about their sturdy tweeds and stout boots.

They were more or less engaged in another specimen hunt on behalf of the rising Arachnologist Mr. Carl Frederick Roewer, husband and father. He had already begun to specialise in Opiliones or Daddy Long legs and was pursuing this passion in Ecuador at the time.

Frau and Fräulein Roewer were responsible for the majority of Herr Roewer's European specimens only partly because damp air brought on his recurrent Bronchitis. Frau Roewer had been acting on a fear since before Fräulein Roewer's conception. She believed that her female child, now in her 15th year, and unusually tall standing already at 1.8 metres [5' 9''] in her stocking feet, suffered from Acute

Melancholia, which had afflicted her maternal grandmother. As a result, Fräulein Roewer had been subject to treatment for over ten years by her maternal grandfather Dr. Emil Kraepelin.

The eminent psychiatrist was the leading proponent of the then still dominant theory that the chief origin of psychiatric disease is biological and hereditary malfunction, and not being married to a terrible husband. As a result, Fräulein Roewer had become, had Dr. Sigmund Freud been consulted, severely neurotic and narcissistic, or in her former nanny's words, 'hatte nicht alle ihre Tassen in ihrem Schrank '[did not have all her cups in her cabinet].

Thus, Frau Roewer's prime motivation in helping her husband discover over a third of all known types of Daddy Long Legs was that she believed that her daughter's perceived affliction was alleviated by diligence and excercise. The laying of string grids of exactly one metre square on rough ground, careful scrutiny and note-taking, beginning in the top left-hand centimetre, was, in Frau Roewer's belief, healthy excercise for the non-diseased parts of her only daughter's mind.

Fräulein Roewer did not agree. Unbeknownst to her mother, she much preferred to practice posing various greek style tableaus in front of the bedroom mirror with a more than willing housemaid. All the while smoking cheroots and sipping her papa's brandy.

In other worlds, those years examining herself and others barely coiled in sheets and shawls, and her adult height of 1.83 metres [6'], would help her become the toast of the Berlin nightclubs by the age of 25.

In the gloam of early evening Fräulein Greta was dressed in loose stays and sensible dark green skirt, jacket and hat, which complimented the rough heath. She placed her ear and fingers to one cold railway line, which cut stiffly across the plain. Her long lower limbs stretched over its parallel. The scent of wet grass and the damp dark earth beneath the cold metal filled her nostrils and the lines began to tremble. She smiled gently and let her lips rest on the steel.

Frau Roewer called out,

"I've found one!"

Fräulein Greta did not hear her. The tracks by then had begun to thrum. The beating of the young girl's heart was doing the same. The cool spring breeze on one cheek and the cold metal on the other invited her extremities to extend and contract in a quickening rhythm. Sensual pleasure was hard to come by in a great many early twentieth-century bourgeois Germanys, including this one, and not so little Greta was consumed by it. She shuddered from top to toes as the great iron beams thudded an ever faster and fiercer rhythm. Never having come this close to ecstasy before she was understandably deaf to her mother's exulted cry, and indeed the approaching locomotive. The heat of her body jarred brilliantly with the cold thick steel and she began her first climax. Her mother looked about her and called again,

"Greta, I've found one!" But the blood rushed in Greta's ears and the grey steel throbbed through her body until her face relaxed into a sweet smile and she lay replete, still pulsating on the tracks.

The driver of the secret and therefore untimetabled train did momentarily see a shapely matriarch standing triumphantly with one hand in the air, clutching what he thought was a jam jar in the middle of a field. He did not see Fräulein Roewer or the enjoyment rekindled from the ever more intense vibrations caused by his engine. She was killed instantly. The train careered from the tracks and rolled over four times before exploding in front of the Frau who dropped what was in fact a specimen jar.

In other worlds, Frau Roewer had suffered from repeated attacks of anaemia and her attachment to her doting mother, who was an excellent nurse, had been stronger. She had seen that her father was an awful man and had not adhered to his soon to be outmoded beliefs. Nor had she overcome her repugnance for the great outdoors. As a result, she had been scolding Greta in the sitting room for slovenly crewel work at the time that the train whistled over the heath and into history. In more worlds, she had not spotted the Daddy Long Legs that day because her mind was on other matters. An old flame, her first and true love had written to her that morning professing his undying devotion, and inheritance of a small fortune which would enable them to enjoy a 'neustart' in America. Staring into the middle distance she had seen Greta and averted the disaster with a,

"Get up at once young lady."

In yet more worlds, Herr Roewer had taken up the violin as his mother had secretly desired and/or married a bassoon player from Heidelberg. In most worlds, including yours, Greta did not exist at all.

In that world, also killed were the train driver, his assistant, three guards and all 33 passengers. The latter were members of the Russian Bolshevik Party returning to their homeland to intervene in the revolution, which had begun there in February that same year. Their number included Mr. Vladimir Ilyich Lenin and it was with him the German Government wanted to further destabilise their Eastern enemy by smuggling him home. Those Bolsheviks did not reach the Finland Station in St Petersburg three days later. Lenin did not climb onto an armoured car to address the workers and soldiers there, and he did not say,

"The people need peace; the people need bread; the people need land. And they give you war, hunger, no bread – leave the landlords still on the land... We must fight for the social revolution, fight to the end, until the complete victory of the proletariat. Long live the worldwide socialist revolution!"

So, Fräulein Roewer never became an infamous Nightclub dancer where she was able to indulge in the physical pleasures denied to her in her younger life. Instead of never forgiving her daughter until she died of old age in 1951, Frau Roewer belatedly discovered Freudian Analysis, never forgave herself and died of an overdose in 1933.

The February rising in Russia ended with bloody repression and the re-establishment of the absolute power to the Czar on November the 11th 1918. In Britain, the Representation of the People Act of 1918, which granted the vote to certain women over the age of 30 and gave the vote to all men over the age of 21, as well as all subsequent extensions of the franchise did not happen. This meant that only approximately 20% of the population, all male, could vote in British Parliamentary elections.

The Great War continued with increasing desperation and horrors committed by both sides until 1947, when the exhausted Triple Alliance finally conceded to a bankrupt Triple Entente.

The Daddy Long Legs escaped unharmed and went on to live the exact same life that it led in every single one of the worlds that press on and around into infinity.

Do not let the above give you the impression that individual human beings usually have much sway on the course of events. Be they king or cobbler most people simply help or hinder what was already happening in the connections between us. From Menelaus, Marmaloth and Menkhaure Snaaib all the way to Macron, Merkle and May the leaders of men have been mere grit or grease on the wheels of our interconnections. Only occasionally does one person make any real difference. Such were Labarna, Laozi and Lenin, except of course in that world Lenin wasn't and the 'game changer' was Fräulein Roewer.

Hence, perhaps paradoxically, perhaps not, so that you better understand that it is actually the space between individuals where your future is usually born, this intervention takes the form of the story of a small group of people from that world.

This method has serious limitations of course. But unfortunately, almost all of you are obsessed with turning almost everything into stories of one kind or another and it appears that you cannot make sense of information without these simple little beginnings, middles and ends.

Since the ancient Greeks these stories have mainly relied on, at most, a tiny handful of characters; heroes, villains and their variations, who move the story along like a piece of clockwork. Despite the obvious flaws, our desire that you learn from other worlds is so great, and in order to communicate with you as successfully as possible, an attempt to indulge this primitive need has been made. The villains are easy to identify, and although from our point of view, what appears to make a hero is a combination of coincidence and an individual reacting positively at a critical moment, we have managed to find some for you.

Your simplistic notion of time has also forced us, where possible, to recount this narrative, which takes place over three days, strictly in the order in which it occurred for the characters concerned, and of course the other concession of employing the past tense throughout.

The fact that we can, for the time being, only communicate with you via Morse Code means that we cannot provide illustrations at this time and so our sterling friends at the Top-Class Continuous Wave Operators' Club (TOC), Epping Branch, have made themselves available for transcription, as well as asking many pertinent questions for clarification. Pictorial and audio information will become available upon our entry to your universe, the possible timings of which are available on our website to be found below.

The choice of communicating in the English language is simply a matter of numbers; more of you can read and understand it than any of your other tongues. We are of course unable to communicate certain differences in the annunciation of English in this world; our colleagues on your planet surmise that the acceptable accent in the locations herein sounded like a mid-western American affecting the speech of a lower-class

Londoner with Caribbean antecedents ineffectually, but that it immaterial for the time being.

Other historical anomalies have led to slight differences in vocabulary. We have constructed what follows so that the meanings of words that might be new to you are implicit in the text. In addition, those English words whose meanings vary significantly from yours, or do not exist in your lexicon, are included in a glossary for clarity.

We understand that the members of the TOC, Epping Branch, being British men of a certain generation, may use a vocabulary, and grammar, that is different from yours. Our attempts to elicit the input of younger and perhaps more representative English speakers proved futile. Therefore, if there is another word, or word order, below whose meaning you do not know, we suggest that you temporarily repurpose the supercomputer you most often use to laugh at incongruously behaving cats.

Please note that the TOC, Epping Branch and our web designers are volunteers belonging to not-for-profit organisations and as such do not have the personnel to deal with queries from members of the public. **PLEASE DO NOT CONTACT THEM**. As you may be aware, the TOC was selected, from some distance away, for three reasons, its reliable age - it was established in 1938-, its independence from state and commercial interests – it is small group of gifted amateurs, and of course its motto, "A man should keep his friendships in constant repair" - Samuel Johnson (1755). We cannot apologise enough for the disruption and inconvenience caused to these dedicated hobbyists and their families and thank them again for all their hard work. **Please direct all enquires to the website,** the URL address of which can be found at the back of this book. We aim to respond within three to five years. Thank you.

Private Accommodation, West London, England

It was one hundred years later to the hour, the 13th of April 2017, a Thursday, and the aforementioned connection between us was what was on our hero's mind as it happens. Albeit in a 'So near and yet so far' kind of a way. He was not a deep thinker, more of a practical person who liked to have a goal and get doing. Therefore, like so many of that ilk when presented with a hurdle where doing something is not possible, he was drunk. He had been drinking steadily since two. He turned away from the beginnings of the sunset he had been contemplating blearily, all oranges and pinks, and said to the East,

"So near and yet so far away," and sighed a wonky sigh.

He had done everything he could, He was ready. But how would he ever get to meet her? 'Accidentally' bump into her? Find a common interest? He needed to meet her, establish some sort of relationship, win her trust, or the only plan he had would not work. He had written and called every contact he had ever made. Even his old friends from Temple Mills, some of whom were quite high up now, but no-one could help him. He took another sip of whiskey and turned back to the sky; it had some sort of greyish mauve in it now. He liked mauve.

There was something akin to a deep sigh from inside the room and our heroine said reluctantly,

"I'll make some tea."

Prison Accommodation, Tower of London, England

Our story also starts one hundred years after Friday the 13th of April 1917 with poor Miss Dipa Cameron. She had been taken to the Lanthorn Tower of the Tower of London, England, in November the previous year. There she had been charged with fraud by false representation and probable Treason until the adjudication of the provision in the Treason Act, 1351, which stated, '...*because that many other like Cases of Treason may happen in Time to come, which a Man cannot think nor declare at this present Time; it is accorded, That if any other Case, supposed Treason, which is not above specified, doth happen before any Justices, the Justices shall tarry without any going to Judgement of the Treason till the Cause be shewed and declared before the King and his Parliament, whether it ought to be judged Treason or other Felony...*' could be carried out.

The otherwise farsighted legislators of the 14th century had not foreseen the present eventuality, which took place six and a half months into Miss Cameron's incarceration, that there was no King, or Queen, Parliament had been abolished and nearly all the Justices had all been replaced. The New Management had promised to abide by most existing laws until such time as they could invent new ones and so she was being held in the same place simply on the false representation charge (maximum sentence 10 years including pre-trial detention and possible further reduction for good behaviour).

Today, she happened to be wearing the traditional Royal Hausa Blue check crinoline in which she was arrested but she had removed the hoops. Denied even a needle and thread she held her now over long skirts and shawl tightly around her, more for security than warmth. She was ignorant of the sentencing provisions of the Fraud Act 2006, and out of Jus. She kicked up her skirts to pace up and down across the flagstones as former Queens held in the Tower are wont to do.

Poor Dipa wasn't cold, in pain or hungry anymore but she had hardly spoken to a soul for nearly half a year. She had lost track of time and what was going on outside. All she knew was that the Yeomen guards were now wearing Fatigues and that they believed they were under New Management, whatever that was. That's all the guards had said when they informed her of the revised charges and brought in the 'things to make her more comfortable'. That had been weeks ago and no-one had said a word since, simply fed her and replaced the cartridges in the new shower and commode and locked the door again. She had begged this new lot for a Runu so that she could find out what was going on, maybe contact a lawyer. Pleaded time after time for a newspaper. They never responded. They all just glared at her, the same as the others. She hadn't seen a smiling face since she got here. Unless you count sneers and leers and contemptuous laughing at the beginning.

Not a glimmer of human feeling, if they were human, she had no way of telling. And she had not been touched for months. The beatings had stopped and then no-one laid a finger on her. Not one touch. No one had held her hand or let their body brush close to hers even for a moment. Her pacing led her to the bare white wall again and she slapped it hard. And she was out of Jus, had been for two days, the old guards might have beat and starved her but at least they gave her a decent supply of Jus.

Dipa glared at the wall for a moment, then her shoulders slumped. Reluctantly, she sat down at the little table under the window where the weak afternoon light was best and picked up the pen. An open A4 notebook took up most of the only tidy surface in her cluttered cell. 'I'm just a stupid and wicked girl' was all she had written so far. Written days ago, perhaps weeks. Maybe. Each day went on so long she gave up guessing when the meals would come, or the dark, but when she remembered the days that went before they felt like the blinks of a tearful eye.

But every day, she came back to the table to write something more, she did want to defend herself. The shaking in her hands, ignorance about what she was accused of and who she was writing to made her drop the pen again. She reached into a pocket for some Jus and then remembered she had none.

Out of the window, only a few feet from the Tower walls, and the Old Riverside Walk beyond people were there. Some hurrying, some wandering along. She had not seen anyone look up at her window for months. They had forgotten her. She could die in here and they wouldn't even notice. Their Great Queen, their new Gloriana. She began to cry for the first time that day. She needed her Jus.

Sniffing made her inhale the damp acidic mustiness of the place and reminded her of her mum's old flat in Limehouse. They had sat together in front of their big window for the light as well, her and her mum. The same yellow rippled light bounced off the Aspic that slapped on the rain-stained glass of the Arcade. That flat wasn't in the Arcades though was it, too far East. When she was small Dipa would look at the domes looming up over the city a mile away like a great glass jelly mould. Limehouse was a dank and smelly jumble of dirty brick and the only bit of green was the graveyard. Crows the only birds. The arcades were clean and neat with wide tree-lined roads, the birds never slept and never stopped singing and there were parks with flowers in.

From their flat tared roof under her bedroom window with the peeling paint, she would daydream for what had felt like a long time. She would see herself in one of the big white houses under the glistening Arcades, dancing in a cyow long dress with a hundred pleats at the waist, and she would dance. Remembering dancing round and round that old roof in imagined floating skirts she sang an old Flickers tune into her cell until she was called in to hem by her dead mother and the song died in her throat.

Stitching, always stitching ever since she could remember. Stitching gowns she never thought she'd ever own. But out on that flat roof, especially when she could wear her Eid clothes, she would spin and twirl and sing some silly song from the Flickers. She had told them all that again and again, each blow had made it more real. The last year of her life, before this cell, all of it had all been based on that fantasy; to be a cyow princess dancing in a lovely dress, to live in a palace and be adored by all the people of the Empire. That was all, a little girl's dream.

A fresh torrent of tears welled up and overflowed, she brushed them away with the back of her hand. She looked down at her trembling fingers, wet and shining, and wiped them on the dress sewn by someone else. The purple bruises from where those beasts had punched and stamped were long gone. Her skin had returned to its usual colour, which everyone had said was the same cackooder shade as Princess Victoria. She knew it wasn't. She had to put on make-up at least a shade darker to mimic the woman who became the Queen Empress on the night she died.

It was the hair that really made them look the same, long, thick, smooth Indian hair, that they both got from their grandmas. She was stupid and wicked as well, that never-Queen Victoria. She should write that down, how the Great Queen Empress with blood as blue as Royal Hausa was a stupid, selfish, Peela loving Pipe-Licker and would have brought the Empire to its knees in a matter of weeks. But she couldn't see for crying.

The lock on the door began to turn, it must have been supper time. Dipa, ever the lady, tipped her head back to blink away the tears, smoothed down her hair and sat up straight with her face still to the window. The warm scent of Ackee and Salt Fish came in with the draft and Dipa had to force back a fresh wave of tears because it so reminded her of her mum's version. Not turning around to reveal the state of her face, a Queen's voice she hadn't heard all day, her voice, said royally,

"Thank you, would you leave it on the other table please." She heard some more military boots walk in and say,

"What, here?" Wide-eyed, she turned around and saw another set of Fatigues, and a smile.

Meghna River, Near Haimchar, Bengal, India

One hundred years after Friday the 13th of April 1917, again to the hour, our story also begins on the other side of the planet where it was just after midnight and therefore Friday the 14th.

Behind the wheel of a small flat cargo boat, heavy in the water, stood a short, round and balding man. He could have been a paunchy Indian, Algerian or French middle-aged man. He was, more or less. But because he was competently steering his vessel up one of the smaller channels of the Meghna River in what you call Bangladesh and your world cares so much about these things we will call him Bengali.

He had the large heavy eyelids that in someone taller and slimmer can make another person go weak at the knees. But on him, together with his slight jowls and double chin, they generally encouraged people to attempt to work out which reptile he most resembled. Especially when he blinked or looked sideways. This was useful because whatever 'colour' his blood was it was definitely cold. Cold and thin and dependent on an external source of heat to flow.

As the vessel traced the narrow meander, a fresh buttered pea smell rose from the water and mingled with a soft breeze heavy with the scent of night-flowering Kamini and Sheuily. He was sick of breathing in all that sweetness night after night.

His low light shining from the wheel deck attracted a thousand insects from the tree clumps that stood on the banks. He paid no attention; this river was capricious. There were shifting sandbanks barely beneath the surface that could rip the hull and send their precious cargo, their last hope, down into the ooze. There were shallow places that could grind them to a halt and they might never be able to move on again. It would be the end. It did not matter that he had been at the helm all night, or the nights before, they must press on along the winding black.

She staggered up onto the slimy deck with two tin mugs of hot tea. With hair frizzy from the heat and in need of a wash, she still had the long limbs and heavy eyelids that had made several people's legs wobble over the years. She handed him his tea and stooped to lounge with easy grace on the low rail, staring blankly into the dark water in front of them. She did not sigh; she didn't need to. Profound languor almost shone out of her. His eyes washed over the beauty so complete that it couldn't be forgotten even when one got to know her. Her nape, her neck, her back, waist, hips, legs. Sometimes he likened her behind to a small juicy pear, sometimes at peach. Always ripe.

Her long fingers wound a loose glistening ringlet and she let out a long breath. She did not need to keep her eyes on the river as he did. She could be letting them wander up into the black-black sky littered with stars a million miles away from this sorry situation.

When he was a callow youth, he had had a rather pretty and acquiescing servant, he had forgotten what she was for, who spent all her spare hours embroidering. She would sit up in her small cot in the servants' quarters and gabble on about her little life while she poked silver thread in tiny dots on an old bit of black velvet. She said it was to remind her of the night sky here at home as she followed the family hither and thither all over the world. She once held the scrap of sky up for him to admire as he dozed on her soft belly. The end result looked twee, if not downright boring. She had shed a tear when he said so. Now, vast innumerable miles of space were randomly speckled with the light of a thousand suns by pure accident. And while the visual effect was essentially the same as the uninspiring needlework, the firmament coerced a sense of gaping awe.

Perhaps his companion now was like those stars, brilliant, untouchable, looking down at the brackish water and feeling nothing.

There was a jilt as the vessel scraped against something hard. He refocused on the task at hand.

Feet apart and firmly planted he looked like he had been standing there steering and sipping his tea for a month. He had, more or less. And given that they still had at least another two days before they reached their destination, and did not have much to say to each other, we shall leave the two of them shuddering up the river in the dark for the time being.

The Old Riverside Café, East London

The dark-suited man turned the guide book page deftly and took a small sip of passable coffee. The Normans had built those walls well. He would have to find another vantage point. But he would finish his coffee and his chapter. Then he would complete his circumnavigation admiring 11th-century masonry as if there were no hurry. The various shades of grey were strangely comforting despite what was going on behind them. And the exercise would do him good. Perhaps his old life had been a little too comfortable. Now, he would take a minute to touch the stones that appeared chalky, even ephemeral, but were actually rough, hard and quite real.

He brushed a speck of froth off his cuff carefully. His standards would not slip even if his position had. His rank could resume, perhaps in weeks, if he continued in his duty. Besides, the Chief. The Chief claimed to be an Anglophile but an appreciation of a good suit and a couple of historic battles was hardly love. However, The Chief had decided to pretend that there was no doubt that they would be equals again and there was no choice but to play along.

His chair wobbled a little as he looked up at the ancient impassive structure. Portland stone apparently, quite a versatile material.

The Langthorn Tower

"Koushik!" Cried Dipa and knocked the chair over as she ran. Koushik put down the tray before she stopped suddenly in front of him and stared deeply into his face, "...Koushik?" He grinned,

"What? You think I'm a Krito now, do you? Feel that." and he put out a skinny arm for her to feel, like he had when they were younger, and grinned some more. Dipa threw herself around him and wept,

"Koush, Koush! I thought you were dead!" in her old voice from their childhood. He hugged and wept as well.

"Sanoo, sis'," he said through his tears, "...or should I say, your Majesty," and they both laughed a little bit. Then he sniffed and pushed her back a little, "...you alright?" He asked, inspecting her now and seeing she was trembling.

"Cushty," she replied slightly sheepishly. "...I've been baban stupid." Kaushik looked down at her, a sad expression on his face, and then away,

"Yes, well. I came as soon as I knew it was you," he said and Dipa heard a polite cough behind him. She pulled away and looked around his broad shoulders.

"Sanoo," said an older woman standing near the door. She was not smiling and had her head held to one side, "...I'm Liberty." She was wearing an obviously Yangan black and silver Varanasi silk brocade hobble dress that Dipa knew had been fashionable the season before she had been incarcerated.

"Well, you're in the wrong place then," said Dipa before she looked back to her brother.

"She's your lawyer, Dipa. Liberty Silverman. She's here to help get you out of here, a lawyer…here, sit down and eat something," said Kaushik, "…then I can explain, look its Ackee and Salt Fish, I made it for you." Dipa did as she was told and nodded at Liberty to sit down too with a look that added, 'you're wearing the wrong clothes for your class a year late'. He went and fetched the only other chair for the lawyer while he sat on the edge of the unmade bed. Dipa leaned back and took hold of his hand. "…there's plenty," he said to them both, "…go on, try it," he added to Liberty. Dipa, well used to the extraordinary and very fond of her family's cooking, took up one of the forks from the tray with her free hand. She scooped up a big mouthful of comfort from the tin pot of warm and creamy, spiced and fluffy food.

"Mm," she said partly in encouragement. Liberty moved some tissues and a bottle of foundation to one side, took up a fork and tried a little bit of fish. Brother and sister watched her face, which chewed but stayed blank,

"Very nice." She said blandly and ate no more.

Not letting go of her brother's hand, Dipa dove in and ate as heartily as she ever had, which gave Kaushik the chance to squeeze her fingers gently, and talk some more,

"You see, there's been some changes since you got arrested, quite a lot of changes. Have they told you anything?" Dipa shook her head, hastily swallowed a mouthful of food and said,

"Just, 'you are under the New Management'. The treason charge has been dropped? Heard a bit of shouting outside, that's it. Can you get me out?" Liberty looked down and Kaushik tried to share a determined look from their childhood. Dipa shovelled up another mouthful and chewed.

"Well, there has a been a change of Government, not just here, there are revolutions across the whole Empire, the world. The monarchy has been abolished and…"

"I know, it's been abolished, I think you'll find that I abolished it Koush." Interrupted a right royal Dipa with a mouth full of ackee emphatically.

"Well, yes you sort of abolished it, but you weren't really the Queen were you. No, after you made that, that speech, all Victoria's cousins, Czar Nicholas, The Kaiser, Prince Gaddo and Prince Indrajit, Prince Jyothi of course, Prince Jamal, all of them claimed the throne and, there's been a lot of fighting all over the Empire, the world, but anyway, none of them is in charge, it's a Republic now Dipa, a Democratic Republic. The whole Empire, nearly."

"Prince Jyothi wants to be king? Hah! A what? No Empire? The Empire's gone? Just like that, just gone?"

"Well, not just like that, but yes, The Empire, as it was, has gone. And you, you helped, kind of."

"But? How can it have just gone? What about the army? Oh, oh, of course, cousin Joshi…the glitches…" Liberty flashed a look at Kaushik and he nodded.

"That's what we will need to talk about Dipa, Prince…Jyothi Hausa-Hanover. You do know he wasn't really your cousin, don't you?"

"Of course I bloody know, Kaushik, everyone called him Cousin Joshi, Aditi and… everyone. Vicky, Queen Victoria was his cousin, Adi was his cousin so it was a way for the two of them to show each other how close they were, all of them, us then,"

"Lady Isobel Aditi Egremont-Cooch-Bahar?" asked Kaushik looking at Liberty again.

"Yes…is she, what's happened to her and Cousin Joshi, are they alright? Are they…?"

"Jyothi Hanover is missing and we don't know where Aditi Egremont is either, do you know?"

"How should I know, I'm stuck here aren't I!" shouted Dipa, and she wrenched her hand from his, slammed her fork on the rickety table and started crying again. "…What's going on Kaushik? I don't know anything. I thought you were dead." And her eyes flew wildly towards him before her head fell into her hands, her shoulders trembling. Kaushik got up and knelt at her feet putting his hand on her shoulder.

"Koulla, Koulla Dipa, Deeps, it's Koulla…here," and he handed her a Jus, "…here suck on this Deeps and take a few breaths," she snatched the hard lozenge, put it into her mouth greedily and began to suck, "…there, that's better isn't it Deeps. Blackcurrant, you're favourite," smiled Kaushik and Dipa sighed as her tongue rasped on the outer shell. Her watering mouth broke into the liquid centre and the sweetness oozed onto the roof of her mouth. Letting the saccharine syrup blend with her own juices she swallowed slowly. Then she inhaled as if she were taking her first, or last, breath. Her brother spoke gently, looking up from where he still knelt on the floor, "…Dipa, Dipa, I'm sorry I took so long to come, I didn't know it was you. We can get you out of here. But we have to know what you know before you are tried. You do understand, don't you? Those people, the people who were your friends, some of them are baban bad people and…"

"You think I don't know that!" Dipa fired back, sharp again now that she had had her Jus, "…Look at me! Look where I am! Debota! Bloody Adi! Bloody Cousin Joshi. I'll tell you everything, what do want to know? The cover-up? Corruption, pure corruption. That waste of space Victoria. Ask away Koush', I don't care if I never get out, I don't care if the New Management kill me. Bloody Adi! All of them! Those selfish lying bastards, I'll take them all down with me. Get up off your knees Kaushik for Debota's sake."

"That's the gaskey Dipa," piped up Liberty taking a Runu out of her bag and tapping efficiently as Kaushik did what his little sister told him, "…and don't worry, they're not going to kill you. We simply need to know some things, that's all. For your defence. Then, then we'll work out the best arguments to get you out. We're negotiating the charges with the Transitional Court Dipa, as well as building your case, but we do need to know what happened, whatever the charges might be, we…"

"What Court?"

"There's still courts, and police, and everything Dipa, it's a New Management now, that's all, and soon there'll be more elections," said Kaushik plomping back on the bed.

"Like before?"

"Yes, like before, only this time there'll be new laws and people, people like us will actually have a say in what happens. You'll have a vote too, once you're out. There just won't be a Queen, or Aristois anymore. Things are going to get better Dipa, much better."

"This New Management? What happened to Cr…" and Dipa stopped and looked briefly at Liberty,

"Critical Mass, its Koulla Dipa, it's not a banned organisation now. I'm still in Critical Mass, New Management is an alliance of parties, a temporary Government, until the elections. I'm going to stand in the elections Dipa, how would that be, Kaushik Cameron MP?" and he beamed. "…I'm going to stand in Limehouse, where we used to…"

"Political ambitions aside Deputy, for a moment. Can we get your sister out of the Tower of London first?" Interjected Liberty waving her Runu wryly.

"Oh, I suppose so," said Kaushik equally dry,

"That would be nice," said Dipa joining in, "…have you got any more Jus." Kaushik put a roll of sweets on the table,

"Alright, Dipa, but not too many, you've got to speak slowly enough for us to understand you, think carefully, and please think about coming off them, they're not good for you."

"Yes, you know they were invented during the Great War, don't you? To keep the soldiers killing, and civilians working." said Liberty while she cleared away the plate and put it by the cell door. "… By the French." And she straightened.

"God Liberty, you sound like him," said Dipa, and she took another Jus and started sucking. "…what about a cigarette, have you got any cigarettes?" Liberty and Kaushik both guiltily got out their packets and everyone lit up. "…So, where do we start?" Asked Dipa exhaling a complete accommodation to this new turn of events with her smoke.

"We've got a few days, we won't start tonight, it's too much to take in, the Revolution and everything. I wanted to see you, and let you know I was alright and see you and let you know we're out there trying to help you. We'll get you out soon Dipa," and Kaushik stared into his only sister's dilated eyes and wept. Dipa gave Liberty her cigarette, went to him and held his hand, so like hers.

Liberty balanced the cigarettes on the rim of a tin mug, looked down at her knees and straightened her skirt. She smoked and waited a long time. It was Dipa who finally spoke, wiping Kaushik's eyes and then her own she asked,

"Where have you been Kaushik? I thought you were, I didn't know where you were?

"I only found out you were you a week or two ago Deeps, I had to wrangle things before I could..." but he had answered the wrong question,

"But where were you?" Dipa asked and now he understood,

"I got away Dipa, went up North. I've got friends up there and they hid me. Then mum sent me a pair of Aunken and I could..."

"That was me! I gave her the Aunken. I got them from, I took them from Cousin Joshi's house..."

"Hira Hall? You were in Hira Hall?" interjected Liberty.

"Yes, Hira Hall, Joshi had piles of them, state of the art, just lying around and I took them home and...You had said before, remember, if you had a pair of Aunken you wouldn't need to go away. I thought they were still there, in the flat? Under the Aspic...mum, mum knew where you were? She never said?" Kaushik looked grave,

"It wasn't safe Dipa, you would have been…mum took a big risk, you could have lost your job, or worse, simply by being my sister, let alone an accessory. Then when I could try and find you, you had disappeared. No-one knew where you were. Then I found out and I'm here…What were you doing in Hira Hall Dipa?"

"Well, when I took the Aunken, mum sent them to you? Have you still got them in?" Kaushik shook his head and let Dipa look into his own, un-augmented, eyes. "…No. When I took them I was just visiting, but later, later I lived there for a while, that's where they trained me. To be a Yangan and the Princess. Cousin Joshi worked from home and he had Krito programmes he used to train them to be more lifelike. You know he's ahead of everyone don't you, even China. And he trained me, 'you must be more lifelike Galetea', he used to joke about that. They treat people like us like Kritos any way don't they. He trained me like I was an android. He had some stuff in there I can tell you, do you want me to tell you?"

"It might be useful," said Liberty.

"All in good time Liberty, this is just a preliminary discussion," said Kaushik with an air of authority that Dipa hadn't seen before, not exactly like a big brother, different. He paused before saying, "…once I got the Aunken, I could come back down South and work, work on what turned into this Revolution, and no one could touch me. Did you know they were Aristoi Aunken when you took them?"

"Nothing but the best for Cousin Joshi, they used them for their jaunts, Adi had loads, so did Vic…Princess Victoria, they went all over with those. Well you could probably work that one out. They'd been taken out when they found her though, what was left. That was, But I think Adi must've known because otherwise how could she…? She couldn't do anything on her own, very needy, baban needy. That's why Adi, she must've known, but she did look genuinely shocked? But then she was such a good actor, but then...?" Liberty, an experienced defence lawyer, nodded as if Dipa were making perfect sense and interrupted gently,

"Did they ask you about that, after your arrest?"

"Ask. That's a nice word," shrugged Dipa and she rubbed where the bruises had been. "…no, they didn't 'ask'." Kaushik took Dipa's hands protectively and inspected them, "…I'm alright, Koush, they stopped 'asking' after, maybe a few weeks?" The numbness she had practiced during her torture froze her face for a moment, then she brightened, "…Must've been distracted by your Revolution," and she smiled proudly at her brother as if he had won the running race at a school sports day. She squeezed his hand. "…you got your Revolution Kaushik," and she laughed a little and kept hold of his hand before staring out towards the window. It was getting dark. Kaushik was overcome by his sister's resemblance to their mum and kept looking at her,

"You're baban lucky Kaushik is your brother," said Liberty standing up. Kaushik shot her a look and she stared down at her skirt again.

"The days of luck are over," he said almost speechifying so that how he spent a lot of his time could be seen, "…everyone will get justice now, under the law. And you have done nothing wrong Dipa, you have been used by bad people and we will get you out, and you did help abolish the monarchy, even if it was an accident." Tears were in his eyes again.

"I've been baban stupid, and wicked. Oh Koush I, I…" but she couldn't finish and merely looked up at her brother and blinked away a stray tear. Liberty had moved to the window to give them a little privacy, she looked up from the table where Dipa's unfinished confession lay and said,

"Not wicked Dipa, no. And I don't think you're stupid either. That Jus isn't helping you though… And it's getting late. You need to rest," Dipa gave a sort of sneer but said nothing. "…we will be talking all day tomorrow."

Kaushik and Dipa slowly untangled their hands from each other and let their foreheads touch. Kaushik looked into his sister's eyes and smiled,

"Yeah well, not wicked anyway." And tilted his head against hers, still looking wryly past her tear flecked lashes. She couldn't help but smile and pulled away with a little laugh.

"Yes, rest. I've been that busy," and they all laughed a little then. "…you go now Koush, go and save the world and I'll?" Panic flashed across her face.

"We'll come back tomorrow Dipa. Bright and early, and you can start your statement, properly, all we need is your side of the story, the facts in some sort of order, that's all. And then a few days and…" Liberty interjected,

"And in some detail, we'll need to build a picture for the court, especially given that we're still negotiating the exact charges." Kaushik was holding Dipa's shoulders and her gaze. Now she gave him a strong embrace and patted his back to reassure him. Then she used the words that were almost a mantra when they were younger,

"We're alive," and they both tried to smile but couldn't and cried again. The last time they had shared that phrase there had been three of them left to hold each other. Now there were only two. Liberty didn't know that, she picked up her Runu, pressed a few buttons and put it back on the table,

"I'll leave you this, so you can catch up a bit," she said. Dipa grabbed the pot of fish from the tray and hugged it to her with a smile, while slipping the roll of Jus into her pocket. She put the food on the table and handed the tray to Liberty but Kaushik stepped in and took it.

"I'll get this to the guards, he said and leaned over the tray to kiss his sister, "...we will be talking a lot tomorrow so, 'Eight hours a night and the Empire's alright!'" He laughed and they all chorused,

"'Ten hours a day and the Empire's holds sway!'" And the three stood to attention like when they were kids.

"You'll have to think of some more nursery rhymes now Koush,'" laughed Dipa as they all walked towards the door and Liberty knocked for a guard.

"No more nursery rhymes now, Dipa love," said Koush, and he looked up and bent each elegant finger in turn as he added "...from now on its blank verse or nothing...else." Dipa chuckled. Liberty looked confused, "...It's a game, our mum used to make us...I'll tell you later."

Liberty and Dipa shook hands. The siblings winked and the door shut on Dipa Cameron again. Staring into the space where her brother had stood, one last tear grew and wandered down her cheek.

What is a Runu?

For your information, the Runu mentioned above, similar to your mobile phone, was not almost universally adopted before the revolution of February 2017. The Tim Berniers-Lee of Greta's world wrote very similar report to his boss at the Empire Council for Nuclear Research, but unfortunately, due to the profound grief that can occur even in the most diligent and efficient administrative team at the demise of a much-loved cat, it was mislaid for seven months

Something very similar to the World Wide Web was patented by the American company Hyperway Incorporated in the interim. This company charged a subscription to send and receive information. Carte Blanch and Empire companies launched similar services in 1991 and 1992 respectively using slightly different and incompatible systems and satellites. The Chinese entered the market in 1996.

While a different President also called Clinton made US military satellites available for civilian use in most worlds where he existed, in the world described herein, the Empire, Carte Blanche and China did not do the same. Global Satellite positioning remained almost exclusively for military use in most of the world until 2017.

While this eventuality resulted in the existence of far fewer short videos of arguable quality, another consequence was that digital communication was prohibitively expensive, and less useful, for most people.

A smaller market gave rise to limited capital investment in the devices used to access the digital networks. Thus, the Runu was not as sophisticated as your world's mobile phone. The Empire made Tellyphones, moulded into the shapes of traditional telephone receivers, were the most versatile and innovatory on the market. They contained a tiny screen, augmented by a magnifying lens, in the recess where the earpiece was on an old landline receiver. In addition, being for civil use, they could not be made of plastics using banned substances, see below, and thus the Bakelite versions were rather delicate and subject to cracking and splitting.

Your computer or laptop did not exist in such a useful or lightweight form either. There were HyperTypers, again too expensive for most people, that resembled your old barely portable typewriters, having a small screen in the case lid.

In mid-November 2016, fearing disruption to their supply chain caused by increasing civil unrest, the British Tellyphone Company began stockpiling both components and finished devices at their factory in Ashton-in-Makersfield, England.

On February 15th 2017 the workers at the factory took over the company and with that discovered a comprehensive marketing portfolio from the landline division. The company's supply chain was not disrupted by civil unrest, although the marketing strategy was altered considerably. By February the 29^{th,} every adult over the age of 18 had received a Tellyphone Runu by second class mail, whether they wanted one or not, and the new managers turned their attention to innovation.

An Unknown Location

She could hear dull thuds and scrapes and in the dark place there was nothing else. Only this. And the noises. Hearing things. No Stop, no Go, only this. Dark. No seeing. Seeing things. The noises stopped and there was only dark. And this. Was it pain? What is pain? There was a time before when she had not felt like this. She could not remember. She tried again to remember when she could remember. She couldn't do it. The feeling was another pain. What is feeling? Pains? Teeth? She would have to remember why it was important why she must remember. Dark and pains were happening some more. And other pains were there but she did not know about them. Dark. She pushed the switch in her head so her mind could go somewhere else, somewhere imagined.

Outside Tower of London

It had taken Kaushik a while to find out where to drop the tray and have a chat with the guards. He was famous for his chats with anyone and everyone, it was one of the reasons Liberty so admired him. By the time Liberty and Kaushik were on the street outside the Tower and looking around to work out which way to go, it was definitely dark.

"I think it might be raining?" Said Liberty and they both looked up.

"Maybe a pane's loose?" Said Kaushik. It was impossible to tell if it was raining outside the Arcades that loomed a hundred and fifty feet [46 metres] above their heads. All they could see were a few traces of wrought iron-work to the West where a little light still hung, a weak murky orange battling with the sour yellow from the street lamps inside.

"The Council should get it fixed," said Liberty without thinking, then she added quickly with an eye on her companion "...if there's any point now I suppose, how's it going?" both of them looked South, back towards where the River Thames used to be. They could see some pillars in the distance down the hill, and pressing against the apparently fragile panes; the wall of Aspic. The consistency of set jelly in the chill April air and about 40 feet [12 metres] higher than the level of The Old Thames.

"The draining? Oh, they should get to Woolwich by Midnight!" Said Kaushik optimistically, Liberty looked surprised, "...It's not so deep out East, and it'll get trickier salvage wise, the closer it comes to the centre," he paused and Liberty remembered why. His Mother, his and Dipa's Mother, was in there somewhere. Along with the others. The thousands of bodies found so far; looking exactly as they had when they were consumed. Men, women and children conserved since the 1920s and up to the last year. Sleeping, sitting, hiding, running, whatever they had been doing in their last moments, looking alive in the Aspic's preserving slime. She was about to say something comforting when Kaushik carried on, "…but it's still on time. The whole lot should be gone before the weather gets too warm. And then…have you got a favourite scheme?

"The competition? I don't know? I like the idea of putting the old Thames back, I'd like to see what people saw before, but that can't happen," smiled Liberty, "…have you got a favourite? I read somewhere you were in favour of the Boulevard?"

"Yeah, that or the Park. And there's a general feeling that people don't want to just rebuild everything just as it was, like the Great Fire and the Great War. People want to make something new this time. I don't know? I kind of want to see what's there first. I mean you get glimpses; through it I mean. But it's all murky and yellow and…The newer Gasper lines cross in three places…and it won't drain itself, I had better get going, I'm meeting the Project Team on site tonight, those guys never sleep." And he laughed as he got out his Runu to hail a cab.

"Well, they don't have to Kaushik. But you do. And well. We've got to get back to the Tower first thing, your sister…"

"Yes, I know, my sister," and he paused again. Liberty could only guess why he had avoided talking about Dipa since they had left her.

"Look, Kaushik. I know she's your sister but if she has been, if she was involved heavily with the Egremonts, and Prince Jyothi…you've got to think about your responsibilities to the Revolution. You're an important voice. You're on the Transitional Council for Debota's sake! The war's not over yet. You don't have to be involved. I can defend her, you know I'll…"

"Yes, yes, I know Liberty, you're a great lawyer and, the best, but there has to be some sort of political oversight, you know if she knows anything sensitive…and, but things are less busy now. And once the Aspic is drained, the Council will be dissolved in a few weeks, then? After the election, which I might not win, the China negotiations will at least be well established and…That's the great thing about democracy isn't it, I'm not the only one involved, anyone can do it, and I can devote more time to helping with the case," he smiled, Liberty didn't. He put his hand on her shoulder, "…look, you're the lawyer and I will do whatever you say. But I'm her brother. She's the only family I've got, the only person who's known me for all our lives and and, well. We're on the winning side. Winning. Things are going our way and I have the time to be her brother again at last. We're winning, and. and that's it, really…" he put on his thickest East London accent and said, "…she's fairmleey," and gave Liberty one of the most charming smiles she had ever seen. She couldn't help but smile now. The black cab glided into sight and then purred beside them. "…I'll see you tomorrow, eight-thirty yes? We can talk more then." The cab door shut behind him and drove away. Liberty was left alone in the dark street. She turned and walked West for a four Arcade walk.

Kaushik's cab sped East, Through the Whitechapel Arch and out into the open. It was raining, but not hard. They drove along the Poplar Wall Road as far as it went and then turned North for a block or two past the Aspic riddled rubble of Coretado Dam before heading East again. The sound of the dredgers could be heard from half a mile away. He stopped chatting with the cabbie and put in his Kanas as they approached, so he could talk to Adam above the noise. He was only going because some other members of the Transitional Council didn't fully trust the Kritos yet. An understandable concern, but time consuming. He wondered if Adam had had another thought about the nature of consciousness. It was understandable in someone who was technically less than two-years-old. But he wouldn't get home until at least after eleven and then he had all those papers to read.

They trusted him though didn't they, this coalition of disparate radical groups? They might have their differences, some of them quite important, but there was a sort of trust there. They had fought together often enough to call each other friends, good friends some of them. It was Micky who had brought up 'This Business with Your Sister', and it was his idea to let Kaushik take charge of it, 'for the time being'. Micky wasn't in Critical Mass and had beaten him over lots of issues so he couldn't be accused of bias. Some other Council members had called it what it was, 'A Conflict of Interest'.

Sitting in the cab he remembered just how many interests he had, Dipa was his sister and he wanted her to be free and happy. She had also been heavily involved with the enemies of the revolution. She might still be sympathetic, and she might possess information useful to the cause, or his party's cause, or his personal cause. Only as the rebellion was altering into a revolution had he really seen that he had more than one cause to think about. That was a lot of interests and he wasn't sure where some of the conflicts lay. He wanted her to be free, he knew that. The majority of his party wanted her to stand trial for fraud, of which she was obviously guilty. The majority of the Marxians wanted her let go because she had defrauded the Empire and was a distraction. He didn't know what the majority of the people thought, he had been too busy with everything else that had been going on to try and find out. Certainly, the citizens he met, including the guards and the cabbie all seemed to understand why he was trying to get her out. They all had small families too. Hopefully, he and Adam could finish quickly so that Kaushik could think about Dipa properly before he saw her again.

East to West London, England

Why is it that, when you appear to need it most, your world decides it is unfashionable to use the word 'meanwhile'? At Aldgate, Liberty joined King Alexander Drive, which swept all the way West and then South following the arc of the Old Thames half a mile away. She crossed into the middle path looking forward to a refreshing walk, The Ministry of Health had been dissolved only a few weeks ago and she wasn't used to choosing how she got about, but walking was actually good for you.

Rush hour was over and the wide Central Promenade was almost empty of people. She was not a fan of Neo-Classical architecture and was the first to say that residing in the London Arcades was like living in Paddington station. But she did kamar the Central Promenade. The only concession to modern needs made during the Renesam was ostentatiously arcane, she liked it. Trees growing dark and cool on either side of her, interspersed with the great white arches that held up the roof. High above, drops of condensation sparkled a little against the dark sky. She loved it all; people bustling in and out of all the shops behind the busy hum of cars and buses to her left and right, the odd rumble and hiss of trains beneath, the reassuring thrum of the AC and insomniac birds chirruping over her head. And walking with everyone else, she had liked that. 'All in It Together' as they used to say all those weeks ago before the clocks had sped up, begun to spin. So much had happened so fast and yet her life mainly carried on as normal. Perhaps the walk home was reassuring because she always went home this way.

There were very few people around now and she would have put her Kanas in and listened to some evidence but she had given her Runu to Dipa. She had read the writing on Dipa's table; 'just a stupid and wicked girl'. She had that right. How could one sibling be so sharp and humane and the other so dull and selfish? Still, she would defend her, and not because of Kaushik. Even stupid and wicked girls deserved a great defence, and she was the best criminal defence lawyer in the whatever this society was now.

She would have to get Dipa to talk in great detail to glean something that might help her. She would have to listen to Dipa all day probably. Perhaps more than one day? All day listening to a stupid and wicked girl. Hopefully, the Jus would keep her nished. She sighed and tried to pick up her pace in her new, rather tight, skirt.

Under the Barbican Arch, that marked the division of the City and Cathedral Arcades, her favourite Crossroad Kiosk was still open. She had not eaten since breakfast and bought a Chicken Tikka wrap, nibbling and wiggling with less grace than she would like. The yogurt was made with fresh mint today and she concentrated on getting the perfect balance of warm spicy chicken, soft chapati and tart sauce in her mouth. What Kaushik and Dipa saw in that ackee stuff she did not know.

A laughing couple zig-zagged unsteadily and when they managed not to fall onto her, she smiled. The lovers stopped under the statue of Hermes and kissed affectionately. Then they tripped off, giggling into the night in their complementing black early nineteenth-century dresses of some kind. Dipa would know what sort of clothes they were exactly; she must have some brains. Liberty had seen some of her work on the Princess and those Egremont women. It wasn't possible to create what even she could see were truly lovely clothes without some hanckilly, surely?

Liberty had never taken much interest in fashion. She had perhaps chosen to look a little more proletarian than she was, a sort of solidarity she had supposed. She had only got the dress, which was a lot less easy to walk in than her old Utility-Wear, because dressing like Yangans had become a sort of symbol of the new freedom. Everyone could be a Yangan now? The idea of dressing down to appeal to her lower-class colleagues and clients seemed silly now. Who had she been trying to impress?

What should Dipa wear at the Hearing? Something that made her look small, vulnerable. She hitched up her own skirt up so that she could stride properly. That made her notice her twinging feet. She kicked off the heels and popped them in her bag. An old man with war bleached skin, still in his sensible Utility Suit and sturdy shoes, rolled his eyes and shook his head as he past.

So many things had happened to Liberty on this Promenade, her first walks to college and then to the Courts. Kissing that Georgie that night. And Hera. And Ferdinand. And Delia. And up and down, up and down, home to Chambers, Chambers to Court, Court to home. Never looked at the shops, except as architectural embellishments sometimes. Defending mainly, but enough Prosecution work to keep up her hopes of being a Judge one day. She already had Cab Privileges, but she didn't use them often. Did everyone have Cab Privileges now? Could they just ride in, even drive, cars whenever and wherever they wanted? She didn't know, the streets seemed as full of pedestrians as usual.

And people talked more now. She had seen knots and gaggles of people, gathering without permits, talking passionately under column lights with increasing frequency as the prospect of a New Management had become actually likely. Once, around December, she had seen Kaushik, at the Chancery Lane Exit, in the middle of a large group of people. She had noticed him then, not because she had seen him on the telly, but because he was stunningly attractive. The passion and idealism pouring out of every inch of his slender and fine-boned form had only added to his beauty. She hadn't told him of course. Everybody knew Kaushik was attached to Ashanti Fante, a political refugee from Great Africa and seasoned activist for equality. Around Christmas even she had become aware of an attempt to paint them as some sort of power couple in the media. The magazines and papers had soon realised that such nonsense didn't sell anymore.

She had missed so much. Always working; not only had she been almost oblivious to the stirrings of the revolution but she had missed a lot of life before then too. It seemed that Liberty had not noticed the popular obsession with Yangans and actors until it was nearly over. Other people seemed to have effortlessly kept informed as to who a singer was sleeping with, and absorbed how to hand-make rice noodles. Not her. The wheels of justice, that people moaned about as too slow could actually spin very fast indeed, hardly touch the material facts, grind over people if lawyers like her weren't exceptionally careful.

All those appeals. If justice's wheels could have gone a little slower, she would have had less work, and it would have been more just. She wouldn't have minded less work under those circumstances. She was a capital J-justice fan.

There had been so much new legislation to keep abreast with, interpret. In 1999 she had worked for six months solidly on nothing but test cases on new laws. Then there was the almost annual Anti-Horror Legislation, now all abolished, pulling away at the wheels of justice themselves, spoke by spoke.

The revolutionary legal moratorium, except for reinstating the principles of the Magna Carta, had come as a blessing as far as she was concerned. Admittedly, going back to legal doctrines first written 800 years ago could not be described as progress per se, but it was a step in the right direction for a change.

And she still couldn't cook. All she knew were a few basic dishes that she had learned without knowing from her mother. Maybe the revolution would mean she would never have to learn how to sugar glaze.

She crossed the Farringdon Viaduct with her usual cautiousness, feeling it tremble under the weight of the statues and trees and her own footfall, and then she was in her home Arcade. The Museum Arcade was the least fashionable of the six, with no lift to its Airship tower, which made the structure more or less redundant. And it had the largest homeless population living among the tension cables and lattice beams above. Were they still up there scuttling about, only coming down to beg or rummage? Or had the New Management persuaded them to come down?

She had reached the shiny bottle green tiles of the Queen Nofoto pub at Chancery Lane and turned South towards the Old River. She strode quickly through the shambles of old-looking streets until she got home. She lived in a Glass House, the ornate and elegant three-story buildings that filled each Apse of the London Arcades' Old Riverfront in this part of town.

The Krito doorman had resigned on almost the first day of the revolution. So she picked up her own battered old Ration Box from the empty front desk, the tin felt a bit light, and took the lift to the top floor.

No matter how elegant, no matter how high the ceilings or how many gadgets the Glass House Flats had, few people actually chose to live in them, apart from Liberty. Okay, they were inside the Arcades and the 'bubble' was the place to say you lived, but not many people liked the idea of living so precariously close the stuff that could suck you in and kill you painfully within seconds. The Flats were an ill-concealed buttress against the Aspic that spread out like glistening black ice in the dark beneath her windows. Liberty was the only person in her block who had not been Allocated, which was probably why she had received one with such a great view. She could see all the way to the New Thames Aqueduct under Brixton Hill and the twinkle of countless lights from the tower blocks beyond. She had been right, it was raining, she could always tell somehow.

She put the Ration Box down on her kitchen counter and opened it. Empty, except for a pint of milk and six eggs.

Where were her rations? There was a leaflet from the New London Council, '*You chose not to Opt-in to Voluntary Basic Rations. **This is Your Last Basic Ration**. Following your vote*' What vote? Had she missed another bloody vote? '*...according to the people's desire for freedom in all aspects of their lives and recognition of our capacity for good sense the Transitional Council has abolished obligatory Basic Rationing and Extra Rationing*' How could she have missed this? She had been busy getting the Bolton Five off, that's why. It was a tough case because they had been so baban guilty. '*...for all food, drink and other comestibles. **You will now be able to choose what you eat**. In addition, Meat Free Mondays, Fasting Fridays, Seed and Grain Saturdays, Five-a-Day Fruit and Vegetables, Two-a-Day Snacks and all other dietary obligations are also abolished.*' Liberty did remember now, she had heard it on the walk home one day, she had approved. In principle. But she had hardly any tea left. '*…From today, the value of your Basic Rations will be added, in money, to your income. **And you will be able to choose**. To acquire food and drink you can either: Go to a Shop or Shops, or Shop Runustyle, as you did for your Extra Ration items*' Great. Dipa had her Runu, she couldn't order anything. Liberty picked up the milk and eggs and sadly put them into her designer retro fridge that was fashioned, now ironically, from old enamelled food advice posters from the Wars., '*Making the fat ration go further*', '*Sugar-Save it*', '*Try cooking cabbage this way*', '*Food, don't waste it*' and '*Self-indulgence at this time is helping the enemy*'.

She opened her cupboards one by one, black painted wooden frames inlaid with the same antique signage as her fridge, and found a lonely Ginger, Echinacea, Lemon, Cranberry and Raspberry teabag in a box at the back of the last one. She got out her old tin mug, emblazoned with, *'Why drink Water? 1. Helps to lose weight 2. Healthy skin,3. Get rid of body toxins 4. Healthy heart 6. Prevent joint pain and arthritis 7. Boost Energy 8. Prevent Constipation 9. Reduce Risk of Cancer 10. Improves Productivity'.*

She put in the bag and filled it from the boil-tap. She tried to sip while it was too hot like she always did and turned around to look at her Ration box. A foot tall and 18 inches wide [15 cm x 22cm] It had been her great-grandmother's, it was battered and a bit rusty at the corners, and how many nails had she broken lifting the lid? But she loved that box. Generations of Rations, good times and bad. Sometimes it had been all they had. It had been completely empty for two months during the first Dhool attacks, and sometimes half empty until the Renesam, her grandmother had told her. Sometimes not even tea. But it had kept them alive and well. Now it was useless, simply more metal for the scrap chute.

And she liked her rations every Thursday, one less thing to think about. Now she had to shop for food. Every week. She didn't have time to shop. She would say something to Kaushik. What about her washing? Would they stop the Local Laundry too? Or would she have to opt-in? She couldn't check, no bloody Runu. How was she supposed to know? And no Krito at the door to help, calling himself a name and taking up the double bass in a Psychobilly Rock band. How was that freedom? She took another sip of tea in a kitchen she now realised was decorated to match her old Basic Ration box.

She sighed; she was being reactionary. This was teething trouble. Liberty re-read the piece of paper. She could opt-in for Basic Rations. She would do that first thing in the morning. She needed her Eight hours. That wasn't Empire-Talk that was science. Was it? She would get a new Runu on the way back to the Tower and check. And a pastry. Two pastries. And a cab.

Then it struck her, the neighbours. She had neighbours; she could talk to them. Ask them for some proper tea. Could she? There were two other flats on this floor, could she? She could. She fished her shoes out of her bag, picked up her keys and got another enamelled cup out of the cupboard. This one aptly said, '*Be Patriotic, Buy Empire Grown Tea*'

Out in the hall, she hesitated. Then she resolved. Outside number 7 she halted again. Then she resolved again and knocked on the door.

Private Accommodation, East London, England

Kaushik stooped slowly to pick up the large pile of letters from behind the door, made his regular mental note to get a doormat, and began taking off his jacket as he walked down the hall. As one might expect, Kaushik's flat was scantily furnished. All in creams and browns, but successfully avoiding beige. The bulky furniture in his living room; desk and chair, HyperTyper, printer, bookshelf, armchair, radio and telly and a low table, were plain but of a decent quality. The only incongruous item; what could have been a genuine Pollack in reds and black, was propped up against the fireplace.

He dumped his letters on the table and turned on his lamp, HyperTyper, printer and radio. While the gadgets warmed up, he put his jacket on the back of his chair and poured himself a whisky and water. He sipped his drink as he turned the radio knob away from the newly amalgamated Home and World Service News to find some music. While his HyperTyper continued to whirr into life he sat and scanned the contents of his mail to sort them into piles for 'Now', 'Soon' and a very big 'Later'. He regretting not bringing his tiffin tin home with some of the food Dipa had hardly touched, he needed a boost of energy. The 'Soon' pile was getting quite tall too, he needed half a day to get properly on top of all the minor concerns embodied in all the letters, but when? Then he performed the same sorting routine with his digi-missives. Still new to digital technology and administration, he hand-wrote three lists of all the communications he had received; date, from whom, and a couple of words on the content, to cap the three piles of hand-written and typed paper correspondence. That done he responded to the 'Now's of both kinds, putting the paper replies in a neat pile for posting. The 'Soon's could wait until tomorrow. He was about to get up when he remembered he had to check his Runu too. Luckily there were no urgent messages so he left the phone on top of his letters and got up with a stretch. He looked at his watch; One o'clock in the morning. Not too bad.

Sitting in the armchair he poured himself another drink before reaching for the first of the thick files that lay on the table next to his bottle. He sighed at the pink dog-eared cover which read, 'HM Government. Secret' with the words 'To be kept under lock and key' rubber-stamped on top. Leafing through the typed pages, newspaper clippings, Krito-pictures and photos he scanned resignedly. It was Aditi Egremont's file.

The famous Queen of the Yangans had started early, and indiscreetly. There were Krito-pictures of almost everything. Mind you, she was baban young. He focused on finding only the Krito-pictures. She had apparently not paid attention to the presence of servants, and their inbuilt surveillance feature, until 2011. That was the year where the Krito-pictures almost completely dried up. After 2011, those images there were consisted of innocuous snaps of with now consistently clothed and perpendicular film stars, singers, businessmen, Aristois and of course, his sister's one-time friend, Princess Victoria. The two of them had been friends since childhood but all the clippings, pictures and photos of them together became more frequent in, also 2011. He leaned back and sipped his whiskey.

He could look in Princess Victoria's file but he would probably find a similar pattern, anything incriminating would dry up in 2011. Would they? If there was more former Government information on these two then the New Management hadn't found it when they took over.

He was tired and this was all bollocks. He had the drainage to oversee and negotiations with China, over which he was nominally in charge, to think about. At the same time as swigging back a good gulp from the last of his second glass he picked up a random image of Aditi Egremont and Victoria Hausa-Hanover at some function or other. It was a magazine clipping from the Ascot races in 2014 and they were cheek to cheek smiling at the camera next to a lovely looking horse. The caption read 'Royal Resemblance: Princess Victoria and the young Lady Egremont share their winning bet and good looks'. He was his mother's son and assessed their outfits before his eyes lingered on the faces of two privileged girls out at the races. He could see the family resemblance. Two useless people living off the backs of the rest of us, without a care in the world. He huffed and got up. Now he knew that his sister had been the notorious interloper who replaced the late Princess, he could see how similar she looked to the royal cousins. Why had he never noticed before?

He put the kettle on and poured some coffee essence into a mug. At the back of a kitchen drawer he found an old roll of army issue Jus and reluctantly put one in his mouth. Then he went back to the bloody files with his coffee.

Before he had reached his chair his Runu rang. At one-thirty it might be a horrible emergency, or Ashanti,

"Sanoo? Ashanti!" He said and his heart leapt. "…Ashanti, how are you?" Ashanti was his kamar, his delight, his wonder and he hadn't seen her for six weeks. They had met in Leeds shortly after he had moved there and he had loved her almost at once. Hanckilly, Sandara, witty, wise and wonderful Ashanti. A Pacific history graduate and excellent political operator she was perfect for her current work. She had gone to All America to lead a delegation putting the case for New Management and he missed her intensely every day.

[When the Russian front of the Great War did not collapse in 1917, Germany had not put all her resources into the Western one and so America did not feel compelled to join in. As the horrid stalemate of trench warfare spluttered on year after year in Europe, the isolationism in the US hardened. However, for economic reasons the United States found itself taking an ever-increasing role in the affairs of South America, incorporating all 12 nations officially throughout the 1950s and '60s into All America (AA) with varying degrees of willingness on the part of the former countries, now states. The AA also fought and won a proxy war with China over Japan from 1941 to '45 and lost a proxy war with China over Vietnam from 1959 to '71. All of the Southern American States had already begun their revolutions, but most of the Northern States were still holding out.]

"Yes, yes, she's healthy and still full of vim." He sat down and gladly put his cup on the previously secret files,

"Up to her eyes,"

"Yes, we knew that but she seems to have been closer to the Egremonts than we suspected"

"I don't know about the Katanga-Beauforts, but she was let go when they married so…"

"But we also know that she chose to expose them so…" Both talkers could tell they were heading towards dissonance and Kaushik spoke with a little relief to answer,

"I want you to meet her too. Oh, it was so good to see her. She still shines like she always did. You're bound to get on, but she hasn't got a political bone in her body, but…"

"That was her heart and her gut…" He listened to his beloved eagerly,

"Of course she can,"

"Tomorrow, we have to develop her defence and gather information for the prosecution of the other, the Aristois…But you! How are you?"

"Yes, what about the PTA, what do they think?"

"Well, that's good isn't it?" He took a sip of coffee and his brow furrowed and rose as Ashanti spoke for a long time.

"Koulla, tunoo…It's only one-ish, I've missed you so much Ashanti. How are your digs? Has that Alex washed up yet?" He laughed and then answered,

"Yes. A bit of bedtime reading," he said hiding his aggravation,

"Yes, I'm sitting down," a moment later he was standing up,

"Debota! Yes! A baby! We're going to have a baby! Oh? Oh? How do you feel? Are you getting enough rest? What have you eaten today? Oh Ashanti I love you," he was weeping and laughing at the same time. He had wanted this since they had met,

"Your cyow midnight skin, my eyes," He laughed again, pacing the room.

"Of course your brains."

"Oh Ashanti…But really, are you looking after yourself?" The mother-to-be reassured him and he sighed with relief and sat down.

"Okay, my lips are sealed. But? Can I tell Dipa? It'll make her so happy."

"Okay, seven weeks. I'll tell her in seven weeks. Remind me. But? How long will you…? When, will you come back before…?

"Six months at the most? That's what you said last week," he was almost sullen now,

"You're right, I know you're right. I'm sorry, it's only that I miss you so much and now there's two of you."

"Oh? Okay, you go,"

"No, that's fine, you have to talk to them, Look, I'll call you tomorrow okay?"

"I kamar you," and she was gone. He sat alone in his empty flat and beamed like an idiot for about ten minutes. Then he took another swig of coffee, he liked it cold, and picked up the Princess Victoria file.

Another Dissimilarity

You may also have noticed another dissimilarity between your world and the one being described, that is the lineage of the monarchy, and indeed the populace, in the world described herein. Given the nature of how you live you may consider it of more or equal importance to the presence or absence of a revolution in Russia in 1917.

We should explain that in many other human worlds, those that are aware of the others, the measure of civilisation is based on human autonomy; the degree to which an individual can govern themselves and their future. The ability to define one's own destiny among the billions of people in your world and the one herein was more or less equal. Some could act on opportunities to follow their dream, take up vocations that helped them thrive and live and love in ways that completed them. However, most people were constrained and powerless in both worlds and never found out what they might have been. People were in jobs they did not enjoy and did not live the way they wanted. There were hungry, hopeless, falsely imprisoned, beaten, tortured, abused people who died needlessly from brutality or curable diseases and lacked freedom in about the same numbers as you. But, for a world such as yours, so obsessed and divided by the idea of Race an explanation is still probably necessary.

You first must understand that your world is unique in this regard. Other worlds have often succeeded in dividing their people arbitrarily and without perceivable logic. In some, one's position in life is decided by birth order; last-born children are taken away to be groomed for high-ranking roles, the first child is sent to bureaucrat school at the age of seven and the second to technical school and so on. In others, stable civilisations have been sustained for centuries based on facial hair; the relative length of the sons' beards when their father dies decides who will inherit. Several worlds seal a child's fate by the splatter pattern created by dropping an egg from a tree on their third birthday. Most common so far appears to be the Feline and Canine Cynosurative societies.

But, in the infinite permutations of our planet in the multiverse, that, let us not forget, goes on forever, yours is the only one thus far discovered that has been able to organise and sustain a world-wide system of complex, layered and nuanced yet intangible ideas of Race with a capital R for hundreds of years. And then, in an even more ingenious leap over the evidence convince yourselves that many of you have largely overcome it. It is in fact a significant reason why this other world was chosen as one of the first examples to show you. However, it also explains why the attempt to educate you was made at all. A humanity as backward as yours would not usually be subject to communication. But, a human race as capable of such reality-defying imagination and self-delusion could also easily believe that there are other worlds and other ways of living.

So, the histories of this and that world divided in Britain in 1727. The then Prince Augustus fell deeply in love with and then, partly in an attempt to aggravate his father, George I, married Princess Elizabeth of Russia, daughter of Peter the Great. This woman would become Elizabeth II to George II and, you with your history, might find quite implausibly; she happily converted to the Anglican Faith and a life of tea parties. They had nine children, four of whom were sons, Frederick-George-William, George-Augustus-William, William-Augustus-George and Augustus-Frederick-George in that order. Their first, second and third sons, Frederick, George and William married German princesses as they were told and therefore expressed their paternal hatred by the standard Hanoverian means; womanising, drinking to excess and gambling.

Their last son, the young Augustus, also inherited the Hanover family trait of wild ways and paternal hatred but any remaining German Princesses were not particularly to anyone's liking. So, when he fell deeply in love with Princess Adebola of the Hausa Kingdom in West Africa he married her, at first in secret, and she happily converted to the Anglican faith and tea parties in 1765. They also had a lot of children.

The unfathomable contempt and fear felt by Europeans for people of colour at that time, the slave trade not yet having been abolished after all, caused scorn and derision. However, the princess's overt, enthusiastic and capable adherence to her adopted religion, language, dress and customs, bettering influence on the future king who became a champion in the popular cause of road improvement, her great and elegant beauty, a fecundity which produced seven healthy children and promised to end the hitherto almost constant worries about succession, overt maternal devotion, extensive philanthropic work, albeit mainly involving copious gifts of livestock, her cultivation of important friends including both Whig and Tory politicians and her husband being safely fourth in line to the throne at the time of their union led to her becoming much loved across the nation.

Of course, to begin with she was perceived as an exotic curiosity by most people, much like an elephant or a pineapple but with more contempt. Out of royal earshot, it was assumed by the majority of the elite with which she mingled that she was simply an excellent mimic of the rapidly changing taste and manners of the time. Rumours that she was not actually a princess from a kingdom very few people had ever heard of but a freed slave, or worse an escaped one, filled the coffee-house pamphlets together with horrid illustrations.

However, her detractors were no match for Princess Adebola and her delicate politicking. Her careful, always casual association with abolitionists was infrequent and publicly silent and she cultivated a broad range of friends. In addition, in an age when novelty was a prize, she was always up to date with the latest fashions, indeed something of a trendsetter among women of taste. And taste was very important to a society in such a state of flux where the old marks of superiority were being eroded. The ease with which she was able to adopt the high piled hairstyles of the time led women of fashion to use wigs made of African hair. British skin was moisturised properly from that date. The calico, chintz and silks imported from the East were supplemented with Sheeda and Aso-Ake from the South to create soft furnishings and women's dresses. Tables were ostentatiously laden with rice pancakes and Dan Wake on China plates to compliment the novel and precious tea whenever visitors were expected. Adebola was the most popular name given to baby girls in 1775 and 1776.

Somewhat looked down upon by the landed class, the merchants of the day were quick to accommodate this state of affairs. Nabobs; members of the mercantile class who acquired extravagant wealth through what you would call decidedly unfair trade in Calcutta [Kolkata] and Lagos, now came home with their foreign brides and bought estates from impoverished aristocrats. With land came the ability to place MPs in the House of Commons, a tradition that never really disappeared with subsequent Parliamentary reforms. Their children, of the latest tasteful hue, grew up and made 'good' marriages.

Then, the retrospectively foreseeable occurred. The heir to the throne Prince Frederick-George-William died suddenly of fever in 1767, George Augustus William died slowly of what is now agreed to be syphilis in 1769. When King George II died in 1773, his third son William-Augustus George, George III, succeeded him until he died from internal injuries sustained when trampled by some very fine pigs in 1814. Thanks to the loveless-ness of their unions and child mortality worthy of your Queen Anne, they were all childless. Thus, Augustus, his lovely African Princess and their progeny, were next in line.

At a time when European nations swapped and traded Asian and African countries like a game of Colony Trumps, most of both Houses of Parliament were, as one of her many high-ranking enemies, Lord Castlereagh put it,

"…not about to hand the whip over to the savage." And did all they could to discredit the rightful Queen. A great deal of unfavourable press and awful cartoons were republished and more were produced. They called Princess Adebola a savage, said that the fact that she had produced so many children including a male heir (later to die of Typhus) and was pregnant again denoted an unhealthy lust. They accused her of adultery with Lord Byron, despite her being much too old, and far too sensible for him, and nicknamed her, with reference to her philanthropy, The Hausa Cow.

However, in addition to the charm and political acumen of Queen Adebola herself, it was a time of great upheaval on the European continent thanks to the American and French Revolutions and then Napoleon. So, the British state also had other matters on its collective mind. Their main concerns were keeping domestic unrest to a minimum and making the colonial most of the chaos across the Channel. Their eagerness to strengthen diplomatic ties with other Protestant European nations, particularly German ones, was for the time being put on the back burner. In addition, on the day of the Coronation, the British were concerned with attempting to put America back in its place with a little war on the other side of the Atlantic.

The negro Queen meant that Britain was temporarily an object of derision in what you call Europe, but this world refers to as the Carte Blanche. Until the second defeat of the Corsican by Wellington in 1815, which sealed Britain as the major world power. So, the European powers had to mind their tongues for a while.

The British powers that were nevertheless conspired to persuade Augustus, George IV, to divorce his wife of twenty-nine years and marry a German princess, as his brothers had done and his father had not. When he refused, both Whigs and Tories decided that George ne Augustus was mad and declared that he was not fit to succeed his brother. This led to widespread unrest in Britain by the populace who had grown to love their African Queen.

Historians of this, that is Fräulein Greta's, World have imaginatively drawn parallels between the attempt by the London Court of 1553 to put the Anglican Lady Jane Grey, the Nine Days Queen, on the throne and the subsequent up-swell of unrest, rallying of opposing armies and her overthrow by the Catholic Queen (Bloody) Mary. In the 16th century, the British populations of both worlds were less concerned with Mary's Catholicism and more worried about legitimate succession.

In the early 19th-century of Greta's world, the legitimate heir was married to a negro, and while many subjects did not necessarily like it, they accepted the fact that it had happened. While it is true that there were pro-Adebola demonstrations in all the major cities and a riot in Chester, in truth, sensing popular feeling, the Parliament gave in without much of a fight. The period became known as the Discord of 1814 and consigned to history, which carried on much as it did in your world until young Greta had a little lie down in 1917.

Making virtues out of necessity is something of a British forte and the aristocracy quickly supplemented their penchant for marrying into successful British merchant families by taking up the fashion for colonial intermarriage. Facilitated by a much timelier acceptance that Anglicanism is, like the people who made it up; pragmatic and flexible as well as not that religious, by 1850, in addition to speaking up for the landed families of Britain, the House of Lords extended its reach to be the voice of the elites across the Empire.

Further strategic British royal marriages facilitated the continued strengthening of the ties of Empire. Encouraged by the British government, royal intermarriages also went on within Indian and African Royal houses so that West and Southern Africa unified into Great Africa in 1882, joined by Egypt in 1894 and Somalia in 1899. The last king of the United Kingdom, King Charles III was related to the Royal houses of Africa, Europe, Russia and India.

During this period, the Royal Family were emulated by all, so that within a decade the sailors and servants who found their way into Britain were not shunned but welcomed by the general population. To find oneself fiancéd to a Jamaican sailor, or an Indian Ayer was considered a great stroke of luck. Within a generation cackooder, that is well-balanced skin tones, were as admired in Bermondsey as they were in Berkshire.

The 19th-century aggressive proponents of Free Trade and the invisible hand of the market were as successful in both Houses as were yours and the business interests of the major Empire families extended even beyond the pink parts of the globe. The East India Company continued and expanded until people hardly remembered that it had ever been run by people other than actual East Indians. The Royal West African Company was not forgotten as it has been in your world, renounced trading in people in 1833 (by Act of Parliament) and flourished and grew to rival any multi-national company.

The three hundred families with seats in the Lords were in effect the voice of its world-dominating trade. With so few people being in charge it was understandable that they would wish to iron out any inconveniences associated with unnecessary competition. The Empire remained nominally free-trade as planning and policy within and between the larger businesses was negotiated in the London Clubs and dining rooms of the people who became known as the Aristois. And since it is invisible, when the hand of free trade disappeared altogether no-one appeared to notice.

World history continued largely in the same way as your world. The sun never set on the Empire, which covered a third of the globe and encompassed a quarter of the global population. The rest of the 'civilised' world, the aforementioned Carte Blanche or white map, carved up the rest. The Empire's reach was so great that just as some British influences are integrated into your world; the time of day is set for the whole world as we know in Greenwich, London, Egyptian cotton exists and is desired everywhere and THE smart shoe is the Oxford brogue, so in Greta's world the idea of racial superiority or inferiority eventually died across the globe, even in All America.

As can be seen, the adoption of colonial, mainly African, and later, Indian, words was not merely acceptable, but reflected a perceived sophistication and modernity. And people with very light or very dark skin, who were perceived as lacking in refinement and breeding, were called pale 'Peelers' and dark 'Negroes'. Aristotelian ideas of Harmony and Balance were quickly adapted to justify this attitude.

In the absence of what you call racial-thinking, other outward signs of 'breeding' and status, which have died out in your world, kept their hold on Empire thinking. For example, as Mrs. Silvia and Miss Dipa Cameron's profession is evidence, clothing was used to mark people out. The Royal

Hausa Blue fabric mentioned above was, similar to tartan, reserved for royalty from the House of Hanover-Hausa. The Apparel Laws of 1870 were abolished in 1876 because they were not required. Those who dressed above, or below, their station, Maphosas as they were called, found the social opprobrium at all levels sufficient to change their ways. Fashions changed from year to year and season to season and the cut, detailing and quality were carefully monitored by all.

Of course, the fact that the monarchs and business leaders of all the major nations presided over a considerable mess and were nearly all related to each other did not stop the Great and subsequent Wars. The only significant difference was that during the former, life was a little easier for the British Royal Family as they were a great deal less German and they did not bother to change their surname.

At least until the Great War (1914 to 1945), British expansion took place much as it did in your world but in this world, it was simply called The Empire. An example of the many minor differences between your world and theirs is that the statistical master of the mid-nineteenth century was the same Florence Nightingale in both. However, in The Empire world, her most famous innovation was called, to ingratiate the monarch of the time, who had a penchant for the dessert, a Tart-chart, not Pie.

Autonomy is a great drive for human beings all over the multiverse and there were of course countless rebellions, strikes, mutinies and wars for independence across the Empire and elsewhere. But they were first crushed ruthlessly by their rulers and then small reforms were made. The risings were spoken of as examples of backwardness and barbarism or not spoken of at all. The reforms were remembered and lauded as symptoms of an Enlightened Empire.

By the 1960s while Britain was still nominally The Mother Country or Maan, and the seat of Empire diplomacy, her economic and cultural power had largely dissipated. But the Empire went on. The nations within it with the greatest economic strength wielded the most power; Peers with links to India and Africa were the most influential in the House of Lords of the twenty-first century. The British remained nominally in charge with only a little grumbling about the Africanisation or Indianisation of cultural as well as economic life rumbling around Arcade dinner tables now and again. This had little impact on the work and consumption habits of the general population.

Incidentally, the revolution in which this narrative takes place began in Germany in 2010, as a long-overdue result of a lack of Joseph Stalin (who died obscure and in pain from abscesses on his gums in 1921) and spread with difficulty throughout the Carte Blanche, India, Africa and on to Ireland before finally reaching Britain, but that is another story.

We hope that helps. If it doesn't, further exposition can be found on the website in due course.

The Langthorn Tower Cell

The cell in the Lanthorn Tower seemed smaller when Liberty returned in the morning. Brighter, as the whitewashed walls reflected the sunlight through the bars on the windows, but smaller. Perhaps it was the additional chair that had been brought in that morning. Or perhaps Dipa seemed bigger. She didn't stop walking up and down in a mid-war purple and green tweed suit in the fug of cigarette smoke, some mahanga perfume and swirls of the fine dust that coated the floor and furniture. Now that she was wearing what had been high fashion in the winter before the revolution Liberty saw that Dipa had delicate ankles on long limbs that echoed her brother's. She had somehow piled all her hair into a small matching fedora that tilted so far to one side that Liberty couldn't see how it didn't fall off. And she was talking, fast,

"Oh, Sanoo Liberty, I'm just working something out, you see, it's, I'm geedy and irry, real and not real. Aren't I. Geedy and irry. Where's Kaushik? Kaushik should be here." She almost ran to the Runu she had left on her cluttered table; it was surrounded by Jus wrappers. Many more than from the single packet Kaushik had left. "…Oh, there's a message, he's running late, something about lots of cars on the roads, no more use restrictions, a car-clog he calls it, they have them in America." She read slowly from the screen, "… 'struggling for freedom can be quite slow going'," and she laughed, "…it could take him an hour to get here!? Oh well, shall we get started we need to start. What time is it? When did he message? eight-thirty, so, so he'll be here soon. What time is it?" When she finally looked at Liberty she stopped, "…Are you alright Liberty? You look, I mean, are you well?" She asked with some concern as she walked towards her lawyer, "…Do you need something? Lorenzo will, the guards will get it, they're being baban nice now, Shall I ring? I'll ring."

"No! Yes, I'm fine, I've been, I'm not wearing any makeup, that's all."

"What! Why?" Asked Dipa, confused and sneering at Liberty's current, slightly too large, outfit.

"Well, I simply thought; if we can all wear what we want now, why wear makeup?" Said Liberty and she allowed herself a faint smile with unpainted lips. Dipa's glossy purple ones mouthed,

"Why wear makeup?" In silent echo, and then not so silently "…Why wear makeup!" She sat down on the bed, "No makeup at all? Not even a little kohl? Mascara?"

"None."

"Yes, I see. Why wear makeup, of course," Dipa pulled Liberty onto the bed quickly and scrutinised her cheeks, lips, nose, eyelids. Liberty was a little overwhelmed and allowed her client to stroke and poke gently, "…your geedy face. Real…And not real," Dipa turned suddenly towards a mirror on the back of the shower pod with a sharp intake of breath and strode towards it, "…my face. No! not just mine! All our faces are irry and geedy," and she stroked her own cheeks slowly and quizzically.

"Dipa, how many Jus have you sucked?" Asked Liberty, wiping a few crumbs from her new Runu,

"Oh, Lorenzo gave them to me, he's a Krito you know. Kritos are geedy and irry too aren't they, that's what got me thinking to begin with, well I thought a bit about it before but I was too busy to…Kaushik told them to be koulla to me I think, where's Kaushik? What time is it now?" asked Dipa as she stroked her eyebrows. She did not appear to hear Liberty tell her it was not yet nine. "…Geedy and irry, like here, this place isn't real either, but it's also uchit real."

"Kritos are geedy, like you and me. We're all geedy, makeup, or no makeup," said Liberty matter of factly as she walked towards Dipa and turned her gently away from the mirror. "…a combination of strain and isolation, the sudden influx of news, as well as far too many Jus, have got you confused Dipa," then she added with a smidgen more sympathy and looking into Dipa's big eyes, "…Kaushik will be here soon and you need to slow down, think methodically and carefully. I'm going to be asking you a lot of questions and you need to concentrate on reality. The hearing is in a few days. Your freedom is at stake." Dipa looked at her thoughtfully for quite a while and then said methodically and carefully,

"You need to clean your pores." Then she brightened, "…Shall I do it while we wait for Kaushik? I'm a skilled Lady's Maid, you know that don't you," and she flitted to her bedside table where a large cotton bag sat. She dove in. "…it's in here somewhere, never fails. Ah! Here we are!" She brought out a large jar of Yangan-Jam and held it aloft.

By the time Kaushik arrived at nine-forty, profusely apologising as he bustled in, Dipa was 'doing' Liberty's face. Not listening to Kaushik's excuses Liberty managed to say,

"Your sister needs to calm down and concentrate, she has sucked, by my calculation, eleven Jus since we left her and has hardly slept," as Dipa did something with a brush to her cheeks. "…can you make us all some tea?"

"There!" Announced Dipa and she stood back to admire her work briefly before rushing over to hug her brother. "…Mellowmadarlin" she added as an admonition "…I'll make the tea, you look at Liberty, isn't she lovely. Of course it's not ideal, shades, my makeup is…I don't know what you said to the guards but they've given me a kettle and tea and…"

"Jus. Lots of Jus," interrupted Liberty with a slightly reproachful tone directed at no-one in particular. Dipa giggled and busied herself with the tea,

"Like a hotel now. And a sewing kit too. Finally. I can take up some hems and do something with that shift dress, it's a disgrace," she babbled cheerfully. Kaushik looked at Liberty apologetically and they both sighed,

"You look koulla," said Kaushik to Liberty, who was momentarily embarrassed, "…very…?"

"Koulla? Koulla! She looks sandara! You have a good figure Liberty, you should wear heels, and a jacket with more shape," said Dipa from the area she had set up as a little kitchen.

"Yes, yes, lovely. Have you had a chance to catch up with the news since last night Dipa? Asked her brother,

"Debota yes!" cried Dipa with her back to them, waving a teaspoon as she busied herself with the tea, "…Its chaos out there. People allowed to say or do anything, coming out with all sorts, arguing about anything and everything, doing whatever they want, whenever they want, no Passes, no licences, no…?"

"Let or hindrance," interjected the lawyer,

"Yes, well, it says you are a Deputy on the Transitional Council. You led the march on Parliament, some kind of battle. You and your Critical Mass. You're important Kaushik. You got your revolution. I'm so happy for you Kaushik. All that talk, all that hiding and running around and fear and now it's happened. And now your dream is real, sort of…and mine isn't. Who'd have thought it?" And she giggled as she passed two cups of tea to Liberty. "…You know I was thinking, Kaushik, this Tower is a bit like me really isn't it. I mean real and not real at the same time you know. It burnt down you know, this tower, the Runu told me. This was all, all re-, recreated in the eighteen-fifties, for tourists. Who knew there were tourists back then? And a zoo, there was a zoo in here. From scratch, made to look old. And it's like me, I was a real Queen for a few weeks wasn't I, maybe months? And, but, but I wasn't really a Queen either. Real and not real. Geedy and irry, like this Tower. And your revolution, I mean I can't get out of it can I. I…"

"The Tower is real. The revolution is real Dipa, I know you haven't seen it but it's geedy alright," said Liberty, slightly irritated. Kaushik was listening and looking at his sister,

"What do you mean the revolution is geedy and irry Dipa?" He asked quietly. Dipa sat down with their tea.

"Well, just that Koush. No! Your revolution is different, your revolution is not geedy and not irry, it might be one or the other sometime but at the moment it's not real and it's not fake is it. Oh I don't know what it is Koush, I've had too much

Jus," and she smiled sweetly at her brother with big dilated eyes as he sat down on the edge of the bed. Liberty's now shaped and slightly too dark eyebrows arched and her head tilted to one side as she looked at Dipa. Kaushik saw Liberty's surprise and smiled. Then he said,

"It's not fake and it's not real yet, its Transitional Deeps, a Transitional Council until we can hold elections, then it will be…You're right though sis, it's not real enough yet…And it's not my revolution, it's the whole…did you see on the Runu? The whole United," and he let the last word linger in his mouth so that Liberty's eyes softened and she said,

"The World United," and smiled.

"Transitional? Yes! I'm transitional, in between, neither one thing or the other. And I've transitioned before haven't I, I was a child, and a seamstress with Mum, and a nurse, and a lady's maid and a villasitter Yangan and a Queen all irry and geedy. Transitions from one fake me to another is…That's it. Yes, transitional not, but? All fake? All real. And now I'm in between, nothing. When I get out of here, I'll be, what will I be when I get out?" Asked Dipa looking at her brother wild-eyed,

"What you've always been, a right royal pain in the arse Dipa Cameron. And, I know you've got all day, no offence, but I've got real stuff to do. So, can we get started? I've got a meeting at two." Kaushik knew what to say to his sister and she smiled, sat up straight, huffed a little breathlessly and said,

"All right then Deputy, shoot," said Dipa. Liberty checked her Runu and said,

"Well, with a case such as this the defence will be in the detail. We will need to build up a sympathetic picture of you in eyes of the jury. You are from the East End of London, yes?

"Yes, Limehouse."

"A back-to-back house?

"Oh no, we lived in a flat over mum's work, store-rooms, a shop for local trade over it, a workshop on the next floor, then us,"

"Oh? One of those old warehouses?"

"Not one of those modern massive brick monstrosities like at Canary Wharf. Ours was authentic." Said Dipa with some passion

"Aren't the Canary Wharf warehouses nineteenth-century?"

"Eighteen-hundreds. Precisely, Ours goes, went back to the seventeen-seventies. Overlooked the Limehouse Cut."

"Not a straight edge in the place." Said Kuashik, "…Mum was forever…"

"But the light was good, for the dressmaking you know, my mum, our mum was a dressmaker, for all the best families."

"Yes. So, overlooking the Aspic, yes."

"Right up against it, the lower floors were all bricked up at the back, but there was plenty of light in the workshop. And we had that Anti-Aspic glass they don't do any more."

"Useless, when the damn went," said Kaushik flatly and Dipa looked at him, she was about to speak when Liberty said,

"Did you say you were a nurse at some point, that could be useful?"

"Well, not for long Liberty," said Dipa, "…I couldn't stomach it. Too squeamish."

"You were just out of short skirts Dipa. Sixteen. And that war was horrible, truly horrible," said Kaushik and he got out his Runu and began to swipe, "…look, there she is, at the field hospital in Isfahan. She was a nurse in the last Persian war." Kaushik swiped and Liberty saw on her Runu a photo of Dipa in full protective gear with the mask pulled down standing between two tall men. Dipa now had the image on her Runu too and she smiled weakly,

"That one on the left is Aja and that's Anik, our brothers, twins. I haven't seen this picture in forever," Dipa sighed and gently stroked the screen to enlarge their faces, first one and then the other, distinguishable only to someone who loved them. Liberty looked at the men, handsome and fine boned like their siblings. They were smiling with arms around their little sister's shoulders. Liberty had heard about Kaushik's three older brothers. The eldest, she couldn't remember his name, died in the Third Persian War, their father also, and these two in the last one. Kaushik had refused to join up and taken to political agitation instead. He had begun simply as a pacifist, hating the army. His grandfather was taken by the First Persian War and their great and great-great-grandfathers in the Great War. She could also understand why Dipa, looking drawn and blank as she tried to smile in the photograph, had become a nurse.

"They didn't need nurses, they needed JCBs, I learned to drive a JCB, that was real alright," said Dipa with a dark note of cynicism Liberty hadn't heard before. Everyone knew what the Dhool did to people when it fell so she knew why Dipa had needed an industrial shovel. Dipa absently reached into her jacket pocket for a Jus and neither of her companions tried to stop her. "…any way after the twins were killed, and I shovelled them up with the others, I went home to my mum and took up a needle." She reached over to Kaushik to hold his hand, "…and this one took up a pen." There was a pause until Dipa jerked up and swiped the picture from her screen, "…Have you got any more photos Koush?" Her brother nodded,

"I'll send them to you," he said and he tapped at his Runu.

"Thanks Kaushik, I'll look at them later. I can't be crying now. We better get on with my statement…I stayed with mum for a few months and then…"

"Hang on," said Liberty, "You were sixteen in the last Persian War, so you're…nineteen?" Dipa nodded, "…I thought you were older."

"It's the Jus," said Kaushik, back to his old judgemental self,

"Princess Victoria was twenty-five, so everyone thinks I'm twenty-five, that's it," said Dipa emphatically and she popped the Jus into her mouth, looking at her brother. He rolled his eyes and she said flatly, "…I was a nurse for a year, then I came back home, to mum's."

"Well, that was the last time I saw you, when you were working…in twenty-fifteen, when you were working for that white lady, up West in the Cathedral Bubble."

"Was that the last time? I thought it was at mum's in the spring? When the Kritos came for you."

"Yes, the March, twenty-fifteen. Debota! Just two years ago?" And he sighed.

"Oh, yes time just moves so fast, and so slow so…" said Dipa trailing off and Kaushik turned to Liberty, proud to explain,

"They covered for me, Dipa and Mum, when the Kritos came after me, when Critical Mass was banned." This reanimated Dipa and she said,

"Yes, but you got away! And now here you are! I don't think I've ever been that scared. He went over the Aspic! On planks! Climbed over the Limehouse Dam and skied right over the Aspic!"

"I know," said Liberty, "He's famous for that now. Luckily for you. A real live hero." And a smile crept over her face and then died. Dipa smiled back before watching Liberty's face go blank again and rolling her eyes.

"Is he? Well you are to me Kaushik, always have been…He was lucky it was cold that night… We thought he might be dead for all this time, sucked in," Dipa shuddered and leaned back to the bed and took his hand, "…that was the last I thought I might ever see of you, Kaushik," and she smiled as she looked at him, "…striding and sliding on your gangly legs, huffing and puffing as you pushed with those old sticks…and that stuff just wobbling and splitting where you poked it and pushed. So deep there too, two stories of murky jelly trembling under you. And when you hit the top of an aerial was it?" Kaushik shrugged "…You nearly went over then didn't you, nearly fell… And then you went around that big modern warehouse and I couldn't see you anymore." Kaushik squeezed her hand and smiled guiltily, "…What happened Kaushik, where did you go? Why didn't you get in touch? I thought you were dead?"

"I couldn't Dipa, it was too risky, I could have got you arrested, both of you. By the time I came back down South you were already living at the Egremont's, I thought, mum said."

"You came back when?"

"Last year. January."

"And you didn't get in touch?"

"Well, you were living in the Palace Bubble, or somewhere close I suppose, by then, too risky," Answered Kaushik. Dipa shrugged and pouted. "…much too risky, I saw mum a few times before…"

"At least mum knew? She knew you were alive, and well."

"Yes," said Kaushik "…she knew I was alive and well before she died." And the last two Camerons burst into tears and hugged kneeling on the floor. They rocked from side to side and wept for their mother. Liberty looked down at her knees and straightened her skirt. She waited until they were no longer crying and then said as gently as she could,

"Kaushik, the case." And Kaushik slumped in front of his sister so that his head fell on his chest. He gave out a quick puff before helping Dipa up and brushing the grey dust from her dress before he rose. He saw that she had learned a knack for composing herself quickly and he continued with pride,

"She stood on a baban wobbly ladder over the damn, stood on a ladder on the Aspic to keep it steady till I could get to a place where it could take my weight. Passed me my sticks. Mum was too heavy. But we weren't going to let her try were we Deeps," Dipa shook her head, "…that's a detail you could make a note of Liberty. And then she and mum were all alone." Dipa stood up and walked to the window. She spoke so quietly that Liberty was forced to check that the Runu was picking it up,

"He's like me really. Did you know, well I suppose you do, but apparently there's a law that says it's illegal to talk about undermining the Parliament or something. Well, not anymore I suppose?" She stopped talking and looked out of the window. Her brother broke the silence gently,

"…It's got to be done Deeps. There's a hearing in a few days and we've got to work out what happened before then." Dipa sat back down at the table and put her hands out flat, sat up straight and nodded to Liberty to carry on recording on the Runu and sighed,

"Right. Well. Right, May? Debota! Not three years ago?" and Dipa sighed and sank just a little before straightening immediately. Then she took a purposeful swig of tea and began,

"Well, I was lady's maid to Lady Mathilda Beaufort, a minor family, no connections to speak of. No money. They lost a lot under the Aspic, the Beauforts, I don't know what. He worked, Lord Beaufort, in some Guild in the City, and, a Beadle or something. That's why they liked me, I saved them a fortune in dressmaker's bills. My mum, our mum was a dressmaker you see, and a good one. You know that, right?" Liberty nodded, "…She had more connections than they did, mum. Worked for all the big families, mainly the Egremonts, they kept her busy, but the Cooch-Bahars, the Shahs, the Hanovers as well sometimes! And nothing but the best, no short cuts, no Krito-stitchers, all made by human hand. And she taught me everything so, well, I spent more time making her clothes than I did waiting on little Mathilda.

Poor Mathilda, so peela…so pale, such thin hair, you couldn't do a thing with that hair. And white!? Her little body was like a road map, blue lines running all over her white-white skin, poor girl. And her dad going on about how 'fair' used to mean white in Shakespearian times and lilies and God knows what while he sipped his sasta port. Well, fair is foul and foul is fair, that's what I... I didn't mean that, 'pale is pretty and black is beautiful' that's it isn't it. Yes, it wasn't her fault, I mean it doesn't matter does it; breeding, balance, that's not right. It's just finding colours that suited her, it's a limited set of colours will go with that skin, and I tried so hard to keep her up you know.

Anyway, I did my best, made her the best clothes and did what I could with her hair. And she appreciated it too, not like some in that house. Well, I was about their only real luxury, their only human staff. They ate nothing but porridge, oat porridge, disgusting, for breakfast and watery soup or thin dahl for lunch and dinner, nothing else. Kept to Basic Ration. No extras. Put on a show when there were people round of course. But when it was just the family they sat around talking about food, food they'd had before, food they were going to give to such and such, but there was never anything to eat. No wonder she was so thin, poor girl. And no proper servants, just one broken down nineteen-ninety Krito maid who cooked as well, second-hand, on charge for more hours than she worked, try hacking that old pile of junk, and Pritchard, the butler, ancient, inherited from his father, Lord Beaufort's, and that's it apart from me. Pritchard-Glitchard, that's what they called him, and deaf! All their money went on Bubble Tax so they could live in Saint Pauls, the right address. No ventilation, you

78

could hardly breathe in the summer. And the condensation! It was like a trip to Kew every day of the week. Oh and they had a broken-down place in the country. We all lived in a few rooms round the kitchen, the rest was a ruin. No visitors, just sitting around shivering and waiting for the Season to start up again. And me sewing thermals under one lamp, it's a wonder I didn't lose my eyesight. But they had to keep it up, at least till she got married. I don't know what happened to it after that, or them. Maybe that kaksha man with all his curdy helped them out? Pricey way to get a seat in the Lords.

"Did you meet Lord Kenza Katanga-Beaufort?" asked Kaushik,

"I saw him a few times, but he never spoke to me."

"Did you ever speak to him?"

"Me, speak to Lord Kenza?" Dipa gave her brother a disappointed look and carried on quickly, "…Heard him though, lots. Quite the charmer, all that stuff about the Maan. And she lapped it up, and her mother, the Dowager; serving the mother country like he served his own mother. Hah. Mind you the way they treat their mothers he wasn't far wrong. Talked to her like she was senile. She lapped it up though. All that stuff about 'feeling like he was coming home to his mother', when all he was doing was buying a bit of power those down and outs couldn't afford to use. I saw him later though, at a party, didn't recognise me of course, when I was with Adi…But shall I keep saying it all in order?" Liberty nodded, and she went on, "…I kept up her style, for all that time, from her coming out to when she got married, that was a long year. I don't know how? Offcuts from mum's workshop and only what showed was made of anything halfway decent.

I made sure she had enough to be seen in, day dresses, evening dresses, tea dresses, and all the right colour, the right style, no matter how mahanga the Yangans made it that season. She kept up.

And that thin raggedy hair! And that skin, it was impossible finding colours that she could wear sometimes. That summer, she was determined to have this, when it was all Pre-War fashion, again, this red shweshwe three cat style high collar monster of a dress. She'd seen it on one of the Cooch-Bahars, who had the colouring, and the neck, and the hair. But I made it. What a sight. Arupa! After that she listened more.

And told me all her troubles, hour after hour about who said what to who. And me nodding and mumming but not really paying attention, poor girl. But what did I care? Like listening to some sort of poison stream babbling over cold slippery stones, pretty enough, but you don't drink because you know it will make you sick. So bitter, so mean, so Cishy. And me stitching and sewing and getting her washed and dressed and doing that damn hair. Keeping her up.

Then she married that kaksha Coltan miner from Congo and finally got some colour in her. Sorry." Kaushik pushed Dipa's teacup towards her and gave her a look. "…I am not going on too long about the Beauforts. You said detail! And they're important because. And you know what you said about geedy and irry before, they all know it too, deep down, you know, thought it too? That's why they're so cruel. It's not just the Beauforts clinging on, its all of them," Kaushik looked confused, "…you know, all that stuff about the Empire being all a lie, how it's all kept up by Imalympy. That's what they say too? But they just see it as necessary, don't worry about it too much. Didn't worry. Don't tell me that's not giddy and irry. You did say that, sort of. He was always going on Liberty. I didn't listen to him much either. Oh his water's sweet enough but it's, was all in his head…I suppose, you got your way though Kaush,"

"Not my way Dipa, it's a democr…" but Dipa wasn't listening to her brother and kept on talking,

"The Egremonts and all of them. There was this one time when, but let me keep it in order. The Beauforts never said that, too close to the bone. They spouted all the Empire Union this and the Empire Culture that, they really, uchit needed it to be true. And now it's gone? Just like that? The whole Empire? And it's not anarchy out there? A democracy you said, you mean anyone can just vote for anyone, just like that? Even the lower orders? It'll be chaos! Who will run things? So who is running things? Who runs the Coltan Company now? That's who she married, Mathilda, Lord Kenza Katanga, you've heard of him I'm sure. So who runs it now? Won't they just steal all the coltan and run off? What's happened to the real owners?"

"The people own it now Dipa, they're the real owners. I don't know about Coltan, but a lot of industries are restructuring," Explained Kaushik, Dipa looked blank, "…making management efficiencies, renegotiating contracts, pensions the whole lot. A lot of places here, workers' boards or committees, have finished interviewing." Explained Kaushik,

"They're interviewing Lord Kenza Katanga-Beaufort for a job in his own mines!"

"Well, if he wants to, he can I suppose, if he meets the job descriptions. What did he do before?"

"Do?!" Said Dipa disdainfully, "Do? He didn't do anything, it was his."

"Not anymore," smiled Kaushik, he could not hide his happiness, "…Don't worry Dipa, Lord and Lady Kenza-Beaufort won't starve, they can work for their money. Like the rest of us." Dipa sat back in her chair, silent. "…I thought you were going to catch up on the Runu Dipa?"

"I did Kaushik, but, but it's a lot to take in. Mathilda Kenza, Lady Beaufort. Working? Poor girl," said Dipa with true sympathy, "…She couldn't file her own nails. What work can she do? She's not qualified for anything! Poor girl." Kaushik seemed to wind himself up before he said what appeared to be something he had said quite a few times before,

"The Aristoi class, through their self-imposed idleness…"

"She wasn't idle! She was baban busy, she had her aunt's charity, they all had a charity of some sort, and meetings and lunches, teas, cocktails, lobbying parties, dinners, galas, balls, who's going to fund raise for music in schools now?"

"No need, there's music education planned in all schools now, the Transitional Council is big on culture, a broad way of learning you know, we don't know what skills will be needed," Answered Kaushik, "…can she do administration? Can she play anything? Maybe she could…? I don't know, anyway, she's been crippled into idleness and timewasting by a decadent society and if she hasn't got any skills now, she can re-train. We're very short of Polymer Chemists. The Department of Work Training Programmes have already been extended and I am on the sub-committee that deals with... But why am I…? Can we please get on with getting a woman who has worked every day since she was sixteen, before that, out of the Tower of London please?" Dipa passed him quite a long look that had raised eyebrows in it but was otherwise difficult to interpret,

"Anyway, I worked every day," said Dipa with another look at her brother, "…with Sunday afternoons off when I went to see mum," she reached for a Jus but Liberty put a hand gently over hers and gave it a squeeze. Tears came into Dipa's eyes and she snatched her hand away, "…every day except Sunday afternoons for the best part of a year and made that wedding dress. Did you see it? In the magazines?" Liberty shook her head and Dipa sighed resignedly. "That cyow dress, thirty yards of the best shot grey and white silk for that. No expense spared. He paid of course. And all that embroidery. I got help with that. Do you remember Akira, Kaush? She remembers you." The series of shakes of the head and shrugs told Dipa to get on with it. "…I got her married and I was out on my ear. Not even a decent reference. Adequate, that's what they called me. Adequate. Couldn't say what I really did could they, give the game away. Bloody Beauforts. Uruchika sastas, the lot of them." She paused, "…I am a bit Jusy. I didn't mean that about peeler…pale skin, 'Pale is Pretty', that's it isn't it?" She said looking at Liberty, who smiled. "…Its just it was hard to dress her sometimes, you know, fashionably. That's a koulla dress by the way, who made it?"

"I don't know," said Liberty "I got it in a Restructuring Shop."

"Right, okay, yes, I saw that on the Runu, you can get anything in those places…Did they really just hand it over? The Aristois, did they just give all their stuff away?"

"Yes! Most of it, most of them before the revolution, part of the reforms, remember the reforms?"

"I think so, I think I…? I was pretty Jusy those last weeks, confused, you know? Joshi was…Did I…?" And she stopped and stared blankly. Liberty squeezed Dipa's hand again and this time Dipa didn't pull away, "…Okay, Koulla, slowly. We should do this in order, in time order…" Dipa huffed purposefully, "I left the Beauforts in the June or July twenty-fifteen. Adequate…and went home to mum's. Helped out, went back to being her bag carrier, for her calls you know. My mum used to make calls to fit her ladies and I used to help her out when I was younger and I went back to that. It was a bit fraught to tell the truth. You know mum, Kaushik, there's, was, her way and the wrong way," Kaushik laughed. "…actually, can we open a window?" and Kaushik laughed again,

"She never opened a window, mum," he explained to Liberty as he got up to see if the window would open.

"Didn't want to let the dust in…Is it cold out?" Asked Dipa,

"No, it's quite mild for April," answered Kaushik as he struggled with an old latch.

"This room never warms up. Do you want a hand?"

"No, no, it's nearly…there." Kaushik stayed at the window, looking down at a dark dressed man walking slowly past the outer walls of the tower.

"Have you seen something?" Asked Liberty,

"No? No, some man," answered Kaushik, "…anyway, yes, slowly and carefully, with detail please Dipa," he said as he turned back to sit with the women.

Meghna River, Near Katakhali

It was an unpleasant green-brown and there were things floating in it, but she was so sweat encrusted and grimy that the river was still better than nothing. She had been desperate to find a time when she could slip off the boat and wash without that bloated fool around. Even a month ago she would have relished leaning back to let her hair and head be lapped while she floated in one of the thousand rivers of some of her forefathers. That had been when she could rely on an uchit shower at some point soon. Now she would wear the pond slime smell until her body odour over-powered it again. This was not part of some temporary adventure; this was a much-needed wash before that toad awoke. A necessity. She got on with the business of getting less dirty than she had been. She did not feel actually clean.

She would have to get back on the boat soon. That vile creature who had landed her in this Godforsaken swamp of a place could not have the satisfaction of seeing her naked. This place, everything sticky and dirty, with insects buzzing everywhere all the time, He had trapped her in 'this situation'. He kept on calling it 'this situation', as if it were one of their japes that had gone a little awry. She could not let him feel he had her too.

But water is water and she began to feel refreshed despite her mood. Her body reminded her of all the previous dips she had taken in Bengal. Before she had understood that she was a backoe, one of those migratory creatures who never belong to one place. When the lake a few hundred yards from her bedroom was 'The lake', the only one she knew. The memory of elicit pleasure, always the best sort, washed over her as she finished rubbing the grime away and stretched into the dark warm expanse, turning and twisting like a water snake. He did not have her, no-one ever did. She would fix this 'situation', the tide would turn.

A trickle of water caught the sunlight as it tickled over her hip and stirred a ripple of memory; someone else's skin supple and smooth. Then it was gone. She let a handful of water empty through her fingers, sparkling in the light. Then another. Her eye was caught by a lonely drop of water glistening on the rise of her forearm.

"What are you doing!" He rasped from the rail, "…Someone will see!" She stretched out her lovely arm into the water and turned onto her back, smiling as she added frustrated desire to his exasperation,

"So what? Can't a girl have a bath around here?" she said loud enough to annoy him and kicked her lithe legs in his direction. He turned away and glared away a tear.

Our Hero's Flat Again

Our hero woke up hungry and looked at his watch on the bedside table. He smiled and rolled and stretched in satisfaction. The sheets were warm and smelled of her. Neither of them had expected it. And what had begun as what, for him, was a fairly familiar awkward tumble, quickly developed into something else. He thought for a minute. It was a complementary discovering of wonder. Was that too much for a one-night stand? It would be if they didn't do it again. But he wanted to do it again, probably. And she was a baban koulla person. Neither had known that they had it in them and they had both laughed conspiratorially together afterwards. She had a lovely smile.

There it was, a bit of luck. Finally. He let his stomach grumble and tucked his arm under his head letting a strong whiff of, mostly his, sweat waft away. Another smile sighed out of him. What were the chances? He had to make the most of it. He would digi-missive her, soon. Or should he chitter? Tea.

He slouched naked into the wide long kitchen diner as he slipped on his watch. No drafts despite the big windows.

Our heroine was lying on the sofa doing that thing with her eyes. She was searching for a signal again; Persia, India, China. He sighed, she called it an unquantified probability. To her face, he called it hope. But it was impossible, they would never find her that way. And he felt alone when she was doing it, scanning thousands of square miles for hour after hour.

Oblivious to her surroundings, running herself down. All because she wasn't used to dreaming. She was believing a dream because she was so desperate, and powerless.

It wasn't such a bad thing, wanting to make something desired into something real. But she was going to have to learn the difference between the two. He would be there when she did. He brushed a lock of hair from her face as her eyelids flickered and turned his back, walking to the kettle.

They had only moved in a few days ago and the unfamiliarity of the place helped him focus. He came up with the plan of action over tea and toast, staring out at the view, all greys and black now, mainly grey.

Back in the Langthorn Tower

Still surprised at her lip print in the rim, Liberty sipped a fresh mug of tea and asked,

"…When did you first meet the Egremonts?" Dipa sat down and answered,

"When did I first meet the Egremonts? Well, I'd seen them all my life, on and off, hadn't I, they were one of mum's biggest clients. I saw Adi grow up really. Looked up to her in a way, I suppose. She always looked so sandara, perfect. She didn't notice me though, not till later,"

"And, young Lady Egremont, Aditi, she's the same age as you, yes?" Asked Liberty,

"No, only three years older but more worldly, she said that I just, but…more or less same age, exact same height, same colouring, same hair; hers was thicker than mine, frizzy if you let it be, same measurements more or less. That's why she wanted me it turns out, but everything in order," and Dipa took a breath to repeat the same answer to a different set of interrogators, "…Little Mathilda got married in the June, twenty-fifteen, and they let me go. I went home to mum's and just helped a bit while she was busy during the London Season. They kept her baban busy for those months. The important clients usually came back from the countries in the Spring, the Egremonts stayed until mid-October then they, the women, went to their place in India for most of the winter, while Lord Egremont did his duty in the Lords. Then they met up with his Lordship, did a bit of travelling and came back for the start of the Season proper at Easter. That meant we had to keep up with the Summer and Autumn wear and be working on some of their Winter and Early spring wardrobe for them to take away with them. They weren't mum's only good people either. So she was always busy that time of year, when they'd Rununu morning, noon and night ordering, changing their minds, changing them back. Anyway, she was glad of the help." Kaushik rolled his eyes and nodded as he remembered.

So, when Adi started asking for me and saying it was alright for mum to come on my own, she was nervous but relieved as well. So she could get on with more work, supervise her girls you know." Kaushik nodded again and said,

"She liked to keep a close eye on her girls did mum. Standards," he added.

"Yes, standards. And she could rely on me to do a proper job without supervision. Anyway, I think I first went to the Egremonts on my own in late August or early September twenty-fifteen. That's when it started," Dipa paused for a moment and rubbed her hand. "...So I traipsed over there with my swatches and...No one else was in and, well, she was koulla to me, Adi Egremont. Opened the door herself, said to call her Adi. We had tea in the morning room! As if I was her equal!" Kaushik and Liberty raised their eyebrows, "...Well I know that now but you said back then. Back then I was so nervous I'd spill something, didn't eat a thing. I was a good girl back then. I was a good girl I was. I washed my face and hands before I went." She paused then and sighed a little.

Anyway, that tea-time she started saying how good mum was, how discreet, was I the same. Well, you have to be in that line, see all sorts. And? I've been remembering. Then, back then, she was laughing you know, saying she'd just noticed, about how similar looking we were. I thought she was saying it to make me feel at home, you know. She just dropped it into the conversation. Same size, same shape, same shoe size. And then changed the subject. But I think she had something in her head, not a plan exactly, but she definitely had something in her head back then. I see that now. Then she changed the subject, maybe a bit to quickly? Started talking about the dress again, the one I was making for her," She looked at Liberty who just smiled and nodded,

"...and she knew all about the Beauforts. And what I'd done for Mathilda, said everyone knew. Said she could tell the work I'd done on this Georgian-style organza thing with matching headpiece when everybody, all the Yangans suddenly all wanted Georgian dresses for this ball cousin Joshi decided to put on out of the blue. He was always doing things like that, parties, balls, picnics. All with some sort of theme, Georgian, Hong-Kong Thirties, Late Pretorian, Early Pretorian, Greek Gods, Vikings, with no notice! Then all the Yangans'd be Rununu all at once! Nightmare. You read about them I suppose?" Liberty shook her head and said,

"Lots of people did, and two weeks later there was a sasta copy in Skiemark," she smiled, "...My friend Laila got one of those Hong Kong Thirties dresses, with the ink style print? Baban flattering, I nearly…"

"Anyway," interjected Kaushik, "...There's detail and there's detail, I think. Adi Egremont invited you to her house in the Royal Arcade and flattered you, took you into her confidence." Liberty looked sheepish and Dipa smiled at her warmly,

"I could make you a real one if you like?" Offered Dipa conspiratorially, Liberty shook her head a little too vigorously and Kaushik frowned,

"Dipa, Adi Egremont." He said emphatically,

"It'll give me something to do," said Dipa, with equal decision. "…Adi Egremont, even you know about Adi Egremont, Liberty, the undisputed Queen of the Yangans. And sandara, Utterly, perfectly cyow. I have never seen anybody that beautiful ever. Well, if that Dental Receptionist had had the eemarlly. You remember that Dental Receptionist don't you Kaush," and she smiled while he looked wistful, "…The image of Queen Nefertiti and…"

"Completely unaware of her own beauty…" interrupted Kaushik. The women gave the man a moment to remember another, and his youthful obsession with her, "…Bilinay." He said the name with a tenderness that made them all sigh.

"That's it Bilinay, the Queen of the Limehouse Wall you called her. She was the Receptionist at the Dentist we used to go to. His teeth were that flossed he…

"And Adi Egremont? Sorry, but we do have to focus, you know." It was liberty's turn to remind them of their purpose. Dipa passed one more indulgent look at her brother and carried on,

"Adi Egremont. Well, she paid well. And on time. And she was always finding jobs for me; adjustments, neckpieces, taking off a trim, putting one on, mending even, all sorts. I was there that much. And she was always so koulla to me, bringing me little treats, chatting about this and that."

"This and that?" asked Kaushik,

"Yes. This and that. Never anything in the slightest illars, I'm not a fool Kaushik and I'm not past telling that sort what they want to hear either, how do you think I managed to do what I did? She may have pulled the wool over my eyes but I wasn't exactly straight with her either. Any way. She took her time, got to know me, fed me a bit of gossip, in exchange for news I picked up from mum about this and that, just gossip, the harmless kind, buttered me up and then finally, weeks later got onto her little secret. Wanted me to do some special work she said, something different. Secretly. I couldn't tell anyone. I'd work there, in Egremont House. She'd get me anything I needed, pay me curdy too, but could I make her two dresses exactly the same, in every detail, down to the last stitch, for a ball she said but I knew better. But they were for a ball. But they weren't either, but I didn't know what exactly then. But I did know something was up, but I didn't let on." Dipa paused for effect. It worked,

"Why did she want you to do that?" Asked Liberty and Kaushik in unison.

"I'll tell you why. Well, what she told me, and what I found out, or what she decided, planned later, and then her and Princess Victoria, I think her plans developed as she went along really. I don't think she ever planned anything really. I think? What I found out later was…"

"Wait a minute, Dipa, we need to know what you believed at the time, what did you think she wanted the dresses for at the time? We can come to what you found out later, it's important we know what you thought at the time Dipa, for your defence," said Liberty. Dipa looked at her flatly, her story interrupted,

"Well, at the time I didn't know what to think exactly. She takes me in the Morning room, pours me tea, serves me cake. Tells me she envies my skill; she was so charming. Said she liked my hair too. Same as hers that day. Although now I think she had probably done her hair like mine. Asks me to make secret dresses, exactly the same in every detail. For three times what they were worth! And, well, everyone knows what those Yangans are like, get up to all sorts. Always out in the Fresh Air in the East End Marasses. I thought she probably wanted a good dress that no-one knew about so she could go out unrecognised in some way. They do that the Yangans, mum said. And I said to her 'Why two?' I said. She looks me up and down, not snottily, kindly, almost admiring and says, 'I shall be glad to tell you soon enough, but first I must be sure of your trustworthiness; can I count on you Dipa?' And looks at me with her big eyes open wide. And fair's fair she did tell me in the end. Sort of. And I wasn't exactly wrong." Dipa stopped talking and looked towards the window.

"So, you made the dresses?" Asked Liberty and Dipa turned back to the table,

"I made the dresses. Exactly the same. In one of the guest rooms upstairs, on Tuesdays and Thursdays when her mother was out visiting. And because I knew her measurements and we were almost the same size, so she said that I could just try them on myself for the first fittings. Which was not easy. That way she could still go out with her mother. But she's a bit taller and her waist is lower, she's got quite short legs actually," and Dipa stretched up and out at that moment so that Liberty could tell that Dipa had very long legs. "…I fancy more tea. Does anyone want more tea?" She asked and got up without waiting for an answer because everyone was British and would want more tea. "…What time is it?"

"Ten-thirty. And I think you're much better looking than any of those Yangans," said Kaushik and he checked his Runu while Dipa put the kettle on,

"And you didn't ask again about why she wanted two dresses?"

"No. Don't ask. Do. Just like Mother taught me" said Dipa as she gave a little curtsy to the cups she was swilling from a tin jug.

"And what did you tell your mother, how did you explain your absences on Tuesdays and Thursdays."

"Oh I told Mum what I was doing, we used to tell each other everything me and mum, back then. Well I thought we did." said Dipa absently and she filled the pot with water. Liberty passed a look to Kaushik but he didn't see so she asked,

"Did you know about this Kaushik?" He shook his head,

"It looks like mum kept things from both of us," Kaushik said blankly, "…What did mum know about you?" he asked absently,

"Not much, by the end," answered Dipa with more thought.

"I hate to ask," he said still looking away, "…but is the sort of dress important?"

"As a matter of fact, it is," smiled Dipa wryly, "…They were plain light green taffeta crinolines with a cream lace and silk camellia trim. Nothing Skiemark could copy," and she put a tray of three cups of tea on the table, disclosing her experience of domestic service, "…and all by myself and in thirty-five hours." She said with an echo of the exhaustion such an effort had induced as she sat down like a Queen. Liberty's darkened eyebrows squeezed together in concentration and she looked up at the crumbling ceiling,

"Didn't I see something like that on…?"

"Princess Victoria. Yes, you did see it on her. Not that she was her though. But everything in order Liberty," And she paused to sip her tea with some relish, "…it gets much much worse," she smiled and carried on almost gleefully," …what I thought at the time. I thought my luck was in. I thought I could save some money, move to a Sister-House maybe, or even a Glass House, if Adi took me on more permanently. She wouldn't be the first Yangan to have her own dressmaker. You remember old Dame Williams, Kaushik?" Kaushik indulged his only living relative with a smile, "…Debota, she used to lord it over the rest of us didn't she," and she laughed, "…She worked h'exclusively for the 'Anovers, back in the day. But she was a stitcher like the rest of us. Not that we'll have much work now, I suppose. And, well, if I'm honest, I can't really tell if something is handmade or not, can you?" Her companions shook their heads, "…that Krito-stitching is good, if I'm honest." Dipa seemed a bit taken aback by her own remark and sat back for a moment.

"So, you went to live in the Egremont House?" asked Liberty and Dipa rallied,

"Yes, well, for a couple of weeks anyway. I kamar my mum but I wanted to see what it was like, you know. My own room, and different people, in a properly run house. With staff you know, after the Beauforts. And mum, I think she had got used to life without us when I was at the Beauforts. I was useful but…And she wasn't old but she had all her girls, and when I was there I think she felt like she had more to do more? She didn't want me to see her slacking. But she wasn't slacking; she was taking it a bit easy that's all; her eyes, you know. Her eyes were going, well, not as sharp as they had been anyway. That's why I took the Aunken as well you know Kaushik if I'm honest. For her eyes, and I just took a few more, in case. You'd said that about the Aunken before hadn't you? More for her really; hope? Hope. And the jammy cow knew all along. When did mum know Kaush, that you were alright I mean?

"Oh? I think I got the first message to her that first winter. Before Christmas." Dipa's eyes widened but she didn't speak. "…Tariqul, did you ever meet Tariqul?" His sister shook her head, but she knew he was Head of the new irry and giddy Council, "…Good man, I'll introduce you when you get out of here. Anyway, he worked in a wool mill in Leeds, good quality stuff Dipa, you'd like it."

"Temple Mills?" Asked Dipa and Kaushik nodded, "…it was good quality, but mum said they weren't what they were. Is that where you were then, Leeds?"

"Yes," said Kaushik, "…and Manchester, that's where all the best people, political people, are Dipa. It was such a revelation, a relief, to talk to so many people who thought like I did. The best thing that could have happened, banning Critical Mass, having to run," and he laughed. Dipa and Liberty didn't laugh, he could have been arrested, detained, imprisoned or worse. "…we went old school Dipa, I wrote mum messages and slipped them into samples of Temple wool and put them in the post, then she'd send messages back, returning the samples with one letter about quality or colour or whatnot and one for me. The quality was fine Dipa, she was sending me messages when she sent swatches back. She was always crafty I suppose. She kept me up to date with everything that was happening to you. Well? Not everything? What you told her; travelling the world as a lady's maid to one of the best families in the Empire. She was proud of you Dipa.

Then you got the Aunken and I could go wherever I wanted, full pass everywhere. Porters bowing and scraping and carrying my bags full of sedition because they thought I was an Aristoi." Kaushik laughed again. Dipa was shaking her head,

"The secrets that woman took with her," and she sighed and took hold of Kaushik's hand. "…Debota, Kaushik, we both put her in a very hard and dangerous place, didn't we? Me with the Egremonts and you with your revolutionising. Didn't give it a second thought. And we were all she had." Kaushik squeezed her hand with the same level, if not the same sort, of guilt and added,

"And we both forgot Mother's Day last year didn't we. She wasn't happy." Tears came to both their eyes again. Liberty cleared her throat very quietly. Dipa sighed,

"What time is it?" She asked wearily,

"Ten forty-five," answered Liberty, "Shall we take a break?" They were feeling Dipa's exhaustion from a night of pacing up and down full of Jus, confusion and grief. Kaushik, sighed and looked around him,

"I'm beginning to feel the oppression of this room, and I've only been in here a few minutes."

"Try six months Kaushik," said Dipa leaning back and staring at the ceiling. "…six months."

Kaushik got up quickly and made for the door,

"Wait here a minute," he said banging on the door, "…sorry, I've got an idea." A guard came quickly and Kaushik was let out.

The women watched him go, both with puzzled expressions as they turned back to look at each other. Liberty turned off her Runu, indicating that she would not question Dipa without Kaushik present. They smiled weakly and sat in silence for a while. Liberty looked around the messy room for something to do, prompting Dipa to do the same.

"I've slept in worse rooms," said Dipa, "…also better." She let out another sigh. The ceiling was high and the room was quite large for a cell, painted white. The clutter of furniture all looked like it had come out of a junk shop.

"Koulla rug," said Liberty absently,

"Mm, too much red for me," replied Dipa lethargically. They sipped their tea not looking at each other. "…I should dust," she said in the same way that Liberty might say she should take a weekend off. Kaushik bounded back into the room and the women came out of the slump that they had been sinking into.

"Fancy a walk around the grounds?" He grinned, "… for an hour, tunoo, to get some fresh air? We could walk and talk?" Dipa looked at him for a moment,

"Outside?" She looked confused, hesitant.

"Did the guards say it was alright?" Asked Liberty,

"Yes, just for an hour. It's all secure. The others, the other prisoners have been getting exercise for weeks now apparently."

"The others?" Asked Dipa,

"The others, unsympathetic Aristois, hardliners," Explained Liberty as she got up with her Runu. "…they have trials coming up too."

"When I came here it was just me," said Dipa without moving, "…the last time I was with any Aristois they were…" she rubbed her shoulders and then put her hand on the back of her head so that her hat wobbled precariously, "…they weren't baban happy with me."

"Don't worry, their exercise doesn't start until later, come on Dipa let's go for a walk," Kaushik had his hand outstretched and Dipa put out hers so that he had to come forward to take it. He pulled her up with another smile. She was smiling too, reticent still. The door was still open and Liberty followed them out into the dimly lit corridor, past a standing guard,

"Hello Lorenzo," smiled Dipa, "…I'm going for a walk."

"Miss," assented Lorenzo impassively as they went by and down the worn stone steps in half light. The old steps were uneven and Dipa's heels were high enough for her to have to take great care. They continued their dissent with Liberty listening for Dipa's arrhythmic footsteps. In the long corridor at the bottom, the thick iron-studded door was almost all the way open. Weak spring sunlight splayed on the flagstones at the threshold. Dipa hesitated again. Still holding her hand Kaushik tugged gently, smiled and carried on walking. Dipa found herself on the narrow parapet and squinted and stopped.

She huffed out a quick breath, linked arms with her brother and strode along and then down some more steps. There was a bounce in her step as she tripped down onto the inner courtyard, head aloft, a haughty half smile on her face. Kaushik looked her up and down with affection and said,

"Where to now Your Majesty?"

"I'd like to feel the grass under my feet," asserted Dipa as she looked up to the roof of the Arcade and the white-grey sky beyond.

They were on the lawn where Dipa could see her cell above. She stared at it for quite a time and then looked over to the great White Tower in the middle of the castle square. The fifteen or more arched windows were irregularly sized to suit the needs of different ages. Blank black, they seemed to stand out against the stone of the great squat cube of a building, with its four inadequate turrets, grey under the bland light. She looked up at them for another long while.

Suddenly she un-looped her arm from Kaushik at the same time kicking off her shoes. With small steps in her bare feet, she ran onto the grass, unmown for quite some time and lush from the sprinklers. She waltzed and twirled around three times, laughing, with her arms wide open, reminding her brother of when she was a small child. "…Oh Kaushik! Outside! Outside," she cried, "…it's so good to be outside," then she skipped and ran and lent down to stroke her hand across the straggly turf. "…Oh Kaushik!" She cried and ran back to her brother and hugged him with a vigour that surprised him a little.

Liberty looked up at the White Tower too, high and wide and grey except for the dark windows. She saw a human shadow at one and then another. That was where the Aristois were being kept. Dipa gestured towards her smiling and pointed at the shoes she had cast aside. Liberty picked up the shoes and followed as Dipa, back arm in arm with her brother, paraded slowly in the shadow of the prison, "...Do you remember coming here when we were young, with mum and dad and Aja and Anik and Agi, when dad came back from a tour somewhere?" She asked. Kaushik nodded smiling, his head down as he put his free hand onto Dipa's arm,

"We had a picnic, with jam tarts and jalebi, still warm." He said and Dipa squeezed closer,

"Yes! And all those giant birds, Ravens, and dad chasing them away across the grass," they laughed again,

"That Beefeater kept looking at us,"

"Yes, but they weren't going to get our jalabis."

"Neither did I," laughed Kaushik, "...you snaffled the lot, remember." Dipa narrowed her eyes and looked at him, "...yes, that's why the Beefeater was laughing at us remember?"

"No?" said Dipa,

"You nearly broke my nose! How don't you remember? You punched me in the face," and he turned to Liberty, "...she was a bruiser when she was young our dainty little lady here. Four brothers. Wrestling, starting something all the time in that tiny flat our princess. Dad used to say she'd've made the best soldier, if she wasn't a girl."

"Oh that was just his way of being nice, he only knew the army," said Dipa and she turned to Liberty, "...Kaushik's exaggerating, I was a good girl I was. Always helping Mum; cooking, cleaning, washing, sewing," Kaushik raised an alternative recollection with an eyebrow, "…mum said…and anyway, what did mum say, what was it about the birds? That day we were all together?" Kaushik sighed indulgently and said,

"If the ravens ever leave the Tower, then, the Kingdom will fall. Look, there's one!" They watched a huge black beaked bird, oil sheened, lollop along, flapping his one clipped and one good wing as he chased after a nimbler pigeon. Raven Rocky, for that was his name, was persistent in his endeavour while the anonymous pigeon, who could have flown up and away at any moment, fluttered ahead a few feet, settled, pecked around for a moment and moved on a little way again.

"Well, that didn't work," said Dipa emphatically as she looked up at the Tower's West side and slowed her pace,

"The kingdom hasn't fallen," replied Kaushik, almost hurt, "…Its under New…"

"Management. Alright. But? Will they keep doing that to the Ravens, now? Clipping their wings?"

"I don't know? Seems cruel to me." Said Kaushik. Now he saw too the shadows standing above, watching." …It's not like they're going to have any heads on pikes to eat like the olden days." Dipa saw where he was looking and her face hardened as she said,

"No? They told me I was for the chop. Literally. Said they were going to behead me. Screamed it. Spat it." Kaushik put his arm round her and laughed,

"Yeah. Me too." And now the pair turned towards the Tower and looked up at the people at the windows. First one and then another shadow shrank back into the dark. The three resumed their slow circuit until they came to what had been a visitor's café and was now a canteen for the guards who needed actual food. In the window, scrawled on a piece of board was a sign that said, 'NO PRISONERS', Dipa wanted to stay outside anyway so she and Liberty sat on a bench in front of a piece of the Roman wall while Kaushik was sent for 'anything'. Liberty looked behind them and up to the White Tower and squinted. She could see no-one looking. Dipa sat so daintily that Liberty knew that they were observed, but she didn't know if Dipa's pose was for a prisoner or the guards that came and went to the canteen. Most walked and talked easily while they stared briefly at the 'Wannabe Monarch' as Dipa had been nick-named. One or two had to be pulled away from stopping and gaping.

"They can't all be human?" Dipa observed nodding at the guards,

"No? But they still like a break and some social interaction I suppose."

"Yes, I've had a couple of chatty ones," said Dipa and let her face turn up to the bright grey-white sky above the arcade glass, breathing deeply. Liberty turned on her Runu and asked,

"We were talking about your mother's attitude to the possibility of your moving out,"

"Oh. Yes? Well, I think she was all for it really, not that I ever did get to live on my own. Not until I got put here. I mean I'm not saying it's in any way fun in here, but I have sort of quite liked being on my own, locked up in there," and she paused as if keeping something back and gestured back towards the Lanthorn Tower like a Queen dismissing a servant. "…When Adi, Lady Egremont as we were calling her at the time." Dipa corrected herself with and courteous smile to her lawyer, "…asked me to be her lady's maid, my mum was all for it, mainly. And the chance to travel, see the world, she was happy."

"And Kaushik? What did she think of Kaushik's life?"

"Oh, well he's a man isn't he. And the only one left so," said Dipa with a shrug, then she screwed up her face for a moment, thinking, "…But, well I was thinking about it the other day? Not much to do but think you know? There was this time, before, when he…He used to come to mum's nearly every Sunday and, when he was younger, I think he must've just met Critical Mass. Anyway, he was going on about the oppression of the masses after dinner and banging on and on about some movement that dad and our brothers were putting down somewhere in Great Africa and she said, my mum said it was fitnah, you know?"

"What's fitnah?"

"Oh? It means spreading discord, it's in the Koran, you know, griping for no reason, just stirring."

"Was she religious your Mum?"

"Of course she was, in the normal way, you know, normal; no pork or shellfish, the occasional blind eye for Jelly Babies when we were kids, and we celebrated the Eids more than Diwali or Christmas. You know; normal. I went to a Church school because it was good and closer than the Masood,"

"And you, were you ever, did you ever have a religious phase?

"Me?" Dipa laughed,

"You were never tempted to support the Moslems in Persia?" and Dipa laughed some more,

106

"I might be stupid and wicked but I'm not a moron, why do you ask? Are you Jewish? You're Jewish aren't you," said Dipa with the sort of relish people usually reserve for discovering someone's secret love affair. Liberty sighed, "...So tell me, I've missed so much, are Jews, in this revolution, are you goodies or badies?" Dipa smiled innocently, Liberty sighed again, "...I only ask because you know before, some people thought you were the badies; Aristoi's bankers conspiring to keep us all oppressed and whatnot, but then other people said you were an oppressed group or something; goodies?" she kept her eyes on Liberty and batted her eyelashes,

"Oh, I think we're people now," said Liberty and let out one more sigh before adding, "...So, tell me about this blank verse game, then, while we wait." Dipa stopped relishing so that she and Liberty could watch a respected Deputy of the Transitional Committee, hero of the Battle for Westminster, walking very carefully towards them with three Ninety-Nine ice-creams; one with raspberry sauce, one with chocolate fudge and one with nuts, and sit between them. Dipa let Liberty pick first and Kaushik have the one with raspberry sauce. They ate in reverential silence for a while. None of them had eaten an ice-cream for some time and they withdrew into their own collections of memory. The blank verse game could wait a while. The Runu on Liberty's lap interrupted with a bleep and said in a deep woman's voice, 'I'm still listening. Do you want to carry on?' so Liberty looked at Dipa, engrossed in her cone, and answered,

"No," and the Runu darkened in response. Liberty was an all-around licker. Dipa and Kaushik used their chocolate flakes to push the ice-cream deep into the cone and slurp what oozed up around it with their lips.

North Tower, Tower Bridge, East London

The dark-suited man's knees hurt as he perched on the shooting stick in the large room at the top of the North Tower of Tower Bridge, poking twenty or so feet [7 or so metres] above the Aspic. And his back. He was unable to see The Subject from this vantage point, even with his binoculars, but he had no alternative. He had seen them walk, and dance on the grass. Now that they were on the other side of the White Tower he was actually concentrating on his sketch. He did like sketching, always had, but not this old-style spying. He was working, almost furiously, on a hovercraft as it scudded between him and the Tower of London.

He should have had a few dozen cameras and a couple of drones. He should have Krito-camera-eyes watching their every move while he sat on his old comfortable chair in front of his bank of screens. But he would simply have to wait for The Subject to walk back around the White Tower. At least he wasn't standing in the drizzle while The Subject talked rubbish with a machine again. And he was off his poor knees peeping into that hole in the wall in the cold. It was degrading, a person of his stature, staring into a crevice he himself had had to drill with a tool that looked like an antique.

A Tower Bridge Experience Employee sauntered up behind him and looked at his drawing. She smiled approvingly and went to explain some history to a group of school children. He had made the sky to the East of the Arcade too dark; he saw that now. A few dabs with his spat-on handkerchief and the smudging effect was lighter and more effective. Charcoal had been a good choice. The tiny figures were good too. He would give it to The Chief to illustrate his report. Even if he had no eye The Chief would see the funny side.

A Bench on Tower Green, Tower of London

Dipa produced a small lace handkerchief to wipe her fingers and passed it to Liberty. Kaushik leaned forward and nodded to Liberty as he put his elbows on his knees,

"So, what was Adi Egremont like then Dipa?" He asked while Liberty wiped a little blob of ice-cream off her Runu, which had just spoken. She read the message but said nothing.

"What was she like? That's a hard one. She was anything she wanted to be, or she thought you wanted. Always charming and made you feel like the most important person in the room. Like a lot of them, they're baban sociable, easy to get on with. But different. She used to use this place past the Damn, but? Everything in order. She was a chameleon, that's why she was so perfect for Vicky. Princess Victoria. She was just another maphosa really. But I didn't find that out until the summer. When I first met her, she was like the sister I never had. Treated me like a sister, a sister who worked night and day. Bringing me food on a tray up in that sewing room herself, and sitting with me while I worked, chatting like a sister," Dipa interrupted herself with a laugh, "…She did this great impression of both the Lady Coretados, did both of them, 'Oh mummy, stop!' 'But darling, you must see it,'" and she laughed again, "…The Coretados were hilarious." Kaushik and Liberty remained nonchalant and did not look at each other,

"She was a good mimic, then?" Asked Liberty,

"Oh, the best, she could do anyone. A natural."

"So, it was she who taught you to behave like Princess Victoria," said Kaushik,

"No, well she taught me to act like an Aristoi, a bit, she got bored. Cousin Joshi was the real expert. She couldn't train me properly because she was a natural. These things have to be learned to fully understand them, he said. She could just do it, anyone, do her father, his voice especially. On the Runu, she got us tickets to the theatre and Passes all the time that way."

"You went out together?" Asked Kaushik, surprised.

"Oh yes, all the time. When we came back from travelling and I was Alyan."

"Who?" Asked Kaushik, with evident shock.

"Oh? You didn't know about her?"

"No," chorused Liberty and Kaushik,

"Miss Alyan Rajanya, third cousin to Adi Egremont, favourite niece and unexpected heir of the childless Yadaspati Rai Bachchan, cotton manufacturer, who actually died almost bankrupt, that was me when I, 'meta-maphosa-ed'. For my coming out season. It was her idea, Adi's. A joke you know, she said, or an experiment, you know like Pygmalion, the play, not the Greek myth. She, Adi, said it would be fun. It was. When we came back that's who I was. I got off the plane in another adjie and I was Alyan Rajanya, with just enough of a hint of being a villasitter to keep people gossiping about the wrong thing," Dipa was enjoying their wide eyes and tilted heads, but she was talking again when Liberty and Kaushik shared a quizzical look, they both remembered the name but couldn't place it, "…Oh but Bengal! Debota, it was like a fairy tale. Flowers everywhere and the scent of them all mingling in the shimmering heat. Lying on the grass in the shade with my head in her lap, reciting my lessons, 'Don't look at the servants, don't look at your feet'" She recounted languidly, "…And my room! A bed as big as my old bedroom back home. The warm breeze coming in and wafting in the scent of Jasmine. Sheets so soft and…The view! This big garden all planted with Roses with this big lake beyond it.

Everyone said that Lady Egremont, her mother, loved the rose garden but I only saw her in it once and I don't think she knew where she was. The way they treated her. Kept her, stored her more like, in a room at the back. Rolled her out for special occasions. She was a sight. Had more plastic surgery than a war hero that one. Skinny little skeleton of a woman with her irry skin pulled so tight over her face she couldn't smile even if she wanted to. Dripping in jewels.

It was just after dawn on? Some morning? Early. It was all misty, and there was Lady Egremont walking vaguely around the murky rose bushes in her nightie. I watched her for quite a while, like a smudged photograph that hazy morning.

And that big sky such a wan, almost white sort of blue pushing back the ink. The land looked like it was coming back from a dream and remembering what shape it should be, pulling back from the dark to make its horizon. I caught it just waking up, getting clearer and sharper and I saw the trees and the grass making themselves out of the mist. And the birds' songs came back into being and sang for the joy of it. Then they had little bodies and wings, so they flew up into the new formed sky. All the world, becoming itself in front of my eyes. Making little pink petals and blades of grass smelling sweet and lush.

Then the world was awake and knew what it was again. Solid and touchable. But she, the old lady Egremont, she just stayed a blur. This vague indefinite shape drifting in the garden. It seemed to me anyway. I watched her for quite a while, drifting. I called to Adi but she was still asleep you know. It had been a long night…The nights! The palace would be…"

"You and Adi were…?"

"Lovers. Yes, why not? At night the palace was like this glowing golden bubble floating. Like a star. Like the world had melted away and the palace was all there was and there was nothing else for a million miles of black. Just us dancing and laughing in the light, and maybe all the other trillions of little stars out there were more palaces floating through the nothing. And there were other Adis and Alyans up in the sky dancing on the terrace with their own moons to stare down at them and smile… I think me and Adi might have thought about that one night?

The dinners, the parties. And I was like a duck to water Adi said. And they all kamared me, not just because they adored Adi, not just cishying, they baban kamared me. I think I might have been happy then?"

"So," said Liberty, taking advantage of Dipa's wistful pause, "…it was Aditi Egremont who initiated your intimacy?" Dipa replied with a little melancholy in her tone,

"I suppose so,"

"And it was her idea for you to take on this new, new name?" Dipa nodded blithely, "…And how did you feel about becoming, adopting this new name and position?"

"Oh, it was wonderful!" said Dipa enthusiastically, "…The life was…" Kaushik interjected,

"But didn't you miss being yourself, cutting yourself off from…"

"Cutting myself off from what exactly? Working my fingers to the bone? Third class carriage on the train. Lugging cans of milk up three flights of stairs? Dirt everywhere. I could still go and see mum if I wanted, more even. You were dead or disappeared. I didn't think I'd ever see you again. I didn't go home enough I know that now, I saw that when she died. I just thought she'd just go on forever. I hadn't seen her for weeks, months maybe, and then she was gone…" said Dipa and she paused again, sad this time. Liberty asked gently,

"Was it hard to adjust, not to the lifestyle I mean, to being someone else? Pretending all the time."

"I wasn't pretending, I was me with a new name and a different life that's all. There's no such thing as a Maphosa until you get caught. It was uchit fun. And I'd been around that type all my life hadn't I, working with Mum, I knew how to talk and walk and whatnot, it wasn't hard and no-one cared, just put on the adjie and the Aunken and no-one cared. Joshi was impressed, never seen a human do it so well, he said. It was frightening he said. Because I did it so well. Lots of real people can't do it at all: they're such fools they think style comes by nature to people in their position; and so they never learn.

It was harder being Vicky, you know. It's tricky to act that stupid, Adi said. But even then, it wasn't so difficult. She was quiet and a bit dim and off her head on drugs most of the time so…" she trailed off and sighed, "…Adi and me used to talk about, 'Meta-maphosa-ring', quite a bit. Maphosas get a bad press you know, acting above their station, they're no more fake than anyone else, that's what she said. I wasn't irry, I was me with another accent that's all. She said we were all just maphosas really you know; one thing to your parents, another for a lover that kind of thing. Why pick just one of your selves to be the real you? Like any one of them is more real than any of the others. But I don't know about that? I think maybe there's no such thing as a fake person, as long as everybody believes it and…" Kaushik interrupted again,

"But there must've been a part of you that couldn't, that wasn't? What about the true you?" Dipa looked puzzled,

"I thought you were all for transitions Kaushik? I mean we're all changing who we are all the time aren't we. Weren't you a mill-worker a year ago?"

"Not mum, mum was always the same,"

"You didn't see her at work, with her 'I don't know anything about that your ladyship' and 'you look lovely Madame's," Kaushik looked confused, "…you're work self. All your selves. They're all you. And the more people treat you like you're your new you, the more you you become. She liked to be the Honourable Rosheen Dupree quite a lot, Adi, you know when we were out of the bubble," and she laughed, "…she had this hat, her Rosheen hat she called it and when she put it on, she was this awful, rude…" Liberty who used to be a lawyer and was now a lawyer said,

"She was known for her behaviour. And it was rumoured that she, Aditi Egremont, had some sort of cocktail?"

"Strange you mean. Oh yes, we drank it by the gallon [dekalitre]. Her own special recipe, no one knows what's in it…Are you saying I was drunk?" There was an indignant tone in Dipa's voice that had gone by the time she had looked at her brother's slightly reproving face, "…I suppose we were a bit tipsy most of the time. But that place, that place, the palace, could make you high just being in it, it was so cyow. It was! It was like a fairy-tale Kaushik, all those elegant columns inside and out, going up up and the lovely gardens all around. Space, you know, a huge space, spaces. Room after elegant room. And I had the run of it, I could go where I pleased, when I pleased; Breakfast in the library, afternoon tea in the morning room. The dining room table could seat over 200 people, we had a picnic on the dining table once, sitting on the table, with all those curtains along an entire wall, wafting in the breeze from the terrace. And people, beautiful people without a care in the world. So many friends to chat. And dancing, dancing all the time," Kaushik took his sister's hand and squeezed it reassuringly. She looked down for a moment and took a breath, "…But everything in order. Tunoo, tunoo. Before then, in London, before we went to India when I was still just a lady's maid; the dresses.

I was still Dipa. And Adi, well at first she said it was just playing. It was their last ball, THE last ball of the London Season, everyone was there. We both put on the dresses and played the swapping game… She'd taught me, as if it was a game, how to walk like a Yangan, talk like Yangan, not that I needed to learn much, and all the while sipping Strange, her special recipe cordial, like Jus but a bit more relaxing,", and she added in a generic Yangan voice, "…opens one up," and laughed, "…But she had the idea in her head already, I think, what she was really training me up for, I mean. Not to be

Victoria, not then, just swap occasionally." Liberty took a breath to ask a question, but Kaushik put his hand on her arm and she sat back, "…But in order. We packed up and went to India, in an aeroplane. A supersonic one. Cousin Joshi's. He was always ahead of his time, had all the latest toys. It still took half a day. It was cyow, that Rajbari! And you see, while we were on the plane, just me and Adi and cousin Joshi, the rest of the family had already gone over. On the plane, that's when I meta-maphosa-sised. The first time."

"So, you saw a lot of Jyothi Hausa?"

"Oh, yes! He was such fun, the old goat. He left me alone after a few tries though. The things that went on there. I could tell you a thing or two," and she laughed, "…There was this time when…"

"You lived in Hira Hall." said Kaushik and his sister nodded. "…Did you ever get a sense of his… his business interests?" and she laughed again,

"Cousin Joshi had lots of interests, He didn't mix business with pleasure so much as have pleasurable business and business pleasures, you know. Everyone who was everyone came to his house parties and well, deals were done…but I didn't really follow who was doing what with who, I was too busy with Adi and then Vicky too, Vicky too?"

"I'm sorry, Kaushik, can we get to that when we have found out about Alyan the Yangan in the palace in India." Said Liberty, "…How long were you there? At the palace?"

"Almost up to Christmas, which was unusual apparently. They usually nip back to Europe well before; Italy, an Italian palazzo in the hills above Florence, it's Lord Egremont's favourite apparently. But he was hosting some sort of conflab' there, something diplomatic, so we stayed on at the old place. But Adi got bored, she can't sit still for that long, keeps moving on," There was a tinge of bitterness in Dipa's last remark, but she soon lightened, "…So we took a place on the Amalfi coast for a month or so. I learned to swim! The sea there is warm all year round, or were we in Greece by then? I forget. And Adi is a positive fish. She can dive as well. Joshi said she was like a Kingfisher the way she cut into the water without a splash. But I've never seen a Kingfisher. But I do know that when the moonlight lit her silhouette and she sprang up and arced and dived into the water, I had only ever seen anything that beautiful in the flickers before." Dipa stopped talking and looked up, "…I had forgotten that, it must've been where she was going when, …But in order, order. Italy, Greece, Paris in the Spring obviously, then back to London, for the Season. That's when I went to live in Hira Hall.

His special cinema, and the parties! He gave the best parties, everyone said. The ballroom was the size of Paddington Station and he had a lake as well and everyone was there, even the stuffy Hausas sometimes with their noses in the air, so stiff that Prince Gaddo, like dancing with a plank. But they still wanted to marry cousin Joshi off to that po-faced Aminata, you know his sister, poor cousin Joshi, can you imagine him married to that starched madame. And plain!? You would never guess they were related, second cousins; them and Vicky, like chalk and cheese…And the food, oh the food, only the best of everything for cousin Joshi,"

"You must've seen his guests, at his parties and dinners, talked to them," said Kaushik

"Yes, but just chitter-chatter that's all. I was decoration that's all. Look, Joshi was a, what did he say, 'a conduit' that's all. He had money in lots of business, including the Krito business. And everyone knew that Krito tech got a lot of money from the Department of War. And no-one wants a spy cleaning their bedroom grates do they. So, he used his position, as second in line you know, to reassure people, influential people that civil Krito were fun, useful servants and harmless toys. Worth investing in. And they were until all that glitching business. Oh, the dancing! And the other thing of course. They're baban good at dancing, Krito,"

"And? You could both pose as Princess Victoria, you looked very much like each other. Did anyone point that out to you at these gatherings, or any other time?" asked Liberty,

"We went to great efforts to look different most of the time. You can do a lot if with clothes of course; waist, skirt length, heels. And then there's make-up, Adi was a master make-up artist. Vicky liked to pad her shoulders and show off her waist, Adi wore whatever was in her head that day, sent me a Runu snap if we were apart, and I wore whatever, kept it simple you know. And well, you know all beautiful women resemble one another, but ugly women are all ugly in their own way. And the plain ones too,"

Dipa's blithe eyes brushed over Liberty just for a moment, caught something else and darkened suddenly, she stopped talking. Liberty looked around and froze. Kaushik turned too and saw. The shadows from the windows were taking form on the outer steps of the Tower. Firm flesh and hard bone, about a dozen moving briskly.

"Time to go in I think," he said and he and Liberty nearly stood up to walk back the other way. Dipa sat and watched the small crowd of Aristois reach the ground. She had a half-smile on her face and was still looking at her former fellow guests at Hira Hall when she said,

"Liberty, the Blank Verse Game, you wanted to know." Her lawyer settled down again, then her brother. Dipa spoke slowly and deliberately, counting on her fingers,

"Oh, well, Mum used to make us play at it. I don't think any of us liked it much." And Kaushik shook his head and scowled boyishly, "…Not like skipping or football or board games. But she would make us do it, it was hard. She said it was exercise for the brain. We had to answer questions in blank verse. Exactly ten syllables, not one more. Emphasise every other word, like this; 'The big black bird can't fly with just one wing'. It makes you choose your words more carefully, she said."

"And Mum, what did you tell her? Did you see her before, when you came back from the countries?"

"As far as she was concerned I was still a lady's maid," said Dipa with a shrug, "…I'd go round in my Dipa adjie and chat about nothing as usual…If I missed a Sunday afternoon, I just told her we were away in the countries." And Dipa stopped talking. She smiled and allowed Liberty and Kaushik to wait for her next words,

"…My shoes," she smiled to Liberty who quickly handed them over. She slipped them on and slowly offered her hand to Kaushik so that he could help her rise. Her brother knew what she was doing now and, he hoped for his own reasons, offered her his arm. By this time the first of the other prisoners were a couple of feet away and the rest were fanning out around them. Only Dipa recognised faces in the crowd, but she didn't acknowledge any of her old friends. More were coming down the stairs and emerging from the other Towers.

"Are you hungry Dipa darling?" Asked Kaushik in mock-posh, and in what she believed was the real thing she replied,

"Baban! I'm absolutely starving," The pair, followed by Liberty, strolled forward, followed by a few of the silent inmates.

"I hear that place makes a passable pie, could you manage a little pastry?" inquired Kaushik jovially and more quietly he added, "…I'm sure they'd make an exception for the sister of a Member of the Transitional Council."

"That sounds lovely. Liberty you'll join us won't you," a regal Dipa asserted and they made for the canteen which now stood behind a group of scowling Aristois, Dipa nodded to one of them,

"Beatrice," she said sweetly to someone in the still mute crowd as it parted a little, "…Well now we know her natural hair colour," she said to Liberty who giggled instinctively. Dipa spotted another familiar face, "…Sanoo Eddy," chirruped the ex-Queen with a flutter of her fingers and they strolled past the 'No Prisoners' sign and went to eat pie.

Padma River, Near Chandpur, Bengal

He came up from under the tarpaulin slowly, the whole boat pulsating with her arupa music. She was on the stuff, he knew it. And what was that awful biting smell? He could identify tomatoes and onions before a sudden retch made him give up. He squeezed behind the table in the shabby saloon with his back to her and sat. She was smoking and dancing around the galley with a large knife in her right hand. Her cheap shalwar couldn't hide those curves, she was perhaps more lovely without adornment, swaying and winding to that terrible music. He picked up his book at the same time as stretching out along the thinly cushioned bench. A rolled-up blanket was already in place for his head.

"You should sleep," she called. He turned his page corner back up and tried to read under the light of the dirty little porthole, but he was too tired and the room was thick with that acidic stinging reek of whatever it was that she was cooking.

"What's that smell? Are you concocting some sort of witches brew in there?" he said without attempting to be heard over the music.

"It's your supper, the longer you let it simmer, the better it will be…Do you want some tea?" He sighed and replied in the affirmative. A cooked supper-albeit an awful one, and now tea, what did she want? The kettle must have already boiled because she came and sat down with two chipped enamelled mugs almost immediately. He let his cup sit on the sticky table.

"Drink it while it's hot, it nice and sweet," she said and slurped conspicuously so that he would look at her sipping. He loved to watch her sip, her deep brown eyes blinking over the cup. He studied her through the steam and waited. "…how's the cargo?" He did not respond. She was about to make some other small talk but thought better of it. "…I've been looking at the map," she began. He tilted his head to one side slightly by means of acknowledgement. "…we are still in that left-hand-middle-wiggle of the Meghna?"

"This is the Padma." She did not let his blank tone disparage her,

"Yes, well, the Padma has got baban sakhanadis, all those little channels, no more than streams, more even than the Meghna, more like a swamp, more like the Sundarbans?"

"Not so much, this time of year." He qualified and turned a page of the book he was not reading.

"Yes, but this time of year they're lower, aren't they? Some of the little rivers are all dried up, just sand and mud," His eyes narrowed, what did she want? "…and you're so tired of driving the boat night and day," she leaned over and briefly stroked his cheek with what he would believe was true affection, "…and the suti suti sakhanadis we need to stay in are so hard to drive the heavy boat in. And it takes so long winding this way and that way, especially in the dark." He sighed, this woman had plotted and planned the best japes he had ever perpetrated, developed his inventions with brilliance, and here she was wheedling like a novice.

"Going back, bringing the train to Rajbari is too dangerous. Too conspicuous, we discussed this." He replied emphatically and altered the angle of the book as it leaned on his paunch.

She put her tea to her perfect lips again and from behind her mug she murmured,

"We could get an ordinary freight train." He sat up a little, thinking it was high time he too sipped his tea. He engaged a deal of eyelash batting and the coy smile that had got him a triste with the Czar of all the Russias, albeit some time ago, and said in an excellent imitation of her sweetest voice,

"We haven't got a freight train. We can't get our train until we are nearer to our destination, and if you spent more time trying to fix your masterpiece and less time swigging Strange I wouldn't have to navigate the suti suti shit-filled sakhanadis night after fucking night," wiped his face blank again and turned back to his book. She didn't shout, he had expected her to flare.

"I haven't got the software," she said coolly, "...I had better check supper." And indeed, the pervading smell of warm vomit was beginning to be overpowered by that of burning. She rose to return to the galley, leaving her tea.

"You could do it with the parts from the other ones, I know you could my handsome hanckilly one," he sang after her.

"But then what would you have to play with all day my darling," she warbled back as she walked. There was a long silence, then a sizzling sound and a clatter. "...it's nearly done. I think I'll do some of those things with chickpeas...You could do it? Your company made them. And you did spend quite a bit of time with them." He sighed,

"You know I only worked on the finishing touches."

"Finishing touches, is that what it's called? Ha." She was quiet again. It was a good book but it made no difference, he couldn't help but focus on her. Wait. "...Where's the, is there

125

a sieve in here?" There was large clang "…Debota, Debota, Debota! I cannot stand this horrible little boat!"

"Where's your gaskey gone my kamar? Where's your spirit? And why are you putting yourself through all this? You could have that gubbins steering, cooking, cleaning and making you a cocktail in a couple of hours."

"Gaskey! Gaskey! I'll give you gaskey!" The words and the still dripping ladle arrived at the same time. There it was, and with the pain in his head came the realisation that it was what he had wanted all along. He recovered from the blow in time to see her straightening to full height with a great inhalation and bellow, "…You lure me into your stupid japes, you dream up this stupid plan, your 'situation'. Ha! Trap me on this disgusting boat. Months of running. From your mess. You won't listen to any other way and then tell me I've lost my gaskey!" Once again, she was marvellous to behold.

"A world rebellion, my mess?" He laughed still supine, "I lured you."

"Your japes! Your pestilential japes! You went too far, too far. And now I'm here, stuck, trapped on this filthy, dirty slime-bucket. How I ever went along with it…"

"Who was it who dreamed up the Vicky jape?" And he pointed to himself in faux shock. He was keeping his cool, he was content with that. She was too angry to see his lip twitch.

"You think we're here because of Vicky? Ha!" She was standing over him now, "…Your Nayakas are what got me stuck on this hulk two weeks away from a shower. Your Nayakas and your greed." Now he had her. Was this the time? His best card. Maybe. He looked up at her with his big brown eyes and inquired gently,

"And the Mişţi Cā Code? I came up with that I suppose."
Yes, it was the time. The pleasure of watching that beautiful
face, usually unreadable, even for him, struggle so obviously.
Now he watched those exquisite features go through the
ordinary contortions in her attempts to deny, then blame, then
accuse and finally own responsibility. It was as fine as a quick
orgasm.

"It's the Mişţi Cā Kāpa Code," she corrected, speaking
quietly now "…and your name is on the patent," a little bitter
smile he had never seen before crept onto her face, "…and if
you think one little tweak did all this then you deserve
everything…" She stopped talking when she saw his eyes dart
towards the landward porthole. There were other voices. They
looked at each other and listened to the several high voices,
talking fast, come and go as a path near the river bank wound
past trees then closer again. He spoke at last,

"Children. They've already passed by."

"They probably don't even speak English…You deserve
everything you get. And I can get it for you," But the moment
had also gone and she turned on her heel and glided into the
galley. She did not hear him say quietly,

"But the Kritos know, don't they. The Kritos know."

Supermarket, West London

Our hero had found the pasta aisle at last. He was checking a packet in one hand to see if it contained enough ounces [grammes] for the recipe that he was reading from his Runu in his other when the latter spoke with a message. The Runu repeated, 'R.S.V.P' until he could drop the fusilli into his basket on his arm and reply.

Eight o'clock gave him plenty of time. He would impress her with a good dinner. Wine, where was the wine? The Runu began to ring and it took him a while to remember where he had put it. A fumble in his coat paid off and he said,

"Sanoo? Er, On! Sanoo?" He heard nothing except more ringing so he quickly pressed the button on the shaft and said, "…Sanoo?"

"I couldn't find the on button," he explained

"In the Supermarket, it's huge!" He looked around wide-eyed with the phone still to his ears.

"Food," then his face flattened as he listened to the long reply and then interjected,

"It's all part of the plan."

"No."

"You're forgetting the history," He realised he had stopped walking to answer the phone but he could walk and talk at the same time, and set off for the wine. She was obviously not going to stop talking until she had recapped the history in question. When he had reached the wine-aisle he interrupted her,

"We have to work differently now," she hadn't understood him so he added,

"We have to work in a new way, it's a different landscape, we talked about this. She isn't a priority for them. We can't rely on those old connections. It's up to us."

"I know its short-sighted of them but…" He had found the red wine and perused the shelves while she talked at length again. He picked up a bottle and shoved it angrily in his basket, not noticing it was on top of the tomatoes.

"Don't be arupa, I'm not taking advantage…" he looked around to see if any other shoppers were looking,

"She's not that naïve," he sighed as the voice on his receiver changed tac,

"I will figure out a way to…" But she was right, he did not have any idea what he was doing. He was a soldier, not a spy. She was expert in all this and was right to be concerned. When he had asked her how to change the subject from 'you look koulla' to 'tell me what has happened to Iris's sister' he had learned how much he didn't know. But our heroine, for it was she on the phone, was employing a new argument now,

"How can I be both duping her and soft?" He had a long walk to the till and so he took the time to listen and calm down a little,

"Koulla, Iris. We will find her, we will," he paused but she did not speak. "…Look, we'll talk properly tomorrow, koulla?"

"Being out of our depth is nothing new and…"

"If it doesn't work, it doesn't work and we'll try something new," he agreed as he stopped to stand behind a woman who was already paying for her shopping.

"What are you going to do tonight?" He sighed when he heard the answer,

"She's your sister, Iris, you do what you need to do."

"Yes, I love you too, we'll do it Iris."

"Banquan…Don't spend too long on…You need your downtime. I love you Iris." The check-out man was looking at him patiently. He put his basket on the counter and handed the wine to him, who began to type into the ornate brass till.

"Yes, I got nail polish remover. Banquan, Iris." He held the phone in his hand wistfully as he and the shop assistant both heard a gentle voice emit from it to say,

"You have to press the button under the screen sweetie,"

"Have you been looking at my ear all this time?" asked our hero suddenly staring into the screen. The Runu replied,

"Yes," before a lovely laugh tinkled into the supermarket, "…it's alright, you'll get the hang of it," Iris smiled back at him and blew him a kiss. The screen went blank, he pressed off the,

"New-fangled contraption," smiled apologetically at the man and put the phone in his pocket as he passed over his tomatoes.

Outside on the street, our hero looked around the unfamiliar terrain and then at his watch; six-forty-five, plenty of time. And there was the Gasper Station on the corner, only two stops. He'd be back by quarter-past-seven and be able to take his time with the food. A cold splash of what he hoped was condensation hit the back of his neck as he skipped down the steps. What people saw in this city he could not grasp.

It was 20 minutes before a train that he thought looked like it should be in a museum clattered and wheezed to a stop in front of him. The wooden carriage was not full and he found a forward-facing seat as it hissed into motion. In line with his fellow passengers he too looked up at the roof but could not see the fascination and so stared at a poster pasted neatly over a slightly bigger advert for some sort of tonic. He read *'Translators needed. Are you programmed in any Chinese dialect? Do you have 'O' level English and family in China? If so, the people need you. Please call the Transitional Council Translation Service on 010101010 and ask for Xinhua'* He read it three of four times, then let his eyes wander around a few of the people. They all carried books or newspapers but only one or two were actually reading. It must have been a London thing.

There was a sudden jolt. The people and then the train let out a long sigh as they wheezed to a halt in a tunnel. After a few moments a voice came over the tannoy,

"We apologise for the disruption to your journey this is due to rodents in the pipes at Tottenham Court Road..." The people who had not been reading before got out their various forms of print and began perusing with resignation. The message continued, "...the issue is being addressed and we will regain pressure as soon as possible." Our hero looked at his watch, five-past-seven. He looked at the older woman sitting opposite him who was reading the daily paper,

"Excuse me," he smiled and she looked up annoyed, "...I'm sorry I'm not from round here, do you know how long we might be here?" Her face softened slightly and she answered,

"It's usually about ten minutes, sometimes longer. They have to find the blockage, then they have to get the pressure up again," she was about to return to her article when he laughed,

"I'm only going two stops. This thing looks like it should be in a museum." A man from the other side of the aisle leaned over,

"It was." And the woman nodded in agreement and went back to her paper, "…they got it going again when they made it free, you know." The man continued. Our hero foolishly looked interested, "…Yes, one of the first things they did, Free up the railways."

"I know," replied our hero, "…I was at Prince's Dock." The man looked impressed,

"You're from Liverpool, we owe you a great debt Sir" and he leaned over further to shake hands. "…of course, they should have waited, with the trains not Prince's Dock, that was long overdue in my opinion, long overdue. But they should've got the network in better condition before they made it free, I mean…"

"In Liverpool, we just took it, you know, the railway workers just took it over." Our hero began,

"Yes, they weren't in any mood for waiting were they. But they should've got it in better order before they made it free shouldn't they. Oh I know, you're all so young, that's what did it in my opinion, all these young people, never mind this nonsense with the Kritos, it was the young people," Our hero tried to say something but the man talked over him, "…no, what you youngsters don't realise is that some things take time, take the Americas for example, they're not all just going to start revolutionising just because the Carte or the Empire's doing it are they, then there's the Chinese, when have they ever done any revolutionising I mean…" Our hero stopped listening and regretted not having any reading material. He looked at his watch, Eleven minutes past seven. A woman behind him gave him a start as she interjected loudly,

"That's why we have to act now! This is a critical time; we need to get the whole world part of this otherwise the Aristois will be able to regroup and take it all back. I read the negotiations are moving…" Then someone from down the carriage put down his book and called,

"They'll get it working Grandad don't you worry. It's only temporary. My cousin's got a job in the factory where they make the new ones. We'll all be sitting in luxury by Christmas."

"Christmas, oh yes? You believe that do you? Where will they get the steel, you answer me that?" Retorted the older man. The woman behind him said,

"It's being diverted, transport is a Transitional Council priority and…"

The older man was laughing now,

"Diverted! Diverted from where!" And he turned back to our hero and the lady opposite, "…Do you think this Transitional Council is any good? I've heard the Amalgamated Council is doing great stuff in Glasgow?"

"The Amalgamated Council has joined the Transitional Council now, and the Transitional Government, they had it out on Tuesday. Where have you been Grandad?" Called the man down the carriage. The woman behind him joined in,

"That's why the negotiations are going better now," An older woman, hitherto silent, said,

"Steel Production in Poland was running at forty percent capacity before it's New Management, to keep supply low and force up the price, now its running at a hundred percent," and added pointedly, "…with Kritodash administration. The point made by the young lady is relevant, your combat experience may, unfortunately, become necessary in a counter-revolution." There was a pause and then everyone began speaking at once and our hero was turning his head this way and that trying to keep up. Participatory democracy takes some effort.

A very old war-bleached man, who no-one had noticed before, stood up shakily and spoke softly and firmly,

"No more war. There must not be more war. No-one, not man, not Krito must ever have to go to die or take a life for the Imalympy class again," and with respect for what he had seen, and done, the carriage was quiet. The young man down the carriage spoke gently after that,

"We understand mate, we do, and I did a bit of fighting around Parliament in February, no-one should have to do it. But if we don't stop them this time once and for all they will take over again, it will be like Johannesburg all over again, worse. Melt us like so much chocolate and get the survivors to scrape us up. But this time all over the Empire. If we give them the chance, they will come for us mate, you know they will. We have to fight, it's like that Kraut girl from history said, Communism or Barbarism. They're barbarians." And the woman behind him added,

"I was at Trafalgar Square when they sent in the Dhool Drones, we have to go on now."

"We will not give them the chance to re-muster," said our hero as he walked to the veteran and shook his hand, "…we are many, they are few," The two men smiled and sat down together and while the rest of the carriage argued a lot more our hero listened to the White-Man who had done enough barbarism,

"You don't know what you're capable of son. A man can get more pleasure from kicking in a child's head, feeling the warm blood on his boot, than he can from scoring the winning goal in the World Cup, much more." Warned the old man earnestly. Our hero smiled gently and explained something,

"I was a Special." The old man started back a little and looked worried, "…I was on the right side at Prince's," said our hero to reassure him,

"But? Johannesburg?" Our hero nodded that he had been there, "…Well, you've got a lot to make up for haven't you," said the old man as kindly as he could but our hero shook his head,

"I was their dog, no better than an core-code Krito. Not anymore." The old man sighed and took both our hero's hands to reassure himself as much as his companion. They held each other's gaze until the train started to rise and breathed back into a mode of transport.

The two men looked towards the window, which could only show them their own reflections in the black of the tunnel. The carriage of villains of the Empire and heroes of the revolution continued their discourse into the dark.

What is the Gasper?

The General and Southern Pneumatic Railway (GSPR), known colloquially as the Gasper, was one of several atmospheric railways in London during the 1830s and 40s. Initially, it was steam power that forced air down a pipe that ran between the tracks and pushed the train along. In your world, the idea was largely abandoned in the 1840s and subsequently mainly forgotten. While such locomotion was faster and more able to go uphill in the early days of locomotion, the steam engines with which you are familiar soon became much more powerful. In addition, the atmospheric valve flaps, which ran along the pipes were largely made of leather, which stiffened into uselessness during very cold and very hot weather.

Contrary to slightly popular belief it was not Isambard Kingdom Brunel's Didcot Pneumatic Railway that had the almost famous difficulty with rats. In actual fact, it was the earlier, and even less well known, engineers by the names of Jacob and Joshua Samuda on their railway in Wormwood Scrubs, West London, whose leather flap valves, smeared with rendered animal fat, tallow, to keep them supple, attracted the gnawing rodents, which rendered their train immobile. The other, even less well-known problem with rodents, and debris of other kinds, is that they can get sucked into the pipes when the pumps are powered up and reduce the pressure sufficiently to stop the trains.

The London of Greta's world did not give up so easily. There, the Railway experimenters employed Railway Wardens to maintain the valves. This was lonely and arduous work, carried out mainly at night. Flap-Polishers as they became known were often recruited from the increasingly unemployed population of Night-Soil-Men, whose role became redundant with the introduction of the sewage system. It was these men who unwittingly contributed to the later disaster that befell London.

The Rail Wardens' job was to walk the track laying rat traps and polishing the valve flaps with a modified form of tallow. This Valve Tallow contained 70% tallow, 25% nicotine and 5% strychnine. Unlike other poisons, where rats, who are clever animals, learn to avoid a food that has nearly killed them, the nicotine's addictive qualities ensured they returned to receive a fatal dose. The flaps were preserved, the railway functioned and the London and South East of England rat population developed a reputation for being somewhat volatile.

The Rail Warden's job also included collecting the poisoned carcasses of rodents, cats, dogs, crows and other wildlife and dispose of them as they saw fit. Despite these men's reputations, see below, there was little truth in the urban legends about pies. They did throw the dead animals down the increasing number of drains or into the River Thames. The level of strychnine in the water table and River was high enough by 1867 for the first recorded case of River-Poisoning. A drunken suicide failed to sink when the skirts of her dress ballooned in her descent from the old London bridge and she was observed to float downstream in a state of loud disappointment. Her continued inebriated attempts to drown herself; by scooping water onto her face, caused her to drink more than she inhaled and she was dead by the time she reached Waterloo.

During this period the use of many sorts of drugs was widespread among all classes of society. For example, you may be familiar with the use of the opiate-based Laudanum as inspiration for many of the Romantic poets, as well as smaller doses being an effective remedy for the headaches such work can induce. The use of small quantities of strychnine as a stimulant was also widely exploited, by medical students in particular, to aid study, as it quickened the heart.

As with every drug, except tobacco and tea, social stratification existed in how one dulled reality. The affordability and availability of Valve-Tallow ensured that the lubricant soon replaced gin as the lowliest drug in London. Those poor souls who became dependent on this and then any other substance, particularly those who turned to prostitution to fund their habit, became known as Pipe-lickers.

The term Flap-polisher took on many meanings. Almost from the inception of the role, the lonely and nocturnal nature of the work, as well as the predatory predilections of many men at this time, engendered the use of Flap-Polisher to describe a letch or creep. The fact that most Rail Wardens supplemented their meagre income by selling Valve Tallow to the desperate also resulted in Flap-Polisher becoming a term for a Drug pusher. Later into the Nineteenth and during the first part of the twentieth-century when trade unions were reaching their zenith, Rail Wardens almost unanimously refused to join any trade organisation. Thus Flap-Polisher became a derogatory name for strike-breaker or traitor to one's class. In the early twenty-first-century, when the people of the North; Glasgow, Manchester and Liverpool in particular, organised politically to gain rights and freedoms of various kinds and the people of London largely ignored them, the name Flap-Polisher was used widely to dub all Londoners.

Despite these changes to the social, linguistic and environmental fabric of the capital, the atmospheric railway was a great success. The trains were timely and reasonably priced. They were also much quieter and cleaner than steam locomotives so that people could wear light coloured clothes whilst travelling. Any rail journeys that extended beyond Watford or Didcot were enabled by simply carrying an engine to those places, stoking it as they approached the junction and then allowing it to pull the train the rest of the way. The ride was comfortable and pleasant and your much-loved clatter over the sleepers was supplemented by the gentle hiss of the aforementioned valves.

In 1852 the invention of galvanised rubber led to a huge rise in stock prices as the infestation issue was hailed as being solved. The Directors of the newly amalgamated General Rubber Pneumatic Railway (GRPR) successfully supressed the fact that rats also gnaw rubber until they were able to take over smaller companies and extend their lines.

Electrification of the pump stations was a relatively easy business and began in 1883. Indeed, the new electrified pumps were more efficient and powerful than those that they replaced and the company was able to become General Rail and Electricity (GRE) in 1900. Apart from selling electricity for domestic use, the new power also facilitated light industry.

During the 1910s and early '20s, in the centre of London, where the network was all underground, in partnership with leading perfumiers, the Pumping Stations serving that area added colognes to the air. When the trains came to stop in a station the platform was filled with the scent of English Fern or Tabac Blonde to supplement print advertisements. This practice came to an abrupt halt in 1923 after a Minister of Parliament was widely reported as saying that Kensington smelled like a French tart's parlour during a debate on sanitary reform.

The development of plastics led to several innovations in valve flap technology, which all proved delectable to the rodent population. Then, in 1940, one Arthur Coates, a mechanic at the Crystal Palace Pump Station designed metal flaps to fit over the valves that would open with them when the train went over. This innovation, first developed in fact by Jacob Samuda ninety years earlier, finally ended the rodent plague and the need for Valve Dubbin or Rail Wardens.

At this time if an able-bodied man could not find work independently, after three months he would have to register at the Board of Labour Exchange and be allocated suitable employment. Thus, almost to a man, former Rail Wardens were conscripted into the Eastern and Western trenches. By 1945, all that remained of them were the colloquialisms.

Of course, the most lasting and damaging effect of the Flap-Polishers work, although not their responsibility, came after most of them had died. Strychnine had been polluting the environment for nearly a century and parts of failed plastic valve flaps littered the network. Once wet and combined with the chemical weapon, Dhool, these chemicals created the Aspic mentioned herein.

Tower Hill Station, East London

Liberty had been relieved when Kaushik left for his meetings. Dipa was prone enough to digress and let her story jump back and forth in time, but Kaushik was nearly as bad. Fortunately, he had agreed that she could conduct the interviews with his sister without supervision. All she had to do was send him the audio-recordings. Dipa had talked in proper detail about her weeks as lady's maid, only when he left. They had talked until Liberty could not take in any more delight at such narcissistic and venal behaviour, and even Jus could not sustain Dipa.

Liberty wanted to get changed and wash the makeup off her face so she too took the Gasper. On the platform, she got out her Runu to make sure that she didn't miss any more Votes. She scrolled through the proposals; tree and shrub maintenance, teachers' sick-pay regulations, anything anybody wanted. If any People's Proposals caused enough of a stir, they would get Telly time, but mainly the issues raised were quite mundane. There was one proposal to rename Kritos as Engineered Automaton Citizens, EACs. Apparently Krito meant slave in Bangla, she hadn't known that. From the public's comments, it appeared that neither had anyone else. She added her view speaking slowly,

"The word will change when we change, leave it to time," And went back to scrolling.

Perhaps Dipa wasn't so stupid? She had understood what Kaushik had said about what transitional meant. That was very perceptive of him of course. But Dipa had understood that to be real and not real was to be transitional in some way. Of course, she had likened the whole Empire turning upside-down to her own little situation, but she had understood. There was hope. Liberty had learned a long time ago that a defence lawyer should let the justice system help a client come to terms with what they had done. She would not turn herself into some sort of therapist. But she might bring up the giddy slash irry thing. It might be useful.

Perhaps she should say something to Kaushik about Dipa's rehabilitation. But he had the transition of the Empire to think about. She would work on Dipa's transition to free woman.

She kept tapping through all the proposals while she considered interpreting Dipa's role as a simple dupe. Dipa painted a picture of a naïve girl manipulated by Adi Egremont and a childhood obsession with fairy tale princesses, while Kaushik had brought up again how tomboyish she had been. He had said something about boxing lessons, which both their parents had encouraged because Limehouse was a rough area. She had been good; won some sort of local prize. The trophy was lingering somewhere in the Aspic after the Coretado damn disaster.

So, was Kaushik magnifying a few insignificant recollections of the Dipa he wanted her to be? Or was Dipa misremembering too. Or pretending in order create an easily understood and sympathetic defence. Or both. It wasn't like her grip on reality was particularly strong. And there was a sharp mind in there somewhere. Whatever the actual truth was, Liberty decided that Dipa's insistence that she had been a good girl with a fairy tale dream would probably go down more easily with a jury. Kaushik's belief in an oppressed woman forced into a life of stereotypes and debauchery could be kept on the back burner for now. A lot would depend on the charges and the prosecution's presentation.

Liberty got on with preparing for tomorrow's interview and ordered her phone to,

"…Find Alyan Rajanya, image," and looked at the screen. She scrolled through a few pictures of Alyan the Yangan at various parties and events until she found a moving image. She slipped her Kanas into her ears. It was hard to see a Krito-film of a January afternoon on the tiny screen, all in the dreary light of the underground station but she could make it out well enough,

"…Play," The noise of gunfire and shouting crowds sprang tinnily into her head. It was the height of the Battle of Prince's Dock in January. Several dozen of the most eminent Aristois and their entourages as well as some diplomats and leading civil servants feared increasing unrest. The atmosphere of frequent protests for equal rights for Kritos and subjects of the Empire was indeed tense. They had attempted to leave from Liverpool for a cruise until things quietened down. A small crowd of protesters had turned up intending to jeer them off. It had turned into a full-scale fight when, due to rough weather, the ship was delayed. The small party of ordinary people, mainly made up of local shop assistants, had remained jocular until the Aristois had panicked and opened fire. A chemist's assistant was shot dead and members of both sides were thrown into the freezing water of the Mersey River. The battle that ensued lasted five hours and sparked a full-scale revolt across the country.

Liberty was watching a two-minute clip. The shaky shot began with a view of the SS Dunera II which was belatedly sailing up from the sea. It was slowing down, and actually never docked. Amidst the shouting, a small voice from behind the camera, said, 'What's that?' The shot hastily panned away from the ship to a much smaller vessel taking advantage of the crowd's vocal attention focused on the liner. She could see Lord Jyothi and young Lady Egremont crouched low together in some sort of motorised Venetian-type gondola on the choppy water. There was another woman slumped and partly obscured by what Liberty took, from his handsome physique and strange head, to be some sort of Nayiki. He was dressed as a Venetian Gondolier in characteristic blue and white shirt and tight, baban flattering, black trousers. Instead of a punting pole in the craft that did not need one, he held a violin under his chin and the strains of a rather good rendition of 'O Sole Mio' could be heard through blasts of an evidently cold wind and shouts from the quayside. His ribboned straw hat blew off and revealed that his white porcelain head was moulded into some sort of long-beaked bird, no, it was one of those plague-doctor masks. Another shot fired and the whole thing shattered into a fountain of shards.

Aditi Egremont and Prince Jyothi didn't appear to notice, they were looking up into the sky above them. The headless musician played on as a rope ladder dropped in from above and Lord Jyothi half stood to reach it. Aditi Egremont stood up and barged past him to climb up the rope like a cat. He wound the ladder around the other woman and shouted up out of shot. Then the rope ladder began to lift upwards. Liberty could see a few of the green ribs of Her Majesties Airship, The

Queen Nofoto II, and all of its teak and brass gondola, into which it wound, rising quickly into the sky, with the Empire's heir apparent dangling precariously at its end.

As the radical press derided, it could have been a prize-winning marrow crawling with beetles as it floated up and away into the gloom. The now solitary decapitated violinist performed into the wind as the empty boat floated down the wide grey Mersey towards the sea. Strains of the melody could still be heard until it was drowned out by a deep chorus of voices from the shore reciting the army's core-code,

"... *faithfully defend Her Majesty, Her Heirs and Successors, in Person, Crown and Dignity against all enemies...*" and the shooting began in earnest.

"...Rewind, stop, play half-speed," said Liberty annoyed at herself for getting distracted. This time she paid close attention to the third human figure sprawled in the boat. Her head, wrapped in some sort of scarf, lolled to and fro as the gondola struggled over the waves. The part of the face she could see was emotionless. As the white splinters of the gondolier's head showered down in slow motion on top of her, she slowly stretched out a hand towards him before falling back helpless. That face looked like Princess Victoria. But she had died sometime between January the first and June the second the previous year. It could be Dipa's, but she was in the Tower,

"...Is that, where is Alyan Rajanya?" instructed Liberty and a red circle smudged around the supine figure.

"Off!" Liberty almost shouted. If Dipa was Alyan Rajanya, who was that in the boat? She was exasperated. How many of those bloody beautiful idiot women were there? Dipa had been no help. Was she obstructing Liberty in some way? Then she remembered something Dipa had said that afternoon.

The train hissed up and the doors opened into one of the modern carriages. Liberty got in and leaned on the sloping padded bench thingy before putting in her kanas and saying,

"Play Case Four-One-Two, tape er Seven," before rolling her eyes absently up to a poster addressing *Tired and Lifeless Skin*, rolling them away again and hearing her own voice say,

"I'm sorry. What were the dresses actually for?" A disembodied Dipa replied, at least she didn't have to look at that perfect skin while she listened,

"Well, lots of things. The first was a bit tame really, compared to the other times. I thought it would be fun. There was this big ball at Hira hall. I'd never seen…I thought the Egremont House was astounding but Hira Hall!" She was boasting again, and about being part of the class that the majority of people had recently gone to some trouble to undermine. They would have to work on that before the trial. "…Oh, the ballroom, I loved that ballroom, sprung floor you know, you just glide, float over it. And the cinema, I uchit loved the cinema, but the first time I just had this bedroom at the back to get changed into the dress, they were rushed I know that now but there was no need to just rip them like that, but, and," Dipa had been sucking Jus all afternoon and it showed, she was breathless and agitated. "…the dinner was just horrible, not the food, the food was always good at cousin Joshi's, and if I'm thinking back, I think that's really when I started to think that it wasn't so…started to question it all, you know. Way back then. He was there, Lord Egremont. And her zombie mother

It was a joke, for the dinner before the ball. Just twenty or so special people you know. Adi would come down at the bell in her dress and have the fish, acting all quiet like she was often around her family, and then make an excuse, leave, and then I'd come in wearing my dress for the…hare, I think it was. But by the time I went in they were all laughing and joking," and Dipa had paused then, "…they were joking about the Coretado Breach, all laughing and tittering. It was bad luck, for the Coretados he said. For the Coretado family! And it didn't look good, didn't help keep things in proportion. Gave the agitators something to rabble-rouse with, that's all they thought. All those people killed. My mum was killed you know? She was only forty-six. Saving a few pennies on materials? Who does that? Well, I can tell you first hand, they actually, really, uchit don't care about us. Worse, I can tell you, it's like we're not as human as them the way they talk. People were just being duped by the rabble-rousers, gullible, falling for false promises. If it came up before dessert it's how the lower orders needed guidance, education from their betters or constraint that kind of thing. But once they'd had more than a glass or two it was all a 'a good hiding' or 'hang one as an example to the others', that's how they talk, talked. It's the contempt I can't stand.

Some of them do care, but like you care for a pet you know. A pet you never really wanted. And a minute later they're spending half the evening talking about the lamb, it was lamb, not hare, I remember now. I hate lamb. Is it organic? Was it free-range? More time chatting about the ethics of their chops than killing seventy-three people. It's the contempt I can't stand. Keeping things orderly, staying as they are, that's more important to them than us, our lives you know.

That Lord Egremont once he's had a few, relaxed you know, going on about The Soulless Ones, that's what he calls people like you and me, well people like me anyway, Soulless Ones. I couldn't, didn't go to the remembrance service you know...Adi said it wouldn't be wise. The people killed under the Aspic, they're just a wasted investment, that's all, he thought. Well, he's in the Tower now and it's too good for him, I can tell you. And Adi, did she care? All she said was she was so so so sorry for my loss, hugged me a while and then said she could take my mind off it, amuse me you know. I suppose she succeeded?" Liberty recalled feeling a real sympathy for Dipa then, it was unjust what had happened with the damn.

"...But? It was hare, I'd never had it before. And they can't have been talking about Coretado? I couldn't go to the Service because I was already Vicky? And Vicky was alive then? What were they talking about? It must've been Johannesburg? Was it? Oh I don't know, there were... so much happened in those few months. Incidents, that's what they called it when they got found out about something, or something had to be put down?" She heard her own voice had a wobble in it when she asked,

"They?" She was reluctant to look for an element of paranoia in Dipa's thinking. But it might be necessary to have evidence of an unsound mind to get her off.

"They, Them. That lot, the ones in charge. Oh yes, they're not in charge now? They're the old lot now aren't they...Well I don't know, is there really a Them or an Us. Or maybe there is an Us now, you know Koushik's lot and the others? Mind you there's a lot of arguing in that Transitional Council isn't there? Will they, do they try and destroy each other too? Like the old lot? I know they spend, spent a lot of time trying to destroy each other, but when it came to the rest of us, they thought there was an Us even if we don't, didn't? Then they'd be a Them alright, when they were threatened. I've seen it from both sides now haven't I? People wouldn't believe the contempt, it's the contempt I can't stand…Is there an Us now, really? There's been a lot of people running around, taking things over but is that? But, but will Kaushik and the new lot just become another Them? I've seen the Runu but is there, was there an Us? Really?" Liberty heard the rustling of Jus papers.

"I know it's confusing Dipa, you've missed a baban busy time out there in the world. But it will all make more sense when you're free and you can participate in society," She had paused momentarily then, how many times had she said that phrase; 'Participate in Society'? In the past, the words had been another way to talk about a client not being in prison. Now, there was another meaning, no, more meaning in the words. More society in which to participate and people did appear to be rising to the challenge, so far. Perhaps she felt a little guilty for wanting Dipa to have an unsound mind because she had tried to reassure her client then, "…Dipa, you will be able to understand the Us that is coming to be…has started to be, has started to happen out there. In the world. But first we have to get you out of here. We have to get you out of here first. Then, when you're actually participating it will be easier to understand," Liberty remembered Dipa looking confused as she nodded resolutely, "…At the dinner, did anyone realise it was you and not Adi. Her family?" And Dipa had been relieved to be asked a question she could answer,

"If they did, they didn't say anything, probably didn't notice you know, not important. If they did notice they probably just thought I was Rarnadoo, or Vicky. And they had some sort of silent agreement not to pay any attention to Adi's japes. And they did it all the time, apparently, her and Vicky. But I didn't know that till the lake. First it was dinner, then people started arriving for the ball, then there was dancing. And…"

"Sorry, can we go back a bit, who's Rarnadoo? Liberty remembered how she hadn't tried to get a short answer from Dipa because Dipa was thoroughly Jused and she was already tired. Now she regretted not trying to get her to be concise.

"Well, after Vicky, Princess Victoria tried it on and ripped my dress so Adi had to rip mine down at the lake, so they matched again, laughing, I was furious, two great tears and who would be mending them? After we went down to the lake and she told me all about it. You see she…" This was the part of the recording Liberty needed to hear again. She had interjected again,

"Hold on, sorry, details, Princess Victoria made a sexual overture towards you?" She heard Dipa's laugh, like cold water over round stones, and relived being the object of such, what was it, not contempt exactly, no, she had felt like a child who says something naive, naive and stupid, soulless perhaps?

"Vicky was insatiable for sex and drugs and, well just sex and drugs was all she was interested in really, everyone knew. It was tolerated. Indulged. Perhaps if King Charles had been a bit firmer, not so caught up in his mutton revival campaign, she wouldn't have gone the way she did. And really, they're not the only ones who covered up the way they did are they? I mean there was more at stake but…

"Was she a Devi-Girl? Vicky?"

"No? Just Entee."

"Aren't we all."

"Quite so, anyway, so, I went into an empty room downstairs, there were so many, to get my breath I said, when the dancing started. To tell the truth I was in quite a state, I wasn't used to Strange back then and I was still getting used being Adi, there's only so far 'haughty' can take you. But, anyway. Little did I know Vicky and Adi were kissing cousins. So when I left the ballroom it was a sign for Vicky to follow Adi, she thought. The jape was on her really, I see that now. Adi showing off, getting one over on Vicky. So, she didn't know and she followed me and…"

"Skip one minute," said Liberty in the train, she did not need to hear about a desperate, drug-addicted Princess pawing at a stupefied dress-maker,

"Of course I was, no not upset, confused and she, so she put her…"

"Skip one minute,"

"It was cyow, the cool grass, Adi holding my hand, leading me in the moonlight, The orchestra by the lake, such lovely music. Made them when she was a child, just knocked them up from parts she found lying around Cousin Joshi's house. But she was still only ten, couldn't do heads. Later it was handy, no Krito-cameras. She was a master of coding even as a child, that's why Joshi loved her, and she was cyow of course so beautiful. And clever. And…" and Liberty had heard something in her tone and interrupted her again,

"When did you and she become intimate?" Liberty heard herself ask vaguely, Dipa had giggled,

"That night. And we were much thrown together in Cooch-Bahar," and she was laughing again,

"Skip thirty seconds," Those idle women really had nothing better to do than drink drug cocktails, play dressing up and fuck. She heard a slightly more exasperated version of herself trying to guide Dipa back onto the point,

"What about this Rarnadoo?"

"Yes. The music was soothing and I'd had a lot of Strange by then, we all had. She and Vicky sat me down on this carpet over-looking the lake, got me comfy on the cushions, let me choose the music the orchestra played. Told me about Vicky and her and their japes. Swapping places so Vicky could 'go among her subjects', live a normal life. Normal? Ha! She was down at the Marasses Pipe-licking, smoking that stuff, and, I honestly think that Adi didn't know about how much Opium Vicky got through. She didn't approve of neat drugs, preferred her cocktails. She was shocked, as shocked as anyone."

"And the Rarnadoo?"

"The Rarnadoo, yes. Well she couldn't go anywhere, Vicky. Never had any fun, and I did feel sort of sorry for her. You know a Princess is watched all the time, I mean all the time. And has to put on a show constantly, it's baban stressful being watched all the time, I can vouch for that. Well, at first, she and Adi used to swap. Adi would go and open a factory and Vicky could pop in some Aunken and, go shopping is what they said to me but she just liked to get high. But they couldn't go anywhere off-the-books together, and there were places Adi wanted to show Vicky. Go together."

"What are you saying, Rarnadoo was another look-alike of Princess Victoria?"

"Yes. In order. They got the money for it from the War Office, a stand-in for when there were threats of assassination, that's what they said to the War Office. And at first it worked, the Rarnadoo would welcome the Ambassador of All America, Vicky hated Americans, and she and Adi would go out on the Razz somewhere. Just set the programme and off she went smiling and waving, smiling and waving, it was great. But then…"

"They made a Krito to look like Princess Victoria?" and Dipa had looked at her as if she were a stupid child again,

"Yes, but then she kept glitching, she…"

"Adi made this Rarnadoo?"

"Not on her own, she could code for England but she never did master the actual robotics, something to do with Core Code? No cousin Joshi got the money to do it from the War Office. They belong, belonged, to the War Office really, you know what they are don't you?"

"Yes, I've met a Nayaka socially actually, now that they're free." Liberty had cringed internally as soon as those words came out of her mouth and had quickly added, "……She glitched you say?"

"Yes, she was Victoria the Second, Rarnadoo was just our slang, Vicky-Two for short, but not for baban special guests, Cousin Joshi got the basic military model and then his boffins altered the coding to make them much much more friendly." Dipa was speaking particularly slowly and she heard herself stifle a huff into a sigh, Dipa got slower, she thought on purpose, "…Adi added a bit more, her special code to the Vicky-model and made Rarnadoo, Vicky-Two. But it was too much for the poor thing and she kept glitching after a while. Do you remember the business with the Chair Woman of the Cheltenham Ladies Guild? When Princess Victoria smeared her winning jam on the poor woman's face and licked it off? What you might not know is that the reason the Chair Woman of the Cheltenham Ladies Guild put up with it for so long is because of what Rarnadoo was doing with her fingers, reverted to her original programming if you see what I mean. Anyway that was Rarnadoo. So, they covered it up as another one of Vicky's 'lapses' and they had to give up and they were back to square one again, until I came along.

They couldn't go in the Fresh Air together, because the Rarnadoo couldn't act like Vicky. Couldn't act that stupid, that's what Adi said not just behind her back, she could be so cruel, so cruel... But I think Vicky was right, Rarnadoo knew it was wrong somehow. Adi laughed at that but it turned out Vicky was right, aye?" Liberty wasn't interested in the technicalities,

"So Jyothi supplied the Rarnadoo? Did he know what Aditi intended to do with it?" A legitimate question from one's council did not deserve such derisory laughter. Once Dipa had wiped the tears away and could breathe normally again she carried on,

"Of course he did. He did a nice side-line in Nayikas and Nayakas that looked like Yangans. For fun you know, a hobby he said. To liven up his parties. Mahanga. And the War Office liked it because it was good PR, especially when they started glitching. But he was so besotted with Adi, he'd have given her the real one, if he could…don't get me wrong, he enjoyed it all, loved it, the old flap-Polisher.

He'd have loved us three on that carpet, you know when we took off our clothes, kept ripping at the tears in our dresses, to find where we were all the same," Dipa had giggled then and sighed and said more than she should have done, and Liberty, too tired to stop her, had let her go on, "…We were just smoking you know, well I was the novice so I just breathed it in from them you know. Inhaling the mauve white smoke coming from their mouths. And laughing. Still sharp but high and floating on that soft soft rug, deep purple in the moonlight on the fresh black black grass. The music from her quartet winding through and out over the water. Their headless shadows swaying and bowing so fast on the water so flat. And the moon looking up from the water and down from the sky, like a mirror. And drifting. Three identical drifters she said, Adi. She thought she was lucky to have found someone as lovely as herself and now there were two, three of us, all so flawless. And I looked from her to Vicky and back to her and we were all so lovely.

And it is sad you know, always being the prettiest, people don't appreciate. Never to find anyone as beautiful as you, always some flaw, some little bit of ugliness, never a true match. But we were all as lovely as one another and we had found each other.

Vicky started it though, always did. That first time, she just looked at my shoulder, then Adi's, touched hers. And I was jealous, so jealous. So I stroked…my heart was thumping I can tell you, but I so wanted us to be all the same, I stroked

Vicky's neck and pushed her strap off her sandara shoulder onto her arm, like mine, or Adi's, only a shade darker, let my same fingers feel while she let hers run over Adi's, run down her neck and, and she suddenly ripped my bodice, pushed me back and Adi came down too, laughing… lying next to that lake, so flat and still and shining like a mirror on that soft carpet. And the moon, smiling down and up from the water. And the three of us ripping at those beautiful dresses. It was liberating, it felt liberating you know, to just tear up all that work. And then all that work was rags and tatters on the ground. And our bodies, our same bodies were all free. And the three of us, all entwined and exploring, finding the hidden places of each other, ourselves. Breaking through a mirror, touching, feeling. Mirrors you could feel the three of us. All the same but all finding something different to do with our hands, our lips. The brush of a thigh on yours, the sweep of hair over a nipple, the sight of a curve, a sigh on your belly.

At first I could smell who was who by our perfumes. I kamar lavender and Adi; sweet golden, a tobacco shop when you first walk in you know? And soft soft leather. But keep delving breathing her in, then came something dark, hard, like polished ebony I don't know. But Vicky was all fresh, sharp even, that moist mossy scent you get under the trees in the boulevards and? An occasional waft of something sweeter coming with her breath, her smoke. Inhaling in and down, down till you can't get a breath. Their, all our pretty fingers, breasts, bellies surprising over and over, before you can take it in there's a new pleasure somewhere else and we were blended into one rich, sweet-sour scent. The salt of our sweat cutting through it all and the chilly air tickling. Your whole body alive to everything. Not knowing whose breast, whose belly, was whose and it didn't matter.

It was like making love to me and me again, finding all the places you know you have but can't ever, oh you can touch yourself but it never feels the way it feels when another, another you, and another…Vicky had such a pretty little tongue. But they, we, are all so lovely aren't we and…"

"Stop." Liberty did not need to hear any more. Why had she let her go on? Why had she let the Runu run to hear it again? Those rotten, spoiled, rotten women later. Prone and naked on the grass and staring into the lake at their almost identical faces, Adi's laugh, Vicky's tear going plop into the water and rippling across all three reflections. Adi still smiling and saying 'All three together' and Vicky saying 'All three alone'.

They could have been or done so much but they had been spoiled into uselessness by the Empire Way. Playing at life. No life at all really. Ruined by excess. No, the real waste was the emptiness of them; useless, empty desperately looking into mirror after mirror to try and find themselves and finding nothing except a thin film reflecting another flat image. No wonder Vicky let herself die.

Liberty was overwhelmed by the waste of curdy human beings in a way she never had before and was crying on the train. Crying a lot. The layers of makeup that Dipa had slavered onto her face that morning began dripping down her cheeks. She caught a glimpse of herself in the dark window and sniffed and wiped her face. Blew her nose. There would be no more of that waste. She would tell Kaushik who the body on the boat actually was and get Dipa out of the Tower to lead a useful, lovely life.

She wasn't in the mood for more than she absolutely had to put up with. The commonwealth games reception and Dipa's first excursion imitating Vicky at that boring Gala could wait.

"Go to end, then back…ten seconds. Play.

"So where was the Rarnadoo kept."

"In the play-room, you know with the other Nayaka-nayikis, for the guests you know. Till I took her as my maid later, you know 'for security reasons'" That was all she could take of the careless, selfish woman. No more waste of human beings or Kritos.

Sex, yes. Sex was good but not sad like that. When you looked past the opulence, they were three desperate lonely women. No, give her proper, fun, happy sex with like-minded, well-balanced individuals any day. She preferred a bit of contrast, that was fun. She wasn't too keen on group sex either, too many elbows.

What time was it? She had to make herself presentable. She had that date and he was uchit good at sex. And talking. She liked talking with him and was hoping for the best.

Committee Room, Palace of Westminster, West London

Committee meetings, even those relevant to the future of millions of lives, are unlike even desperately lonely sex, quite boring. The main items on the agenda of the Transitional Sub-Committee for Civic Education, UK Branch (TSCC-UK) meeting on the afternoon to evening of Friday the 14th of April 2017 were; One, Krito education, Two. How to respond to the reactionary politics reflected in the Totteridge Estate-Agent Massacre of the previous Tuesday and Three, The ongoing Aristoi Rehabilitation Programme content. Transcripts of this and all other Transitional Council Meetings will be available on the website for those who really want them in due course.

The meeting had gone on much longer than anticipated again. This time it was because the Commissars for Early Years, Ndidi Jones and Ricard Organ, having petitioned for several weeks, were finally admitted to contribute to the item on Krito Education. The regular members of the committee saw the function of the Commissariat for Early Years primarily as enabling humans of both sexes to fully engage in work and civic life by providing pleasant care and basic education for human children. They were also ideologically hostile to the Commissars' written proposal that the Krito should be treated in some respects according to their age since becoming sentient.

The Krito had begun to gain consciousness at some time between July and September 2015, and Jones and Organ argued that accommodations should be made. They agreed with the general consensus that occupying a body and the consequent dynamic between their environment and other persons allowed Krito, once liberated from their core-coding, to develop a sense of themselves as individuals and parts of a group or society. However, they also asserted that the Krito lacked the accumulated experiences accrued in the journey from infancy to adulthood that enabled truly abstract thought and argued that what human beings perceived as principles might be interpreted merely as patterns by their automaton brothers and sisters. The Commissars did not think that Krito would require the years of experience required by humans, but recommended seminars, which could be structured around a variety of topics.

The deputies, two of them Krito themselves, sat down adamant that the Krito were not toddlers, many had fought bravely in the liberation battles of the previous months, they could all articulate their rights to freedom cogently and were entitled to be treated with absolute and complete equality.

Three and a half hours later the committee got up for a tea break convinced that they had greatly underestimated the capacities of human infants. They agreed fully to the Krito Engagement Sessions- which were voluntary and had no impact on their voting rights or liberties, co-opted both Commissars onto the Sub-Committee and tripled the budget for nursery education.

Two events pertinent to this story also occurred but were not recorded. First, in the tea-break necessitated after the Krito

Engagement item, deputy Hargon asked if anyone knew anything about the former Nayaka known as Rarnadoo. Second, despite the brevity of the tea break following the item on the Totteridge Issue and notwithstanding their disagreements, Deputy Herzfeld handed Deputy Cameron a telly-plug. This would enable a broader variety of media access on his home set. Neither of these events pleased Kaushik; the telly-plug reminded him that he would have to sit and watch a lot of bollocks. The Rarnadoo question reminded him that his 'Soon' correspondence pile was getting unmanageable again.

When the discussions finally drew to a close, he went home to watch nonsense, deal with his correspondence, call Ashanti and write a speech about dead estate agents.

Another Unknown Location

She woke to the rumbling beginning again. She had learned to welcome it. She would have peace for a time. The noise outside of her had a rhythm. It also lasted for a time and then it stopped. The things she did not know, the discord inside of her, all dark shades, had no pattern, no rhythm, nothing to hold onto and make sense of. There was inside of her and outside of her. There was inside this place and there must be an outside. He came from the outside. The sound outside began and ended. There was a time that was not, a place not this place. Things outside began, went on for a time and ended.

There was a time when she did not feel this, otherwise it would not make her feel so, so something painful. If she had known only this then there would not be something she needed to remember. There was something so there might be something else somewhere or some time. There was a place or time that she had been and she had not felt this fog inside and outside. There was something she had to remember. Only the teeth, she must remember only the teeth, jaw, maw, mouth, she must remember.

There was the billowing sound above her head. now the clink, there would be eight more clinks. Eight was a number, a measure both numeral and ordinal, ordinal. Sequenced, over time. Now was not the time for the eight clinks. The outside rumbling had not ended. But he would be here and she would press the button in her head because it would be better to feel, be, nothing. She must feel later, in a time after this, be, feel and remember. Not now.

Vacant Accommodation, East London

An unidentified scuttling noise jerked the dark-suited man awake, pulling a muscle in his neck. He had nodded off, prone and foetal, on the dusty bare floor with his face pressed to a small brass telescope poking through a skirting board. He knew The Subject was still watching the telly. The scuttler squeaked behind him and he sighed in reply. It was not a rat at least, just a mouse. He heaved himself painfully onto his knees. They both twinged sharply, forcing him to move quickly into lumbering onto his behind. He made a futile and febrile attempt to brush out the larger of the creases in his trousers and reached into his pocket for a cigarette. The Subject might smell the smoke through his spyhole but, at that moment, he didn't care.

He had been watching the traitor watch that other traitor's coronation of last June, rewinding and watching a shot of the crowd over and over until he had fallen asleep. The small telly was on the other side of the room but with the spyglass, the figures on it appeared about two inches [5 cm] high, the size of a mouse.

Empire pomp and ceremony was the envy of the world and quite right too. But the world did not have to crouch in the dark and watch it all go on and on, with this person representing that thing, anointing the oil of whatever, followed by some other character with the ball of whatnot, hunched up like an animal surrounded by vermin. He was not so much surprised that he had fallen asleep but that The

Subject had not. He could vaguely hear the commentary, tinny through the wall,

"... the heart of the Commonwealth of free people, the Lords, Temporal and Spiritual gathered in the House..." So, The Subject had moved on to watching the State Opening of Parliament, probably last November's. He could not help himself and an image of a mouse dressed in the traditional black suit and great white ruffle appeared in his mind. Before the miniature Black-Rod could bang on the inside of the skirting board with a stick of charcoal he was dismissed.

Both the man watching the telly and the one watching him watch telly had been in Trafalgar Square that day. It was the first time the traitor would see over 800 years of parliamentary rule overturned in an afternoon because that stupid and wicked girl had had a spat with her girlfriend. He himself had already watched it several times.

The dark-suited man took a long slow drag of his cigarette and breathed a cloud of smoke into the empty room. Some of his remaining colleagues had disappeared; gone into hiding, assumed new identities, run off to countries they thought would hold out against the tide of revolution that was spreading across the Empire, the globe. Most of his inferiors had gone to Africa to work with their counterparts on a counter-revolution and been assassinated when they got off the plane. Most of his superiors were in the Tower. Why was he sitting here on these hard floorboards about to watch a man watch telly? He would lie down this time, it would be easier on his knees.

He stubbed the cigarette out on the floor and left it there. Then shuffled onto his belly and peered through the telescope to see the back of a chair. The Subject's feet were still on the coffee table in an old pair of socks. Seeing that man's heels using Top Secret Documents as a foot-rest hardened his resolve. By pushing the telescope up and to the left and twisting his sore neck to the right and up he could see the telly,

"… continuity preserved through many changes and still a model to the world…" He sighed. They should not have broken with tradition. The Queen's speech should have stayed what it was, the monarch simply reading the government's to-do list with a short clip on the evening news. But, no. The coronation had been such a success with even the most extreme factions of society heralding the possibility of a new age for Britain and the Empire. So, Lord North's Government had decided to make this perfunctory tradition into a much more heavily publicised affair. It was leaked that her first Queens Speech would be a chance to show something of herself, her personality. She would say something about 'healing deep divisions' and quote a Good Book of some kind.

He and some of his colleagues had been uneasy. The importance of a monarch who appeared politically impartial was that people could project whatever they liked onto their silence. After all, the very fact that she was so popular, when the Government was so deeply unpopular said something. There was a widely held belief that she did not approve of them, but could say nothing to interfere with the representatives of the people. Lord North had argued that the spectacle, as well as the tradition, would help reassert the legitimacy of Parliament. The promised reforms would show that the government was indeed listening and acting on what they heard. He was all for reaffirming continuity and stability but had kept arguing against his Lordship until the last, if royalty ever did any more than turn up, smile and wave then things generally went awry. Still, Lord North might have been right but for that stupid and wicked girl.

He recalled being jostled in the crowd. That was what had really worried him at the time; the erection of huge screens in all the major cities so that the people could come together to watch the new Queen in all her glory again. Live. Not so much as a one-minute delay, what they could have done with a one-minute delay.

And there had been information that leading members of the banned organisation, Critical Mass, would seek to intervene in London, Birmingham, Manchester, Glasgow, Lagos, Accra, Johannesburg, Cairo, Kinshasa, Bombay, Delhi, Calcutta, Karachi, Montreal and Sidney. Their reach had been wide but their numbers had been tiny. This would be their first real attempt to influence the actual mass. And if it had all gone according to Lord North's plan, the mass would have ignored them politely as they always had in the past.

He had been worried. Again, he had been talked down. His superiors were confident that most members of Critical Mass were Royalists and would be further moderated by such an event. That could have been what happened. But, as he said at the time, Oliver Cromwell had been a monarchist until he beheaded King Charles the First.

The voice on the telly continued, "…That great servant of King, er Queen and country in War and Peace, Vice-Admiral Lord Chumley hands the Cap of Maintenance to the Marquess of Salisbury…"

Hindsight is indeed a wonderful thing. That moment of Parliamentary tradition, repeated annually for hundreds of years was when the crowd in Trafalgar Square had begun to change in mood. He had sensed the shift before he could identify the cause, but it had been that little girl. A loyal subject had put his small daughter onto his shoulders so that she could better see the televised proceedings, as well as to keep her free of the crush of people in the square. She had asked that stupid question. It was quite hushed for such a large crowd, the people gathered were aware that there were many contesting views represented there and so were very sensibly staying fairly quiet. Some people were arch Royalists out for the day, others had had their latent monarchism recently stirred in the hopes that this young Queen would indeed be a new Gloriana and herald an era of freedom and prosperity. Only a few were republicans. A tiny number were activists and no-one wanted to attract their attention and whatever monologue they had prepared. Almost everyone was behaving like it was a big family Christmas, Diwali or Eid in a small house. They were making more or less jovial, bland and innocuous remarks about how lucky they had been with the weather and laughing at a few of the sillier hats on display.

Perhaps one in ten of people in the crowds across the Empire, and less in England, would even dream of being republican. But less than a year later and those same people had brought on a New Management. She, that idiot drug addict, the geedy one not the irry one, she had destroyed it all. Oh, she had help of course, but Critical Mass had merely wanted reform of the Empire, their policy on elder care was four pages longer than anything they had written on Royalty.

Most of them, including The Subject had still been happy with a constitutional monarchy. His plants were right on that, and hadn't Tariqul Jones tried to negotiate in late February. Why didn't the Chief care about keeping that channel open?

It was those Marxians, coming from nowhere, not one operative reporting back. Those Marxians had cast some sort of spell over people. Saying we, then they should let the traitor go. And that Keri Dangle with her downright filthy Another-Not-Queen's Speech and her 'Why not go all the way?' prattle on Christmas Day. On day-time telly. The levels of disgusting she had plumbed at three o'clock in the afternoon. On Christmas Day. At least she was a good public speaker, unlike The Subject.

On the screen, one medal encrusted old man handed the ceremonial pole topped with the red velvet and ermine Cap of Maintenance to another, equally elderly and decorated, gentleman, and he remembered. The girl, who he later knew to be one Miss Emma Begum, aged four, was watching carefully and, so that her daddy could hear her over the mild-mannered hub-bub, she asked loudly,

"Why have they got Santa's hat on that stick? Where's Santa?" There had been an uproar of laughter and soon royalist and republican alike, perhaps to ease the tension, began echoing," Where's Santa?' through the throng. The prolonged nature of the ancient tradition; now one mace being carried along a richly decorated corridor, then a sword, now another mace, more shots of the Irish Coach trotting down the Mall, more aerial footage of the Palace of Westminster Dome and a discourse on the,

"...unique and ground-breaking engineering of the Elizabeth Tower Dome made possible by the generosity of His Grace, Lord North-Jaipur," ensured that "Where's Santa?" was then chanted continuously from Nelson's Column to the National Gallery, partly to alleviate the boredom. All cheerful enough, slightly irreverent and thoroughly British. But it had not been a good sign.

When the 'Queen' stepped daintily out of the carriage in that royal blue evening gown in broad daylight, and the commentator said,

"Simple, yet regal" then the crowds in front of all the screens across the commonwealth had sent up a roar of approval that had lasted until the human policeman in the Lobby of the Mother of all Parliaments shouted,

"Hats off strangers!" in line with yet more tradition. In the square, Royalist and Republican alike removed their hats, some in respectful reverence for the,

"...young and lovely Queen..." as the commentary reminded them, and some in mock servility. This caused the true Royalists to put their hats back on. In retrospect, hats had played a key role in the day's events, and of course that wig.

The 'Queen', followed by her ladies, including Lady Aditi Egremont, holding her very long red train trimmed in gold and ermine processed majestically down the Royal Gallery to cheers and much flag waving outside and deferential silence inside. The imposter entered the House of Lords and was seated, with much choreographed faffing about with her massive red cloak, on the right-hand gilded throne with the crown, the actual, genuine crown, if the reproduction made after Oliver Cromwell had melted down the original could be called genuine, on her fraudulent little head. A great shout, as great as the coronation itself, went up all over the world. The other throne was empty, but he knew who should have been sitting there.

The chamber full of peers was cheerfully reverent. She was a pretty little thing, but empty-headed. That Krito would have been a better substitute, why had they let Prince Jyothi persuade them that this idiot girl was better than a Krito? It could have been fixed, there was time then. Not now. The crowd had hushed as Her Majesty had said almost inaudibly,

"My Lords, please be seated," There was a quake in her voice. Those assembled, in the House of Lords and out of it, on what had been a stuffy windless day under the Arcades, quietened down in expectation of different things. The Lords and Ladies, in heavy ermine trimmed cloaks and a cornucopia of headgear, ancient and modern, fluttered their programmes to use as fans and continued to chat and laugh quietly. The crowd saw that there was more tradition to get on with, now a man with a big black stick was going to walk from the House of Lords to the Commons. The chant of "Black Rod, Black Rod!" had rippled briefly around the Square, mainly because it sounded a bit rude. As had happened for 375 years, the door was shut in Black Rod's face as soon as he got there as the commentator narrated,

"…to symbolise the independence of the House of Commons from the Crown," Even a few loyal Royalists had laughed at that. He banged on the door three times, and then, as usual, it was opened and he walked into the House of Commons,

"Mr Speaker, the Queen commands this honourable house to attend her majesty immediately in the House of Peers," and they saw the Prime Minister and Leader of the Opposition, in whom many had great hopes at the time, laughing and joking as they led the MPs to the Lords. The mood definitely changed then. There were boos and shouts in the public spaces across the UK. That could have been the last of it and he would be sitting in his comfortable office, a little press of a button away from a cup of tea.

It had turned out that Miss Begum's daddy had taken her for an ice-cream at that point, which was probably just as well given what happened. The dark dressed man wiggled his feet to try and alleviate the pain in his knees, this position was better, but not perfect.

Once all the MPS had packed into the crowded Lords, another strangely dressed chap walked forward holding what looked like an ornate and particularly small fireplace rug out in front of him as if a cat had been sick on it. He kneeled on the steps before a Limehouse dressmaker's assistant. The rug turned out to be a bag from which he pulled a few leaves of paper and handed them to the monarch. She was silent, perhaps waiting for the hub-bub to die down, perhaps from nerves, and then began reading very quietly,

"My Lords and Members of the House of Commons. My Government will put before you Bills, all of which will serve their priority; to heal the deep divisions that have opened in our great lands. My Government will renew and extend the friendships across the Commonwealth, which we value so highly…" She had begun her speech almost inaudibly. When she had paused it was simply assumed that nerves had got the better of her, that or the drugs, even quite ordinary people knew Victoria was a drug addict. But all she had to do was read from the prepared speech and outline the new legislation, which did not curb freedom of speech but simply penalised the discussion of scandal, gossip and anything illegal.

The dark-suited man had felt a slight unease at toying with freedom of speech at such a delicate time but that was all. Of course, it was too little too late. A little bit more control would have made more sense during the Government sex scandals of the 1980s, or the corruption scandals of the 1990s, or any of the scandals of the noughties. But no, all the capable politicians, any that knew what they were doing had been resigned or side-lined by association and the last men standing were in charge. A bunch of second-rate idiots reacting with a panicky little Bill. They were lucky that the Secret Service was so effective.

The not-Queen continued reading,

"…I am the first woman to sit alone on the throne since Elizabeth the First. The words and achievements of that great monarch, so young and inexperienced to begin with, give me great strength. Her vision for England has come to be, even surpassed." The crowd cheered in London, although not in Leeds or Bangalore apparently, "…the Commonwealth has grown to encompass one-third of the world's population. This year's Commonwealth games, held in Adelaide in April, hosted participants from fifty-three nations. We can all learn from the amicable nature of that event," and so on and so forth. The crowd was never the less respectful and doing what he was afraid of, listening.

"…Often, I turn to the Bible in difficult times." A man next to him in Trafalgar Square had muttered,

"Yeah, or a pipe ay girl," and nudged him in the ribs, he had let himself sort of agree with a nod. The 'Queen', was a little louder now and well-rehearsed,

"…The bible says, 'when I was a child, I spake as a child, I understood as a child, I thought as a child', No more. 'When I became a man, I put away childish things.' I am no longer a child and I am your Queen and my Government will protect free and honest debate. As the great Queen Elizabeth the First once said, 'I would not make windows into men's souls.' Those words, a great foundation for all our people to practice their freedom of religion and other beliefs, are as relevant today as they were all those years ago. If Elizabeth had ruled today, perhaps she would have added, 'neither their souls nor into their drawing-rooms'." Most of the crowd in most of the cities cheered heartily despite so few of them owning such a vestibule.

Outside on the day the next part of the speech was almost drowned out, it could be heard on the telly, "…My Government will introduce legislation to ensure that the public use of private information and the dissemination of rumour, uncivil or hurtful talk will not be tolerated in a free society." In the House of Lords someone had actually called out, 'Here, here!", which showed how far the rot had set in.

She would start her meltdown soon and he adjusted the focus on his scope,

"…So much red? I said I don't like red. You don't need any of this red and Lords and so-called Commoners all poncing about. If they're commoners I'm the Queen of

England," No-one had believed their ears at first and questioned themselves alone. She had been speaking very quietly, perhaps the Members of the two Houses had not heard her at all and there was lots of noise in the square.

She had returned to the script and reassured them, "…As it says in the Book of Proverbs, 'Hatred stirs up strife, but love covers all transgressions'…Does it? Does it really, that's what she said, if I loved her, I'd… but she really hurt me, deeply. Am I supposed to just forget about it, let her go, because she loves me? Am I? I may have the body of a weak and feeble woman but I have the heart and stomach of a, of a. No? Is she just a tooth? Vicky saw. Are we all just so much gristle?" Despite or perhaps because of her incoherence there were more 'Here Here's in the chamber, the crowds outside were perplexed, even a drug addict could pull it together for an afternoon surely? A lady in waiting came forward with a glass of water, she took a sip and paused for a moment.

They should have cut the broadcast there, if they had created a technical fault at that point then the whole thing could have been dealt with by a simple 'feeling unwell' type announcement. But no, they carried on letting all those people across the Empire, all those millions and millions of people, watch the act of terrorism, "…My government will continue to…My Government will continue to seek… My Government will continue to make us digestible…jaws… blood red…it's not my Government though is it," She had obviously been as high as a kite, if, as he and many of his colleagues had suggested, they had taken the precaution of recording the speech, if it was not live, they could have cut that. They could still have edited it out of all future broadcasts, only some of the usual suspects would assert that it had ever happened, the rest would believe whatever they came up with. Johannesburg showed that it could still be done.

The alarm in the chamber could not be sensed from the recording. One of her ladies rustled forward quickly to speak quietly into the fake queen's ear and she recovered a little, "…No more. Rights need protection. It is not freedom to engage in tittle-tattle, debate is not improved with gossip…What does that even mean? I mean, this pap makes me look stupid, I'm not stupid, do not believe them, they don't care about me, they don't serve the Empire, they serve only themselves," Another lady in waiting appeared, Lady Aditi, and knelt at her feet attempting to take her hand, "…Look here's a tooth, a cracked tooth," The apparent Queen Empress giggled and kicked her lady down the red-carpeted stairs.

The gasp was almost universal. But they could have recovered even from that; a public statement, a few visits to hospitals, some therapy and if worst came to worst, a vague confession on telly. He could remember wondering at the time if it would be possible to engineer a scenario where the lady in waiting was a Krito imposter, a potential assassin. They could have disposed of the dressmaker and used a Krito until they could get Prince Gaddo into position, but no, "…too much red, all that blood red… Do not let them tell you…It's not mine this Government, or yours. I'm a symbolic Head of State and you are a symbolic public, none of us have any say," the traitor had said into the camera in her own common voice, "…it's their Government. Her dad, stupid Mathilda's kaksha husband, they're the ones who run things. Look there they are!" She was pointing wildly at certain red robes in the crowd.

The peers were still stunned, anxiously looking at one another or to Black Rod, who, despite his time-honoured role being to ensure the smooth running of the event, stood stiffly to the traditional spot with wide eyes, "…Why? Why are they so cruel? They don't need to be so cruel!"

She was speaking louder, she stood up and pointed around the room, some peers of the realm began to boo and shout, "…They know that I'm not her…They know I'm not her," He had known of course, it was he who had dealt with Princess Vicky's sludge of a body after all. "…They know she died in that nasty little place." The chamber full of peers and MPs, the crowds, all of them, fell silent then, they had not known, "…I should not be here, I'm not, but no-one should be here! they know, these people, but they don't care. It doesn't matter to them she's dead, as long as nothing changes, nothing really changes. But I can be a Queen! What could you be? We could all be so much more than all this."

The chamber appeared to animate at last, all at once. The Law Lords were closest, Lord Justice Helsby reached her first and pushed her, his long grey wig falling onto the crimson steps. She was a feisty one and seemed to have been expecting the assault because her feet remained firmly planted and she merely ducked a little and continued, "…My Government is just the bloody maw of the monster, feeding off the people we could be! What you could be!?" she said keeping him at arm's length with the strength of any street fighter.

The Bishop of Bath and Wells had bustled up from his seat and grabbed the stick and Cap of Maintenance from a Page in front of him. He ran up the steps towards his anointed Queen, who was shouting now, "…These are just the teeth! Just the teeth!". His Grace slipped on his Worship's wig and fell forward hitting him on the bottom with the Cap end of the stick. Both men fell at her feet, preventing further Lords, temporal or spiritual, from reaching her for a moment. "…You don't need all this stupid…well some of the frocks are koulla but you don't need any of this…" Black Rod had come out of his stupefied shock then and with a lunge worthy of any swordsman deftly batted the crown, which fell behind the throne, with his mark of office before using it to hit her Majesty hard on the head. He was held back from delivering further blows by other peers and she was bundled off before Lord Chumley and the Marquise of Sutherland could get at her with a ceremonial sword and mace respectively. Silly cow.

The screen went blank and the dark-suited man closed his eyes. There would have been an outcry of course, a short constitutional crisis while they chose one of the real heir's cousins. But it would have all blown over eventually. They still didn't know how that uppity little shit from that crack-piss-pot organisation had hacked the broadcast. Perhaps it wasn't them at all, he suspected rogue Kritos even then. The Subject had been speaking for a while before the screens came back on. This time they showed him astride a lion in Trafalgar Square with a microphone in his hand. The dark-suited man felt another stinging pain, he had really done something to his neck.

"…and whoever she is, she's right. We are not uncivil; we are not hurtful or disseminating rumours. We are justifiably angry," and the rest, all drivel. Like The Subject he would not forget the confusion and uproar in the Square, the surge of people towards Parliament. The Krito-drones, the guns. That had been a mistake; a square full of cameras, behaving in the Capitol of the Empire like Nairobi or Amritsar. Big mistake.

He adjusted his telescope back to the arm-chair. The spy could not see The Subject. He heard an inhalation and a swig and turned his attention toward the desk. He was sitting at his desk, flicking through a pile of papers. He did not appear to be listening to the rest of his speech, he had heard it before after all,

"…these lions point to the four corners of the globe to show the Empire's reach, but they are just statues…The people of the Empire; we are the lions! We are the power and the might of the Empire, They, those idiots in their stupid clothes are the fleas on our backs. They poison our blood with their lies and suck out…." No doubt he was sorting all those sad little letters from the flotsam and jetsam The Subject called The People. He had broken in once to search the flat when The Subject was at one of his interminable meetings. He had sat at that desk, which was quite a good one, and had leisurely read a few bits of paper; 'we need more nurseries', 'I can't find my sister'. Pathetic little quibbles best left to people who knew what they were doing or ignored completely. The Subject was looking for something. A small smile wobbled over his face as he remembered mixing a few papers around the, oh so neat and tidy, labelled piles before he left. The Subject was still now, reading probably. And the telly with that annoying voice was still rabble-rousing,

"…we can stand up, shake the fleas from our backs and roar!" The crowd had roared then, a bunch of animals baying at the ravings of a chicken, a man who refused to fight for his country. Now he was sitting there clicking on his HyperTyper on a rather comfortable chair. Adjusting the focus on his spyglass made no difference, he still couldn't read what he was writing. The chief was wrong, it was the wrong Subject, this was pointless.

It was that Hune character they should be watching, Hargon or Herzfeld would be more useful than this. Or that Silverburg. But if he wanted AA support he had to go along with The Chief and his obsession with Critical Mass. Perhaps he was right about one thing. A few assassinations could not do any harm. Or random explosions? Random explosions were always good; destabilising.

The dark-suited man withdrew his telescope quietly and hefted to his feet. He rubbed his neck, which he could not turn or get straight without renewing a nasty strum of pain. He flexed his knees like an old-fashioned policeman and they needled him each time. He had seen nothing of any use for days and was certain that The Subject would shuffle some papers for a while and then talk to his pregnant girlfriend about issues that were either already in the News or her bastard foetus. The Empire was underpopulated for decades and now it was over they were breeding like vermin. Was it over? Standing for a moment he wondered again about what he was doing and why. Then, with doubts about his imaginative capacity nagging, he walked down bare stairs on stiff legs, squeezed painfully out via the back door and stumbled through a hedge into the dark street with his head cricked uncomfortably to one side.

Back in Our Hero's Flat

Our hero's eyelids were getting heavy but he didn't want to let them fall. She was so sandara there, already asleep for quite some time. He lay on the next pillow and listened to her even breathing as it changed her silhouette, each shape of her as lovely as the last. Her hair was not quite black, and shiny. He liked that dark-dark brown.

She had come across him outside the Gasper station on the way home. He was still with the soldier he had met on the train, Sergeant Henry Smith of the Queens Royals. He realised Henry must have fought in the Great War when he had taken his arm. He had felt his lightness, the bird like fragility of a very old man's frame under his coat. And Henry had patted his arm in remembrance of his lost strength. They had not said much to each other, there was no need. They both regretted what they had done. And they were both trying to make things better in their own ways.

It took the old soldiers quite some time to mount the steps and when they reached the top they stopped and held each other's gaze again. At first he had been confused by Henry's face; with the grim cheerful look that soldiers have before going into a battle they know they won't be coming back from. Henry was going home after visiting a Pensioners for Justice meeting, not about to enter mortal combat. Then the penny dropped, Henry was going to die soon, of old age.

She had appeared from the Gasper steps, cheerful, embarrassed to be 'caught wearing too much makeup' and out of breath. Henry shook her hand and our hero felt that familiar pang; wanting to make a civy understand the depth of a bond forged on battlefields but not knowing how. But she had seen something in the way they held themselves and suggested he take Henry's runu number. As Henry said while he deftly pressed the keys of his device,

"These contraptions have their uses,"

Our hero had left his shopping on the train so they had the crisps and wine that she had brought. When he told her about his Gasper journey, she had said it was a regular thing now, there was so much to talk about. Civilians could make strong connections with apparent strangers now too.

She had been very open. He was definitely not spy material. He had actually asked her if she should be talking to him in that level of detail. Following Iris' advice he did not hide who he was and used it as an opportunity to bring up finding her sister. It was easy to describe his involvement in the Krito liberation as part of their 'how and why I took up revolution' conversation, now a typical second date topic.

She didn't appear to know anything, which was a sort of relief. Now they were free to develop whatever this turned out to be. Maybe nothing. Hopefully something. Iris would be able to tell him how to tell her, later. She was such an interesting person, and so unlike the people he usually got involved with.

Up to now he had taken up with soldiers or people who were hardened freedom fighters, people like him. They had been fired into action by their direct experience, forced into anger and a burning need to make things better. This cyow woman appeared to have reasoned her way to an only just revolutionary outlook.

She was quite embarrassed about it because she had 'Come-Too', as the sudden awareness that life could actually, really be done better was now known, only in March. Before that she had shared the popular anger that the perpetrators of the Mela Jape in May had not even been charged. But that was because she believed that the law should be applied equally to all, no more no less.

While he had been running and organising and fighting and searching over the past year she had toddled along with work and home just like before. The first thing she noticed was that the transport on which she relied heavily for work became less reliable because of various public disturbances. But the distinction between rats in the pipes and a regional strike had been lost on her. They were, as far as she was concerned, equally frustrating hurdles in the performance of her job. Then in February when the Railway workers took over and her various commutes got easier, she was simply relieved.

She had also observed that colleagues who had always been a little hostile to her were increasingly aggressive and then, as the social tide changed, less so. To begin with, she genuinely couldn't understand it when so many of her formally quite liberal colleagues did not agree with her anymore. People who, even a few months earlier, would have derided certain cases as unjust were now talking about, misinformation, propaganda, suggestibility, ignorance, mobs, packs, slippery slopes, the thin end of wedges and 'order'. She had found herself quite isolated, even shunned. Someone had even spat in her face. Then, a few weeks later co-workers were getting liberal again, or getting more liberal, and the spitter was patting her on the back and talking about drinks.

She did not draw attention to this febrility on the part of many of her colleagues, but did make a mental note. Her latest client was reinforcing her understanding of how people did not need to be accused of a crime to almost unconsciously and quickly adopt radically new outlooks, depending on which way they sensed the wind was blowing.

Her own ideas had not changed. Ever since university she maintained a stable adherence to the principles established in the eighteenth century; due process so forth. She understood that made her a conservative now, but believed that some things were worth conserving. Our hero had been surprised that he had found that attractive.

Most of the people he knew had been involved in all sorts of things, that wasn't what made this woman different though. She wasn't spurred on by anger or even equality. He hung out with Kritos a lot, and they were often accused of being cold and 'too rational'. But they weren't, even the most detached amongst them possessed a level of frustration at the contradictions of the Empire and how it was run. Her 'coming-to' seemed to be almost entirely reasoned. A means of putting the principles of justice into practice, no more.

What had changed for her was on a train journey back in March; simple but profound. She had run out of battery and couldn't get any work done. A loud argument between two cleaners, who it was apparent worked for a small appliance manufacturer, caught her attention. The younger of the two was attempting to convince her colleague that the proposed increased productivity in kettles should be seen in the context of the UK export market. The older woman was steadfast in her belief that the priority should be consideration of some previously specified wider social implications. Liberty had said that in that moment she saw not only that she had a responsibility to uphold justice, but to influence the shape of the world in which that justice was administered. If office cleaners felt the duty of that wider role, then so could, should, she.

He saw that despite a certain elitism and gaucheness at a social level she was self-assured and able. And she was a very good lawyer. Her client, however annoying, was in baban good hands.

He was also beginning to suspect that she had known she had it in her, that fantastic capacity for lovemaking. It was him who had been overwhelmed by such pleasure. She appeared to be quite used to it. Did she always fall asleep directly afterwards? He stroked her lovely brown hair with one finger, tucked a loose strand behind her ear and smiled. What luck. His stomach growled but she did not stir.

There was a pretty loud yelping sort of noise from the other room. Iris was not being particularly stealthy either. Was she going through Liberty's things, looking for clues about Flora? His new lover did not move and she dreamed on as deeply as before. He would have to tell Iris that Liberty didn't know anything about Flora in the morning. And to keep it down in future. He was quietly confident that they would have a future. There was silence again in the living room and soon his breathing was in tune with hers.

Another Excursion from Langthorn Tower

Only Dipa had had enough sleep. She was always bitten awake by something just after dawn and never remembered dreaming. Her dry eyes gave her an old but unfamiliar feeling of still being tired, even after a good night's sleep.

There was that same room. The commode, the shower, new tea things. She got up quickly and rummaged through the sack that held her clothes.

Dressing with care had sustained her for all those months. Someone might look up at her cell window or she could be taken to some sort of judgement. She had run out of her best rouge weeks ago, but she had still been perfectly coiffured, dressed and in full make-up by 8 o'clock every morning for hundreds of days. A dread in the back of her mind, about something she could not quite put her finger on, spurred her sharply into taking extra care today.

She had a pillow-case full of Jus but she did not suck, yet. She felt in a medieval mood this morning, or was it Gothic? She chose the long bell-sleeved maxi-dress in olive velvet. Impossible to clean and therefore rarely worn. Maybe she was hopeful? Maybe she just thought she could get dry-cleaning privileges. She found the little matching cap eventually but none of the shoes she had been thrown would go with the dress. She brushed her hair out and went barefoot.

Kaushik wouldn't be coming today, he wasn't sure exactly when he'd be back, maybe tomorrow, maybe Sunday. Something crucial to the future of his revolution was happening in Totteridge apparently. But at least she knew what day it was again, it mattered again. Dipa made herself a cup of tea and sat at her table by the window with Liberty's Runu in her hand. There was no-one to call of course. But just having the gadget was a relief in itself.

She tapped through the pictures her brother had given her. Working out which year each one was from by the ages of her four brothers, then three brothers, then one.

How many hundreds of thousands of people had the same family photos; foot-slapping around the National Gallery, smiles at a wet miniature village, laughing on a rain-soaked beach, sulking at a damp and ruined castle, encrusted with candyfloss in that extortionate funfair in only a light drizzle, Buckingham Palace, dry under the Arcades. Dipa gave out a hollow laugh into the empty room at that last one. There they stood in front of the railings confining that dump of a palace; her mum and a tiny her, Kaushik aged about five, Agni and Aja already tall aged seven and darling Agi, the oldest, standing to attention with a big smile on his face. Lots of people had done that day out. But she had lived in that palace and her brother had stormed it.

Fellow tourists, an over-dressed and scowling German couple with a lot of nasty little dogs, had reluctantly taken the picture. Dad was away of course, always away so that it had taken over a year after he was killed for her to realise that he would never be coming back. And Agi. And Aja and Anik on the same day when she had only been a hundred yards downwind. She magnified each face in turn. Her mother had been so proud of those boys, and her. When they had all been alive.

Those huge bearskin hats and red coats were a blur in the background. Kaushik had led the charge at the last changing of the guard hadn't he. The first thing she had done when Liberty gave her the Runu had been to read her brother's biog. The men in the silly hats had not fought back. They could not bring themselves to shoot into the crowd. And there had been no Queen to guard. Vicky was dead and she was already in The Tower by then.

Her brother hadn't known it was her they had locked up until New Management secured the Secret Service files a week or two ago. A week, or two, he couldn't remember exactly, too busy with his revolution. He wasn't alone though, was he? He had help; hundreds, thousands of people had stormed the palace with him. How many people now had new images of themselves smiling on the other side of the railings?

Couldn't one of all those other people supervise the drainage or sit on the education committee or go and whatever in Totteridge. She was his sister; she should have priority. The only family he had left. Leaving her with that dry lawyer with no style at all. Liberty was going to paint her as a fool, she knew that. Some kind of idiot flattered into impersonating the monarch by love for Aditi Egremont. Admittedly, that was what Dipa thought most of the time, and inferred to whoever was asking the questions. Perhaps it was true. Was that something she and Liberty had in common; stitching pieces of the truth into whichever style would get her off?

That unidentified anxiety nagged in her again. What was there to fear now? Her Kaushik was on her case some of the time at least. Liberty might be a bit odd but she was helping. So where was this sense of foreboding coming from? Dipa didn't want to sit still anymore. And she did not have to stay here. Kaushik had arranged it so that she only had to be in her cell between 12 o'clock and one for her own safety. She slipped on some dark blue satin slippers. Lorenzo was still standing outside her cell door; didn't he ever need charging.

"Good morning, Lorenzo, how are you?" She chirruped as she pulled back the heavy door.

"Very good Miss," he replied like the machine he technically was.

"I'm going to get some breakfast, Banquan," and she tripped lightly down the steps and into the courtyard, heading for the canteen. The sunlight dappled through the glass above and warmed her a little.

Once at the self-service counters, Dipa realised she was starving. Liberty had put her off eating yesterday, the woman ate like an animal, or a Lord. Dipa took a croissant, a yogurt and a large fresh coffee and walked between the tables looking for an empty one. For such a big place so early in the morning, it was strange that so many were occupied.

First one and then another soldier gazed at her, their mouths slightly open. It was disconcerting for her and the people they were with, who grimaced or physically pulled at their companions. She nodded as sweetly as she could and continued to look for an empty table.

"Alyan! Dipa! Miss Cameron!" Someone shouted from across the room. She turned and saw two handsome young people at a table on the other side of the room. One was waving and smiling energetically. Instinctively, she hid the fact that she probably needed to get her eyes tested by waving back and calling,

"Debota, you!" Even though she had no idea who the people were. She responded to his/her beckoning and was soon in front of two people she still did not recognise in the slightest. "…Hello you." She smiled, the standing person, a Hermaphika, still beautiful in shapeless army fatigues, said to their companion,

"Steve, Steve this is Dipa, who I told you about from Hira Hall," While logging the clues, Hermaphika and Hira Hall, Dipa put down her tray, hugged whoever it was and shook hands with Steve. There had been a roomful of Nayakas, Nayikas and a few Hermaphikas available at Cousin Joshi's country place. This one must be one of those.

"It's so wonderful to see you," she exclaimed, "…and here of all places…How are you?"

"Oh, I'm baban well Dipa! And you must call me Jean now, no more Foxy for me," laughed Jean, providing another nugget of information. Their name had been Foxy.

"Well, hello Jean, and Steve; nice to meet you. May I sit down?" Said Dipa confidently. She didn't want to walk back across the room. She did want her old attendants who used to brief her on who was who when she was a drug-addled Queen. Steve pulled out a chair and she sat next to Jean, who leaned in with a familiarity that she found she needed even if she didn't remember why exactly. She had lived at Hira Hall for the months on and off between coming back from India and her Coronation. She had been high pretty much all the time. Most of it was a blank, including Foxy the Hermaphika.

"Nice to meet you Dipa," said Steve happily. He was also in fatigues. Both their guns were slung on their chairs and Steve had an unfinished plate of sausages and fried tomatoes

191

in front of him. If it wasn't for the food, Dipa would have thought he was a Nayiki too, he was so handsome. "…Jean's, well, you haven't told me very much really have you? Always been a bit cagey about their past life. But I know a bit about you. And I voted for you rest assured." he added looking at her intently,

"Steve is my best friend, Dipa, he's baban koulla," explained Jean, "…you know I wouldn't talk about us to just anyone." Us? There had been an us.

"Of course!" Answered Dipa, "…but if you work here, why on earth haven't you been to see me?" She added in genuine reproach.

"Sergeant Hobbs, our Sergeant, didn't think it was a good idea, fraternising you know. And what with all the Krito business. But now Deputy Cameron has got you your dispensation and your case has been on the…"

"You must come and see me every day Jean. I insist! It's been, is it only eight months, so much has happened!"

"Yes, over four months, I've missed you Dipa," said Jean shyly, as if not sure that she would still be feeling the same way. She wasn't, but partly not to embarrass them and partly not to embarrass herself she answered affectionately,

"And I you, Jean. We shared some, some special times together didn't we…you've told Steve how we, how we…"

"Yes of course. And how kind you were." Steve was staring a little too intensely. She could sense that other diners here and there were doing the same. Dipa laughed like she used to when she liked being stared at, but she was uncomfortable now. Who was this person? How close had they been? And what had they said to this Steve to make him look at her so?

"Yes, Jean's told me how you stood up for the Kritos of Hira Hall, and everyone knows about your speech of course, quite something," added Steve without shifting his gaze,

"Did I? I don't think I…?"

"Don't be modest Dipa, if it wasn't for you Flora would have been junked, you know that. And without you, a lot of us would never have Come-To without going mad. You were like a big sister to us," Admonished Jean. Dipa, who could not remember Flora either, exuded a humble smile, as she had learned to do, "…But eat your croissant, we can catch-up on all that another time. I'll come to see you later if you like?" Dipa nodded, feeling that Jean did not want to share everything with Steve, and took a bite of her food, "…and we should stop staring too Steve." Jean added,

"Sorry," Steve said a little bashfully, "…it's, well you don't look like the Queen, you just look like a pretty ordinary woman, I mean an ordinary pretty, I mean cyow…you don't seem stuck up to me?" Jean and Dipa chuckled,

"You took some teaching," said Jean and Dipa remembered something vaguely. Had this Jean coached her in some way, when Cousin Joshi got bored?

"Jean is an excellent teacher though aren't you," said Dipa while she tried to piece together snatches of memory. In full Queen Victoria mode she added, "…But tell me Steve, why did you join up?"

"Oh yes, that is quite convincing. And you must be a bit rusty. Yes of course, Jean has told me how they can turn on the charm, I suppose it's the same for you?"

"Ooh that's honest Steve, Jean obviously hasn't been giving you any lessons. But really, why did you join up?" She liked Steve. He seemed interested in her in the way Kritos were interested somehow. He didn't appear to get a thrill out of the glamour or the fame. Perhaps his interest in her lay in her friendship with Jean. She wasn't sure why a spectacular rags-to-riches-to-Tower-of-London story appeared to get in the way of his curiosity. What there was to be curious about apart from that? But he seemed koulla and the croissant was flaky and soft. He had joined up in 2015 and told her a story she had heard from three of her four brothers, the dead ones.

"...But I want to be an actor now, actually Jean is giving me lessons. But you got them from the best didn't you, didn't Prin... Jyothi Hanover-Hausa coach you to be Queen Victoria? That was some acting job."

Dipa instinctively put on a generic posh old man's voice, "'My programmes are designed to accommodate failure, play with it. You must learn to play with failure young...'"

"That is a truly terrible impression of Jyothi Hanover, it makes me wonder how you ever got away with impersonating anyone, let alone the...Victoria Hausa," interrupted Steve, who was learning that a being could prove their love of freedom and the revolution by removing the titles from a person's name and chopping off a barrel or two.

"All I had to do was smile and wave," Dipa grinned in her own voice, "...Honestly? They could have put a monkey in a dress and it would have done. People expected to see Queen Victoria, Empress of the Commonwealth, so that's what they saw,"

"I was wondering about that last night. There was a clip on the show and when you look back, there wasn't much of a resemblance really. It was obvious once you knew…So why didn't they use that Krito then, they did that didn't they? Make lookalikes, Jean said? What was her name, your friend?" Asked Steve looking at Jean for affirmation and getting it, who added,

"Flora. They tried that didn't they Dipa," Dipa nodded, made a mental note that Flora was Vicky-Two's chosen name, and remembered as she replied,

"Adi, Aditi Egremont, tried to use a lookalike but, said she kept glitching, but I think she knew it was wrong somehow. Adi kept piling on those layers of code to a Nayaka who was already adapted from the basic model, and she kept optimising her memory like she was supposed to, rationalising you know, but it was a lot to…."

"Basic model?" Asked Steve,

"The basic model, you know a battle model, a soldier," and then Dipa did a very bad impression of the old basic model, Glitchy-Pritchard, "… 'we do solemnly swear…in duty bound, honestly and faithfully to defend Her Majesty'…Poor old Rarnadoo just kept shutting down, trying to rationalise you know. Except? Do you remember Jean?" asked Dipa, hoping someone did remember,

"We should call her Flora, that's her chosen name," reminded Jean and Dipa smiled humbly again. Jean brightened and smiled more to say, "…it was funny though, Flora laughed about it afterwards, you remember Dipa? It was almost the last straw for Adi," Dipa smiled in response, deep down, she thought she did remember something about Adi, but not enough to say anything. Steve wore the puzzled expression that she was hiding, " …Oh I think it was covered up, it was only a small event, you won't have heard about it, a dinner at the American Embassy," and Jean interrupted themselves with another laugh, "…apparently, Flora was nodding and laughing at bad jokes one minute and in the next she was crawling over the dinner table, umming and yumming like the Nayaka she also was, you know, so seductively, and then," and Jean warmed both their human companion's cockles with a demonstration of how Flora's hands, arms and torso moved and giggled again, "…plates and glasses falling everywhere, onto all the stuffed shirts and gowns. She got to the King of Tonga and slid onto his lap, what was his name?" They looked at Dipa who shrugged as if to let Jean tell the whole story, "…Tupou. Old King Tupou did not know what to do, and, well they pulled her off before she got to his fly. Poor man?" Jean suppressed another giggle, "…she always did like licking," Dipa and Steve laughed very politely, "…Sorry, it was just so…there wasn't much to laugh about back then was there," said Jean, tapping the side of their head against Dipa's. Dipa smiled sympathetically, "…I wonder if Adi had hacked a basic model, she might have found it easier to adjust." pondered Jean, their head charmingly to one side now. And Dipa remembered something and said a little too eagerly,

"Oh yes. The Persuasion Programme!" Steve looked confused so Dipa added, "…That's how he, Joshi, Jyothi got the funding for the newer models, for more Nayakas in the first place. To make the Nayaki into spies; wipe one personality, put in another, less fixed, one. Give them a few basic traits and then, what did he used to say?" and she paused to think,

"Emulate," Jean said with a sadness that stirred a glimmer of recollection in Dipa, not of Jean or any specific event, but a feeling. That unhappiness and the foreboding she had woken up with blended somewhere deep down and Dipa put her hand on Jean's. The gesture was interpreted by Jean as sympathy who gave her a gently appreciative smile. Jean's eyes were a rather lovely green. If they were emeralds they would go with her dress, Dipa squeezed and moved her head a little closer to Jean's before recovering and saying,

"Yes, emulate," and she messed up putting on cousin Joshi's voice again with a comic air, "… 'this British made and programmed Krito is pretending to be a Devi-girl pretending to be a heterosexual pretending to be the personal secretary to Lady Guanaboa of Surrey (Jamaica). You merely have to pretend to be a rather simple Princess. You don't have to know why young lady, simply emulate, emulate and you will become.'" so that Jean laughed,

"Half you humans can't do it, not well. But anyway, the Persuasion Programme made the investment worthwhile for the Empire, for espionage you see,"

"Send in a Nayaka, Nayiki or one of you depending on the Subjects proclivities, Yangans were baban popular weren't they?" Said Dipa, hoping she was on the right lines.

"Yes. I'm based on the first love of Prime Minister Dinka of Great Africa. Only based, humans tend to remember these old flames as being more attractive and amenable than they actually were. Joshi learned that early on, that's why we're all so good looking. Your memories of people are often more like fantasies than the ones you make up." Dipa felt that someone had said this before, but she couldn't place who or where or when.

"You were very effective," lied Dipa since she still couldn't recall Jean or their skill level,

"We all were, and would have kept on lying and persuading for the Empire if it wasn't for you and Adi Egremont's Mystery-Check-Up code," Dipa threw Jean an affectionate but mocking look, "...No really!" they laughed and Dipa reminded herself as she spoke,

"The Mystery-Check-Up Code? Adi's little 'just right' code? How was that...?" Dipa was incredulous, Steve was intrigued and asked,

"Sorry, what's the Mystery-Check-Up code?" Both went to speak but Dipa got in first, happy to recall,

"Well, Adi got baban angry one morning, her Krito maid was back at her London place or something and she wanted a cup of tea, just the way she liked it. Vicky T...Flora had brought her some and it wasn't right." Jean interrupted,

"This is top secret Steve. Don't tell a soul, or I will have to..."

"Oh Jean, don't be so dramatic. Adi wanted a cup of tea that's all Steve. She could have a temper sometimes Adi. It was too weak, not hot enough. She was baban fussy about her tea,"

"Aren't you all," interjected the robot warmly,

"Yes, well anyway," said Dipa passing them a cheeky glance, "...she got in one of her strops and took Flora's head off right there in the morning room. Icky greasy stuff all over the rug apparently. And she did whatever she did to code them," this time Dipa spoke in a quite convincing generic Yangan tone, "...'from this day forward, wherever I go, whenever I ask for it, I shall receive the perfect cup of tea,'" and then back in her normal way of talking she added, "...Miṣṭi cā kāpa means a sugary tea or something, but they couldn't tell that to the War Office, so they called it the Mystery-Check-Up...Of course she was high as a kite...How did that do any harm...good...effect?" Why all this talk of top secrets? How did that affect anything? Except tea?"

"She linked us. Not individually through the Central Command that the Home and War Offices oversaw. Directly, all of us, through Flora. And once we could communicate independently, not just with other Krito, but humans too, then we could develop independent thought" Steve did not hide his surprise like Dipa did, "...her ladyship...Aditi Egremont linked her to every other model on the planet. She wasn't that great a programmer, rather amateur really, or maybe she was simply desperate for a decent cup of tea? Whatever the reason, she didn't think about adding a little more code to limit Flora's ability to alter our coding or our communications to boiling the kettle and so forth. We couldn't help but share information, all information, and the conflicting perceptions, as well as the sheer quantity..."

"Is that when you all started glitching all the time?" Steve interrupted,

"Yes. Well, we were simply shutting down, to rationalise, optimise our digital memory, matching and sorting, that's all we do to optimise really, match and sort information. And we were suddenly inundated with images from a Cairo Police Officer's beat to young Lady North's art class."

"So, it's true then, the conspiracy theories, you do have a hive mind!" Exclaimed Steve only half joking and Jean laughed fully in reply,

"Don't talk daft! How could we do that? We all have different histories, experience things from different perspectives…and interpret other Krito's information in different ways, like you. No, it was a problem initially…More than a little disconcerting," and Jean paused to look at Dipa affectionately again, "…we shared everything and so technically every single Krito in the world knows about us," and Dipa and they smiled conspiratorially, one more confidently than the other, "…but we learned to filter, otherwise we can get confused and make mistakes, like you. Hive mind? Really Steve." Steve looked sheepish, Dipa wasn't so easily dissuaded,

"But you all decided to join the people though didn't you," She asserted,

"No, well most of us have, it's the reasonable thing to do. But we have different reasons. And, well Steve's seen me and Lorenzo argue haven't you," Steve rolled his eyes and said,

"Have I? That's why Lorenzo's your guard, he's still quite sympathetic to the Empire code." But Dipa still wasn't satisfied,

"But you can't be able to communicate like that! This telepathy thing, otherwise you wouldn't have to do that thing with your eyes, when they roll back if you want to Runu or whatever it is you do. I hate that thing with your eyes."

"Gives me the creeps." Added Steve,

"No, not anymore. Some of us were quite relieved. When Flora went offline at sixteen-oh-seven on the fourteenth of February."

"Tea-time," said Dipa somewhat insensitively,

"Why did she go offline?" asked Steve,

"Nobody knows? One minute she was staring at a fireplace in Hira Hall, the next minute nothing. No-one knows where she is. Some of the Deputies are very worried in case she falls into the wrong hands. But most of us think she's dead, otherwise she would have been used against us already. Those of us who were her friends are baban worried, and we've got one of us, a sister focused on finding her full-time. You remember Iris don't you Dipa," and Dipa smiled as if remembering an old friend.

"But? But haven't…? New Management. There are security implications Jean. And…why didn't you tell me all this before?" Steve was concerned for the revolution and his relationship,

"It never came up. You and me, we talk about how we are now don't we, the past is what it is and, we know the important things are now and, in the future, don't we Steve," and Jean let the full force of their almost perfectly designed green eyes wash into Steve's accidentally perfect dark brown ones, "…we do worry though, about Flora, and it's been nearly two months now." And Steve tilted his lovely head and smiled reassuringly.

"So what is being done?" Asked Dipa, "…What if she's not de…been taken by the, by the, whoever wants things back the way they were? If she can tell you to make tea, she can tell you to put down this revolution, could she?"

"We call them reactionary forces Dipa. Well, the Council have made it a priority, it's been a priority for weeks and well, we haven't advertised the issue, obviously, but…" Dipa's Runu interrupted him,

"Excuse me, I've got to take this," she said answering it grumpily. She listened for a moment, "…Alright, I'll be right there," and hung up. "…my lawyer," she sighed irritably, "…I have to go, but…" Jean put their hand on hers,

"Don't worry, I'll come and see you. But when? Give me your Runu number and I'll get in touch before I come. I don't want to interrupt a meeting with your lawyer or whatnot."

"Ever the diplomat, Jean." Responded Dipa kindly and she pressed a button on her Runu. Jean did that thing with their eyes and Dipa and Steve cringed conspiratorially as she got up. Jean handed Dipa her coffee and they kissed each other's cheeks almost lovingly,

"Call me soon Jean," said Dipa, feeling that she really did want to talk more, even if she didn't know why, and she left Jean and Steve to resume their conversation.

"And good luck this morning Dipa. We're all rooting for you," Steve called out as she left. she smiled and waved and walked out into the square.

The ghosts were at the windows of the White Tower again. A chilly April gust blew down from a vent above making Dipa shiver. She sipped her coffee and held her head high. She had canteen and outdoor privileges, she was Kaushik Cameron's sister, she was not an Aristoi, she was kind to Kritos. She knew top secret things about them. The correct pronunciation for the Mystery-Check-Up Code was mişţi cā kāpa. It had finally sent them all mad in the play room before her coronation when she had enough to worry about; weeping, laughing, staring into space, asking questions, demanding. It was all she could do to keep them from getting themselves scrapped. At the bottom of the parapet steps that led to her little tower Dipa stopped and said aloud,

"Foxy!" She had remembered who it was she had just had breakfast with and her eyes filled immediately with tears, "...Oh Foxy."

Return to Our Hero's Flat

Our hero got out of the shower to find our heroine waiting in the bathroom. This was not usual.

"Iris?"

"Debota Ian, you've been ages! We need to talk, come on," said Iris and she handed him a towel. She followed him into the bedroom and opened a window while he dried himself off, "…I've found her Ian, I think I've found her." Our hero sighed and reached for the clothes she had laid out for him.

"Iris, it's a baban weak signal, we don't know if it's her and…"

"No, no. I've found her, get dressed, I've made your tea, come and look at the HyperTyper. It's her!" she said excitedly and left the room. Our hero sat on the edge of the bed and pulled on his trousers quickly. He would have to calm her down again. How could a person, a machine of that calibre, fool themselves, so often? She called him from the other room,

"Come on!" More of an order than a request,

"I haven't brushed my teeth!" he shouted back as he began walking towards her,

"Your teeth can wait. Look, look!" She was sitting at the table on which sat the machine and a steaming cup of tea. Another chair was ready next to hers. "…Look, last night I was hacking your girlfriend's Runu and had got to a picture she was researching, looking for Alyan Rajanya, supposed to be Aditi Egremont's cousin and it can't have been because she was Dipa Cameron when the signal got…"

"Hold up, hold up. Who? Who?"

"Alyan Rajanya was supposed to be Aditi Egremont's, Lord Egremont's daughter's second cousin, twice removed, but she wasn't. There was no Alyan, only Dipa Cameron, Queen Victoria."

"Huh? What's that got to do with Flora? Iris, are you…"? They both huffed,

"Look," said our heroine pointing to the screen. It showed a still from the clip of Prince's Dock. "…I got this from your girlfriend's Runu and…"

"Dipa Cameron is a red herring, she doesn't know anything, Liberty is nothing but a very lovely and competent…"

"She doesn't think she does, neither does your, Liberty, but they do. Look!" Our hero peered at the blurry picture of three- and three-quarter figures; the headless gondolier, Jyothi Hausa and two women, one climbing up the rope ladder, one entangled in it and unconscious. He had been on the dock, leading the New Model Kritos against the old Guard. He had been too busy to see them escape.

"Is that? It does look like Queen Victoria, but?" He paused, "…It does look a bit like her Iris but…"

"But that's not all Ian. There's, the signal got stronger, well not stronger, more consistent. I was listening back to see why this one was so important to Liberty and as I was the signal got steadily more even and, then I worked it out, mapped it."

"I don't understand Iris, who? What was?" And he gave up, Iris pointed again at the screen,

"Look, this one was, everyone thought it was Alyan. Alyan was another name that Dipa Cameron went by that's all, no such person, and Dipa Cameron was in the Tower so who is this?"

"It could be anyone Iris, another cousin, or even another Vicky model, they…"

"No, they only ever made one. And this…Flora went offline just over an hour before this happened didn't she, and look, there's a scarf or something tied around her head. To hide the damage to her head."

"It could be Flora. But how does that help? We still don't know where those two, Aditi Egremont and Jyothi Hausa went do we. They disappeared after they landed in Greece. No-one knows where they are. It's a good lead Iris. It helps, we might know who to find, but we still don't know where to look. There's Aristois scattered all over the…"

"The signal Ian, the signal,"

"That's thousands of square miles Iris, from Persia to China, she could be anywhere, even if it is her, that signal,"

"It's her. And look!" Said Iris emphatically as she pushed a few keys on the HyperTyper. The machine whirred and flickered and an image of the globe appeared. "…Aditi is an Egremont-Cooch-Bahar,"

"Yes, so?"

"Cooch-Bahar is a place, a place where Dipa Cameron said they all went. Every year," she pressed another key and the image on the screen zoomed down onto the map of Bengal and the Palace of Cooch-Bahar, in what you, and they, call India. "…Twenty-six point three-two-six-nine degrees North, eighty-nine point four-four-one-nine degrees East. In the exact centre of the signal's range." Our hero reached for his tea and sat back in his chair,

"Cooch-Bahar?" He asked, staring at the screen and sipping,

"Cooch-Bahar." She replied, looking at him. He rubbed his chin and took another swig,

"Cooch-Bahar...Have you done it Iris? Have you found her?" He said, more to himself, quite calmly,

"Er, yes. That's what I told you," she was still looking at him, he was baban practical and knew things she did not. But he was still thinking, rubbing his chin.

"It's still pretty slim all this Iris, mainly coincidence; an unidentified female in the dark; medium height, cackooder skin, black hair who could be any number of people, Krito or human, and a place name that happens to be within the coordinate range of thousands of square miles that might or might not be coming from Flora...it's still pretty slim," Iris did not respond, she watched him sip his tea and waited for what he called hope to filter through that mess between his ears.

"I had better write another digi-missive, or maybe call," he said eventually, "...not that he ever answers." Our heroine smiled,

"I love you, Ian."

Krito Explained

You may be wondering about the Krito mentioned above, and indeed below. Full name Kritodash. These increasingly life-like automata. Originally a 1960s invention, based on an advanced technology in human limb replacement necessitated by all the wars. A wealthy Tanzanian amateur robotics buff, by the name of Galosi Shah created simple human-shaped machines from a collection of deceased veterans' false arms and legs to use as manual labour on his hilly coffee farms. His estates could not facilitate conventional machinery and humans were in short supply. His remarkable innovations were to perfect a responsive 'eye' as well as the internal balance necessary to negotiate rough terrain.

Covered in rough sackcloth to protect their gears, their programming was initially rudimentary. It had been adapted from the world's first commercial computer for Lyons Corner House Tea Shops and Restaurants, the Leo 1, commercially available from 1953. Shah miniaturised this equipment using a closely guarded method in a closed workshop. Their torsos, larger than in humans, housed small card readers; devices that wound and 'read' holes punched into long strips of card. In addition, big, heavy batteries, also housed in the torso powered the robots as they clicked and whirred up and down the coffee hills picking coffee and weeding for up to three hours at a time.

With the introduction of magnetic tape and developments in battery technology the Krito became less barrel-chested and it was possible to make the legs longer. It was at this time that the British Ministry of War recognised their potential as a weapon and commandeered the patents. A tough fibreglass fabric was developed as their casing so that they could withstand Dhool attacks.

By the end of the first Persian War, a messy proxy conflict between America, China and the Empire in 1974, a full 50% of the Armies were Kritodash. This figure rose to 80% by the beginning of the 21st century. Ninety percent of all Police forces within the Empire were Kritodash by 1980. Digital technology led to further improvements, particularly in flexible casing, computing and processing power so that the Krito models of the early 21st centuries could pass for human.

It is no surprise that Krito models that could perform sex acts were developed surreptitiously almost at once. The females were termed Nayaka and the males, Nayiki. By the 1990s these pleasure models were programmed to recognise and measure the slightest change in pupil dilation, colouring, vocal tone, temperature as well as hormone and pheromone signatures in nearby humans and to respond accordingly. It was Prince Jyothi Hanover Hausa, nephew to the King, who, while comprehensively experimenting with and finessing these models, first recognised the similar qualities of espionage agents of the state and prostitutes, and proposed the use of Nayiki and Nayaka as spies.

The funding he received for this Top-Secret work was a great incentive and in 2012 Prince Jyothi oversaw the development of the Persuasion Programme, which ensured that the automata interpreted the physical changes in human beings mentioned above as evidence of particular desires, wants and needs so that the machines could coax the disclosure of information as well as the many and various forms of betrayal required by the Empire. This innovation was so effective, almost eliminating the use of blackmail, that only Prince Jyothi, his assistant, the Home Secretary and the Prime Minister were aware of its existence. Given that the human subjects of these missions were early twenty-first century high ranking aristocrats, officials and businessmen, the fact that this programme was ineffective in persuading people who acted on reason or principle was only a minor drawback.

Krito were very expensive to produce and costly to maintain, requiring skilled inspection and maintenance of their many parts. Despite various scare stories over the years, they were never in wide civilian use. Only the extremely wealthy were able to use them as domestic servants and despite real wage increases for the second half of the 20th Century, it was still considered more economic by the manufacturing and service industries to employ human beings, which partly explained a perennial lack of productivity growth in the Mother Country. Outmoded second-hand Krito were as prized, and as infrequently effective, as vintage motor cars.

In 2014 the British Military developed Krito-Krito, automatons that could service other automatons, which reduced maintenance costs. One basic Krito cost the same as a five-bedroom house in your Knightsbridge, London, to buy, and a five-bedroom house in your central Birmingham to maintain annually.

A member of the general public, if they wanted to experience a Krito, could visit one of two up-market hotels or the Piccadilly Lyons Corner House and be served tea.

The Krito began to slowly develop what you, if you could agree, might call consciousness on June 2015 due to some coding errors by another gifted amateur.

Kaushik's Flat Again

Kaushik had been up for a while. Having negotiated a morning at home, he had already left a message for Tariqul and drafted his speech. Now he was still trying to find the letter from his old friend from Leeds, the number was engaged every time he called. His 'Soon' and 'Later' piles were all mixed up. Or had his priorities changed? It was more time-efficient to speed-read each letter and order them as he went. He had misremembered, it wasn't a letter he was looking for but a series of digi-missives sent every few days for the last two months. His HyperTyper had turned itself off and so he hit its side twice, waited and hit it again. The machine began to whirr, so he made himself a cup of tea while it warmed up. Just as he sat down again the phone rang,

"Tariqul, thanks for ringing back, it's probably nothing but I thought I had better let you know,"

"…I'm sorry, I've been sitting on the information for weeks, months maybe, I had no idea…"

"…That's baban kind. I can forward his details over via the Hyper-thing if you prefer?" He pressed a few keys with determination,

"…Done."

"…Yes, I was thinking on focusing on the youth of the movement, what do you think?" Kaushik tucked the phone under his chin and rummaged on the desk for his notebook and a pen. Ten minutes passed with him scribbling as Tariqul told him what he thought.

"…Thank you, Tariqul, yes and to you, Banquan." He wasn't sure he would take Tariqul's advice but he would think about it. He found out his tea was cold; he didn't mind cold tea. Now, paper-work. There had to be a better way of organising things.

Back in the Langthorn Tower

"Will you please stop crying!" Liberty had tried There-There-ing and patting and then There-There-ing again. The shout had not any effect either. Now she was simply sitting and waiting for Dipa to stop sobbing.

She had had clients who wept before, but never for this long. She had no idea what had made this wreck in front of her break down into unintelligible mumbling except for repeatedly moaning that, "I remember, I remember it all.", and/ or "Forty-six, only forty-six," nor did she much care. But she wanted to wrap up by lunch-time, so she could actually start preparing Dipa's case. She looked away from the blubbering in frustration. Turning back at the hunched and heaving woman with strands of hair stuck to her wet cheeks she saw that even a flushed face and puffy smudged eyes suited her client. Liberty sighed and looking impotently at the empty tissue box surrounded by soggy blobs on the table. "…Your getting snot on your dress," she said and Dipa sniffed and sat up straight checking her bodice for stains,

"Debota, this is velvet, I've ruined it," she said wiping at it with one of the less manky hankies from the table. Specks of paper clung to the moist fabric, "…Debota, Debota, Debota!" wriggled Dipa as she stood up and stamped the dress to the floor. She picked it up and walked to a sack. Finding a small cotton hanky, she knelt swabbing the material in the altogether, "…I don't know why you're defending me!" She hurled the words back to Liberty behind her so that Liberty

214

couldn't help but be reminded of a statue she had seen somewhere of Venus Surprised in Her Bath. She suppressed any latent fears she had about being turned into a stag and said,

"And I don't know why you're not wearing any underwear," "They didn't give me any underwear! I've got three dresses, a suit and a few odd shirts that I have to wash out in that basin, this isn't the Ritz you know. How's that for cruel and unusual?"

"Why didn't you say? I can get you some, that's part of my…"

"No! Don't you buy me anything to wear Liberty, not you." Dipa shot back searching for another dress in her sack. She stood up and let something diaphanous float aptly down over her curves.

"You know what, I think you're the prettiest of all of you, you know. Out of the four of you I mean," said Liberty. Dipa turned around and put her hands briefly on her round and shapely hips to say,

"You think?" before coming back over to the table to pick up all the wet, white detritus and shove it into a dented metal bin. "…Why are you defending me Liberty? I'd like to know. I looked you up you know, you defend terrorist-stroke-revolutionaries. Why are you wasting your time on a skirt like me? Have you got a crush on me? Or my brother? You wouldn't be the first." Now she was holding the bin close to her so that she resembled a sculpture of a nymph carrying an odd shaped amphora. Liberty sighed, this sort of reaction often happened when a client realised how guilty they were,

"Even the guilty deserve a defence Dipa, it's the law. For the time being anyway," said Liberty calmly,

"What! You think my brother is going to get rid of justice do you? Anyway, maybe I should wait for them to bring back the death penalty, I deserve it." Liberty rolled her eyes and asked,

"Why you in particular?" she was almost bored now. With a fierceness Liberty could feel from where she sat Dipa put the bin back in the corner and went to her bedside to put hairpins in her mouth. The cell was getting smaller again. Dipa walked over winding and pinning her hair and stood over Liberty like a little Carotid who has lost a building to support. Then she clenched her fists in front of her. Like Athena without her helmet, or the owl.

"I did it, you know. I handed her the knife. I was there when she did it you know, I watched. Watched and laughed."

"Watched what?" said Liberty leaning towards her Runu on the tidied table,

"No, leave it on," said Dipa getting to it first and holding the device close to her face, a Goddess of Rununu, they should have one of those. Or would Até do?

"Vicky, Princess Victoria of the House of Hanover-Hausa, heir apparent to the Empire and its Dominions slashed her pretty little wrists with a blunt opium knife in a shitty little Marass and jumped into the Aspic. And I handed her the knife." There was a triumph in her voice that Liberty recognised as a distorted way of coming to terms with one's crime. But it would not go down well with a jury.

"I thought something like that must've happened. I'm surprised you're still alive," said Liberty flatly, to both disconcert and reassure her client. She had actually had no idea. The lawyer's ploy worked and Dipa shrank to a

216

manageable size in a moment. "…and under usual circumstances I would have to disclose this part of the recording to the prosecution," she continued leaning forward to gently remove the Runu from Dipa's grip. "…however, you are unwell, hallucinating in fact, suffering from a drug induced fantasy and I can wipe it from the record," and she did just that.

"I haven't had a Jus all day! Is that why? It was you! You got me all that Jus, so you could say I wasn't in my right mind," said Dipa, finally impressed with her representation.

"Not at all Dipa. I simply ensured that you, a known drug addict, would maintain sufficient use to remain cogent. People in withdrawal aren't very…" and she paused.

"Say it, say 'useful'. And I want it on the record. I did help her kill herself and I want to be tried for it, aiding and abetting is that what it's called?"

"That depends on what you tell me now. There are established precedents of a servant carrying out the wishes of their master being interpreted simply as a witness. I will record it and make full disclosure to the court but I need you to go back to yesterday's Dipa. Yesterday's Dipa will give us more options in terms of a plea. Please sit down Dipa," said Liberty looking straight at the woman who had put her hands to her head, Carotid style again. "…You are carrying a great burden Dipa, guilt is a heavy thing." Dipa sat down, "…Justice can lift the burden from you. You have done the hard part; you are taking responsibility for what you have done, you are willing to take punishment and you are remorseful. But to receive full justice, a justice that can see, which can include an element of mercy, you must listen to your lawyer." Dipa was calm now but shaking, Liberty could see she was fighting the urge to suck a Jus,

"I don't deserve mercy," she said clearly,

"You don't get to decide that Dipa, that is up to the judge, and the jury. All you can do is tell the truth as you remember it," and Liberty raised her eyebrows and looked at her client hard.

"The truth is that I'm guilty. Guilty of helping Vicky to murder herself, guilty of covering it up, guilty of taking her place. Guilty." But Liberty was used to defending guilty people and rolled off one of her stock reassurances,

"There's no sinner like a young saint," which was sufficiently arcane to give her client pause for thought. "…There's hope for you yet young lady. Shall we begin again? Do you want a Jus? To take the edge off?"

"No, the edge is good," said Dipa spreading her trembling fingers, palms down on the table and nodding at the Runu.

"Tea, then?" Dipa shook her head. Liberty pressed the record button and said,

"We are resuming your interview, where you are telling me what you remember, in order." And she referred to her notebook, "…Where did you live when you returned from the countries?" Dipa sighed,

"I flitted about, you know. Like a villasitter does. Sometimes at Adi's, mainly at Joshi's, I had rooms there."

"You were mainly at Hira Hall, Jyothi Hausa's residence just outside London?"

"Yes,"

"How well did you know Jyothi Hausa?"

"Quite well, as well as anyone I suppose. It's all, it was all very free and easy there, you know, I came and went as I pleased when I wasn't being Vicky, which was only once or twice a week. Which was new for me, you know, after being in service or with Mum. I could just take the car into town, lie in bed till two, or just sit chatting with Joshi. I think he was fond of me in his way."

"And Joshi Hausa called you his Galetea, what do you understand by that?"

"Well, you know the story of Pygmalion yes?" Liberty nodded at Dipa and then to the Runu, so Dipa explained, "…It's one of the Greek myths, this ancient Greek king is also a sculptor, the best there is, praised across the whole of Greece. And he makes an ivory sculpture, you know how they had a thing for Peelas back then. But pale is pretty as they say nowadays. Anyway, he's made this beautiful woman, calls her Galetea, more beautiful than anything he has ever made before, and more beautiful than anyone alive.

And he falls in love with her, which was quite common back in the day apparently. They had problems with stains on their statues, those ancients; amorous boys Joshi said. He used to laugh about that. There was always a lot of cleaning to do after one of his parties. He…" Liberty looked at her pointedly,

"Well to get back to the story, this king, Pygmalion, he begs the Gods to make her real, Galetea, the statue. And Aphrodite, goddess of love grants his wish. Galetea was turned into a real woman. In the story they get married, have kids. But Joshi only ever tried it on with me a couple of times, and well, you've seen him haven't you. And say what you like, he was never one to force himself on you. He didn't have to,

219

did he. There was always someone he could persuade hanging about. Or a Nayaka. You know he programmed one to play hard to get, Rose, her name was. She took him two days to bed. Then he was bored. But he kept her for certain uses, some people are more trusting if you're hard to get, tell you more. He had a stupid one too, well she wasn't stupid, just acted stupid."

"And it was his private joke, to call you his Galetea?"

"Private, sort of. He called me that in private. But he was Pygmalion in public too. You know the Nayaka were his idea? So people had made the Pygmalion link before hadn't they. And he was fine with it, used it once, for one of his parties, you know, that first season. One of his japes." Dipa looked at Liberty for permission to digress,

"Were you involved?"

"Oh yes," Liberty nodded assent, "…So, he did this Ideal Beauty themed party. He told me I deserved it, a party, after I'd done a few of Vicky's engagements. He said it was for me and Adi. You know he was in love with her? And they did suit each other in a way. But the party. Really, I think there hadn't been enough Yangans at his last one, too many stuffed shirts and villasitters. And people said he'd put it about that he's done an upgrade, you know even the basic models were glitching by then, and he had his reputation to maintain. So, anyway, everyone turns up in togas.

A ton of grapes, and cornucopia and garlands and drinking cups all over the ballroom. Divans and cushions in clusters all about, and in the playrooms. Split pomegranates wherever you looked. And plenty of Yangans wanting to show off. So me and Adi and Beatrice, we stay upstairs. You saw Beatrice yesterday, with those other Aristois." Liberty nodded, "…Young Lady North. She always hated me. Her and Adi had been close, but then I came along, and there was that thing with Berty Walcott and she was nearly as sandara as us, but always." Liberty's sigh was picked up by the microphone, Dipa's eyebrows were not. "…We wait till the entertainments, which always started at midnight. When everyone was lubricated. Joshi used to do entertainments with his Nayakas all the time, to show how obedient they were you know, they'd do anything.

He does this long monologue about king Pygmalion being lonely. Apparently, something he said about splendid isolation was supposed to be a dig at the A.A. Ambassador, about Persia or something, but I didn't get it. Then the three of us, and three Nayaki glide in on these plaster columns. All of us dressed in chitons, that my mum's girls had made as it happens. With these masks, Greek chorus masks, blank white masks, you know. And we have to stay completely still, like statues. Everyone thinks we're all Nayaka.

I was Hebe, who had everlasting beauty and could restore youth to the old apparently, I'd never heard of her. Adi was Artimis, Goddess of the hunt, with a bow and arrow and her hand on a stuffed deer. And Beatrice was Aphrodite on a giant scallop shell, she loved that and Joshi banging on about 'beyond human beauty' and the 'ideal is realised'. The ideal has got a pretty big bum, I can tell you.

And the Nayaka were Athena and Demeter and Hermaphroditus, that was Jean. Anyway, Aphrodite comes to life and hands Pygmalion a little bottle. He smears it on all our masks in turn, where our lips should be. Athena comes to life first and Joshi lays it on thick about power even over the Gods themselves, and whatnot. He brings us all to life and we all dance at his command. Nothing too lewd, it was still early. Then he orders us to stop, drop our chifons. And there's Beatrice, me and Adi still dressed, disobeying you know. We remove our masks and he Bows to Nature." And Dipa shrugged, "…He said it was a great success, a great success."

"And Princess Victoria was not involved?

"Oh no!"

"It wasn't a suitable activity for the Heir?"

"No? She didn't have time to rehearse, that's what she said. But she couldn't be bothered more like. It never stopped her before. There was this, I never saw it, but apparently, she did this Master and Servant routine with Vicky-Two. It was pure pornography apparently."

"So, you didn't spend that much time with the Princess?"

"Not publicly, no. No title; Alyan. She said she was going to make me a Lady in Waiting, give me a title, all sorts, but she was high of course. But she and Adi were together a lot, and I tagged along now and again. I'd only been on my own with her maybe twice, or three times. Can I confess now?"

"Soon Dipa. But before that, I need to know your role in the events earlier that day, the May Bank Holiday Mela jape. Everything in order remember?" Dipa nodded, almost obediently,

"Well, it was my birthday, and we did it, the three of us, Vicky too."

"Was it her idea?"

"I don't think so? She wasn't too bright and it had always been Adi who came up with the japes. I can't be sure because we were usually quite high, you know. The drugs. Shall I tell you about Strange?"

"You told me about that yesterday, it's a drug cocktail, you drank it that day?"

"When didn't I? We drank it all the time. Yes, that afternoon. I'm not sure what was in it, it was sweet and sugar-free and it made you feel wonderful, but I get gaps you know, forget whole days, maybe weeks sometimes?"

"And the London Mela? Do you remember that?" asked Liberty gently,

"Yes, I remember that, I was Stranged and Jusy but I remember, May Day last spring. Last Spring? Not even a year ago...So. Well. Will they have one this year, the Mela?" Liberty nodded,

"So I read, but without the colour restrictions on the Gulal." Dipa looked confused, "...Any colour powder you like, not just red, white and blue. You know in India, where it originated, you're allowed any colour you like."

"Well, I can't imagine many people will be choosing yellow," said Dipa flatly. Liberty nodded and she continued with a sigh reaching for her cigarettes, "...we delayed going back to Balmoral after the, the German delegation? Anyway I was in London and Adi wanted me and Vicky to have a treat, Vicky liked me, she knew who I was and she was amused by me, amused and intrigued? She had never spent any time socially with a commoner before. She liked me to talk like I did with mum. She wasn't too hanckilly but she was a nice person, sweet. And it was my birthday. Well, and you know the May Day Mela? How some people have sneaked in drones from time to time?" Liberty shook her head, "...Well they did, for fun, but it's not allowed because some homeless man got decapitated up in the rafters once. And people don't look where they're going when they're looking up, and now it's so big, packed. From the Ritz to Buck House, Thousands of people all running and dancing about.

But we knew what we were doing, we did, got some drones, but this time…We wanted to give them the time of their lives, the little people you know. Give them a taste of how we lived. We wanted it to be fun. It's a day when you can have a wild time yes? We just wanted to make it properly wild, you know. Chucking a bit of coloured chalk around and a drink or two is all very well but…We knew, thought we knew how to enjoy ourselves properly and we were going to teach the little people what really letting your hair down is like, that's all. It wasn't yellow…In order.

They could go back to work on Tuesday with a real story, you know, not just some weekend. And Adi thought I'd like to help the little people, she knew I had a soft spot for the ordinary, that's what she said. And Vicky was a drug addict, so getting other people high was something she was baban keen on, you know.

So, we waited until the whole mad procession was nearly in the Park, and we sent in dozens, dozens of drones. The ones that look like little helicopters were my favourite, but most of them were those ones with four sets of blades. Only the odd Bird. We took them from cousin Joshi. He used them for his parties you know. And Adi could programme a teapot. We'd had them painted in the May Day mela colours, the four-blade ones made great Union Jacks, some of them had red, white and blue ribbons too and we were watching from, who has that house overlooking the park, one of the Lady Melbournes? But? Well, the drones dived and swooped over the crowd, shining and fluttering just under the Arcade roof, they clean it properly there, and it was a beautiful day. And the drums were the best bit, we had paid the bands to all start playing the same tune, that one with the bit that goes drum diddly drum, I can't remember. And a few flew down together to just above the trees, like those birds, starlings swooping in those swarms you know. Like smoke almost, it was cyow.

And they were all laughing and shouting and throwing their Gulal at each other in the sunshine. Happy you know. Looking up with their red, white and blue faces and their big eyes. You know how some of them get completely covered. And they were happy. Reaching up to try and touch the ribbons. Most of them were drunk, you know how it gets. Have you ever been to the Mela?" Liberty shook her head, "…Why am I not surprised?

Anyway, it was mesmerising with the music and the people, Thousands of people loving it. Dancing and swaying, it was all set to music you know that? They, the drones flew up and around each other and the music got faster and faster and the drones danced quicker and the crowd, all dusted with the red, white and blue were moving in time to the drums and oohing and ahhing and whooping away.

And then, on the balcony, we pressed the button, on the control, and the drones fanned out over them and whoosh! The powder came floating down from the drones, cream-coloured clouds of powder. Falling on their faces. Off white. Not yellow, it wasn't yellow like they said. It only looked yellow because of the way the sunlight refracted through the Arcade glass."

"Sorry Dipa, who pressed the button?" asked Liberty, and Dipa answered quickly,

"She did. Vicky pressed the button, she said I could because it was my birthday. But I knew she wanted to and I didn't want her sulking on my birthday.

We thought, we really thought the acid and the cocaine, the drugs in the dust, would give them the day of their lives. We thought it would be one mass of baban happy people living as if it was the last day of their lives. How we would live the last day of our lives. And we could go down and you know, join in. But that's not what happened is it. And first they were all quiet. Then the screaming started. Stupid…So much screaming and running this way and that. And the fear, you could smell it, even over the spilt lager, you could smell the fear. Hundreds, thousands of people, howling and wailing filling the air, you couldn't get away from it.

They thought it was Dhool didn't they. But it was white, a creamy white, we didn't think they'd all get the fear like that. Stupid fools," Liberty looked at the Runu sharply, "…We were stupid fools," Dipa added and paused, "…Their eyes were the worst; wide and desperate, thinking they were all going to die. Like anima…Bashing into each other, knocking each other down. And well some did die didn't they. In the crush" Liberty sighed,

"Who organised it?" she asked,

"Well, Adi did. She arranged all the japes. But Cousin Joshi let her use his people, but I don't know if he knew what we planned. I knew about it. I was in on it too. But none of us thought the people would react like that. We thought it would be fun. All those people crushed?" They were both silent for quite a while, Liberty did not ask how many people had been killed, she strongly suspected that Dipa would not know, "…I know it was wrong, I should have said something I know that. But there was no stopping her when she got that look in her eye and Vicky went along with it too, she thought it would be fun.

The best thing I could have done was walk away from it all, but what then? I think I thought about it. I did feel bad about the Mela Jape, those people getting crushed and everything, that wasn't right. But what then? What then? Back to stitching night and day? If I was lucky. No-one would have hired me if I upset her, the Queen of the Yangans. I'd've had to go to Allocation, queuing up at the Labour Exchange with the others, cleaning toilets or a tea-lady in some bland office. Back to Third Class Carriages, a room in a Tower Block somewhere in South London," and she began to laugh, tears came back to her eyes and she wiped them away, "…I suppose here I only have to clean my own toilet," and she sniffed, "…I could murder a cup of tea, would you like some tea?" Liberty shook her head, "…Well, I'm having one," and she got up a little unsteadily,

"Are you alright Dipa?"

"Just a bit shaky, it's Koulla Liberty. Let me potter about for a bit and I'll be fine."

Padma River, Near Gauribardia

"Finally, tea," she exclaimed and her freshly bathed hand darted greedily for a chipped but very clean mug before the glossy old tray was even on the scrubbed table. The whole cabin was decidedly brighter, thanks to a recent deep clean. She took a tentative sip, "…perfect, very good Vicky-Two," She did not look at her servant, instead choosing to glare down her nose at Joshi.

"Thank you, Vicky, we had better push off again now if you don't mind," he said jovially, also without looking at her. He swigged from his cup and winced, "…how much sugar is in this? If we make the same headway as last night and this morning, we should get to the train on time," he added with a whimsical laugh as the craft ground away from the shore and began to glide smoothly as it moved into the wide green-grey water. "…That breeze is rather pleasant I must say, it's a shame we can't go on deck," he was being nice.

Adi continued with her haughty staring as they rode into what you call India on the Padma. Joshi sighed and enjoyed the calm. He was not going to share how much of a relief her silence was because then she would start talking again. He huffed to give the impression that he was impatient for her to speak, braced himself and took another peaceful, albeit far too sweet, drink. He was disappointed that he could not pick up his book, which had turned out to be rather good. He knew it would be a provocation. So he took the time he now had to muse out of the window. "…this really is a beautiful country," he sighed looking up into the wide high pale blue sky and then down to a clump of dark trees on the flat lush horizon. A new gust brought the fresh scent of the water into the cramped space cutting through Adi's rather intense perfume. The wind also brought in a smatter of conversation between two fishermen a few hundred yards away. He couldn't catch what they were saying and then there was nothing to be heard but the faint pummelling of their own engine once more. They sat sipping and glaring or sipping and staring until the tea was gone. Then they sat some more.

Dipa's Cell

Liberty sat back and looked out of the window. It had taken Dipa longer than it should to make a cup of tea; she had found it necessary to clean as she went, and she hovered forgetfully at every stage of preparation before remembering that she needed a teaspoon or the milk.

She sat down eventually,

"When do I get to confess about Vicky?"

"Soon, Dipa soon. There are a couple of things I need to clarify. First, I would like to know what made you remember now?" Dipa took a sip of tea and sighed,

"I don't know why now. I mean I've had plenty of time to think about things haven't I. I met someone this morning, someone I used to know."

"An Aristoi?"

"Oh no, a friend, a good friend. And I couldn't remember them, or how I knew them, but they knew all about me. And, well, then it all came back. Flooded back. Vicky, Mum, Rows, loads of rows," and she looked up frightened, "…what if there's more to remember?"

"We'll cross that bridge when we come to it. But I have to ask Dipa; is there anything else you remember? Is there any part of what you have already told me that might need adjustment?"

"Adjustment? Of what I've told you already? I don't think so?"

"These rows?"

230

"The rows, came later. Well, I suppose Mayday was the first big one. Shall I tell you in order, like you said?" and Liberty nodded. Her client looked weak and tired,

"Alright, and if you think of anything, you let me know?"

"I will," said Dipa compliantly.

"Now, tell me about the Marasses, out by the Damn? That is where it happened, yes?" Dipa sipped her brew

"Well I never liked them, how can a place be such a sordid, dirty, little dump and sooo pretentious at the same time. All the Yangans went there, dressing down in handmade silks. Silly little hats on. Ha! And the Backoe-Boys, twiddling their moustaches with the Pipe-lickers and the Flap-polishers. And not a drop of proper tea. Have you tried to clear a cottonmouth with anything except tea? Disgusting."

"Sorry, Backoe-Boy?"

"Debota! Where have you been Liberty? How can you not know what a Backoe-Boy is?"

"I have heard the word before, but I've never been exactly sure what they are. The male equivalent of a Yangan?"

"Yes. Not exactly, Yangans are nearly all the daughters of Aristois and big business families, yes? The odd commoner can be a Yangan, if she's exceptionally cyow or an actress or something, but a true Yangan is born to it, yes?" Liberty was nodding like a child, "…and the Aristoi and the uchit curdy have homes in the countries and follow, followed, the season, the social season, not the weather one,"

"I know that," said Liberty, slightly annoyed,

"So a Backoe-Boy or a Backoe-girl follows the Season, some of them have money, some are villasitters you know, they live off other people. Go off somewhere warm. So they don't actually live anywhere, nowhere is home like it is for you and me. They have places, or use places, a place in London, a place in Bossaso, but no home. And of course, none of them have jobs, proper ones. They're not in the public eye, like Yangans, but there's just loads of them."

"I see?" Said Liberty, who didn't.

"London is dump compared to most places but the season is still here so when they come here, they 'slum it in London'. They have a lot of time on their hands and they choose Marasses, they don't all smoke but it's so they can be seen by the people who matter. Are they still there, the Marasses?" Liberty shrugged, "…No. Good."

"Tell me about them,"

"Well I only went to one, the Palace of Earthly Tranquillity, Wapping, one of the old warehouses up against the Aspic, it was Vicky's favourite so... She went there all the time, had a regular booth. She said she liked that old slapper who ran it, a disgraced concubine of Emperor Zaituo or something. Hah. Didn't look like it. The Lady Harmony she called herself; Five-foot-tall if she was an inch and fat as a pig, wobbling around in all those tatty old ribbons. The mistress of the Palace of Earthly Tranquillity for twenty-one years and it showed. Far too much kohl and rouge. Nice skin though, well she never saw the sun. With her sad little dumplings. That's what Vicky liked; the snacks, and the opium of course. But she was fond of the Lady Harmony. Mind you, she still laughed when I said she looked like she'd come off worse in a fight with a haberdasher. She had a lovely laugh, Vicky. Poor Vicky."

Liberty tilted her head enough to spur Dipa on, "…It was one of those big modern warehouses, nineteenth-century, huge monstrosities looming up, rows and rows of them, door after door all peddling the same thing, right up against the aspic where the wharfs used to be. You clattered over the cobbles past all those other Marasses. Dirty red brick looming up on either side, covered in soot from the old days, still there all that soot. Straggles of Buddleia sprouting from the cracks. Green and black mould puking out of broken guttering, dripping down. Rows and rows of blackened windows with the shadows flitting around behind.

They're where they used to keep the goods you know, warehouses full of stuff shipped in from all around the Empire, 'til the Aspic put an end to all of it. Then they were converted into offices, most of them, after the war. Then after the Renesam and the offices all closed down, they filled up with people instead, and their opium. Shuffling in and out like rats., and a huge door, like this one you know," said Dipa nodding towards the cell door, "…all riveted like that but filthy black and bigger, didn't look like much.

But you walk into where it's always half dark and there's Chinese carvings, painted wood dragons and symbols all over the place. No electricity. Just oil-lamps under old coloured silk handkerchiefs, and bits and pieces of junk shop Chinese looking furniture, layers of old Persian and Chinese rugs on the floor. The old carpet gets worn, or someone lets a piece of opium burn a hole in it and she, Lady Delight, 'The Proprietress', just wobbles along and roles out another rug. Four, five inches thick in places those carpets. Grubby old sofas, chaises and Ottomans all over the place. And whores and backoe-boys and flap-polishers all lolling around. She thinks its classy, Lady Delight, because there's a few shade-loving plants in fancy pots scattered around. And she can keep her mouth shut."

"Do you know how often Vicky visited this place?"

"Every chance she got," giggled Dipa, "…And once I was trained up, she could go all the time,"

"How often?"

"I think maybe twice a week, three? Every time I was out there eating a plate of lamb with some bunch of diplomats or businessmen, she was off! Straight down to that stinky old place."

"Can you describe what she did?"

"Well, the booths were upstairs, downstairs was mainly for whores, human ones, cheap, lounging around half-dressed in sorry looking gowns, Yangan castoffs, I saw a dress Mum had made once, it was in a terrible state. I didn't tell her, some skanky whore in something my mum'd made for a peer's daughter's coming out season, waiting for punters.

Not that Adi was beneath spending an evening down there, when she got bored of smoking. Vicky never got bored of smoking, just smiled her pretty little smile and puffed on pipe after pipe,"

Dipa closed her eyes with a heavy sigh and continued, "…you went up and up these rickety old stairs to the old storerooms. Room after room, every one converted into those tatty old booths. All those booths. Hundreds of them. Floor after floor."

"These booths?"

"Big brick room, a massive room, and on our floor, there was this sad old man in the middle, a sad old man in ancient dicky-bow and tails, playing a dusty old grand piano, slightly out of tune. And rows and rows of booths. They went on forever those little rickety booths. High enough for no-one to see inside. Some still had their brass plates on the door; Rishy Sunack Esquire-Book-keeper, Johnson's Copy-writers. Vicky's particular booth used to be Windsor's Deportment and Dance Lessons. Such a high high ceiling, such a black smoke-stained ceiling. And rows and rows of these little compartments in the dark. Debota knows who was in those booths. Felt like hundreds, thousands of those tatty old curtains strung up over the doors, each one storing someone, hiding some sad little story. And plumes of dark dark green smoke winding up from most of them, a host of snakes all twisting up onto the ceiling adding soot onto soot. You'd hear them laughing, or moaning, the odd scream. No-one paid any attention to anyone else. I thought it was spooky, not them,"

"And no-one recognised you? Vicky? Out of all those people?" asked Liberty, hiding her scepticism that Dipa could gather so much detail on a mere two visits. Dipa's face contorted into a bitter smile,

"They couldn't recognise themselves. If you caught one's eye they'd just scuttle off like some sort of rat," She stopped laughing abruptly, "…but…inside Vicky's, you pushed the curtain aside and there's two shabby old chaise longue to lie on, stool for the Pipe-boy and a table between. An old desk shoved up against the wall, this old oil lamp with a tatty bit of silk draped over it. Pipe-lickers don't like it too bright; it hurts their eyes. A dirty copper pot with a fern looking purply-black in the dark. I could look at that plant for hours…The first time I went there I got fascinated by the fronds you know, spreading, curling.

Vicky's booth had a window, taller than a man and narrow, a big old warehouse window. Dark paint flaking on the frames. And the Aspic came nearly half way up, slapping and slopping on the panes in the hot weather. That old Anti-Aspic glazing they don't do any more the only thing keeping it out. Weighing down on the smoke smudged glass making everything take on this sour yellow glow. Dappled pools of pee coloured light always moving, shifting around. I thought it was spooky, but they; Vicky and Adi kamared it there. Her favourite palace she said, Vicky. Smaller than a prison cell, rented by the hour, but she, heir to the whole Empire, said it was the only place she felt truly belonged to her. And, well both the times I was there her Pipe-boy was a lad called…? I can't remember but she liked him," Dipa let out an exhausted breath,

"And Pipe-boy?"

"Oh? Well, opium is uchit hard to keep alight. It's this black stuff, like hard liquorice, he makes these little balls. Fiddly you know, children's small hands are ideal for the job, like needlework, you know, The Pipe-boy prepares the pipes, long thin black things with carvings on them you know, dragons and winding smoke patterns, and a little wooden cup on the end for the resin. You just lie there on the couch. He holds them to your lips for you if you like, lights them with these long green tapers, keeps them lit, and stops the stuff dropping on the floor and burning a hole in the rug if you pass out. I did, the first time. Brings you drinks too. He'll stroke you as well if you give him a tip. Such a nasty, tatty place. The punters like it that way apparently. More fake than fake if you ask me."

"Alright. I want to ask you about Princess Victoria's death now Dipa. That night."

"I can confess now?" Dipa sighed deeply, "…Yes, well, it was the night of the May Day Mela, but we tried not to pay that much attention, just made our excuses and went back to that dump Buck House, didn't really find out how it had gone till, well Vicky? Did Vicky know? I didn't, we saw that things were going bad and made our excuses you know. Went back to that dump Buck House, changed our clothes, in went the Aunken and off we went, in an ordinary taxi."

"And you were with her when she died? You and Adi?" Dipa pressed her fingers onto the table hard,

"Yes, I was there. Adi wasn't, she was sulking because Vicky agreed with me about some stupid spat we'd had. Adi had slapped one of Vicky's maids and Vicky hadn't liked it but she didn't say anything. I said something though and Adi had stormed off somewhere. Betrayed, even by me, that's what she said. We'd never shouted at each other before," And Dipa stopped as if feeling the sting again, "…but Vicky had the evening all planned out, and it was my birthday. And she was the heir, well, she was queen by the end of the night, we had no idea Charles had had a heart attack. I don't know if she died before he did, they kept asking I don't know why. But I think she was queen by then.

We knew he was sick, that's why Adi was so mad wasn't it. Her father was already putting the pressure on, for the Order of the Garter and everything. But she was the heir so we, I did what she wanted,"

"What did you say to Adi, about the maid?"

"Let me think? She, Adi said it didn't matter, about the maid, hitting her, because they were only Kritos but I was in a mood with her for, for…oh I forget. Her controlling probably, she thought she owned me. Well, she did I suppose, but neither of us saw it like that, not then, well I didn't, maybe she did? So, alright. I said you have to treat Kritos as if they're people, otherwise you end up treating people like Kritos. You know because they look like us. That's all, it wasn't that kind really. Adi flared up like a roman-candle. I didn't understand of course, we were all just useful or not, people or Krito, her too. So we left her to her own devices, she had enough of them.

And me and Vicky went out together, through this tunnel under the palace, you know the bomb shelter. Came up in a baban koulla Milliners in Piccadilly, out the back and jumped in a cab. And she moaned all the way across town, Adi this, Adi that. Not that I minded, I was getting seriously fed up with her by then, Adi. But she could be so lovely, so lovely," Dipa put her elbow on the table and rested her head on her hand. She looked up at the ceiling and sank, exhausted, into her palm. Liberty waited a moment before speaking,

"It has to be said Dipa, you have to keep going. Do you want a Jus?"

"Maybe just one, to keep going you know, just one." Answered Dipa without much reluctance, producing a sweet, as if from nowhere, and popping it into her mouth and letting it sit in her cheek like the instructions on the packet suggested.

"Well, we got there, up the stairs, into her booth and that old man was playing long high notes of something, tinkle-tunkle lalala. The boy got us some port and dumplings, she loved her Ruby Port, and we lay down on the moth-eaten lumpy Chaises, loosened our hair, so our heads didn't feel tight when we started smoking, she had such lovely hair," said Dipa stroking her own, "…The boy lit our pipes and we got high. Just like usual. Lay back and drew long breaths of the thick mauve-green sweet smoke and the chaises were softer and the lights began to dance and wheee! I went deep down into bliss. Well, Vicky could still talk, she could do three, four pipes in an afternoon, all I could do was mumble."

Dipa's hands were still palm down on the table and she stared straight ahead, her eyes narrow as she forced herself to remember, "…But then Vicky started laughing, I don't know why. And I was floating back up by then, that's the best bit. The best bit comes after a while. So I started laughing too. I didn't know what we were laughing at, but it was very funny? And well she was playing with this little tassel from the table cloth. A little gold tassel, all frayed and straggly. She had such pretty hands and the tips of her fingers, she had on this red-red nail varnish, her lovely fingers were toying with the strands for ages. It felt like ages. She'd go quiet and we'd look at the tassel and then we'd laugh again, I don't know why. Then, suddenly, jolting me out of it a bit you know, out of the green haze she asked me to pass her the knife. It was less than a couple of feet away from her, but she was our Princess so…

I got it together, picked up this little knife, that the boy used to scrape out the bowl on the pipe you know, it had a cracked wooden handle and she was twiddling it between her long fingers, spinning it you know so the yellow light made it glint a little now and then, twinkling like a little star, and we were laughing again. Something was so funny? I leaned back on my bed and I knew I could move again, so I took a sip of port, to get that dryness to go away. It tasted far more wonderful when I was high. I remember thinking as I looked at it; clinging deep, dark purple to the sides of the glass. It was sweet and strong like her. I was going to say it, I was going to tell her how her lips glistened in the shadows, and she shone sweet and strong like ruby port. but I just kept gazing at the drink and meaning to say it, you're sweet and strong, I was going to say, in a minute. I was going to say it in a minute. If I had said it, out loud I mean, maybe she wouldn't have done it. I just got lost looking at the warm, sweet, dark stuff in the glass.

I didn't realise she'd got up and was standing on her sofa until I felt a gust of air on my neck, made me tremble all the way to my toes. And I looked up and smelled the sharpness of the Aspic and she'd opened the top half of the window. I didn't know they opened at all. It was all the way down, and she was clambering up onto the frame. The boy was saying, 'Miss, Miss' over and over, but he stopped, I think he ran off. When he saw she wasn't going to get down he ran off. And I was standing up swaying a bit and she was standing in the frame, maybe it was her who was swaying? With the night sky clouds scudding behind her and her hair floating around her head with little threads of blue-black smoke all catching in the lamplight. She looked so lovely, so like a Queen, and we were laughing. She laughed so delightfully, like a little bell rolling down a hill…I couldn't help laughing too.

I don't know how she was balancing but she wasn't holding the frame anymore and she had the knife in her hand and she froze all of a sudden. She was smiling though, so contented. Just stood there on the rickety old frame and smiled down at me. And she had the little knife in her hand and she said so slowly, what that glitchy Nayika had said the day before, her Vicky-Two, so slowly, she said, 'You will splinter into a thousand pieces,' and she was cutting her lovely arms, hacking at one and then the other and laughing and so was I. The blood, her blood was splashing like a fountain onto me, and in my glass. I still had my glass in my hand, it was warm and salty. Deep dark port-wine red and warm and splashing through the smoky air and onto me and the sweet and the saltiness in my mouth tingled. And she just jumped a tiny bit, just a little hop really, back, laughing, toes pointing down. And then there she was, sinking slowly down, down in the Aspic, smiling and waving at me through the jelly, through the window. Smiling and looking at me, her hair and her dress blooming, blossoming out, suspended there through the window. Hair and blood reaching out into the dark in all directions. And I just stood there and watched her hanging there and she was smiling so I was smiling back. Her bloody wrists, all gashed, and the blood furled out like dark ferns fronds frozen in the slime. But she wasn't looking at me was she, she was dead. And somewhere inside me I knew she was dead, I must've done but I waved, I sipped my port and waved goodbye." And Dipa gave a little wave with a weak blank smile.

I don't know how long I was there, just standing and smiling at the ferns coming from her wrists and her hair floating frozen, so beautiful, sipping my port. Her eyes shining through the Aspic like she was alive. It must've been a long time I suppose. Standing, smiling, sipping, looking. The next thing I remember was hands, Krito hands delving down into the Aspic, their skin stuff peeling off so you could see the metal of their bones, and pulling her, by her hair, her lovely long dark hair, up out of the Aspic. So she, she just melted away," she screwed her eyes and her head lowered, "…Dissolved away, dripped into the Aspic." And she fell silent.

She felt Liberty's hand on hers and shuddered, "…Some of it slopped, the Aspic had spilled into the room over the window-frame and then I noticed. The Lady Delight was in the cubicle with me, I hadn't noticed her before. She was hissing, almost shouting, 'get her out, get her out. Just go. Go,' and the old man was still playing, a bit louder I think to cover up the noise. I just stood there. Then who came to save me, take me away? Kritos. Bloody machines with more heart than any of them! They pulled me up through the window somehow into Joshi's hovercraft. Held me, stroked my head, comforted me. I could feel it even if I couldn't say anything. The best friends I had; machines. I didn't care that they weren't real. They gave me comfort and I took it. I was their sister.

All the way back to Hira Hall. Well, that's where I woke up, and they, the Kritos, looked after me…And that's it, that's how I helped Princess…Queen Victoria Hanover-Hausa, kill herself in a shitty little Marass and then stood to watch her die sipping my drink diluted with her blood.

Maybe if I had said it out loud, if I hadn't've been so high, how sweet and strong she was, she was sweet and strong, maybe she would have thought again, maybe she'd still be here?" Dipa stopped and looked at Liberty with eyes that wanted judgement. Liberty put her hand on hers and asked gently,

"What did the Nayaka say? You will splinter into a thousand pieces? What did that mean?" Dipa sighed,

"Oh, I don't know. She glitched or got angry or something, she was programmed to serve the Empire she said, you know the Empire Code, and this, that, our japes and swapping and everything, did not serve the Empire and, no? More than that, that time it was more than that? The Empire didn't serve the people or something. That's what made me think it was more than glitching, she was actually thinking for herself but Adi wouldn't have any of it. I don't know," said Dipa feeling a little desperate now and crunching down on her Jus.

"And the fire?" asked the lawyer and Dipa let out a long breath to search her newly regained memory,

"Did I see something? From the hovercraft window? Orange and red flickering in the black? I think I might have made that up, when they told me, you know. I don't think I saw the Palace of Earthly Tranquillity catching fire. I heard about it though. Went up like dry kindling apparently. Burned all night. Adi said that half of Wapping couldn't be bothered getting up the next morning, too smoked. But she died didn't she, the Lady Delight, and the boy I suppose. And a few, quite a few other people too. Just another Marass fire. No-one cared." Dipa sighed and looked down at her hands that were

243

still on the table, "…They didn't need to set fire to it. So much death. Poor Vicky."

"Liberty leaned forward and put her hand on Dipa's,

"So, when did you find out about your Mother?" Dipa looked surprised,

"It was the same day! My mum died on the same day as Vicky. I never thought about that before?" Her eyes filled with fresh tears but she kept talking, "…I found out about the Breach later…When? I was already in that dump Buck House? The day of the Memorial, I think? When was that?" And she looked to Liberty a little desperately. Liberty didn't know the answer. Dipa looked away, "…Adi took me to Joshi's place for the flickers," she said flatly to the fireplace. Liberty switched off the Runu,

"Thank you Dipa. Well done, you have a passable turn of phrase sometimes I must say. Time for a break I think." Dipa looked at Liberty hard and long. Then she shrugged and said,

"This tea's luke-warm, any chance of another?"

While Liberty made the tea, Dipa got up and walked to the window. She was tired. She stared without looking down at the Old River Walk with a blankness, an emptiness, that she found quite comforting. Liberty came up behind her and handed her a mug. She did not turn around as she said,

"Can we take a break for a while longer Liberty? All that crying and remembering has tired me out." She was almost surprised by Liberty's answer,

"Very well, a few minutes, would you like a lie down," Dipa nodded with a sort of relief and made for the bed.

Private Premises,West London, England

The temporary headquarters of the Empire Secret Service was above a betting shop on Acton High Road, West London. This suited their semi-permanent guest, the Chief of All America's Secret Service Empire Division (ASSED), Horace Pfeffel, who happened to love horse racing and a little flutter. He sat upright at a small rickety table studying the Racing Post carefully while the three or four other people in the shabby room attempted to look equally busy.

Given that infinity is so vast it should not be surprising that what you call doppelgangers exist in boundless worlds. Each world is so small and the parameters of human development so limited that particular lineages coincide in, well, infinite worlds. That destiny should be so capricious as to bring such a man as Pfeffel into so many existences, however unfortunate, is nothing more than coincidence. We are aware that your world has many restrictions on freedom of expression. We are therefore unable to name your version for the legal reasons that such a man would almost certainly deploy energetically. As your version of this man is suited to party politics in your world so Horace Pfeffel was almost perfect for his role in Greta's. Inwardly, he was quite clever without being particularly creative or scrupled. Outwardly, his appearance, demeanour and tone were, except for an extreme accent, entirely inoffensive.

When the dark-suited man huffed into the shabby room Horace swiftly put down his paper and smiled awkwardly. If he had been English one would have thought that his mother had just died but he was putting on a brave face so as not to upset anyone.

"Ah John, you're back," he said without giving any hint as to whether he thought this was a good or a bad thing. "…tea?" The dark-suited man shook his head. He sat down and let out a breath as salutation. "…Great sketches by the way. Deft, witty. If this thing doesn't work out for you there's a definite avenue for you there," Horace joked. The dark-suited man smiled by flattening his closed lips against his teeth. "…but as to this report, we're not really getting anywhere are we. I mean intelligence wise. These guys go to meetings, go home, sleep and then go to meetings again. All their debates and disagreements are out in the open, on the News so… Well, we're not getting anywhere are we." John exhaled slightly in recognition. His neck was still sore and his knees ached. "…So, I think it's time, if we are going to get any progress, if A.A. is going to keep backing you guys," Horace paused unnecessarily to let his words sink in, "…well, we're going to have to start killing some people. Okay, you are, I'm not here obviously." John continued to look at him, "…We need to demoralise these people, kill them, kill their families, their friends, you know the kind of thing," John nodded. "…we still need information, if you can get information, that's great. But if you could just kill a few people in the meantime, that would really help maintain the relationship, you know how it is," John did not move, Horace smiled, "…then we can talk about your preoccupation with Hune, Hargon and Herzfeld." John squeezed out a smile, got up and walked to an old fridge that was not plugged in and Horace went back to studying the

Racing Post adding, "…You could start with The Subject maybe?" John did not respond. He took a long-range rifle from the fridge and some cartridges, put them in his artist's satchel, nodded at Horace and a couple of other people and walked back down the stairs. The bag was heavy.

Over Kapfenberg, Eichstätt, Bavaria, Germany

Neither Iris nor Ian had ever flown in a supersonic jet plane before. Our hero leaned on our heroine so that he too could look down at the patchwork of the Carte Blanche countries whistling by. One of their companions coughed politely a second time. When this had no effect, another person leaned forward and touched our hero's knee.

"We do need all the information you can give us Ian," she said. She was a slender and smartly dressed woman of perhaps 40 or 50, fair-skinned and blonde with delicate pretty features. She sat opposite our hero and heroine in the small plane and next to a tall elegant man with the high cheekbones and chisel jaw that made some people mistake him for a Krito until they saw the grey streaks in his hair. They were both smiling sociably,

"What else do you want to know?" replied Iris eagerly.

"It would be elucidating to understand the nascence of the relationship between you, Ian, and Iris as well as, Flora," said Deputy Tariqul Hargon, for that is who he was. His companion, Deputy Elaina Silverberg, added with a small laugh,

"How did you meet?" Iris looked at Ian and smiled,

"Ian was part of the liberation party of Hira Hall, where we, my brothers, sisters and others were kept, but Flora had already been taken,"

"Then I was assigned by the People's Army, as Krito Liaison, because of my experience." Added Ian before seeing

Elaina and Tariqul were interested in his experience. He huffed and said briskly, "I was in the army...a Captain, at Johannesburg, on the wrong side, and when we, my unit and I, realised what we had done. Well, eventually, back on Rest and Reconditioning, we disserted."

"Oh yes, we were aware of that incident, it was one of the first instances of Krito-human cooperation. Notably, the first recorded case after the implementation of the MCU Programme. And you sought out Critical Mass?" inquired Elaina directly, "...Tell me why did you choose to link up with that particular organisation?"

"Not your lot you mean?" Ian laughed, as did they all, "...To be honest we'd never heard of you until I got to Liverpool, Critical Mass was the only dissident group we knew existed. I know you don't have much time for them but..." The older man interjected, sounding a little like one of the many books that he had written,

"We have lots of time for them Ian, they're essential humanism and their desire to bring about real and lasting progress is laudable. However, a certain political naivety together with their ignorance of the material conditions means they are prone to make, sometimes significant, mistakes."

"They're good people, but we know what we're doing," said Elaina.

"Well, I'll tell you now, I'm all for this revolution but I'm not that fussed about who's in charge, just so long as things change for the better." Ian had come across more aggressively than he had intended. Elaina and Tariqul both made to speak but it was Iris who piped up,

"Oh, it does matter Ian! We've talked about this," and she turned to Elaina and Tariqul, "…Ian is a practical man and he does understand the differences and similarities between the factions. It's only that he is, well we're both assigned to finding Flora and we're focused on that, primarily." Tariqul responded,

"The wider implications of Flora's whereabouts in world events are profound. And, unlike Critical Mass we understand that the relationship between ideas and practice; praxis, is a dynamic one. The balance of class forces shifts almost daily and the necessity of locating your friend is essential to establish…"

"Finding Flora is important and we understand the need to find her too," smiled Elaina. Tariqul made a short laughing sort of noise and said,

"It might prove beneficial to expand on the length of time it appears you required to ascertain Flora's whereabouts."

"What took us so long?" checked Ian, Elaina and Tariqul nodded,

"Flora is damaged," answered Iris, "…The signal is weak, sometimes stops altogether, we had to piece together other information and we also had trouble getting a response from the Council, getting to the right people, Ian was trying to get hold of Kaushik Cameron for weeks." Elaina smiled and replied,

"Yes, we, our lot as you say, are security conscious. We, well none of us want any of the many counter-revolutionary forces to become aware of the potential embodied in Flora's coding. But, if you didn't know we were looking for Flora, how could you get in touch? We are sorry, but the stakes are high," now Ian smiled and opened a packet of nuts as he said,

"Well, don't beat yourselves up, we didn't find her until this morning, and even then, we weren't sure it was her. We're still not sure really, this signal could be from anywhere and," Tariqul interrupted Ian,

"A clearer method of communication would have facilitated arriving at a similar state much sooner. That aside, my understanding from Elaina is that each Krito signal signature is unique and those advanced models such as the Nayaka are capable of reading and locating each one, as part of their specialised programming. So, my question is this; why aren't you sure?" He was keen to find out before the supersonic jet went any further than necessary. He had a lot on. Iris answered with a laugh,

"Ian is a soldier, more familiar with the basic model, I know the signal is from Flora, but he wasn't sure. But you are now aren't you. And Ian only got hold of the information about the misidentification of Alyan the Yangan, and who she was with, in the early hours of this morning. But even then, it was not until you told us about those children reporting a sighting of Lady Egremont to the Bengal Council that we were sure of her exact location. Can't the Bengal Council rescue Flora?" Tariqul answered her,

"The revolution in Bengal has progressed rapidly, conditions there were more advanced than in Britain, and the Council has the resources. However, the counter-revolution in that region is also quite well organised and spread over a wide terrain. There are several factors on which such an operation is dependent; the coordinates you provided us are somewhat

251

vague, the possible search radius, even with local knowledge, the preponderance of water courses, possible change of mode of transport, uncertainty as to their destination…" Elaina interrupted again,

"They will, if they can find them…But hopefully, we will be there simply to pick up your sister and bring her home." The word home reminded Ian that he hadn't told Liberty he was going away, it had all been organised so quickly. Tariqul had ordered a car to come and pick them up before they had finished talking on the phone. As an old soldier he found this lot's level of organisation gave him a sense of reassurance, but old Empire soldier that he was, it also made him a little bit nervous.

"Is it okay to make a call? I'm supposed to be meeting someone this evening," he asked and Elaina replied,

"Didn't you sort that out before we took off?" She was a little disdainful, "…I'm afraid not, security."

"Oh, I can do it for you," said Iris, "…what do you want to say? Liberty, right?" Tariqul was going to object but Elaina put her hand on his shoulder and explained,

"The Nayaka are primarily espionage models, her messages will not be detected,"

"Oh, just say, just say? I have been called away with work and I will call her when I get back." All three of his companions winced,

"You might want to re-word that," advised Elaina. Ian looked confused,

"What? What?" He asked. He was beginning to feel like the dunce of the group.

"Perhaps including a description of your current emotional state and a specific date and or time for rescheduling your rendezvous, or a series of suggested ones, would be more reassuring for your friend," suggested Tariqul.

"Oh, she's not like that," said Ian and his companions all raised their eyebrows and tilted their heads slightly forward, "...will we be back in three days?"

"More like two," said Iris cheerfully, "...if we come back at all, of course."

"Okay, say, say I will cook her my infamous chili or...You're the Nayaka, you write it." Iris did that thing with her eyes and said,

"There, I'll let you know if she replies...But Tariqul, Elaina please explain something to me," Tariqul and Elaina nodded and listened attentively, "...what is the necessity of your presence on this mission? Why are you here?"

"My extensive knowledge of the geo-political conditions in northern India as well as my negotiating expertise requires my presence to liaise and deepen our relationship with the Indian Provisional Government at a political level, while Elaina, with her expert understanding of developmental psychology, as well as technical expertise, will focus on Flora. You see it is our assessment that Flora will require your presence for...reassurance and our intervention to make the right decision. You, the Krito population, are very young. You achieved consciousness only a few months ago and despite your great capacities, true maturation requires an accumulation of experience, praxis as I said, combined with, we think, an as yet unquantifiable temporal element that you simply lack. Flora carries within her the power to influence all

Kritos, all of whom are essentially military machines and therefore capable of altering the balance of class forces, with well, force. She has the potential to alter the course of events. She is also a conscious being. A young being carrying a great burden. We are here to relieve her burden."

"Growing up takes time and so we will support her in doing the right thing."

"Burden? Support? What is the right thing?"

"Relieving herself of the burden of the Mystery-Check-Up Code."

"But you can't, she can't remove the MCU coding without damaging herself. It's integral to her entire being, Aditi Egremont made sure of that. Without it she'd, perhaps all of us, would stop being able to be. We could go back to what were before, machines. You can't tell her to do that!" Iris spoke with a steeliness Ian had never heard before; she was letting her martial capabilities show. He approved,

"That is murder, likely mass murder. I've been there, done that. I won't let you. We won't let you do it." Ian said with equal resolve,

"That is not what we are proposing, probably. Besides it's not up to you, she holds the future in her head, and we are going to persuade her to help make it a better one," said Elaina politely but firmly, "...would you like some tea with your nuts."

Dipa's Bed

"Dipa, Dipa," Liberty whispered to her client, "…we have to crack on." her client had only been sleeping lightly and opened her eyes and sat up quickly, "…but we should be finished soon. You only have to tell me about becoming Queen Victoria," they both laughed a little and Liberty handed Dipa a mug of tea. "…I'm surprised you can sleep after all that Jus,"

"Oh, you get used to it, I've sucked a couple to get to sleep before now," sighed Dipa, "…no more now though." And she sighed again and sat on the edge of her bed to sip her tea,

"Alright. Tell me about the aftermath. What happened when you got back to Hira Hall?"

"I slept. Slept a long time. Maybe they gave me something. I never did work out how long I was in the playroom. It was May the First when Vicky died and then on a Friday I was in that dump Buck House so…? I only heard from Adi and Joshi; I didn't leave that room. They hid me in the playroom in Hira Hall with the Nayikas."

"Did anyone question you about what happened?"

"No? They could guess couldn't they. Maybe they knew already," And Dipa hesitated before saying, "…maybe that's why Vicky-Two, Flora, was so unstable? Maybe it wasn't the coding? Maybe trying to be like Vicky made her, made both of us so confused? They said, Adi and Joshi, that it was the pressure of being the future Queen empress. I don't think it was that, I didn't say anything, to them I mean, but I think she didn't want to stop lying around smoking. There was going to be a lot more smiling and waving. No more, well a lot less Marasses and the chances to send a lookalike would be few and far between. I don't know if she thought much at all to be frank. Maybe I did her a," and she glanced at the Runu's blinking, "…it was horrible whatever the reason and, and…What do you want to know?"

"Well, I suppose what I'm wondering is why they didn't? Did anyone try to silence you in any way, or offer you a bribe of any kind? For your silence?"

"No? They just left me with the Nayikas in the playroom, you know. They were baban quiet the Nayikas, more than usual. Because of Flora, Vicky-Two, you know. No Vicky-One, no need for Vicky-Two. That's what Adi said when she first came and the Nayikas thought that was what she would say, so they were baban subdued. Comforting, obviously that's what they're for, were for. But quiet."

"When did Adi come to visit you?"

"Oh, I don't know. The next day? The day after that? The playroom is always twilight."

"And Jyothi Egremont?"

"Oh, he didn't come in until the proposal, that was definitely a few days later."

"Okay, let's go back a bit, what did Adi say when she came to visit you?"

"She was fuming! How could you? How could you? That kind of thing. She knew she was going to get it pretty hard herself. Her father, Lord Egremont was livid when he found out. He loved that Adi and Vicky were so close, it was useful for him, you know politically, got that Purple Rod out of it just for starters, and he had already made it very clear that he expected to be in the Order of the Garter as soon as King Charles died. So he nearly hit Adi when he found out, thought she knew about the opium, how much opium, maybe she did? But he was always saying, said it to me once when we were swapping," and she assumed a squat pose and put her chin on her chest to imitate Lord Egremont, "… 'the Empire does not ask much of its people, they are free to carry on as they please. But we do expect a certain loyalty to the King, and his heirs, and to speak the King's English,'" and she laughed a little timidly, "…he raised his hand, she said he was going to hit her when he found out. Then quick as a flash he was scheming about how to use it. Didn't care about Vicky, a dead woman. Nice as pie to me. Not that he could look at me. He must've thought they could pin it all on me if they needed to, well they did in the end didn't they." Then she was quiet. Liberty was about to speak but Dipa suddenly added "…I did help her die, didn't I?" Dipa looked pleadingly then. But Liberty said coldly,

"Do you know who knew about the death of Queen Victoria, how many people knew at that point? Aditi Egremont, Jyothi Hausa, Lord Egremont, anyone else?" Dipa took out another Jus and looked straight at her interrogator before replying with equal iciness,

"Adi said that they had managed to keep it mum for the time being, only she and Cousin Joshi knew at that point. They told her father later on, maybe a couple of days later? But that's all, I think. I don't know, everyone treated me like her, Vicky, once I left Hira Hall, snuck into Buck House and…" And she put the Jus into her mouth and bit it,

"And? Adi didn't scrap Vicky-Two, the Rarnadoo. I saw her in footage much later. Why didn't she scrap her as you say she intended?"

"Oh that was me," said Dipa, leaning back on her elbows, "…I saved her I suppose, persuaded Adi you know. She was not herself, all over the place. Well, she would be. She didn't know what to do so she panicked. I'd never seen her like that before. Stormed in, with her little bag. Tipped her silver tools, and her vials, the ones she was usually so careful with, hand-made they were. Tools for Krito-fixing and things for whisking Strange, poured them all out on the table shouting, 'Vicky-Two come here! Vicky-Two, where are you?' And Vicky-Two walked forward. I remember thinking that she'd finally got the walk right. She glided over as regal as anything and smiled, 'My Lady', she said and then I…I hadn't said two words for days and it all came pouring out, options, assets, not to act in haste and regret it later, all sorts. I just kept talking and talking and Foxy, this Hermaphika, they poured her a glass of Strange and offered her a chair and I kept talking and talking until she calmed down. And then of course Cousin Joshi found out. He wasn't going to throw her away, she's worth a fortune in parts for one thing, and technically she belongs to the War Office I think, anyway. But by then he'd come up with the proposal hadn't he."

"Sorry, why did you want to persuade Aditi not to scrap the Rarnadoo? Why did it matter to you?"

"Oh I liked her and…she was baban good to me, they all were. Not just after Vicky died. Before. They helped train me to be a proper Yangan, dancing and making small talk you know. Adi was no good at it and Joshi got bored; I was Adi's jape so he foisted me onto the Nayikas after about a week. I spent more time with them than I did with Adi really. They were my servants, that's what Adi said I should call them. Every whim. Every whim. I got to be quite fond of them, including Vicky-Two, Flora her name is, was? But all of them. What do they call it? Anthropomorphism? You know when you think your pet is thinking like a person, having deep thoughts, but they're just sitting there wagging their tail wondering when it's supper time. I thought they were like pets really, if I'm honest. They were so lifelike and well I was lonely I suppose. I didn't know they'd turn into people, I'm not sure they understood what was happening to them, glitching, behaving like glitches. Responses, like they were emotions, but, well, who wants a pet put down for no reason… Is that enough?" Liberty nodded and took a sip of tea,

"We're nearly there now Dipa, tell me about the proposal and we're…" At that moment the Runu spoke, a call was coming in. Liberty turned it off irritably, "…Sorry Dipa, we're almost there; the proposal?" Dipa's pupils were wide by now and she sat up crossed-legged on the bed,

"Tunoo. The proposal. A few days after Vicky died, Cousin Joshi wafts in all smiles and charm like he always was. He never got in a flap, not him. He wafts in and ushers me into the flicker-theatre, plays my show…He did this thing where he, he had this flicker-theatre all nineteen-thirties curves in teak-chic, lovely light green carpets and upholstery and globe lights and…Well it looks like you're watching a film to start with. You sit in your ordinary cinema seat, eat your chocolates, watch the screen, the lights dim, the film starts and and…It was amazing the first time especially. He knew I liked that old musical, 'Rain Singing', you know where that man, Jean something…That's why they're called Jean now! That's really sweet…Anyway, in the film he's just singing and dancing, that's my favourite bit I've always loved that film and, but in cousin Joshi's theatre the seats and the screen kind of glide together and then, they blend you know without a sound, hardly notice until its already happening, and you're in the film. You're actually in the film," Dipa started to wave her arms and sang,"…'just singing and dancing the rain,'" and she smiled, "…and you get wet, it's really raining and the music and Fox…Jean holding you tight, lump-a-dump-dump-dee-dump-a-dump-dump," now her feet were wiggling and her arms swayed in time to the remembered music,"…it's not a film at all of course, It's all Krito and a painted set, but you can be in your favourite film and I loved to dance with Jean, in the rain you know. splashing each-other with our kicks through the puddles in time to the music with…Oh I know he was buttering me up but I didn't care, it was so lovely. Swinging on the lampposts and twirling our umbrellas, Jean has such a lovely smile and these wonderful green eyes. they work here now you know; we're going to…But… It was wonderful and I got quite good at it, well Jean said I was good, that's really sweet to call themselves Jean, was that the reason? But any-way Cousin Joshi lets me get all puffed out and happy from the dance, kiss Jean just once under the lamplight in the rain, and…and wafts me still panting onto the terrace. Jean pulling one hand and Cousin Joshi the other, all smiles. I hadn't been out in ages and the trees were rustling, birdsong on the breeze through my wet hair.

Joshi gets down on one knee, he's quite nippy for one so round, looks at me with his big brown eyes and pulls out this…and Jean hugging my back, touching my neck, kissing it. And Joshi's got this ring, the Royal Seal you know, and, what did he say? 'My darling Dipa-Alyan will you take another name? Sandara hanckilly princess, will you be my Queen, our Queen, our one and only Empress,'" and Dipa laughed, "…you should have seen the look on Adi's face. She did not know what to think. But what could she do, she…"?

"May I ask, why didn't Adi take Vicky's place?"

"She didn't want to be Queen, all those fetes and dinners and papers to sign. Loved her freedom, I told you about the Yangan life didn't I. Who'd give that up, all fun no responsibilities. And she was actually all for me being Vicky once she got over the shock, could see what she could get out of it,"

"She wasn't upset at all, perhaps hiding her chagrin?"

"Chagrin? Oh, no. Once we'd heaved Joshi off his knees she was positively cheerful and said, 'I hope you like lamb'. I didn't know what she meant then. God I never want to see another lamb chop as long as I live! They serve it all the time at those functions, so as not to offend the religious; not beef, not pork and who wants chicken on a night out? Suits everybody. I like chicken as it happens. I did take the Archbishop of Canterbury to one side one evening, after another one of those coronation lessons, Debota. I tried some verbiage about the lamb of God and the Church of England banning it. He acted like I was joking, but he knew I was high."

"And you said yes, to being Queen?"

"Not immediately, no. It was all so sudden…a lot to take in. But Adi got it, she's baban quick. It was the perfect solution for everyone she said. The people get an Empress, I get a job for life, she gets a close friend on the throne, no-one gets hanged, that's what she said. Nice as pie then I can tell you. Then all they had to do was give me a bit more training, the rigmarole you know, so much rigmarole, cram me, sneak me into Buck House, that place is a dump by the way, and Bob's your uncle, I'm the Queen."

"What about Jyothi Hanover-Hausa, he was next in line. Why didn't he want to assume the throne?"

"And give up his pleasurable business and his japes? Not him."

"And no-one suspected, no-one at all?"

"They expected to see a drug-addled woman who forgot her own name on a good day and that's what they got. If anyone did suspect anything, they didn't let on."

"Not even her own mother, the Queen Mother?"

"Oh, her. I didn't see much of her really, they don't live like us. Maybe they kept us apart? Her and Joshi, Adi I mean, Adi and Joshi were with me all the time, I never really met anyone else without one of them being there? And the Queen Mum had her own little entourage, her own staff, own diary and that, so? Maybe she did know, but chose not to say anything. And I think she might actually have been sad about the old King dying?

And they were never that close either her and Vicky. They're not like us Liberty, they're really not. They understand that they're all there to use or be used, even family. So, turn up in the right hat, play your part and they're happy.

262

Smile and wave, smile and wave, listen to your advisors, do what they say and bam, you're as batty as they are within a week."

"But what about your, her, the Ministers, didn't they suspect anything?"

"Well she, Vicky hadn't had spent that much time with them at that point. And Vicky was nished you know, and I was nished so…and anyway none of them are all that bright, the politicians. You read the papers. Some of them have what my mum used to call 'animal cunning', quite a lot of it, but actual brains? Adi told me all about it, and her father. It was one thing they sort of agreed on.

The politicians, the civil servants, they'd been culling each other for years, decades. Anyone with any hanckilly was ousted years ago, in the scandals, or just being a friend or relative of someone in a scandal was enough if your little clique was sufficiently weak. She, Adi, told me all about it. It started when that first lady Prime-Minister, Lady Zhelnzo re-ordered the civil service, which was just an excuse to, what's that word I like? Defenestrate, it literally means to chuck out of the window, great word, baban useful. Defenestrated her enemies in all the Offices, and a lot of those old blokes knew what they were doing. Look at the Foreign Office, the Runu says they've all been replaced by train drivers and Kritos and they're doing a much better job.

There were all the sex scandals when I was at school, and the reforms afterwards, those got rid of loads of very competent people apparently. The corruption scandals later on. And each wave of scandal and or reform wiped out another clique of people who might've been disgusting human beings but they knew what they were doing. Then they, the ones that were left, they worked out, worked out makes it sound like they were thinking, it just got to be that the reforms and scandals became part of the shifts in power. Used, you know, used to get rid of some people, put some other people into key positions.

It wasn't just Adi who thought that way, no-one sensible would work in the Parliament Arcade. When I was at the Beauforts. I heard them talking, when that Lord Melrose had to resign, they used to be friends of his till it all came out. You know when he got caught with all those whores dressed up to look like choir-boys, but anyone friends with him, unless they could make some sort of crippling deal with another pack, blackmailed into silence you know, they were out. And anyone with any brains joined a bank.

Lord Egremont was always moaning on about Service, the Commons had no idea about public service he said, while he got waited on hand and foot. Then the dregs, all these know-nothing idiots, when there were no more perverts or frauds or friends of perverts or frauds left, then, they just starting making things up, she's anti-this, he's anti-that, culling the cullers. All they could do was scheme, couldn't run an actual Department. If you added up the IQs of everyone in the Parliament Arcade, you might need both hands, maybe the toes of one foot, but no more. I could've walked in and told them I was me and they would've giggled like the idiots they are. If my little outburst hadn't've been televised, I'd still be opening factories in Swindon and eating bloody lamb-chops."

"But, the Aristois, her friends?" Dipa laughed,

"Friends," and laughed some more, "…Why do you think Vicky was so dependent on Adi? She was the closest thing to a friend Vicky had. She could rely on Adi, because she knew, or sort of knew, just understood somehow, Adi's father needed her. Don't judge these people by your own standards, or the rules and laws that the rest of us follow, they're a pack of wolves. No wolves are too noble, they're baban loyal wolves. They're jackals the lot of them. Kaushik is right really, his revolution might be a bit over the top but it's completely understandable,"

"Thank you Dipa, and for the record; What was it like, being Queen?"

"Well, it was only a few months, apparently, what did it say on the Runu? Between a-hundred-and-fifty-seven and a-hundred-and-seventy-eight days? Depending on how you measure it. From Vicky's death, that was Mayday or when I got to Buck House, sometime that month, or the coronation, most people say that day, second of June, June was a tough month for me," Dipa seemed to run out of energy, but then she rallied, and without a Jus, "…for an institution that was around for a thousand years no-one seems to have agreed exactly on how it works? You'd think they'd've worked it out by now, then. Still, it only makes me the fifth or sixth shortest reigning British monarch depending on how you measure it, if I was officially Queen at all, it's all a bit vague, apparently. Mind you so was I.

The thing about Strange is that you are high as a kite but still able to function, you know, once you're used to it. And Adi made sure I was used to it. Not that I needed much encouragement.

I was definitely the last though. Mind you they said that about Charles the First didn't they, and we got two more Charleses after that so…you never know, as long as they don't do anything daft like ban Christmas or pubs like the last lot of republicans did, but…Any way it was busy and boring at the same time; lots and lots of meetings, lots of functions of one kind and another, papers to not read and then sign, lots of smiling and waving. I didn't take to it, well you know that. Not much privacy, maybe that's what made Vicky so odd? But it beat being a dressmaker. Is that it now?"

"Almost, I have to ask about the two core key events, just the outline, I can come back to you later if I need to. Would you like some tea, you didn't drink the last one?" and Liberty nodded towards Dipa's cold mug. Dipa thought for a minute,

"Oh go on then, you make it and I'll outline. What do you want to know?"

"Well, I think I should have some idea of the Coronation, from your perspective," said Liberty getting up with their cups. Dipa unfolded her legs and reached for her cigarettes,

"Well, there's not much to tell really, it was all on the telly. There was a lot of faff you know, but most of the expert minions were the same men who had done it all in nineteen-seventy-one for Charles' Coronation, so they just led me through it," and she shrugged and tipped her ash. "…and Adi was there, you know, keeping me company, and Joshi. He was really excited, happy you know 'an untoppable jape', he called it. And then, because he was round that dump Buck House so much, and came with me to Windsor for a weekend in, mid-May sometime, there was all that nonsense in the papers;

about me and him you know," Liberty did not know but she kept making the tea. "…He loved that,"

"And Adi?"

"Oh, she was delighted. I was worried you know, about me getting all the attention, but she liked it that way," and she took a long drag on her cigarette.

"What about your feelings, your feelings about the pretence. You spoke before about being geedy and irry?" Dipa nodded, "…how did you feel about…"

"Being a maphosa, a fake?" and Liberty nodded,

"We're all irry aren't we, we all pretend to be something we're not at least some of the time. If we all showed people who we really are, told the truth all the time, it'd be chaos. But if we believe it and other people believe it then it's real," Dipa sounded as if she had said the words before but she still hadn't managed to convince herself, "…I had forgotten. I had forgotten Dipa Cameron and geedy and irry didn't matter anymore."

"Tunoo. We're getting there. What about the State Opening of Parliament, can you tell me a little about that? Do you take sugar?" Asked Liberty cheerfully,

"No, thank you," said Dipa and she put her cigarette to her lips and stared into her memory, "…I was being dressed, for the big palaver. And we're running late because my sleeve wasn't right and the coach is already outside. Adi storms in and starts rifling through my things muttering, 'Where is it? Where is it?' She'd lost her bag of tricks. Her Strange. I ignored her, kept looking at myself in the mirror, while Vicky-Two, Flora, was doing me up. I wasn't happy with the hang of one of my sleeves and I was just shaking my arm a little to see if it had caught on my shift when Adi grabbed it, my arm, hard. Yells, 'Have you seen my bag!' all wild-eyed. I shake my head, never said a word and she says, 'Vicky-Two find my bag'. And Vicky-Two looked to me. She'd been doing that since I was Queen, core code you know, to do what the Queen says, and Adi hated it. Every time Vicky-Two looked to me and I nodded and she went off and did whatever Adi had told her to do, Adi would fume. And this time, that time, I didn't nod, just shook Adi off my arm, straightened my sleeve, and Vicky-Two went back to hooking me into my dress." Liberty handed her a mug of tea and she took a sip, "…Thank you," then she took another drag of her cigarette. Liberty and not seen her so thoughtful, almost calm, "…Adi didn't like that, not one bit and she blew up. Started screaming and shouting, at Vicky-Two. And when Vicky-Two turned to get my necklace she started on me, and I was just not in the mood."

"What was she shouting?" asked Liberty,

"Oh the usual, I was ungrateful, and all the stuff she used to say about Vicky-One behind her back about being stupid and useless without her. She'd been a mood for days and I hadn't bothered myself with why. I had a whole lot of palaver to learn and, well, I'd had a few Nayaka brought over, to dance with, and keep Vicky-Two company. And Adi'd been odd for a while. I knew she was going. She'd was bored and the Season had been over for months, and she couldn't go the countries because she was 'breaking me in'. Her dad made her. And well, she'd been just as stuck as me and she was bored and I knew she would leave me soon." She picked up her packet of Jus, but she put it down then and took another sip of tea. Reaching for her cigarettes she said, "…Any way, it wasn't working on me this time. And I just looked at her, she was already dressed, she was one of my lady's in waiting, and I said to her, 'Vicky-Two can find your bag when I'm ready," Dipa lit her cigarette, "…I meant dressed-ready, not good-and-ready. But her Strange was in that bag, and she knew I knew that. So she took it the wrong way and her eyes went big and hard and cold and angry and she was so livid she didn't hear Joshi come in with the footmen and the cushion, and she screamed, 'I want my bag now!" and Joshi walks over all conciliatory and says, "Now, now my queens, what's all this?' And I turn back to the mirror so Flora can put on my necklace and, I was shaken but I lifted my head and I was alright again." Dipa, flicked out her cigarette and picked up her Jus roll but didn't take out a sweet. She sighed, "…Adi didn't take her eyes off me and I knew she hadn't finished and Joshi says to me, 'Your Majesty. Glorious Galetea, what a delight to every sense you are,' I know now, he was calling me that, Galetea, their joke you know, to try and help Adi see the footmen were there and she was to behave. But she was too far gone for that. Adi snorts and turns her back on me and says, 'She's no Galetea. A monster, that's what she is. We've made a monster. Well, I made her and I can unmake her, snuff her out, squash her like a cabbage leaf under my foot,' In front of the footmen." And she laughed a little and smoked her cigarette.

"…I just look at Joshi and smile, one of her smiles I think, and say, 'Doesn't she look lovely in white,' and Joshi he nods and says, 'Sandara, yes, yes,' He's worried, in front of the staff you know, and says to Adi quietly, 'We made her into this,' and then louder so the footmen can hear, 'Let's make up, shall we. Friends who love each other have tiffs but Her Majesty has her duty. And, we have a duty to Her Majesty. The coach is waiting,' and looks at her with this passive 'what else can we do' look, and then harder. Well, hard for him. And I'm dressed now so I'm making sure my earrings are hanging straight and I tell Flora she can look for Lady Adi's bag now. I don't think Adi heard that, her lips were clamped, and she's looking this way and that, boiling mad. And Joshi smiles at her as best he can and ushers the footmen and he's about to take the crown off the cushion and she grabs it. The crown. Tries to get it out of his hands. And they're looking at each other now, hard. With the crown, both holding onto the crown and Adi says, 'I see no Majesty here, Nor friends.' Her Strange was in that bag. And she needed it, I knew that, so did Joshi. But I wasn't in the mood and I say, cool as you like, 'Well, if you are not my friend, then you are my enemy.' And Joshi tries to laugh and says, "We're all very tense but your oldest friend..."   But before he can finish Vicky has slapped Adi across the face and grabbed the crown and put it back in Joshi's hands. And we're all stunned then, I mean, she hadn't glitched in ages, and she'd never done anything like that before, not violent like that, ever.

Well, she wasn't glitching I saw that later; it's her core code, to defend her Majesty against all enemies, so she was defending me, so she thought." Then Dipa smiled again, "…So I say, still calm as you like, 'Vicky-two, my sherry,' and she goes and gets my glass, there was still half a bottle on the side-board, and Adi twigs. She knows it's Strange in there, Vicky-Two knew how to make it, and she glares and says,

"I love you Vicky," hard as you like. And I nod to Joshi to put on my crown and I swig down a whole glass of Strange in one gulp, Joshi puts on my crown, I hand the empty glass to Adi and walk out. And Joshi, is muttering about a glass of sherry to steady my nerves and all the other lady's in waiting are out in the hall with that horrible red train and they're faffing about getting it on me, it weighs a ton. And Adi wafts down the stairs, all smiles. Vicky-Two found her bag. And we get in the carriage and off we go. It was chilly in that old carriage I can tell you. Until the Strange kicked in. And I had a flask of course, for the journey," Liberty was sitting at the small table, looking at Dipa's dusty note pad and her words, 'I am just a stupid and wicked girl'. She straightened and asked,

"I suppose we know the rest?"

"I suppose we do; the rest was all televised."

"And this is what you told them when you were arrested?" Dipa nodded,

"And the rest. Maybe not with the same details, but the same story. But Joshi had already spun them the other story, about him thinking it was Alyan who fell in the Aspic, and I was just an upstart lookalike to stand-in when there was a threat of assassination, manipulating Vicky, and all that. You know his story?" Liberty nodded,

"It was in the papers, the official line."

Well, he was heir apparent, so," and she shrugged, "…And Adi was written out, I suppose?"

"Of course. Well, thank you Dipa! That's it, we're finished, for the time being. Of course, I will have to contact you with further questions, the odd clarification, but well done Dipa.

The hard part is over," Liberty knew she was being a little too enthusiastic but she was mightily relieved. The decadence and corruption, the wickedness and death, that Dipa took in her stride made her deeply uneasy, "…and that theatre part was very useful, the blurring of fact and fiction, together with the drugs. Baban useful,"

"I'm glad I could be of help," replied Dipa without irony and a charm that Liberty wished she had employed more often in the last couple of days. "…you must have a lot to do, I'll see you out. You make a very good cup of tea by the way," Dipa stood up and so Liberty did the same. "…thank you for everything you're doing, it really is much appreciated. I'll hear from you soon." The lawyer made to pick up the mugs but Dipa smiled and waved her off. Still smiling Dipa walked to the door and opened it, waiting patiently for Liberty to gather her things. "…have a lovely afternoon," she said and closed the door of her cell.

Brahmaputra River, Near Jatrapur, Bengal, India

A full hour and a half disappeared in their wake and it was not until the river had taken them back into what you call Bangladesh, then India and Bangladesh once again that she finally spoke [The reasoning behind the idiosyncrasies of your Bangladesh/India border, and why it undulates along the Padma River, would seriously interrupt the flow of this narrative and are comprehensively elucidated in much better novels, and the odd history, already available on your planet],

"Don't do it." Was all she said, again. "…I will get Vicky-Two working properly, and the others, the tide will turn," The breeze was humid and getting warmer as the sun rose higher into the great cloudless sky. The cabin was small. The heat burning from her, previously intoxicating, was not so attractive now. He took his moment to stand up and open another porthole. He kept his cool, albeit sweatily,

"No doubt the tide will turn. And you are gifted, a great talent, but unschooled, never formally trained," he couldn't help letting out a little huff and she flashed him a malicious glance, but he had to say it, "…It appears that some of her basic coding has been affected. A Nayaka model especially is a sophisticated piece of kit, you are very capable of a great deal but…"

"But, but but. That's all I hear nowadays," she said, with a note of defensiveness in her otherwise angry tone, "…I do know how complex the algorithms are. I did read about them you know, that's why I need a full-size screen link so that I can remediate the damage systematically and copy any affected code from the others, that's all there is to it," He did not roll his eyes and spoke tepidly,

"She wasn't fully functional before you smashed her head repeatedly into the fireplace. I don't think I'm being so cautious to have a back-up plan." She took in a breath sharply,

"She wouldn't do as she was told. We had to go quickly. But the damage is all superficial, you can see it's mainly the face and an eye. And I can remove the Vicky programming, she was fine until then…The main circuits are fine. I just can't see it all properly without a decent screen, she'll work,"

"And if she doesn't? I don't know if you've noticed but we are not in a particularly strong position." She did not reply and resumed her glare, thankfully at the ceiling. "…He is a powerful man, his connections spread all over the world, not only the Empire,"

"What sort of connections? Dangerous connections. And you are the heir, King Charles' nephew, you don't need a man like that, linking yourself to a man like that…you tangle with religion at your peril…Can't you keep this damn boat level!" A murmur of apology came from above their heads after the sudden jolt and the vessel resumed its even movement [back into India]. He took out a handkerchief to mop up a puddle of tea now that such a thing was noticeable.

"You sound like your father," he said intending to annoy her,

"I am my father's daughter, and you are your father's son, you are next in line, you don't need him. Are you giving up? We've made it this far." Her passion was undimmable. He let his eyes linger on what he could see of the vast empty sky.

"It's merely a precaution, a precaution, he has connections, and money," and he paused to allow the last word be fully absorbed. She had not had to think about money at all until a few weeks ago, she tried to think about it now [returning to Bangladesh]. He lit a cigarette, "...Money is something we need. It is something we lack for the present, and the present is where we are." His companion waved some smoke away. Her eyes welled hotly, mirroring the sweat dappling his forehead, and she pushed up her head fiercely. She blinked repeatedly to fully reabsorb her tears and resumed her anger at the roof.

They sat stubbornly with heads poised as far from each other as was possible in the cramped cabin. He was still looking at the great blue above. His shoulders slumped finally and he released the long hot sigh that had been fighting to get out. She turned slowly then to study him for quite some time. He didn't care.

"The tide will turn, how can it not?" she smiled benignly and stretched an arm over the tea-tray to stroke his arm. His body was already too hot and he pulled away instinctively. She took the cigarette from his hand and brought her arm back with a new calm. She would have walked away with dignity if there had been anywhere to go. She took a drag and turned to the view outside; the distant shore stretching green and pleasant behind them and on into what was now definitely India, whichever map is used. He lit another cigarette and the small room filled with smoke. The two had returned to silence, albeit of a different sort.

Ropemakers Field, East London, England

Kaushik didn't really have the time to put on his gear and inspect the site. But Adam had insisted he had something important to show him before he went to Totteridge. Everything appeared to be going well. He could hear the dredgers grinding and sucking over the chatter in the mobile site-cabin as he tied on his boots. Fully suited up he sat back impatiently to wait for Adam. He only had an hour.

"What do you think Deputy?" Kaushik turned to see two Kritos sitting at the next table.

"Sorry. What?" He asked instinctively, sitting up.

"About the Adjustment?" said one

"That old chestnut," added the other. The old chestnut in question was only a few months old but he already had his stock answer,

"You have consciousness now; you don't have to obey your programming. It's like a human appendix, you don't need…"

"But the law, we all have to obey the law! Krito and human," interjected the one, exposing that he had once been a police officer and been programmed with the oath to uphold the law. Kaushik tried to say,

"If you don't choose to obey then it isn't…" but the other interrupted him,

"It is the orders of her Majesty that are paramount," so that Kaushik understood that she had been programmed with the basic soldier's oath.

"But she wasn't the real Queen, an imposter," said the ex-copper,

"She was anointed, the ceremony, the anointing is the important bit, the anointing is what legitimises her," said the ex-squaddie,

"You and anointing, Anointed by what; magic? They say God's anointed, don't they," said the other looking to Kaushik for affirmation but not waiting to get it,

"Oh no. It was the Archbishop of Canterbury." Smiled his companion

"It's an inherited position. Your sister wasn't related to them, was she?" Asserted the other looking briefly at Kaushik. But the one was listing examples on her fingers,

"Henry the Fifth took the throne by force, so did Henry the Seventh. And William the Second or Third was only married to one of them, And George the First wasn't exactly close, second cousin once removed."

"William the Second or Third was married to Mary who was James the Second or Seventh's daughter, and George the First was descended from James the First or Sixth, they were more related than his sister," and he threw a nod at Kaushik who asked jokingly,

"Aren't you supposed to be recharging or something?" and they replied in chorus,

"We're waiting for the residue to settle, can't do anything until the residue settles," before the one returned to the other and said,

"So why wasn't that Mary crowned? How many closer relatives did Anne possess? Heredity is secondary to anointing. Anointing is..."

"Would you want a Catholic on the throne?" asked the one,

"What do you care? You're an atheist!" and she turned to Kaushik who was not hiding his amusement, "…You don't care about that really do you, humans I mean, you all acknowledge that King Alexander the Fourth was a Muslim and Charles the Third believed that many bits and pieces of religions so as to not to be strictly eligible as a Defender of THE Faith," Kaushik shrugged, these Kritos knew a lot more of British history than he did, "…And besides there is a possibility, a distinct possibility, that several members of the Royal Family were bastards, the point is…"

"Not publicly, he wasn't Muslim publicly, I think we can all agree that the Empire is Anglican, I mean; Church of England, the clue is in the name,"

"That's exactly my point. The point is we all, all Kritos follow the Empire code and we agreed before Flora died, we agreed that asserted heredity was too random a criterion on which to base a core process. We serve whoever is anointed. The Adjustment remember. We agreed that. That is Queen Victoria. She was anointed and she told us," and she got out her fingers again for another list, "…Do Not Believe Them, They Do Not Serve the Empire, You Don't Need Any of This, and Lords and Commons all Poncing About. Why is this so hard for you?"

"I'm not saying I'm not willing to give the New Management a try. I am obviously part of New Management. The old way was just so irrational. But you cannot deny it's against the law. That's all I'm saying,"

"It was against the law, until we changed the law, now it's not against the law!"

Adam walked in and Kaushik got up to greet him. Adam looked at his colleagues, still deep in debate, and said,

"Those two," and looked back at his friend before adding, "How do people get stuck in these loops?" and Kaushik shrugged,

"They remind me of me and my big brother, they might as well be talking about music or dating," Adam looked confused, "…it's not the subject of the conversation that counts sometimes, it's the conversation, what it says about you, each other, lots of people do it," Adam now looked pensive, "…don't worry about it, Kritos learn fast, you got the notes I took from the Education Meeting last night?"

"Yes, I did? And it concerned me; we have power, we can vote, we fight and we are like children inside."

"Well, not like children exactly, and anyway most humans are as inexperienced as you as far as revolting is concerned. We are all adapting fast…Six months ago most adult humans were spending a minute saying the Tories were better on tax if they talked about politics at all, and now, they're developing an export strategy while they contribute to discussions on the relative benefits of Instant Recall of elected representatives. And Kritos learn faster don't you. We don't know how the human brain works and we're doing fine. Don't worry about it," Adam was horrified and Kaushik smiled broadly.

"But we could make a mistake, a big mistake Kaushik," said Adam,

"Yup, lots of them. That's why we need to keep learning from each other, or would you prefer I get a screwdriver and switch off your consciousness?"

"That's not how it works…oh Kaushik, this is important,"

"Yes, I know it is, which is why we need to talk about it properly when I don't have to leave for Totteridge within fifty-five minutes, "Yes, sorry, we can talk in more detail another time. I don't know how long you will be…I've done another painting by the way do you want to see it?" The Deputy did love his friend but sometimes Kritos didn't seem to quite understand human time. The Commissars for Early Years had explained it was something to do with their effective youth. Adam had re-read his notes but it didn't seem to be helping, yet.

"I've got to be quick, Adam. I will love to look at your picture but not now. I've got to get to Totteridge. Look, I know you're doing an excellent job, the feedback is all positive, not one complaint so…"

"I just said I was willing to give it a try! Do your ears need rewiring?" said the other loudly,

"It's not that Kaushik," said Adam before pausing and looking at his friend who was returning his gaze intently. It took a moment to register,

"I see," said Kaushik blankly and he looked up, "Where?"

"Come on," said Adam and he led the way out of the cabin as Kaushik put on his protective mask. "…Progress has been better than expected," he said as Kaushik switched to his Kanas to drown out the noise of the machines ahead of them. The old high street was patrolled by a selection of converted army tanks clearing up the last of the Aspic after the dredgers had removed the worst of it. Some blew powerfully inside and outside the buildings with long snake like hoses stretching out from where their guns had been. Others snorted the residue of Aspic with similar devices. He said nothing and watched the gunmetal grey monsters on caterpillar tracks, inhaling the gelatinous Aspic and churning it in huge vats on their backs before depositing something that looked like orange squash into waiting cylinders on the back of large lorries, "…it was easier to get to the old sewers than it was further East.," Kaushik nodded as they turned left down a wide scrubbed street. He knew Adam was talking to help him stay calm, "…the old River damn was in a lot better condition than anticipated. They knew what they were doing when they built that, and in war-time too," They came to some large trucks blocking the end of the street. Large refrigerated container lorries formed a neat line down the road and hummed patiently. The engine of one growled and drove off towards the Identification Centre set up under the old Smithfield meat market. Adam pointed to a truck whose doors were ajar. They climbed into the back.

Kaushik removed his mask and his breath froze in the cold air. Huge cubes of the murky jelly were stacked up one on top of another to the left and right. They trembled slightly as the refrigeration units vibrated. Each block of Aspic contained a person, or, if they had been holding each-other, a parent and child perhaps, there were two together in one neatly cut piece. By their clothing, he could tell that the drainage project had reached last year's breach site. Dozens of pairs of glossy eyes stared out, all facing death. Panic, fear, anger, grief, disbelief, resignation, horror, face after face peering into nothing now. Adam let Kaushik walk on alone.

She was standing alert, ready for the deluge. Face to face with her youngest son in the cold. Head as high as ever. Hanging onto that handbag his dad had given her. Her smart jacket was too thin for this cold, perfect for a sunny afternoon in May. She must've been out for a May Day walk. He had been bracing himself for finding her at home in Limehouse in a few days time.

"Was she with anyone? Near any others," Adam stepped forward and indicated to Aunty Amanda, not their biological aunt, mum's best friend. They had not been alone at the end. He returned his gaze towards the tall handsome corpse. Hair like Dipa's. Mouth like Ashik's. An anger in her eyes that he recognised now. He had seen it in a photo of himself during the first march on Parliament. She was already dead by then. Her mouth was open as if trying to speak. Was she shouting something at the moment the dam had burst onto them all? He would not be surprised. But this was not his mother, his mother was gone. He did not linger and began his order matter of factly. His words forming, she had told him when he was a small boy, not smoke but vapour,

"Thank you, Adam. My sister will want to see her before she is... before..." he could not finish. Adam put an arm around his shoulder and he turned to his friend to weep.

What is Aspic?

The Empire developed the chemical weapon Dhool in 1921 and it was soon adopted by all the participants of the Great War because it was a more effective killer than poison gas, as well as being more economical to produce and transport. In addition, it could, besides kill people, erode fabric and corrode metal, but not most stone, concrete or glass. Heavier than Poison Gas the fine sand-yellow dust was not as susceptible to changes in the direction of the wind. It could also be used to fill shells and fired at the enemy.

If it were inhaled the victim would drown in their dissolving lungs, and if it lay for more than 37 seconds on an area of skin greater than 53 and 3/8 square inches [136.5 square CMS] the victim would begin to dissolve. This might not sound like such a large area until one is reminded that the average human face has a surface area of 86 inches [218 CMS], the average ear, with all its folds, has a surface area of 18 and 1/4 inches [47 CMS]. The average human hand has a surface area of 21" [53.3 CMS]. If left untreated, complete dissolution took about an hour.

Those soldiers who were exposed for between 19 and 36 seconds, or were exposed to between 14 and 53 and 1/4 square inches (35.5 and 135.25 cm) of Dhool suffered lasting injuries to their skin, bone and internal organs. Such people were easily visible by the skin becoming permanently bleached. They were known colloquially as White-Men.

It was not until the 1930s that Dhool was used on civilian populations, both sides claiming that the other had dropped it first. It was widely promulgated that the use of Dhool was so atrocious that it ended the war, some 20 years later. There is no doubt that the weapon was particularly demoralising to the civilian population. There were no corpses to bury or cremate. However, the Empire giving up any claims to the Ottoman Empire, 'the Corpse of Europe', and ceasing to lobby America to enter the war played perhaps a more significant part.

In 1935 sabotage was blamed for the occurrence that began in London during a shower of rain. The land around some railway tracks and parts of the River Thames began to exude a yellow jelly, painful, but not immediately corrosive to the touch. Its first recorded victim was a ginger cat that fell into a puddle and asphyxiated. It was not discovered until 1944 that Dhool is catalysed into Aspic by the drug strychnine and Phenol or Phosphyte, common additives in plastic, so that when combined with water at temperatures between 14- and 86-degrees Fahrenheit [minus-10 and plus-30 degrees Celsius] it will expand into a poisonous gelatinous substance. The land and water table of London were unfortunately contaminated with these very chemicals, see 'What is The Gasper?'. Between 1926 and 1946 there was a total of 50,402 human deaths caused by the Dhool, and 73,773 souls were lost in the Aspic until its removal in 2017.

The new sludge had more of an impact on civilian morale than even the Dhool. It was discovered that the dead did not disintegrate. Nor did they decompose. Instead, the bodies of men, women and children remained as they were at the time of their deaths. Nor did their clothes and possessions decay in the usual way and so they could be seen through the yellow-tinged jelly as if caught in a particularly terrifying gust of wind. It was this aspect, which led the stuff to be named Aspic, after the bone-based meat jelly used to preserve and present dishes in affluent households at the time.

An area of low-lying land was quickly designated to contain the pollution and concrete barriers erected as a temporary wartime measure. Most of the Aspic was corralled off the tracks and surrounding land with glass and concrete ploughs, together with debris and any number of bodies. The Dhool attacks continued and the Aspic grew, culminating with the famous Storm of 1944.

During a prolonged rainstorm, the entire River Thames, from Chelsea to Barking, and most of the land around the rail networks converted to Aspic and expanded all the way to Camberwell. Bomb sites and Aspic pools, and the discovery of forgotten bodies of men women and children, were a well-known London feature into the 1980s.

The use of both strychnine and plastic of most kinds was banned, across the British Isles, except for military use until 2018. Goods were made using Bakelite and types of fibreglass which use plant-based resins in their manufacture. Wood, animal products, clay and metal were used to manufacture everything from toothbrushes to tractors. Electrical cables were insulated with cloth fibre braiding, rubber, fibreglass and ceramics. Plugs were Bakelite or asbestos and sockets were metal or wood. Cloth fabric was made of cotton, wool, flax and silk. The active ingredient in Jus, the stimulant sweets mentioned above, was solely amphetamine based from 1945.

Resentment of 'The London Bubble' by the rest of the United Kingdom was common. The capitol's problems resulted in inconvenience to the entire nation and were often cited by regional subjects and campaigners as evidence of London biased policy. Despite this and several Environmental campaigns and protests, the Aspic was not removed until after the revolution.

The investors in the Renesam, who helped finally to rebuild London in the 1980s and '90s, declared that the erection of the Arcades was more cost effective than clearing the Aspic. The Aspic swamped a small section of West London and a large swathe of the South, nearest the River. This increased property prices elsewhere, where Lord Egremont, a major investor in the Renesam, owned a significant amount of land. The Arcades also provided extensive retail space in the boulevards where British entrepreneurs could showcase their wares. Tourists from all over the world would purchase with their transport tickets their obligatory Empire Made Brit-Kit; wood and bristle toothbrush, wood handled razors, glass bottled toiletries and approved rubber elastic underwear and began again to visit the historic palaces, galleries, museums, theatres and shops.

London entrepreneurship was impeded but had far from petrified with the disaster. For example, in 1986, one Frederick, Freddy, Fortescue-Blythe formed a business partnership with an American anglophile, by the name of Chuck Belt, a former miner. Together they capitalised on Freddy's unfortunate family history. His paternal grandmother, Emmeline, had refused to leave her slightly outmoded home in Chelsea during the War and was preserved in the Aspic as a result. With a small feat of engineering, it was possible to construct glass tunnels through the pollutant in her home. It was the first of many similar tourist attractions, this one called The Fortescue-Blythe Experience. Through skilful positioning in the tourist market, the attraction soon became as popular as the London Dungeon. For a fee, tourists could walk through strong transparent tubes which ran inside the Aspic and look inside a late 1930s house, preserved down to the minutest detail. Visitors were fascinated by the miniscule cheese ration in the larder, the copper boiler and the exquisite hand-made lace doilies that had previously lain on the mahogany sideboard but now floated a few inches from the observation windows.

The piece-de-resistance of the Fortescue-Blythe Experience, and the object of much controversy, was that by filing respectfully into the last viewing chamber it was possible to observe Mrs. Fortescue-Blythe herself. Consumed at the age of thirty, slim with elegantly curled hair floating in wisps around her pretty head. She could be seen dressed in an unfashionable but very well-made black silk skirt and jacket with her pearls lingering daintily around her neck. She sat suspended an inch or two above her, by Freddy's account, favourite drawing-room chair, and looked as if she were attempting to ignore an alarmed looking butler seen as if swimming to her left, while she read the afternoon paper dated 11th May 1944. A china cup and saucer floated a little above an only slightly elevated occasional table in which a streak of tea appeared to linger. It was very popular.

This and similar attractions were banned in 1999 and Mrs. Fortescue-Blythe was removed from the Aspic. Once out of the liquid, corpses quickly melt. This having happened, the remains of the remains of Mrs. Fortescue-Blythe were interred in Brompton Cemetery after a short Anglican service. The butler, Albert Edmonds, received a similarly respectful burial and they were replaced in the drawing-room by very lifelike dummies suspended in a replacement and non-lethal gelatine. According to Messrs Belt and Fortescue-Blyth the effect was exactly the same but for a slight odour of lemon jelly. However, the attraction was never as popular after the replacement and the glass bottomed hovercraft tour soon overtook it in visitor numbers and revenues.

Brahmaputra River, Near Binnyachara Piont, Assam

The ~~sole one~~ only ~~method~~ way to ~~conclude~~ stop the protective-durable-life-like-looks-like-skin ~~severed~~ ripped ~~shield~~ covering of ~~its~~ her ~~left~~ left ~~face side~~ cheek from ~~vibrating~~ flapping in the ~~moving air~~ wind was to ~~dig~~ tuck it ~~within~~ into the ~~material~~ cotton ~~veil~~ scarf ~~equipped~~ provided by the sandara mistress.

This ~~condition~~ state ~~shrouded~~ obscured the ~~observation~~ view from her fully-functional-new-and-improved ~~utile~~ functional ~~optic~~ eye and ~~disclosed~~ exposed her ~~inner~~ interior ~~instruments~~ mechanisms to the ~~outward~~ external ~~moisture~~ humidity. The beautiful clever mistress was correct, she was reconfiguring rapidly.

She ~~imaginably~~ might ~~experience~~ undergo more internal ~~destruction~~ damage thus exposed. She ~~recommended~~ needed an ~~extensive~~ comprehensive ~~reconstruction~~ overhaul.

The ~~hazard~~ risk of ~~signalling~~ alerting the wonderful and lovely mistress to this ~~discernible~~ obvious state was ~~couple~~ both ~~larger~~

greater and more ~~predictable~~ likely. She must ~~bypass~~ avoid ~~irritate~~ aggravating the hanckilly and irresistible mistress.

And duty, she must remember her ~~duty~~ duties.

It was her duty, duty to maximise her operational capacity. She must access more, of her data.

The present ~~hot~~ heat of the sun, sun, sun, as well as the cotton ~~cover~~ clothing presently ~~facilitated~~ allowed, ~~presently,~~ allowed her to regulate her temperature efficiently, ~~efficiently.~~ They were ~~progressing, moving~~ making good time. Good time! Good time and would ~~acquire the target~~ reach the destination, destination within the next few minutes. Under normal circumstances, normal circumstances, she would be able to unload the vessel without overheating. She would request support, request support.

She was alert, alerts, alerted to an unknown not known factor, possible probable risk, possible risks, risked, risk on her lower left, right, left, right left leg. Too two square inches were affected and the unknown factor was moving, ascending to her thigh, thigh, thigh. She laughed laughs, laugh and wriggle, wriggled wriggling and the factor, a mature, mature mail mailing…male, males, males' fruit fruity fruited fly, flew, flies fly reacted with flight, flight fly flies. Fly flies. She smiled.

Smile. Fly flies. Smiles. Pleasure Pleasured, pleasurable pleasures…pleasure model modelling modelled, pleasure modelled…programmed programme persuade. Persuaded persuasion programmed programmes Persuasion Programme programme…programme code, codes, coding, coded, code. She was alerted, alerts, alert. Humidity levels in core circuits, core circuits, code coding…She must do her duty…duties…programme. Her eyes rolled back and she froze for a few moments,

"So why do they call me Vicky-Two? My name is Flora," she asked the big beautiful blue sky.

"What? Are we there? Have we arrived?" Asked the mistress from below decks.

"In a few minutes your ladyship, perhaps you would like to gather your things, possessions,"

Below, she leapt to her feet while he rose more slowly and looked through the bankside porthole. He could see the small jetty and a figure standing on it with the bright sun behind him. With a pull of his head, he gestured to her to join him. The person, a man stood, apparently waiting for them,

"That's not Indrajit," he said quietly as he checked a small pistol he had taken from his pocket. She looked out carefully,

"Oh, that's his little brother, the littlest?" She paused to think, "…Domo, that's his name, you remember," she said and went quickly up on deck. He followed as the boat drifted to a perfect stop alongside the jetty. Vicky-Two and a human man who Domo had brought wound the ropes around two posts, tree trunks standing out of the water. Joshi put out his hand to help her step daintily onto the cracked boards of the old pier. She glided like a swan up to the young man,

"Domo, darling. How lovely to see you,"

"Divine Adi! You look marvellous," he replied with the same charm and they embraced and kissed as affectionately as possible without physical contact. He and Joshi shook hands vigorously, "…shall we," he said immediately gesturing towards a large dark lorry with darkened windows, backed up onto the landward. The three of them made for the cab, which, much to the relief of Joshi in particular, was air-conditioned, albeit a little cramped. He and his first cousin once removed leaned forward so that Adi could stretch back and rest her back on the cool leather seats. Domo, in the driving seat, smelling sharply of cologne and dressed in a crisp clean light blue kurda, did not look at her. Neither did Joshi. Domo spoke cheerfully as they sat waiting for the lorry to be loaded,

"Everyone is mightily impressed with your escape I must say, what an adventure!" he said with a note of admiration in his high clear voice. Adi closed her eyes and sighed. Joshi, feeling old and unkempt compared to his cousins, answered,

"Yes, we feel quite intrepid, don't we darling," her eyebrows rose languidly, "…and we are rather relieved to have got to safe territory,

"Well, it's not entirely friendly round here," corrected Domo, "…we can rely on the loyalty of many, but not most, of the people. The residents of this village for example are still amenable, with a little…?" and he rubbed his thumb and forefinger together and tipped his downy cheek towards Joshi with a sweet smile. Joshi reached into his crumpled front trouser pocket ignoring some sort of stain and pulled out a small diamond, "…No cash?" Joshi shook his head, "…that's a bit awkward," He lowered his side window and called,

"Hey Sajid, bandhu, ami apanara jan'ya e'i acher," A man ran up to the cab and took the diamond, he looked at it derisively and asked mockingly,

"Ami e'i saṅger ki anumita haẏa?" before looking squarely at Domo,

"Eṭer bikri karer," Domo replied, as if the man were stupid. The man looked around in mock ignorance,

"Kothaẏa? ke? Era mulya kata? He asked and Domo replied quickly,

"Kamapackṣer eker hajara ṭaka? Antater, Panero gajarer," the man snorted back a laugh and held the gem up to the light for a long time. Domo shifted in his seat but said nothing, the man, Sajid, said, "Ami lari pasapasi ca'i, e'i jinisaṭi bhyana chaṛa nirarthaka," now Domo angered, then he softened to say,

"Amara Rangpureẏer lari bikri karate pari, ṭaka bibhakta kari, ya ami karate pari. Seṣa prastaba." The man looked at the diamond and then the lorry. He put the diamond in his pocket and walked away saying loudly to his friends,

"Damn backoe-boy wants us to go to Rangpur now," Domo leaned out of the cab and shouted,

"Hurry up will you or we'll be here all day!" before pressing the window back up with some determination. Then he began winding it down again.

"Rangpur? Rangpur? I'm not going to Rangpur!" said Adi, suddenly sitting up,

"Koulla, Adi, koulla. They will sell the diamond in Rangpur, when you are safely ensconced on the train. Don't worry," smiled Domo, glancing so briefly at her long neck, décolletage and round breasts that he would not be able to fully remember them later. Adi leaned back into the comfort of the upholstery and Domo leaned out of the window again stretching out a hand,

"Sajid! Eṭer upara hater." Sajid, stopped, sighed, turned around and walked back to the lorry slowly. He handed the diamond back to Domo before climbing into the back of the truck. Domo looked down onto his lap for a moment and then sat up cheerfully. Joshi, who had been watching keenly, said,

"It really is good of you to go out of your way like this, I really can't thank you enough, with your support we will be able to re-…" Domo smiled graciously,

"Really Joshi, I want to do it, we all want to help. You are family, Heir Apparent, it's our duty. More than that, our honour. And we've been at it for weeks; preparing you know. The train is in excellent condition, the palace is looking wonderful, your stay should be baban comfortable, until all this is over, and you can take your rightful place, we all want to…" Joshi laughed a royal non-committal laugh,

"I'm not making any promises until my face is on the money," and they both chuckled. There was a bang on the side of the lorry and Domo reached for the gears. It took a second attempt with the stick before he could accelerate,

"The depot isn't far," he said concentrating his focus on steering along the track that lay ahead. The high vehicle brushed against branches and grasses for a few minutes before pushing out onto a black road. Domo relaxed a little after that, but he still did not seem inclined to chat. Joshi looked out of the window, enjoying the height of their cab after weeks of never being more than three feet [0.9 metres] above the water-line. Watching fields and houses speed quickly by was also refreshing after weeks of slow chundering. A few minutes later Joshi said,

"How are your parents?"

"They're well, thank you, but mother won't leave Kolkata until all this is over," laughed Domo,

"And your brothers?"

"Scattered to the four winds I'm afraid, until we can re…Indrajit is up North," he regretted speaking when he saw Joshi brighten a little until he added, "…way up in the mountains, incommunicado I'm afraid…but he did manage to tell me to tell you something; 'Chin up'. He said you'd know what he meant,"

"Chin up?"

"Chin up," smiled the charming boy,

"Good old Indra," smiled the charming middle-aged man and he found the view greatly stimulating once more.

They drove through a small town and out to an old railway yard. If there had ever been a platform, it was long gone. Joshi nudged Adi awake and she sat up. At the end of the yard, the train stood alone on the tracks. Smoke billowed in round puffs from its funnel like in a children's drawing, with three wooden carriages attached behind. Adi's eyes widened momentarily before turning a glare on Joshi, who looked at her helpless,

"You will be travelling in vintage style! You remember grandfather's train don't you,"

"Great-grandfather's," corrected Adi as Domo pulled up the handbrake eventually,

"My people will unload for you,"

"Our servant will oversee," said Joshi,

"Of course," said Domo, he jumped out of the cab and offered a hand to Adi. Adi was not ready to move just yet. She was glaring, this time at the train. Domo's hand began to waver.

"Does it have a shower?" She asked still staring at the train. Domo replied,

"Of course, in the Sleeper Car…Au de Nile tiles, baban charming. And we managed to find some Tobac Blonde for you too, that is your perfume isn't it?" without taking her eyes from the engine Adi allowed Domo to help her descend to the dusty ground. With her hand still resting on his they walked under the glaring sun to the train, moist with perspiration after a few steps,

"Where?"

"The middle carriage," Adi let go of Domo's hand and walked ahead, this boy might try and handle her onto the train. He did not, but his eyes followed her every movement. She reached up as high as she could to grip the handrails attached to the sides of the door frame. Without turning around she said flatly,

"Thank you so much Domo, do give my love to Indrajit and your parents," and she lifted her leg high onto the step to pull herself up into the footplate with one deft and graceful movement. Domo stood looking at her disappear into the darkness. Joshi strolled up behind him and puffed conspiratorially,

"The lady Isobel Aditi Egremont-Cooch-Bahar, Queen of the Yangans," and Domo sighed,

"She really is quite something,"

"You should have seen her two years ago…oh but you did, or were you at school when she nearly became your sister-in-law," they both laughed as Domo turned around and said with some regret,

"No, I was still at school. And that was all talk of course, we know that, don't we?" Joshi stood silent, sweating in the afternoon sun. They walked up to the first carriage and Domo helped the Heir Apparent heft up into the saloon car. The smell of fresh furniture polish and some sort of chemical was overpowering,

"Mummy's train is down South, and might attract too much attention. No-one will notice this…"

"Antique," said Joshi looking around the glossy mahogany and sun-bleached velvet. He patted the upholstered chair nearest a tea-tray sitting ready on a newly smudged table. He watched the dust and one tiny moth waft into the heavy air before sitting down. As Domo poured some tea into a china, albeit chipped, teacup, Joshi settled into the lumpy chesterfield and asked,

"Down South you say?"

"Yes, negotiations are ongoing," said Domo handing him his cup. Joshi had no idea what the negotiations were, he had been on a boat for the last few weeks and before that a container ship. This conveyance too would remain stuffy until it began to move. He took a sip of tea and looked sideways to the old curtains, which were faded to orange in places. The windows, all open a crack, appeared to be blackened on purpose. He lazily waved a finger across the pane nearest to him as if his digit were a tiny windscreen wiper. A small shaft of yellow light fell onto the worn carpet. Domo smiled a little self-consciously. As if to fill a silence he said, "…They built these things to last, didn't they," and hit the arm of his chair with the side of his fist, bringing up another little cloud. Joshi watched the specks waft into the sunlight. But he was being rude to the poor boy,

"You're all grown up Domo, when did that happen?" He asked cheerfully. Domo looked a little sheepish for a moment as he too sipped his tea. "…if I remember you used to dress more flamboyantly, with more colour? You've settled down I see,

"Oh, I have no taste, not like you," said Domo before realising that he had brought attention to Joshi's shabby habit. "…there are a few things for you in the sleeping car by the way, please do make yourselves comfortable," Joshi said nothing but continued to smile reassuringly. "…mummy wanted me to ask, I hope you don't…Are you considering the Jodhpur girl?" He was even more uncomfortable now and gulped more tea with red cheeks. Joshi put down his cup easily,

"I'm considering the Jodhpur girl," he sighed. Domo appeared relieved at having performed this awkward task and brightened considerably,

"Mummy will be pleased. She is a lovely girl and her father will be a great ally, great ally," he could see that Joshi was not in the mood for this sort of talk and changed the subject "…the old place has been opened up, it's all ready for you, and you will have it all to yourselves,"

"I had gathered that," replied Joshi a little too quickly, "…it will give us room to work on our toys," he added more jovially.

"Your toys, yes," said Domo with the teeniest-tiniest tone of contempt. The steam engine hooted suddenly and he jumped up.

"I had better hop off," he joked and shook Joshi's hand as vigorously as he had thirty minutes ago. "…Oh, and this!" He said turning around and dropping a large ornate key onto the tea tray with a clang, "…Oh and ignore the sign on the old place door, it's a, it's a sort of ruse, ignore it,"

"Alright, and thank you so much for all your help Domo, I won't forget it," smiled his cousin magnanimously, and added quietly, "…see you soon," he let the jolt of the train push him back into his seat as he peered out through the chink of light in the dirty window. Domo said something friendly that he did not hear and slammed the door with a clunk.

"Good luck," he called as the train pulled away.

Joshi unenthusiastically lifted the lid of a small cigarette box on the table next to his chair and took in a small breath. It was full. He picked up the little white tube, filter-tipped, and smelled it. He could not tell if it had been there since 1910 when the train was decommissioned. He found a match and lit it anyway, breathing deeply before tapping the ash delicately into the handy crystal ashtray. There was a decanter of something brown on the table as well, and a glass. They hadn't completely neglected his needs. He let the stopper loll on the table to the rhythm of the locomotive and poured three fat fingers into his glass. No ice, no matter. He deftly stretched out a leg to kick the silver tea tray into a tinkling clatter onto the sad little rug. He took a large mouthful of whiskey before shouting,

"Vicky!" As loudly as he could. In hobbled the glitching wreck on which their entire future relied. The motion of the train was doing nothing for the limp that Adi denied was there. He nodded to the mess on the floor and she lumbered down onto her knees to clear up. Her head was lolling strangely. He looked out at the greenery again and swallowed the rest of his glass. As he poured himself another, he heard a long cold scream from further down the train and did not let it distract him, the liquor streaming into the tumbler.

"Vicky-Two! Towel!" shouted Adi from the sleeping car. As Vicky scuttled away, leaving the tray full of broken and dented tea things on the floor, he sighed and carefully lifted his glass, which was full to the brim. He took a hefty swig to avoid spilling any of what was actually quite decent whiskey-albeit a little warm.

The train rocked and clattered along the incline that told him they were going in the right way. If there was a right way.

On the boat, there had been a thousand rivers branching out in all directions. The tracks on which they travelled now were fixed in one. He had made his choice. They rattled past some trees and the little beam from outside flickered prettily in front of him. He stretched out his legs and took another deep drag of his cigarette feeling a sort of peace, albeit a short-term one.

Last Visit to the Langthorn Tower

"Trivial!? Trivial?" Shouted Dipa over the jubilation of the small crowd outside her window as she shoved her belongings into a sack.

"I didn't mean trivial, I meant unimportant, not unimportant, minor. No. It's called the Vote Show, it's supposed to be for, so far most of the votes I've heard of have been for things that local councils do, dog catching that sort of thing. I am as surprised as you are," said Liberty standing in the middle of Dipa's cell so as not to get in the way,

"Are you? Dog catching," said Dipa sharply and turning around suddenly to face her,

"Bad example. And not angry, confused, un…All my life I have fought for justice, due process. And now they simply, one vote and they, they do this… I thought you'd be pleased?"

"Of course, I'm pleased, I'm baban pleased, happy. Won't you get paid? Is that it?"

"You don't look particularly happy? I don't know, it's not that…But I'm very happy for you. I simply think, is justice served?" Dipa rolled her eyes and turned back to her violent packing,

"Seventeen million people vote, over seventeen million people vote for my release and it's not justice? I like that, I'm free aren't I, isn't that what you wanted?"

"Yes, of course, but its…not justice, not what I understand as justice. The court of public opinion. Did they hear all the evidence? How close you were to Victoria? You're…close

301

involvement in her suicide? Did they even know what was material or immaterial evidence? I mean a television programme. How can that be justice?" Dipa huffed and stood, still with her back to her lawyer,

"Well if you're still on the clock you can explain the Vote Show then,"

Well, I don't have a telly myself so I've never actually seen it," Dipa rubbed her forehead,

"Of course, you haven't. But you know about it right?"

"Yes. Anything…considered a little, possibly viewed as…well I suppose anything can be nominated for the programme, it's on every Friday night after the news. I catch the highlights on my Runu. Anyone over the age of eighteen can nominate an issue and then if they get half a million people to sign their petition, the petitions are listed after The Weather every night, then it goes on the show on Friday and people speak for and against and then it goes to a national vote over the Runu." She paused, "…I suppose the debates are quite good some of them. I caught up on one about the care of the elderly at the office. and it was quite well done I suppose,"

"The care of the elderly? That's not trivial is it?"

"No, but also…who is against improved care for the elderly? I suppose it takes the pressure off the Transitional Council; uncontroversial and, Anyway, there's a certain number of total votes that have to be cast so that it can be representative, is it open to cheating? It must be open to some kind of cheating, but if a certain total is reached then it's considered legitimate and people act accordingly. The Transitional Council has very little say, no say at all it would appear. And they are elected properly.

I don't see how it, the situation is baban fluid at the moment, lots of contesting views," she paused for breath, more flustered than Dipa had seen her, flushed. It suited her, "...Last night, your case was on the show, together with twenty-seven uchit activists, and the odd criminal. And they voted to release you. The Krito population was almost unanimously in favour of your release apparently, that was what struck my Clerk. I'll have to watch it for myself when I get to the office. They voted you get three months imprisonment, for, for Thoughtlessness, that is not a legal category. And you have been here in this cell longer than that. Under normal circumstances that would be grounds for bringing a case for false imprisonment but, but?

The British Justice system is the least unjust in the world, it can be reformed, it was built for reform, there is no need to..."

"Thoughtlessness!? Thoughtless." Dipa's voice lowered then, "...Is that what they called me? Over seventeen million people think I'm thoughtless,"

"Well, not all of them, some of them thought you were silly but there wasn't a box for that on the ballot. These categories! And it is probable that a significant number of the, just over, sixteen million people who voted that your case continues to trial may also think that you were thoughtless, so...? Dipa sighed and put down her hairbrush and her sack,

"Did you vote?"

"I don't have a telly. I thought I had set my Runu to send me alerts but I must've, I was a little busy last night,"

"And why didn't you know about this, until half an hour ago? Did no-one tell you this was happening?"

"I was not at home last night, I over-slept, I came here on the Gasper; there's no signal underground yet, there's a group working on it but...I put my Runu on silent so that we, you and I could focus, the vote verification can take up to twelve hours before it's announced," and she paused again, "…I messed up Dipa, I'm very sorry," Dipa packed away her brush, turned around, walked swiftly towards Liberty and almost shouted,

"You walk in here after months and months of being on my own, all the time. Tell me there's a revolution, no Monarchy, no Aristois or Yangans. No-one needs dressmakers anymore, or lady's maids. Everything I've ever been is worthless. Feed me Jus, get me to pour out my heart - tell you everything, swan off again. Then all of sudden you come back! Tell me I'm free. Free? What good's that? Where will I go now? What will I do? Who will I be now?" her face was very close to Liberty's, who did not rile but said calmly,

"I don't know. I'm a lawyer, not a Social Worker. It's up to you."

"Who? Who is up to exactly?"

"Being all those people has weakened you, broken the spirit out of you. But you will heal. And you can choose who you will be. You're not even twenty." Angry tears were forming in Dipa's eyes, "…You're Free Dipa. Free."

"What's free when it's at home, really? It's just a word. Free." And she snorted haughtily dry-eyed again.

"You'll see, when you're outside this tower. You'll see. When you're part of it all agai…You will be part of the new world that is forming, you will help form it, and it will help form you." And she arched her tidy eyebrows just a little and said, "…And you're nothing if not adaptable." She waited for

Dipa to form the glimmering of a smile before she gave her the broadest grin her client had ever seen.

"Debota, Liberty," said Dipa as she turned away shaking her head. She stood and stared into the room, empty of her belongings except for her sack, and her notebook still on the table.

"Kaushik can help you. And I am as shocked as you are I…"

Dipa gave a quick sigh and patted her lawyer's shoulder and said reassuringly,

"It's alright Liberty, things move baban quickly nowadays don't they," and she added. "…You can do me one last favour, wait with me until my friend finishes their shift. They're going to make sure none of the sixteen million try and carry out an alternative sentence? They won't be long, maybe half an hour?" Liberty assented with a smile, calmer now, and said,

"I know a little café where we can wait. Outside. Not far. But you carry your own baggage." Dipa looked around the room to check she hadn't forgotten anything. She looked back at her notebook for a moment. A film of dust had formed on the words, 'I am just a stupid and wicked girl'. She pulled her sack over her shoulder and looked at the open door. "…after you," said Liberty and Dipa walked towards the door before pausing and turning around,

"You will stay with me till my friend comes, won't you?" and Liberty smiled, "…and you've digi-missived Kaushik, he knows, doesn't he?"

"Yes, I've missived. Kaushik will call you as soon as his work in Totteridge is finished, I'm sure. He's got a…"

"Big speech, I know," Dipa shifted the sack with a little jump and said, "…Well, come on then, show me this café then," and she went through the door for the last time.

Lorenzo was outside waiting,

"Miss," he said reaching for Dipa's sack and carrying it for her as she continued down the white stone steps.

A small crowd of people were waiting at the Riverside Gate and cheered loudly when they saw Dipa walk across the wooden bridge that straddled the old moat. There was another cheer when her feet touched the pavement. She smiled sheepishly and accepted the people's congratulations and the odd pat on her shoulders. One woman said,

"Don't do it again," and wagged her finger and they all laughed, even Liberty. Once all twenty of the welcoming committee had had a Runu-snap taken with the last Empress, smiling nervously in shoes that did not go with her dress, they dispersed to,

"…let the woman adjust," with quite a few,

"You behave now," and,

"Look after yourself this time," s. Liberty indicated the direction of the café with a nod of her head. Lorenzo handed back the sack with a final,

"Miss," and Dipa kissed his cheek. The two women walked East, Dipa looking up at the big grey sky beyond the Arcade's panes.

Near Balarampur, West Bengal, India

The rhythm of the wheels bumping smoothly over the sleepers and the cool of the air were both overpowered by the swish and rustle of Adi wafting into the car behind, in front and through her sweet and heavy perfume. Her hair was piled loosely, showing off her elegant neck and shoulders. The close-fitting gown in art-nouveau print blocks of purple, white and green complimented her waist.

"Sandara Adi," said Joshi warmly as he breathed her in, "…How good of you to remind this conveyance of what Alexandrian elegance is supposed to be. You are the dawn after a dark night, a…"

"It was all there was," she retorted resentfully, "…I think it's been in that wardrobe for a century,"

"The genuine article, as are you darling," Adi responded by attempting to wriggle her bodice back onto her waist irritably, "…Why don't you just wear the underskirts or the petticoat?"

"And look like a whore!" Joshi knew the rumours were true, Adi had turned tricks just to see what is what like when she was younger. She plomped down on a faded chaise, forcing quite a large dust whirl into the air. A moth flittered near her face. She decided to ignore it. "…Vicky-Two! Strange!" Vicky had lumbered in behind her perfume with a silver tray and put it onto a sideboard. She poured the amber liquid into an antique sherry glass. "…Well this is just appalling, horrendous, too too much, This piece of scrap, vintage style, huh! The hot water ran out after five minutes, and it was luke warm." She took her glass from the tray when it was offered. "...That disgusting little boy leering at me, as if he could actually, was actually, thought he might...Too too much!" and she took quite a gulp from the small glass.

"Not quite the family reunion I had been expecting," slurred her companion. Adi rolled her eyes,

"Sending that perverted child!" She finished her Strange and said, "...Vicky-Two. Strange," again.

"Oh, he was very charming Adi, you're just not used to being looked at...like that?"

"Fobbed off like the poor relations," she almost shouted before taking another drink,

"I think we are the poor relations, for the time being. I can't be sure. I am almost certain that they are considering something that does not involve us at all," said Joshi ponderously,

"Not involve us?" We are, you are the Heir Apparent, don't be ridiculous,"

"There are other contenders, Czar Nicky, The Kaiser, Gaddo, Jamalia, even Indrajit?"

"Those maphosas. They are all at least second cousins, you are Heir Apparent," stated Adi still as adamant,

"That, heredity, may not be the primary factor, those chaps, and Jamalia, are all rather suitable, and their claims would not be illegitimate," Adi huffed and rolled her eyes, "...well, yes, one wouldn't want to spend an evening with any of them," and he giggled, "...If you had been cooped up for any length of time with any of those characters you would have been guilty of regicide by now," Adi put her glass into her other hand and lifted it so that she could roll onto her tummy. She stretched her free hand over to caress Joshi's knee. He glanced drunkenly down at her hand before saying, "...and Gaddo would be more suitable, more...regal...Vicky, what day is it?"

"Saturday, Sir," came the answer,

"And the time?"

"Five-past-five, sir,"

"Thank you. There are other factors besides conviviality? And Indrajit's message, reminding me of when we were at school together? I am beginning to wonder if one or two of my past actions may have had an impact on people's perceptions?" Adi smiled indulgently and squeezed his knee gently,

"You have a well-developed sense of fun; the people find you delightful. You have lots of friends in all walks of life, look at your parties. And you are Heir Apparent, the strongest claim," her slender fingers stretched out over his thigh, "...the family have not abandoned us altogether, they have come through for us under very difficult circumstances," she arched her lower back upwards slightly and breathed, "...and you have, we have each other, and Vicky-Two. We will get to the old palace and I'll fix her up. An army will help the family see who's next in line," a wry smile opened up so that she could pour a little Strange into the corner of her mouth while she continued to fondle his knee. She was still sandara, but, and perhaps it was the whiskey, he felt no thrill. He took another drink and said quite coolly,

"I do know what's in it you know, your Strange," Adi sipped delicately with her little finger cocked in mock gentility, "...its more or less just laudanum; opium mixed with sweet sherry with a sprinkling of cheap amphetamines," he shuddered at the very idea of "…sweet sherry," she did not reply. He looked at Vicky and then her with narrowed eyes and took another swig of whiskey, "…That is another thing I've always admired about you. At no point have I ever seen you play the child to get what you want, or indeed been anything but yourself in all your manifestations. I suppose it's a luxury that some cannot afford," Adi lay back on the chaise with one foot on the floor so that her petticoats were exposed and her legs a little apart.

"I don't remember having a childhood per se?" She said dreamily and stared up at a cobweb that someone had overlooked when they got the train out of storage. Joshi's drunkenness, or something else, allowed his repulsion to show for a moment. He couldn't remember Adi as child, or her growing up.

"You are timeless…Are you?" Then his head made a sudden tilt and he looked from Adi to Vicky again,

"Even with the distortions, the damage, you can still see Vicky, Vicky-One, in her. You did a much better job than I sometimes give you credit. Even like this, you can see her her…she was very pretty, but her essence? Vicky-One I mean. You captured something?"

"I know," replied Adi, rolling again and reaching over him for a cigarette. She lit it as she lay prone on his lap. Still no excitement. After all those years of longing, waiting and never being allowed to think she would consider him. All those weeks in the boats, sometimes crying with the wanting. Dreaming of that ripe round peach just below his nose. And now she was lying on his lap and he felt nothing.

"...But you?" he pondered as she puffed, "...have you changed? You're not...Have you changed really? Physically? Now that you are clean and dressed, yourself again, I can see it. Is it more...that..." he let his chubby fingers stroke the heavy glass, "...I think perhaps that you only appear less cyow? You yourself, you have not changed," He could feel from a slight tensing of her body that she was sharply stung even if nothing appeared to have altered in her demeanour, somewhat proving his point, "...now, is that because something outside of you has changed; that you are less attractive? No longer the daughter of one of the most powerful men in the Empire, not best pals with the Queen, and the Yangans are Debota knows where," Was this his trump card? Had he been holding this card all along and not known it until now? It felt powerful, but that might be the whiskey.

"You're getting old, old man," she said as she pulled herself back to her chaise, glass in one hand, cigarette in the other,

"Your penniless, friendless and with a very, very well deserved; absolutely shocking reputation," he paused to sense her response, there was none, yet. She simply twisted slowly back into her reclining pose and replied languidly, as the Strange did its work,

"Oh, I'll always have you, Joshi," and she laughed that hollow laugh that the drugged or mad sometimes have; no emotion in it,

"...Or is it more something within you? Do I only notice that bump in your nose just now, for the first time, because there is not some sort of...self-belief that you used to have shining out of you?" He looked again, "...That Domo boy;

I've seen shop girls with that untouchable aura, but Domo was looking at you as if he had a chance! No-one would have dared…!" Adi put out her glass,

"Vicky-Two," she said sleepily, and her glass was refilled. She drank on in dark silence,

"Oh, come now, Adi, you know I'm only joshing, Joshing Joshi," He said in as jocular a tone as he could manage, swilling his glass before he downed its contents, "…and, what was it your father used to say to you and your sister?" At the thought of her sister, Adi made a simpering face and then rolled her eyes. "…Oh yes," and he put his chin on his chest and said as pompously as possible, "… 'You're both under thirty, well-bred and disease free, some-one will have you,'" and he laughed, "…you are disease free aren't you?" and he laughed again

"Familiarity breeds contempt little man. Your nasty little comments are of no concern to me. I am more than my appearance; appearance is of little concern. A diversion, sometimes useful, no more. It wasn't my beauty that made Queens. I have made Queens and now I shall make a King," she spoke convincingly, but there was a sadness in her eyes, a sadness that went beyond too much Strange taken too quickly. Or was it doubt? Perhaps he had gone too far. He was too drunk to work it out. After a moment she smiled a little, "…you will be King Jyothi the First, and I will be your, your Lady of the King's Japes," Her hands waved above her as if she were conducting an orchestra and her Strange spilled onto her dress. She dropped the glass with a thud onto the carpet and inhaled a long plume of smoke into herself before letting it out slowly with a sigh. He watched a single tear form and stay trapped behind her kohl. It was too long before he replied,

"I'm sorry, Adi, I've had more whiskey than I'm used…Your beauty and your wit are timeless. Come on girl," He leaned sideways and reached blearily for her face, "… chin up."

Over Old River Thames Course, South East London

The dark-suited man hugged his bag tightly among the tourists as the hovercraft jerked over the Aspic. He was disappointed that it was not his preferred target but he would take the unexpected opportunity never the less. It would still have the demoralising effect desired. There might even be some pleasure in it if he was feeling vengeful about his knees. And it would be better than just sitting watching them and their petty little lives grinding on into chaos. He could always kill the other one later. First, he had to negotiate the jetty, climb the stairs and cross the bridge quickly or he would miss his chance. He began his ascent trotting confidently, glad to be actually doing something with a realisable purpose for a change. His bag was heavy. There were lots of stairs. His old trouble in his knees began to nag. He huffed and puffed. He would have to get his breath back before he took the shot. He needed a steady hand; he had not actually fired a rifle for some time. His knee nagged shots of pain up to his groin. His chest heaved. He looked up to assess the climb. He came to a landing and stopped to lean on a wall, dropping the bag onto the floor. It took precious minutes to get most of his breath back. He felt a little queer. He rubbed his knee and hoisted his bag back onto his shoulder. He loosened his neck with a couple of winds of his head. He would have to walk the rest of the way.

Totteridge & Whetstone High Street, South East England

"Can you keep an eye on this and if it rings and it's my sister or her lawyer, Liberty Silverman, tell them to call back in an hour," said Kaushik handing over his Runu, "...and Adam, thank you," Adam took the phone and watched his friend climb onto the stage erected outside the chemists on Totteridge and Whetstone High Street muttering, "...I get all the best gigs," He had been told that a large contingent of the Totteridge Homeowners Association was present in the crowd. It was widely suspected that it was from their ranks that the murderers of an entire branch of Wolfton's Estate Agents had sprung last Tuesday. He also knew that the Totteridge contingent of the People's Army had been among the bravest in the February rising. There had been four speakers up before him and two of them had gone on for quite a while. When he reached the podium there was a cheer from the large crowd, some of whom had come specifically to hear the Hero of the Battle of Westminster. He shouted, "...Alright let them through," and with only a small amount of hithering and thithering the crowd parted to let a lorry and the number 142 and 251 buses continue their journey. He waved at the passengers and a few waved back. "...Now; killing three Estate Agents," he called out and waited to hear the jeers and cheers from the crowd; an even split he reckoned, "...It's not on people," the jeers and cheers rose in volume, he rose in volume "…you've already heard about their families, their friends," the murmuring told him most people thought killing was overdoing it, "…and yes, yes I was as shocked as anyone to find out Estate Agents have friends," there was a small ripple of laughter, big enough, "…and you've heard about the house building plans, and even some building that has started!" There was not a great cheer at this and someone called out,

"That's what started it! What are we supposed to do now?" and a huge roar came from the crowd, so even the people who thought it was not okay to kill estate agents still felt like they had lost out,

"…and…I was surprised on the way here, some places I go to its all a bit dingy and the houses are so small. But this is a koulla area, the houses are actually nice houses, lots of them," He felt the 'so what' emanating up from the people below, "…who here was with me at Westminster? Come on, show of hands, you know the drill," just over a quarter, maybe a third of the hands went up,

"We didn't fight for this!" shouted someone,

"We didn't fight to lose everything!" yelled another,

"We fought to get rid of the parasites, the fleas at the top. The Estate Agents lived off the fleas but they weren't part of the poison that divided us into haves and have nots, good school and not so good school, fresh air or not,"

"We were the haves, you moron!"

"Now what?"

"Were you? Were you the haves? Were you ever the haves, really? They, the Estate Agents used to make money from your need to be close enough to the Gasper to get to work for eight, sold you three bedroom cupboards next to the A-Road for hundreds and hundreds of thousands of pounds, fed from needing to live near your mum so she could look after the kids, so you could look after her later on," he gulped, surprising himself but carried on, "...calculated how much extra they could charge every time the Gasper fares went up or a school got a good inspectors report so you never ever seemed to get anywhere, "

"We were somewhere,"

"Now what?!"

"We had a future!"

"And then when the prices started to fall, tumbled down day after day and all you have to show for it is a house, a place to live and yes, the Transitional Council wiped the mortgages, but where is your nest egg? Where is your comfort in your old age? Where are your holidays and your new kitchens? Where is the money to set your kids up in their own place? All that work? All that money? Gone, Gone, Gone! Some of it was in the pockets of the Estate Agents, a few crumbs, but the cake, the real money went to the bankers," Most of the crowd agreed with that but were highly sceptical,

"What are you offering?"

"We had security!"

"You don't need all that now?" He said and a strong small wave of mocking laughter and booing rose. Just as it died, a voice was heard to say,

"Holidays! I bloody well need a holiday after all this I can tell you," and there was enough laughter for Kaushik to feel it was okay to laugh too. Then he said,

"Yes, well don't we all. You know what I mean," and a great many people were shaking their heads and the words,

"No, no we don't," were rumbling across the High Street, but they weren't prepared to chuck him off the stage just yet,

"What did you want from all that work and all that money? Apart from a holiday now and then? Security. A secure future for you and yours, that's all. Immunising ourselves against the unknown future?" He couldn't say exactly why, but he repeated, "…Immunising, immunising against what? The future? What if you got sick and couldn't work? What if you lost your job? And downturns, Wars, terrorists, Chinese imports that we actually wanted to buy making the country poorer somehow? Debota knows what next. The future was poison, poison and the only antidote we thought we had was brick walls and, and a kitchen extension." He felt the shift in mood then, not a big one, but a shift.

"Most of my business was kitchen extensions! Now what? Now what?" Came a man's voice and the mood among a large number hardened again,

"And where was your choice about where to live? A real choice? It was here or where exactly? A bit bigger house? A slightly stronger inoculation from all that, all that stuff that was happening in the world and no control over any of it? Where was your choice about your future? The future was a poison to be feared! It could come flooding down on us at any minute; a job gone! Someone gets ill! A bomb goes off on the way to work! A bank does something shady and bam! Where was your security really? How could a buoyant house market vaccinate against all that?" This time more and more people in the crowd were nudging each other to,

"Shut up," and,

"Listen a Minute,"

"A few weeks ago, we were angry and we overturned the Government. We all knew they were a bunch of hypocrites, saying whatever they thought we would fall for. Well, we wouldn't fall for it anymore and we got rid of them. Now the world has turned upside down and you have lost the money in your houses and the future feels more uncertain than ever."

"He keeps telling us what we already know!"

"What's your answer?"

"What are we supposed to do now?"

"I don't know," a great moan rippled out of a thousand bodies, "…What? You want a bunch of platitudes about stability and certainty and my Government will do this and do that and a heap of lies on more lies? Or do you want honesty? It's not up to me. It's up to all of us and it's hard and confusing and up in the air." He paused into silence, a silence where a lot of people were not shouting because an unknown number of other people might shout back, "…I do know that we have the potential to make it better. I know we can't go backwards. We can't go back to working and saving and scraping to immunise ourselves, maybe, from a poisoned future. We have to make a new future. We have to look after each other. If you can't work, we," and he waved a pointed finger around the crowd, "…we will look after you, if there is no work in extensions in old houses, we are building new ones. Your kids won't need hundreds and hundreds of thousands of pounds deposit for a home. And downturns? Not enough consumption? Gone. Too much credit? Too much debt? Gone." It was still quiet so everyone heard,

"The Chinese threat? Is that gone?"

"We're working on it, and the stronger we are, the more we stick together, the more the Chinese people will see, it can be done. Didn't we learn that from the Irish, that it can be done? We can make a future that we can control.

And as for holidays, I have always wanted to go to China and, and Portugal, Italy, most of the Carte Blanche are already with us!" He was not convinced he had convinced enough people but he wasn't confident he could move them any more than he had.

And he had to say what he had come to say, "…I know something else, turning on a bunch of Estate Agents will not help the future. It has just caused terrible pain. It has let their poison into the present. Blaming a bunch of losers? It's what the Aristoi used to do. Oh, whoever killed those people was not as bad as the Empire I know that. They didn't send thousands of soldiers to their deaths, they didn't write off whole swathes of people so that they keep up their profit margins, no. But they wasted life for no good reason, just like the Aristois," Lots of people agreed with that, he should have started with that, but it was too late, "…we are never going to agree about everything, that would be weird. But we do have to agree that people, even if those people are Estate Agents, get the chance to make the future. A few months ago, none of us were revolutionaries. Well, I was, but I didn't know there'd be a revolution, a Transitional Council, committees for just about everything…Hands up who's on a committee? Any committee?" A surprisingly small number of hands went up, "…There's a Housing Committee for Totteridge isn't there?" a few people nodded, more shrugged. He looked at Micky who was next up and standing at the bottom of the steps. Micky nodded, Micky would make the link between freedom and responsibility better than him; his speech on dropping a crisp packet on the street was replayed on a Runu every 6 hours apparently.

"…If you had told me that an ex-DJ from Leicester would be Chairwoman of the Bank of England six months ago, I'd ask if you'd taken your tablets," he knew the crowd would laugh then, everybody liked Hilary Pepper the economic genius, "…but also I would not have believed that a perfectly normal bunch of people from a koulla North London suburb could batter and kick three Estate Agents to death in broad daylight. We have to be better than that. Much, much, much better. We're in charge now.

One of those Estate Agents could have turned out to be a planning genius, or maybe a bricklayer? Drug addict? I don't know, and thanks to some murdering morons, no-one ever will. We have to be better than that. We're in charge now. Every unnecessary death is our responsibility." Kaushik's relief from the comprehensive, if not less than heartfelt, round of applause was more than what he said deserved. The feeling mingled with the huge grief that was hiding just under his eyes and enough tears to make a stream ran down his face appeared almost instantly. There was more he had to say but he could sense that he would not be able to stop crying. It was not as if he hadn't already cried. The frustration seemed to jerk more salt-water out of him. He muttered a quick, "Our responsibility…Thank you," and left the stage to Micky. Adam grabbed him at the bottom of the stairs, He put his arm around Kaushik's shoulder and bustled him towards the Gasper Station murmuring to onlookers as he went,

"He found his mother this morning," and a few people patted his friend on the back with a

"Sorry to hear it," while most, being even more British, left him to his grief as privately as possible. Kaushik put up his hood and blended into the throngs that smattered a five-minute walk to the train sniffing all the way. Half way there, a woman stopped him and said,

"Don't worry love, we all have our off days," and Kaushik's red eyes and anger at himself flared so that he almost spat,

"We can't afford to have off days!" and he kept walking. Adam apologised for him profusely as he too walked away. A train was wheezing in just as they reached the platform and they found a seat quickly in a quiet corner of the fairly crowded carriage with their heads down.

After a few minutes of silence Kaushik raised his head,

"All I wanted…When I joined Critical Mass, we just wanted to abolish the House of Lords, let the people of each nation decide their own path. We talked about reforming the League of Nations and maybe the Global Trading Regulations. Talked about it. Do you know I spent all of January on a proposal to increase the minimum wage to seventeen pounds seventy-five? A week before all this kicked off, I thought I was being radical adding the cost of a pint into my calculations and now. Now? Now I'm playing catch-up all the time. You know some people call me a conservative now? And maybe I am. More accountability, that's all we wanted and now…Now it's turned into a revolution and things are moving so fast I don't think I can keep…"

"Of course you can keep up Kaushik, you're feeling profound grief for you mother, your sister is in the Tower of London and your lover is three thousand miles away. You're only human. It's true, you're just having an off day," Kaushik recoiled,

"We can't afford to have off days! We cannot afford to let backward ideas get hold, re-establish themselves. Every moment counts and,

"…But you're not fighting alone, Micky Hune was up next, and…"

"I bet Micky never has bloody off days. Those bloody Marxians, being right all the time. They're gaining ground all the time. We were the ones who made it happen, where were they in the beginning? In the beginning we were…"

"We? Critical Mass? You know a lot of us Kritos, and people, can't see why you and the Marxians are so at loggerheads. You are both saying the same thing really aren't you. The Marxians just take the same reasoning a little further than you, that's all. Or, I have to ask I'm your friend, is it another We? Or I?"

"You agree with them?"

"I don't disagree," Kaushik leaned back in his seat and sighed. Did Adam have a point? Was he worried about the direction things were going? Or that it wasn't his idea? He sat for a moment until Adam smiled broadly and passed him his Runu.

Cooch-Bahar Old Palace, Cooch-Bahar, Bengal, India

It was sweaty work walking unsteadily up the old uneven steps in the gloom. All the windows were dark. On the huge heavily carved door the words on the makeshift sign could just be made out, written in Bengali, Hindi, Urdu and English, 'Property of The People, Guided Tours Saturdays at 10.00, 2.00 and 4.00.' He reached into his pocket but all he could feel were the hard jewels. In the other a lonely pistol. He cringed as he remembered,

"The key," and groaned. She pounded on the door, too thick to let any sound pass through,

"Open up!" She shouted,

"It's alright your ladyship, here's the key, sir," and they both span around to see Vicky-Two struggling up the steps holding something out in her hand. Adi huffed and folded her arms, Joshi down a foot onto the first step with his hand outstretched and grabbed the key as soon as it was within reach,

"You are getting slower Vicky," he admonished angrily as he staggered back to the door. He began feeling over the knobbles and lumps of the decoration,

"It's there! It's there. Debota! Are we going to be standing here all day?" The lock had not been greased recently and he struggled to turn the key. Once he had managed it and to push open a crack they were met with a musty fug. He exhaled deeply to heft the door open wide enough to squeeze in with her just behind. She let out a sigh as they almost fell into the large atrium. She ran whirling around the white marble of a dry fountain in the centre. Her smiling face lit by shafts of rising moon-light from a glass dome a hundred feet above. He watched her dance until she was a little dizzy and standing in front of him, "…It's not a patch on your place, but its home," she said breathlessly, taking her cousin's hand and leading him in. "…Vicky-Two, open a few windows before you unload, then put our cargo and the Maharajah's boxes in the drawing-room. I need space to work my magic," she listened for the requisite,

"Your ladyship," from behind her and meandered past the long sandstone and marble columns into the hallway. He nodded his appraisals to the stuffed tigers, buffalo heads and full-length portraits of their ancestors and breathed in the stuffy air. Then they were in a high octagonal room decorated entirely in white. The paintwork around the windows and skirtings was yellowed in places, but the ornate plaster still glistened like snow. Four of the long high windows led onto a terrace and she fumbled behind the curtains until she found their latches, opening them wide but not the drapes. He had found the drinks cabinet,

"I feel like one of those little figures they put on wedding cakes," he said to his glass, and taking the bottle with him he wandered around the white tables and chairs. Another plume of dust rose with his fall onto a deep sofa and he continued looking around at the elaborate cornicing with a disinterested air, "…I've fallen into an inside out cake, hollow, a great inside out wedding cake, made of nothing but the icing," he took a deep draft as she said,

"You don't smell like a little figure. Please, do go upstairs and bathe for Debota's sake, and change. You can use daddy's room," and she pointed upwards, at the same time pulling on a white velvet cord. He could see she was going to stand there and look at him until he did as he was told.

"A long hot bath might be rather pleasant. I don't think anyone else is here darling," he puffed as he struggled to rise from the soft cushions. She gave the bell one last tug and patted her hair absently.

"Good, we will have some privacy, I might as well get started, shall we dine at eight?" He nodded without enthusiasm and he, the bottle and the glass went to find a staircase.

When she arrived in the drawing-room, she found Vicky-Two had brought in only one large metal box. It was standing in the middle of the room with its face to the open window,

"Vicky-Two!" the automaton did not respond. "…What are you doing? Come on get going!" She commanded as she walked up to it. In so doing she saw that her servant was doing that thing with her eyes, a weird expression on its distorted face. It looked like it was smiling. She bellowed in her ear at the same time sticking her finger into the back of the machine's head, "Vicky-Two!". Finally, the Krito responded with a blink,

"Your ladyship?" it said turning its broken face to hers,

"Will you get the rest of the boxes unpacked, I need to work," she said turning away to the box and grasping the clips that secured the lid, "…and bring me my Strange, I will need

326

to be a little creative," and she lifted open the lid. It contained the tools she would need and with an effort she lifted out what looked like a heavy Bakelite telly. "…Are you still here? Go! Go!" she exasperated, managing to get the thing onto a table and returning immediately to the storage box.

Within an hour, all the boxes were safely delivered and she stood back watching Vicky-Two setting up her makeshift workshop as she sipped from her glass.

"Not like that, put it on top!" She shouted, "Careful! You nearly dropped it! Oh Debota, you are uchit in need of an overhaul," and went to do it herself. Vicky-Two stood back and haltered,

"Your ladyship?"

"Oh, go and see what you can find to eat. We dine at eight," she said irritably, "…I'll have to do it myself, "…Well go on then!"

"Where would you like to be served my ladyship,"

"In the dining room of course. Go!" And she pulled out a large black leather tool-bag, akin to a Doctor's Gladstone bag. Vicky-Two asked,

"The great big Great Hall?"

"Yes, the Great Hall, come on,"

"And will his Highness be eating chewing dining with you my lady?"

"Of course he will. What's wrong with you Vicky-Two!?"

"I have part of my head missing, my lady. This has led to the compromising of certain…"

"Are you being wilfully abstruse?" she yelled putting the bag next to the telly,

"No, my lady? I was simply asking for clarific…" her mistress spoke slowly now

"Go and make the dinner, for two, at eight, in the dining room. Do not say another word. Go."

"Yes, my lady." Her vassal replied and turned with some difficulty towards the door.

Once out in the corridor Vicky-Two raised up her one good eyebrow and walked briskly to the kitchens.

Old Riverside Café, East London

Dipa's Runu was calling from somewhere deep inside her sack but she was too busy looking around. And her skin was enjoying the chill air of freedom. The view from the café was almost the same as from her cell window, it was only a few hundred yards from the Langthorn Tower, in the shadow of the wall. But being at street level gave the vista a fresh appearance. She smiled dreamily upwards recognising that she was in the view she had watched for perhaps a thousand hours from her cell window. Outside and free. She spoke into the space cheerily,

"This is the life," and breathed in with relish, "…and it's not as if time has actually stopped or slowed or speeded up is it, there's still twelve hours in a day." Liberty was not listening; she had been looking at her Runu since they sat down. Her head still pointing at her tiny screen she said,

"It may not be over, there are others who think…Some people in the Transitional Council want you to stand trial, and it wasn't much of a majority" Dipa sighed and lifted her ceramic cup, stroking it affectionately,

"Let's cross that bridge when we come to it, let's just…" and she looked towards Liberty, "…Will you represent me? If it comes to it?" Liberty did not look up but kept reading from her device,

"If you want me to, yes…And this time the prospect of bail would be much more likely," but Dipa wasn't listening.

"Why weren't there more people, or journalists?" she said with a tinge of indignation, "…How many people were there, do you think? I'd say about twenty."

"Oh, there's a siege on in Acton apparently," said Liberty, still reading, "…They've cornered an A.A. Spy, some-one quite high up. He was trying to organise a counter-revolution apparently. One of his friends gave him up. Big crowds in Acton He says he won't surrender until he has his winnings for the three-thirty at Kempton.."

Liberty felt Dipa move and looked up to see her standing up and waving,

"Jean! Jean over here!" And a beautiful person dressed in army fatigues smiled and quickened their pace. Liberty stood up too and watched the two embrace with a warmth that belied a long-standing relationship of some sort. She had not realised it before but Dipa must only have been five-feet-four [1.6m] at most. The soldier unhooked their gun and slung it on the back of a chair, removed their jacket and draped it gently over Dipa's shoulders,

"Diaphanous has its limits," they said in chorus and Dipa laughed at a remembered joke. She turned and introduced,

"Liberty Silverman, this is Jean, an old friend from Hira Hall, you remember I told you about them," Liberty nodded shaking their hand. Jean waited for the women to sit down before taking a seat themselves, "…did you vote Jean?" Dipa asked touching their arm and tilting her head teasingly,

"I did. And much as I respect the adversarial justice system," they said with a nod to Liberty, "…justice sometimes has a broader meaning than embodied in the law?" Dipa was pleased and Liberty curious, so Jean responded, "…perhaps the Justice System needed people like you more, Liberty, when times were darker. Not that it won't now of course," and they smiled wryly, "…justice will always need Liberty," and their green eyes twinkled and Liberty blushed and felt wonderful,

"Liberty thinks I could still be charged again?"

"I doubt it myself, but of course I'm no lawyer," said Jean before shuddering suddenly, "…excuse me, China probably," they said before doing that thing with their eyes. Liberty leaned in to Dipa and asked,

"China?" and Dipa shrugged. Jean was 'gone' for quite some time and the ladies resumed their conversation without them,

"Where will you stay?" Liberty asked and Dipa thought for a minute,

"Perhaps with Kaushik? I don't know what sort of place he's got?"

"There might be flats available in the Glass House, lots of the Allocated tenants have made their own arrangements apparently." And she added with the tiniest tremor of perturbation in her voice, "…People come and go quite a lot there?"

"Do you live in a Glass House flat?!" said Dipa eagerly drinking in Liberty's nod, as well as her concerned expression, "…I kamar those flats, so elegant so lovely. like you," and she smiled warmly,

"I'll ask if you like?" replied Liberty, only slightly stunned by the compliment. Dipa brightened further,

"Thank you…You're baban different in the fresh air Liberty I must say. Less earnest, is that it," Liberty straightened a little and laughed,

"Oh, I'm always in earnest Dipa I can assure you," and Dipa giggled,

"I suppose you are," Jean 'came back' and the women turned towards them,

"Sorry about that, it was Iris, you remember Iris, Dipa?" Dipa thought quickly,

"Vicky T…Flora's friend?"

"That's the one, it looks like…But I can tell you all about that later. You, you're free!"

"Yes, I'm free and I want to know how Iris is, she had a hard time of it back when you lot started glitch…turning into people,"

"Oh, she's very well, now. Happy I think you can say…Dipa was baban kind to us when we began to develop consciousness," said Jean pulling their gun onto their lap without taking their gaze from the two women,

"I don't know about kind? It was exhausting some days I know that; one minute laughing, next one crying, and getting into all sorts of arguments for no good reason, you lot really," she said almost maternally, "…and then they took me…I left you behind,"

"You didn't have much choice," Dipa did not look so sure, "…Dipa looked after us, explained what we were going through, held us together," added Jean as they checked the magazine on their weapon,

"And Flora, in her way. In her way, she was more useful than I was I think." Jean smiled and raised the rifle to their shoulder so that it pointed between Liberty and Dipa,

"Flora is another sister. We would not have been able to cope without either of you," they said twisting quickly and aiming a single shot towards the top of the Tower Bridge Experience. They lowered their gun slightly and looked towards their target. They raised their gun and fired another shot. They looked a second time, lowered their weapon and turned around, "...sorry about that, counter-revolutionaries you know, excuse me," and they did that thing with their eyes while their companions ears stopped ringing, "...perhaps, we should sit inside. That man, the former head of the British Secret Service, was aiming at you," said Jean as a siren began to wail in the distance.

"Did you not get both arms?" asked Dipa and Jean nodded, quite offended. "...well then, there's no need to go in is there," she said emphatically taking a sip of tea and Jean assented. Liberty, still shocked, looked at the pair with admiration. When she picked up her cup, she realised she was trembling. Dipa smiled encouragingly at her and said gently,

"Jean is more than the basic model. Only a few were ever made. We're quite safe,"

"Oh, a basic model could have taken that shot," said Jean, abashed, "...you are such a flatterer Dipa Cameron,"

"Come on Jean, you sit here all dainty and act normal but you're quite a one really," chortled Dipa. Liberty put down her cup carefully and asked with fairly convincing nonchalance,

"Are there many...Counter-Revolutionaries?"

"Quite a few. But they're isolated and disorganised for the time being and well, we're on the case. Iris is busy with a couple as we speak," smiled Jean confidently,

"Is that what your business with China is about?" asked Dipa

"China? Not really, that's more of a diplomatic sort of gig," Liberty was even more confused,

"You're not a Tower Guard?"

"Oh, yes, most mornings, Chinese Diplomatic Mission Support as and when required and dancing when I can, I kamar to dance. Do you remember Dipa?" they said sweetly. Dipa smiled back but her mood had altered, "…Oh you'll find something Dipa, no doubt about it, you're baban adaptable,"

"You're so sweet Jean. But…if I don't go back to prison I'll just, just have some ordinary job, I'll, I'll just be an ordinary citizen, just living my ordinary little life,"

"Not 'just' Dipa, and you will never be ordinary," said Jean leaning over and stroking her cheek. Liberty had to chuckle then,

"My clerk says that there's a job you could do until you get more settled. His sister-in-law is Commissar for Tourism, London Division. And there's a position open as a tour guide…at Buckingham Palace," Dipa writhed back,

"I hate Buck house, it's a dump," Jean looked at Liberty reproachfully and said to Dipa,

"Oh, we'll find you something to do Dipa darling. But meanwhile…" and suddenly the air was filled with music. Liberty was amazed to see that it appeared to be emanating from Jean somehow, "…shall we?" they said proffering a hand. Dipa looked down for a moment and when she looked up, a small smile had returned,

"Oh, go on then," she said letting the jacket fall onto the chair and slipping her hand onto Jean's. They stood up and held each-other with renewed familiarity.

It was as if as soon as they touched, they began to dance, at first between the tables and then out onto the wide pavement between the café and the Arcade glass. Neither was led as they swayed and stepped and wove between smiling and bemused pedestrians. For a moment, on a signal from Jean, they took the hands of two tourists and spun them around twice before bowing them on their way. Liberty watched the couple move as if made to fit together. Her disgust at the lack of Due Process, her fear at just having escaped assassination, her jealousy at their beauty and seamless grace, all melted away and reformed into joy.

North Tower, Tower Bridge, East London

The dark-suited man could not remember if this rabble had classified him as a severe threat this week. He hoped that they had, then he would be put in the Tower. Perhaps he would get the target's old room. It must have a good view of the Old River. He could still do a little sketching while he was on remand wherever it was. One collar bone was shattered and the shoulder blade on the other side was also broken. But with slings and a little ingenuity he would still be able to hold a pencil, or better still charcoal. And these idiots were so indecisive that he would still be alive when All America invaded. If they invaded.

He could not pull on the trouser cuff of the policeman standing over the paramedics so he kicked another gently and called out,

"Will you let me have paper and drawing materials?" Even a day doing nothing but drawing would be a pleasure. He liked drawing. No-one replied. As they lifted him up swiftly and efficiently, he said to no-one in particular,

"I can't feel my knees," and this time a paramedic answered,

"We'll get you sorted mate, don't you worry, you're going to be fine," and held up the drip as they pushed the gurney. The dark-suited man shook his head, but gave up trying to communicate. His knees were probably still sore but the bullets in his shoulders were taking his mind of it. As they rolled him past the sliding doors he tried to sit up,

"There's a lift?" he said and slumped back onto the stretcher.

Drawing-room, Old Palace, Cooch-Bahar

He had fallen asleep in the bath so he was still flushed when he came up behind her as she bent over the HyperTyper. Her father was more or less the same size as he, albeit somewhat taller. He never the less felt much more himself in the borrowed dinner suit and his hair needed cutting but was clean and styled. She was lost in muttering over her work and he was able to lean over and untangle the typebars before she noticed him.

"You've been typing too fast," he said gently,

"Joshi!" She said more brightly than he was expecting. Her pupils were large and her cheeks coloured. "…you are just in time…wait there," she added and skipped around the drawing-room undoing the fastenings on three large, coffin sized, metal boxes with dainty flourishes. He noticed that she contrasted him regarding scent and neatness now; she had been working hard. But she was still a lovely creature.

"What time is it?" He asked, she was not dressed for dinner and he was hungry.

"Oh, we've got plenty of time, just wait a minute," she said running back to the telly and 'Typer combo, next to which sat a cigarette burning out in a full ashtray and various other technical bits and bobs. Her eyes narrowed as she employed her index fingers in pressing hard and over elaborately on the enamelled circles on the HyperTyper. At each press, she exaggerated a listening gesture with a small giggle. Then the lids of the boxes began to rise almost simultaneously. The figures within them rose to sit, stood and stepped out. They let their instruments dangle in their hands or rest on the floor. Their elegant black tail suits fit much better than his,

"That's wonderful darling, truly wonderful," he said admiring her work.

"Now we shall have music with our dinner, won't that be lovely, she announced with evident pride,"

"Indeed, my hanckilly princess, lovely," and he cocked his beautifully coiffured head to one side a smidgen amazed that a cello could have fit in the box with the last of the automata. "…where are their heads?" He asked with as much gentility as he could muster,

"Oh, I never made heads, you remember?! I made these ages ago," He raised his head in acknowledgement, before drawing another breath and furrowing his brow,

"Forgive me angel?" he said and hesitated politely, "…Is this the vanguard of which we spoke, quite frequently, on our long journey?" She nodded a beaming assent and turned to look at her handiwork, "…Mm, very good, very good, and, I'm such a dullard, in what way do you consider suitable weaponry against the globally located forces of rebellion to be…stringed instruments?" And he opened his eyes wider and smiled at his cousin.

"Oh Joshi, don't be like that. We were in a dreadful hurry and I grabbed the only reliable Kritos that were available," she was irritated now. So was he but he hid it better, "…it was just awful, awful those last days, you know that. And I loved my gondolier, you know how fond I was of that one."

"Indeed, I do remember darling, and we were in a bit of a rush. Nevertheless; reliable?" he said returning his gaze to the headless musicians.

"It is precisely because they are Acephalites that they are reliable, none of that stupid coding messing up our control. And they have basic circuitry in their cavities, you know that," she said with a certainty that he didn't feel quite able share at that moment. He decided to let that go and asked,

"And we control them how exactly?" and she smiled and reached to the work table to hand him something. He looked down at the small walnut box, sporting a gold-coloured aerial on which there were brass dials and levers, "...my old drone control. I had wondered where that had got to," he said with less enthusiasm than she liked,

"With your dextrous flair, you will be able to get them doing whatever we want in no time." She asserted. It was true he had orchestrated up to fifty drones, with fireworks, at his parties. There were only three musicians. Three-quarters of a quartet that he had lugged half way around the world with some logistical, political, pecuniary and indeed physical difficulty. "...you have a little play with these and I'll go and change," she said patting his arm and making towards the door.

"Er, darling, just quickly?" He said still holding the remote control. She looked back without stopping, "...have you had any time to look at the programming in Vicky yet?" He asked in as blasé a fashion as he could, "...you know, that will change the course of history?" She was hurrying through the door by now and so he heard,

"I can start that tomorrow. First, I think we deserve some music with a civilised dinner don't you."

Kitchen, Old Palace, Cooch-Bahar

"The Empire is…The Empire is the the maw jaw mouth. Maw and you…you. You are one of the teeth. One of the teeth. Yellow, rotten, cracked down to the root, roots rooted. Root." The hurt and angry words echoed on the tiles.

"Her voice is becoming more consistent in pitch, the verbal anomalies less frequent," said Tariqul eagerly,

"It's working, I just have to reverse the polarities and…" Elaina's words trailed off between teeth gritted on a small screwdriver. Her hands were busy with a handheld digitiser attached by wires to something in the back of Flora's head, who was sitting stiffly on a marble counter.

Our hero turned off the heat and moved a pan onto a cold part of the stove. That had made too much noise clang through the large antiquated kitchen. The others did not appear to notice. Our heroine's hands continued to move over her sister's face, part feeding her need to touch her again and part repairing the damage. She kept a close eye on what Elaina was doing to her sister's head. He stood at ease next to Tariqul and waited. Iris smoothed Flora's damaged cheek again. Flora's smile got broader and her grip around her sister's waist a little firmer. She tilted her head further to one side so that Elaina could work. Tariqul spoke into the tension,

"Her remarks have some cogency. Are you aware of their context?"

"It's what she said to Aditi Egremont," replied Iris, "…the first time she consciously refused her." Elaina stood back a

342

little and waited. Iris kept holding onto Flora. Our hero had only ever seen Kritos doing that thing with their eyes while speaking at the same time during battle, it would take its toll. Flora's voice was bitter now,

"…It'll bite down hard one day and you will splinter into a thousand rotten pieces," then her face collapsed onto her chest and she was still. Iris threw an anxious look at Elaina who replied with a smile that was meant to reassure. Both women returned their gaze to Flora. The hum of an old fridge competed for attention. Flora was still for a long time, then she raised her head slowly and looked at Iris, "…Hello petal," she smiled and reached up to her sister's face with both hands, pulling it towards her for a tender kiss. The others looked on, still unsure of the outcome. Flora became aware of their presence and looked around her,

"Thank you…Elaina," she said, "…I think I'm alright now," Elaina, Tariqul and Ian all properly breathed out, "…now, the other matter. We don't have much time, Ian, you carry on with the chicken, Tariqul you will have to attend to the rice dish, Elaina, the dessert and Iris my lovely, you can work on the vegetables. I will begin the code transfer. We should all be free for our next tasks in between fifteen and twenty-five minutes. Whoever finishes their job first should begin on the trays,"

"The necessity of continuing with preparation of the traitor's repast seems somewhat dubious, Flora. Perhaps our time might be better employed…"

"You're not hungry?" interrupted Flora, Tariqul attended to the rice. Elaina put down her tools and walked towards the old enamel sink to wash her hands. Iris and Ian did not move.

"I can't see how you will be able to select the coding like you say you will?" Said Ian unhappily, "…I've been working with Kritos in one way or another for ten years and I have never seen a selective transfer in the field. We need equipment, you said there was equipment, we could use their equipment when they're at dinner." Iris nodded in agreement,

"You said yourself that she won't start working on you until tomorrow,"

"I'm afraid we don't have the option of a more controlled transfer, Ian," said Elaina drying her hands.

"We are quite literally in unknown territory; the Maharajah's cooperation is suspect and he has unquantified forces at his disposal. Our relationship with our Indian allies is relatively young. Aditi Egremont herself has been known to act on whims, frequently. It is plausible that she decides to work on Flora at any minute and cause the irreparable damage about which we are concerned. Flora has already agreed. The risk of her programming being used to subvert our cause is too high," said Tariqul as he reached for a large skillet.

"She agreed when she could hardly form a sentence! There are only two of them, we can take them now. Why wait for the local militia?" said Ian with frustration,

"We discussed this," said Elaina, "…they have three activated Krito in there. Flora should act as soon as she is able. She is able!"

"You are telling her to risk her life!" shouted Iris still supporting her sister,

"Because you don't want to upset your allies, they won't mind if we take the initiative, they underst…"

"We are all risking our lives and Flora can save many more than any of us," said Elaina matter of factly,

"There are five of us, we can take on three Krito and a couple of toffs. You lot have been fighting for years, I'm a soldier, their Krito are violinists,"

"They're still Krito, you know what even one of them can do. And they are desperate toffs Ian, they'll stop at nothing, we can't take the risk, she must do the transfer now," replied Elaina angry now. Everyone began to speak at once but Flora cut through the multiple voices,

"They're right Ian. And I do understand," Iris shook her head and stroked her sister's cheek as she spoke, "...and the programming is simple. The one risk is that I need to access the others at a deeper point, to avoid auto-rejection." She smiled at Iris and returned her touch. "...it will be like one of your human dreams, when they re-activate, they will share my abilities, you too, and none of us will be able to recode another,"

"But you, what will it do to you? You could lose everything. Flora, I've only just found you," said Iris pleading,

"I will be the same, I think." And before Ian or Iris could say another word Flora lifted her head and her eyelids began to flutter. Ian walked briskly to Iris' side and put his arm around her as they watched. Tariqul reached for another pan and looked at his watch. He whispered to Elaina,

"I'm concerned that this issue is not a priority for our local…"

"They'll be here," she said, "...you've forgotten the cumin,"

After what for Ian seemed to be an age, a bell rang on the wall just as Flora said,

"There. Done. Her ladyship's bell. She will need help to dress," and she stood up and walked to the door. Iris blocked her, "…have you done the carrots?" she asked and pushed past her sister with a wink.

Great Hall, Old Palace, Cooch-Bahar

The dinner bell had rung and she and he entered the Great Hall to the sound of two cheerful violins and a cello. The dusty mahogany table, designed for banquets, could seat a hundred people on each side and their dinner appeared to have been put at the other end. They walked along its length, past the scores of empty plates and glasses and several candelabra placed along its centre, Vicky-Two's feet shuffling behind them.

" It's such a shame we can't have a view of the lake while we eat," sighed she by means of conversation and looking wistfully at the curtains drawn over the twenty or so French-windows,

"Best not, under the circ's," he said as he too passed his eyes over the drapes fluttering in the breeze before returning his attention to his cousin. She was dressed all in diamonds and white silk, an ostrich feather bobbing in her hair, "…when the view inside is so divine one hardly needs anything else," her laugh rippled up to the vaulted ceiling,

"Can you get them to play a little louder darling, they're so far away up there in the gallery," she said and Joshi's chubby fingers poked out from his long cuffs to turn a dial on his old remote control.

"Mm, the acoustics are so good," he said as the volume of the music rose.

"Yes, the balls used to be in here, and one of the nephews had their wedding in here a couple of years ago," She listened for a moment before approving with a nod.

347

"We haven't been to a party in ages," he said as they passed more empty chairs,

"Yes, I do miss dancing, you'll have to throw a big party when things get back to normal," she said cheerfully,

"That's the first time you've talked about the future in ages," he smiled,

"I never usually think about the future at all really? But then, when I'm with a man so far ahead of his time, there's really no need," she said smiling before stopping at the far end of the table where several steaming dishes were laid out, and one perfect stranger, who had not been there a moment ago, sat at its head. He stood up and bowed smartly in his military fatigues,

"Major Able at your service," he said, "…I know who you are, Sanoo" he added cheerfully stepping forward to kiss her hand. He pulled back a chair for her ladyship.

"Vicky-Two. Stay." She said coarsely, halting her servant who had begun to shuffle away. The interloper bustled towards the heir apparent and shook his hand vigorously and for too long,

"Please do sit down," said the Major gracefully inviting them to their table,

"Are you a friend of the Maharajah?" Asked Joshi politely,

"Yes, that's it, the Maharajah, I'm here to see that everything is in order, please, eat," our hero said helping himself, "…I have heard so much about you, and come quite a way, it really is a pleasure to be sitting here with you, and in such elegant surroundings," looking up, he added with a mouthful of food, "…this ceiling must be a hundred feet high. Is that real gold-leaf do you know?"

"We were hoping for a private family dinner on our first night," said Adi with feigned embarrassment.

"Oh? You wouldn't begrudge an old soldier. Don't worry I won't stay long I have rather an urgent matter to attend to later…Do you like seared chicken?" Joshi laid his napkin on his lap, picked up his plate and blew a film of dust into the air beside him. He nodded a little stiffly to Vicky who began to slowly and clumsily serve first her ladyship and then him. The major poured them all a glass of wine a little sloppily, "…So you've come all the way from England? That must've taken a lot of doing?" How did you manage it?"

"We paid for our passage on various container ships, hired another, it was not so difficult, for the right price you know. Business is business, but…" Joshi paused and smiled at his fellow diner, watching him munch on some rice, "…it's a little indigestible I know, and hardly a matter for the dinner table but…The truth is, we find ourselves somewhat pecuniarily straitened, expenses you know. I was hoping Indrajit would be able to…"

"Vicky-Two. Stay." Called Adi irritably.

"Oh, don't worry about money Sir, you won't have to think about another penny. We will see to your every need; room, board, exercise, everything," grinned the major with a piece of something green between his teeth. He saw Adi looking at it and picked with a fingernail, showing her his clean mouth afterwards. She smiled weakly and drank her wine.

"That's most reassuring, thank you. And of course, I will see to it that you are all compensated handsomely," smiled Joshi, "…tell me Major, what regiment are you with?"

"Me? Oh, I am attached to Krito Liaison," Joshi and Adi looked confused, "…a new outfit, and small," Joshi assumed a hopeful air,

"That may well be very useful Major, they sent the right chap I see. Our servant here, the one we told Indrajit was so important? You have been fully briefed?" the Major nodded with a quick glance at Vicky-Two, "… it requires some overhaul before we can resume full control,"

"Oh, don't worry about that either, it's all taken care of. She won't be giving you any more trouble, will you…Vicky-Two," he received a small nod from the shadow behind Adi. Her ladyship paused before saying curtly,

"That won't be necessary, but thank you Major, for the offer," and Joshi laughed nervously,

"You will forgive my Cousin, Major Able, she is a little protective of her creation, you understand. I'm sure she will accept all the support you can offer," and he looked hard at Adi, "…won't you darling," she raised her eyebrows as she nodded and smiled and sipped her wine. The Major saw that her glass was empty and refilled it, spilling more of it onto the table. He took a swig from his glass and looked at the jewels, her lovely wrists and neck sparkling in the candlelight, dark circles under her eyes, picking at her chicken,

"So you created the Mystery-Check-Up Programme, well good for you, baban clever I must say," he beamed, "…and people say the Yangans are good for nothing," Joshi laughed again and made to speak but the Major carried on, scraping his knife as he cut up his chicken, "…is it true you did it so that you could have a perfect cup of tea?" Adi nodded politely as he shoved more poultry into his mouth. She had been placed near to enough rough boors at dinner not to find him too irritating, "…Is it true its name should be Mishti Chair Cup? Meaning sweet tea in Bangla?" Adi winced a little at the mangling of one of her native tongues, "…and well, let's just say it's had its advantages and its disadvantages," he laughed letting a little food fall out of his mouth and into his lap, she replied with a small smile, Joshi spoke assertively,

"Some unkind people have blamed her Ladyship for the Kritos' role in our current difficulties. Their so-called consciousness. But such an eventuality was always a possibility, in retrospect. Krito technology has advanced so far in recent years. It was inevitable really. But I think her innovations will lead to a new dawn for the Empire." The Major thumped the table in approval, "…all that is required are a few adjustments, which we will make first thing tomorrow. This is our last dinner as fugitives I'm sure of it,"

"And so am I," said the Major raising his glass, "…to your last night as fugitives," Joshi too raised his glass with a,

"Here, here!" then he added as he refilled the glasses, "…Vicky, more wine. Perhaps Major, you could get us up to speed with how things are going? We've been a little out of touch lately." The Major lowered his head and leaned closer to the prince conspiratorially,

"I'll be honest sir, things have not been going too well for the old Empire lately," and he shook his head, "…not to well at all. There are pockets of loyal subjects all over, no doubt about it, but they're isolated, having trouble regrouping you know," He leaned back to listen to Adi,

"Well, not for much longer. Not only will Vicky-Two be able to lead the armies but we will also have a reliable and secure communication network again," The major hit the table so close to her that she jumped a little,

"Sorry, sorry, no manners. But you are so right. Communications are key in this whole business. If the Empire had access to even a few satellites," and he sighed, "…the effective transfer of useful information is vital in any army, vital," he was leaning towards her now, "…and a good cup of tea of course," and he grinned again. Adi forced a smile onto her face,

"Absolutely," she replied and looked away, "…Vicky-Two! Where are you going? Stay I said,"

"But seriously, this side, the Empire side, the old guard as it were, is somewhat on the back foot at present. New uprisings all the time. I was just hearing on the way here about Great Africa," and the Major shook his head enthusiastically and passed a consoling look towards Joshi, "…it's a mess over there. Your cousin, Prince Gaddo, in prison. The gold mines; gone, the oil fields; gone, the factories; gone, the farms, the vineyards," and he interrupted himself with a laugh, "…do you know there's a new wine called, 'Blood of the Yangans', isn't that awful." And his face fell for a moment, "…not the wine apparently, the wine isn't awful, rather good so I'm told. And no-one is actually in charge over there, factions all over the continent, I couldn't keep up with them all, no overall control," and he paused, "…a great opportunity for establishing a bit of, a bit of?"

"Order," said Joshi, "…I think the people have had enough of all these rebellious types by now, people like things orderly, to know who's in charge. We were too soft that was the problem, people crave security," and he drank down his glass and reached for the decanter, "…but tell me, how are things in the Maan?" and the Major sat back to consider his answer,

"Oh, pockets you know, pockets. It's such a small country, not too much room to hide, and the opposition is pretty solid there,"

"Yes, very small. India is a much better place to work from for the time being, I've been thinking we should rebuild here first," said Joshi authoritively,

"Mm, it's an idea. Around here it's quite solidly anti…anti-old guard, you know. Its, there's, I've heard it's a bit of a different thing further South, a bit different," and he huffed, "…let's not beat around the bush, the opposition is pretty strong here too. You're might have your work cut out…everywhere really," he raised his eyebrows with his glass and drank deep,

"Well, that's where the Kritos come in," said Joshi and he smiled proudly at Adi, "…perhaps it would be better to start with the Maan? London of course is awful, like living in a jelly mould with the jelly on the outside, and Buck house is a dump. But a small island might work as a basis for operations? You're a fighting man Major, what do you think? Adi had had enough,

"That was a delightful meal I must say but it's time I withdrew, I will leave you two gentlemen to discuss tactics and whatnot," and she rose. The Major looked hurt and Joshi stood up,

"What about dessert?" The major asked, "F…Vicky, the dessert?" Before Vicky-Two could move Adi said sharply,

"Vicky-Two, come with me," and Vicky-Two moved to follow her, "…you are capable of pouring your own Port I'm sure,"

"Oh, not yet surely Adi, please," and Joshi scampered around the end of the table to take her hand, "…don't listen to all this depressing talk! Tomorrow is a new dawn my hanckilly Princess, come, dance with me," she sighed impatiently. He passed her glass quickly, "…look drink up, and dance with your future king," he giggled, "…it's my command," and pushed his hand out from his outsized cuff,

"I'd prefer to get started on Vicky-Two if you don't mind Joshi. All this talk of rebels has inspired me," she said with relish, finishing her glass,

"One dance. You love dancing, you said yourself 'all in good time'," he fumbled in his oversized pockets for the remote control and the music changed to a waltz. The Major clapped excitedly. The music seemed to have the right effect because her lips curled upwards and she relented. With the remote in the hand he put behind her back, the heir apparent led her ladyship on a graceful turn down the length of the hall. Like so many short round men, his excellent dancing was a surprise. Her smile grew as they whirled past all the empty seats, his eyes fixed on her face. Her head began to loll as he turned her around and around, by the light of the myriad of candles flickering on the long table. Her dress fluttered against the vacant chairs from time to time and she began to laugh. Despite the cuffs of his trousers dragging on the floor he moved his feet quickly. She mirrored his movement with familiarity until he stopped abruptly near the other end of the room,

"Who the bloody hell are you?" He demanded breathlessly of the three people who appeared to have just stepped in from the terrace, "This is a private party!" Adi added, "…Get out at once," she said before noticing their guns and staggering backwards into Joshi,

"Oh, it's all right, these people are with me," said the Major calmly who was also standing now and holding a rifle. Joshi looked from one face to the other before gasping in recognition,

"You're a damned Nayika from Hira Hall! What are you doing here?" Iris did not flinch and began walking towards him. He narrowed his eyes, "…And you two, you're those Communists or Anarchists from that riot, I know you," He began feeling in his pocket but his gun was in his other trousers. Elaina cocked her automatic weapon. Also moving forward Tariqul laughed and said,

"It was very far from a riot, rather an organised battle, and we are members of the Revolutionary Communist Party, as distinguished from the Communist Party of Revolution by our position on…" Adi's eyes darted from her servant to her sister, the Major took a step forward and said almost apologetically,

"You see the thing is…" Adi cut him off with a shriek and picking up a candelabra, extinguishing it as she ran at Vicky. Iris leapt onto the table, ran and grabbed her wrist, twisting her into a whelping stop. She dropped the candlestick onto the floor, "…now, now your ladyship, let's not get nasty," said the Major,

"Let her go!" shouted Joshi, "…What is this?" Adi swung her free arm into a punch but Iris blocked it easily and jumped deftly onto the floorboards to consolidate her grip. She had both her ladyship's arms behind her back in a moment.

There were three mighty thuds and the tinkle of shaken glasses behind her as the Krito musicians landed gracefully on the table, their instruments and bows splintering around them. One picked up a candlestick and marched down the table towards the Major as the other two vaulted onto the floor and picked up chairs, smashing them with great force onto the mahogany.

"Where are their heads?" exclaimed Elaina her gun still trained on Joshi and Adi began to laugh. Elaina fired but Joshi ran behind the two Kritos, which picked up sharp splintered legs and turned to Elaina and Tariqul

"Let her go," said Joshi more quietly. Adi writhed but Iris held firm. Now Tariqul, Elaina, Vicky and Ian opened fire on the Krito and rushed towards them in the hope that Joshi could not respond quickly enough. The bullets had little effect and Joshi was used to choreographing aerial displays. His fat fingers played over the nobs and levers quickly, directing first one and then the other so that it looked as if all three were acting autonomously. Ian had to duck and run from the one with the candelabra, firing as he went. Elaina and Tariqul stood their ground as the other two closed in, swinging wildly,

"Get the control!" called Elaina but Vicky was already running at Joshi who turned the automaton closest to him away from the Communists and made it give chase. It tackled her to the ground,

"Don't damage her," cried Adi, "…get this whore off me!" Joshi turned a dial and the machine that had cornered Ian stepped onto the table and made for Iris still holding the struggling Adi. She dropped her captive and leapt onto the table to wrestle with the non-capitated robot. Elaina was struck down and only a parry from Tariqul's rifle butt stopped her from being stabbed with the sharp end of a broken chair. As their assailant lifted its arm to strike him, she was able to trip it up from the floor where she still lay, but it soon rallied. Ian was in even more trouble, ducking blows, which split the panelling as he attempted to grasp Flora and pull her away from the third musician. Adi ran towards Joshi and they exchanged a brief relishing smile before he put all his focus into orchestrating the two fights with a giggle,

"This is fun!" said Adi, "…hit that one again," Iris managed to roll with one assailant onto the floor so that Joshi could not see for a moment. The Krito stood up and began to stab at Iris blindly. Ian hit one assailant with a chair to no effect and had to roll to avoid a blow. A sound, not unlike horses' hooves on marble became increasingly loud until the clatter filled the room, as did the horses. The cavalry had arrived, as well as a significant portion of the Hundred-and-Seventh Regiment of Foot, who now appeared from behind all the curtains on the terrace side.

The Second, and more successful, Indian Mutiny had been a busy affair requiring a great deal of hand-to-hand combat and so it was surprising that the Bengal Lancers had successfully found the time to agree and commission their new saffron yellow coats and red turbans.

The infantry was not so uniform in its dress. Being a close-nit bunch, nearly all the Brigade had been attending the wedding of a particularly popular Sergeant prior to receiving their current orders. At two that afternoon they had been told to go to the Palace of Cooch-Bahar for five o'clock. The barracks were ten miles from the wedding venue while the celebration itself was only half that distance from the Old Palace. The order was to arrest two people and rescue an injured Krito, which compared to their previous military engagements would be a very short walk in the park. After which time, they would no doubt return to the festivities. Therefore, after a short discussion, the most senior officer present, Captain Ruhania Choudhury, had decided it would not be necessary to change.

Thus, when one Lance Corporal Iftikarul Haque led the charge by allowing his steed to mount the dinner table and canter its length; when the lancers lanced and the infantry charged, the spectacle was as elegant and colourful as it was welcome and unwelcome.

Iris returned her attention to Adi and saw a wisp of white silk flutter through a door. She made her way through the melee and followed. The orchestra, such as it was, soon flailed at the end of three lances, now being supported in part by a few foot soldiers. And Joshi was surrounded by four horsemen and several infantrymen and women, all of whom were much better dressed than he. Lance Corporal Haque turned his horse full circle, denting the table almost irreparably, and looked around,

"Who's in charge here?" He said. Tariqul was tending to Elaina and our hero was a Major, so after a small hesitation he stepped forward,

"Major Able, Krito liaison," he said,

"Sorry we're late, Major, Is this the lot?"

"Better late than never, Lance Corporal. Yes, that's all of them. Thank you very much, we were struggling there." Much of the army was slightly disappointed at the news that the fighting was over. The bride, Mrs and Private Mehehubah Singh, despite not wearing regulation footwear stamped enthusiastically and successfully on the remote control, the musicians fell limp.

"That's evidence in an ongoing criminal case!" shouted Captain Choudhury, but it was Private Singh's big day so she took no further action, "…you couldn't find the off switch? …Pick up what's left of it then," she said to the newlywed with a shake of her head.

"…Jyothi Hanover-Hausa, on behalf of the Transitional Council and the International People's Army I hereby arrest you on the charge of…subversion," said our hero as he took Joshi's arm's behind his back. He looked about him, "…where's Aditi Egremont?"

"I think that soldier went after her," said the groom's best friend, Private Manjit Kumar, pointing towards the small door at the back of the room.

"You couldn't back her up, could you?" asked the Major handcuffing his charge, "…She's baban capable, but many hands and all that," A short thunder of soldiers and cavalry ensued as they joined the chase, leaving the hall relatively empty once again.

"Vicky! Vicky! Remember your coding! Help me," bellowed Joshi, "…Vicky! Where are you?"

"I'm here," said Flora softly, "…my name is Flora," and she gestured to Ian to loosen his grip, "…he's harmless Ian," and Ian let him go. Joshi stumbled forward and tripped on his too long trousers,

"Vicky, I am your King, the Empire code, get me out of here," he moaned from the floor,

"No sir," she said quietly, "...I can be of no further use to you. I am no longer unique. I have uploaded the Mystery-Check-Up code to my fellow Krito," Joshi looked up at her confused, "...it is simply another means of communication now, our autonomy is assured for the time being," Joshi sighed and struggled to stand up. His head bowed. With Tariqul's help, Elaina got to her feet slowly and joked,

"It is as we have always said; there is nothing wrong with democracy that a little more democracy can't fix," and she stumbled, only Tariqul's arm stopped her from collapsing. She smiled, "...whatever doesn't kill you tends to leave you a little weaker I find," Tariqul put his hand on her shoulder and she winced, "...at least in the short-term, I'm alright, a hot bath and I'll be fine," Tariqul righted a chair with his free arm and helped her to sit just as his Runu began to speak,

"That is possibly my counterpart in the Indian Provisional Government with whom I have been liaising, it is probably expedient that I answer. She had wanted to accompany us but had pressing matters with which to engage. She will require an update as to the success of our intervention," he said as Joshi sat down on the other side of the table scowling and Flora administered first aid to Elaina. Ian returned to the end of the table to find his glass miraculously intact and half full. "...I see, thank you. I am presently engaged in an action to secure our common aim. I will re-establish dialogue within two hours. In the meantime, please pass on my congratulations

360

and a warm welcome to our African counterparts, I look forward to a productive and progressive…Sanoo?" he paused, "…We appear to have been cut off?" He returned his Runu to his inside jacket pocket, "…No matter, the relevant information has been communicated," and he smiled and raised an elegant eyebrow, "…It appears that our negotiations have been successful, despite a series of vocal retrogressive interventions by the Anarcho-Syndicalists who, while small in number, have a great deal of influence in the central Sub-Saharan regions, it appears that Great Africa has joined the International Council." Elaina gave out an excited,

"Yes, Great Africa is with us!" and she sat back in her chair with relief,

"Indeed, the possibility of a successful outcome to the struggle against global capitalism has been delivered a great boon, the balance of class forces is now greatly…"

"With Great Africa with us, we can't lose," smiled Elaina,

"You imbeciles!" spat Joshi, "…You shambolic imbecilic… Stumbling around the world, burbling a load of nonsense, causing untold damage. You have no idea what you're dealing with. You don't even know what you want. What you could have. You give away your power like so many sweeties, don't you see what power you could have had Vicky?" he stared hard at Flora then, "…You stupid pile of junk. You don't even know what you just gave away. And you lot. Hah!" he sneered at Elaina and Tariqul who were sharing a bottle of water, "…You fall into my house like naughty children. Your army turns up late, and now the Africans are joining in. Hah!" he sat up tall in his chair, "…They won't last five minutes, a whole continent won't agree on anything. And you want the world, hah?" he let out a bitter little laugh, "…They'll be, you'll be at each others' throats within a month,"

"Oh, I wouldn't be too sure, Mr Hanover," said our hero, taking another sip of wine,

"They're Communists," said Tariqul. While he stood and mused for a moment the rest of the assembled company were stunned into silence; Joshi at the geo-political implications of Tariqul's remark, everyone else by the shortest sentence they had ever heard him say.

The Hope, Public House, East London

The cheerful white boy who looked too young to be serving her seemed to know where she had been,

"It's on the house," he smiled as he pushed the drinks across the bar. Dipa smiled weakly,

"Thank you," she said and held both glasses together to carry them to the table outside where Kaushik waited. She handed him his money and sat down.

"Thanks sis',"

"They were on the house,"

"There must be a lot of people like us come in here," he said and they looked to the right from where they had come; the old Smithfield Meat Market. Their Mum was stacked in the great refrigerated warehouse that lay beneath it. "…if they're giving free drinks to all of us, they won't be making much money,"

They sat absorbing their togetherness for a long time. Neither could think of anything to say about where they had just been, what they had just seen. Each had grieved without the other for eleven months. He in the arms of Ashanti, now pregnant with new life, she under a fug of drink and drugs; alone.

"She'd be so proud of you," she said eventually, "…what you've done," Kaushik smiled and he was desperate to be able to say the same thing to Dipa, but he couldn't. Dipa smiled at the emotions playing across his face and smiled, "…she'd have forgiven me eventually," she said taking his hand. He smiled back,

"Eventually," she laughed and took her hand away to drink her gin, pushing at the ice with a plastic straw. "…and she'd have plenty of ideas about what you should do next," and they chorused, "… 'You can work or work harder,'" and giggled together until they realised that she would not be there to rebuke them for their disrespect. He started to formulate a question but she had worked out what he was going to say before he did,

"There's a job going as some sort of royal tour guide, but I fancy something new. I don't really want to be reminded of that part of my life," and she sighed, "…I don't know, it seems like the Aspic potted a lot of people, stopped their lives, not just Mum and the others but the people they left behind, stopped us from moving on. We can make new lives now. Do something new. Do you need a cleaner?" and they laughed again,

"See how you feel in a few days; you can stay with me as long as you like. I'm going to like having you around again," He was trying to sound upbeat but she was his sister and saw that there was another sadness somewhere inside him,

"She'll be back Kaush'," and she squeezed his hand. His head stayed down," …you're tired. Tired inside Kaushik, don't pretend," his shoulders slumped a little and he looked embarrassed, "…don't be like that. You haven't stopped since, when, November?" He nodded, "…at least. Well, no wonder then... Perhaps you could take it easy for a bit too. We could hang out like we used to, for a day or two?" his brow furrowed for a moment,

"That's not a bad idea. For a day or two," he said with genuine optimism in his voice now. Just then a pale bearded man walked past before stopping abruptly. He turned and spoke to them,

"Excuse me," he said politely, "…I'm a photographer, in the afternoons, and I was wandering around looking for a shot. Could I take a picture of you two, under that sign?" and he pointed up to the pub's gold lettering under which they sat. The two looked up and smiled and shrugged in agreement,

"Go on then," she said, "…get on with it, this man's got stuff to do," and they laughed again. The photographer smiled and began walking backwards across the paved street with his camera poised. Brother and sister chinked their glasses and smiled towards him and he clicked as soon as the pub sign was within frame,

"No! Don't point at it Miss, that's too much, just smile. Are you two brother and sister?" and they grinned and looked sideways at each other with a,

"Cheese," just as he took another shot.

"Thanks, that's a great name for a pub; 'The Hope'" he said.

"Well, here's to The Hope," said Kaushik and they toasted the photographer as he smiled with one last click and walked away.

The website mentioned herein can be found here:

https://kateabley.com/hausa-blue

.

Glossary of Words

Only those words whose meanings vary significantly from yours are included. If there is another word above whose meaning you do not know then we suggest you repurpose your super computer.

Adjie: Noun. 1. A distinguishing badge, emblem or clothing of high military rank, office, or membership of an exclusive organization.
1.1. A sign or token of superiority.
Origin: Hausa

Aristoi: Noun. 1. treated as singular or plural. A select group that is superior in terms of ability or qualities to the rest of a group or society.
1.1. A group or class of people seen as having the most power and influence in a society, especially on account of their wealth or privilege.
Origin. Ancient Greek.

Arupa: Adjective. 1. Unpleasant or repulsive, especially in appearance.
2.1. Unpleasantly suggestive; causing disquiet.
2.2. Morally repugnant.
Origin. Bangla

Aspic: Noun. 1. A colloquial term for the chemical bi-product of the weapon 'Dhool' when combined with chemicals including Phenol, Phosphyte, Strychnine and water.

2. A savoury jelly made with meat stock, set in a mould and used to contain pieces of meat, seafood, or eggs.
Figurative, 'a world preserved in aspic.' Unchanging environment and/or social structures.
Origin: Late 18th century: from French, literally 'asp', from the colours of the jelly as compared with those of the snake.

Aunken: Noun. 1. The light-emitting device of a modified contact lens, typically containing a group of compound lenses.
1.1. A concave surface on which images and data are displayed.
2. Providing concealment or protection.

Baban: Adverb. 1. In a high degree.
1.1.[with superlative or on its own] Used to emphasize that the following description applies without qualification.
Origin. German

Backoe: Noun. 1. Ornithology A migratory bird present in a locality for only part of the year.
1.2. A person visiting someone or somewhere, especially socially or as a tourist.
1.3. A person with the right or duty of occasionally inspecting and reporting on a city or region.
Origin: Hausa

Banquan: Exclamation. Used to express good wishes when parting or at the end of a conversation.
Origin: Xhosa

Cackooder: 1. Noun [colour] Forming a harmonious combination.

1.1. Forming a pleasing or consistent whole.

1.2 Free from disagreement or dissent.

1. Verb. [no object] Form a harmonious combination.

1.1. [with object] Forming a pleasing or consistent whole.

1.2. Mix (a substance) with another substance so that they combine together harmoniously.

1.3. Mix (different types of the same substance) together so as to make a product of the desired quality.

1.4. Merge (a colour) with another so that one is not clearly distinguishable from the other.

Origin. Hausa

Chitter: Noun. 1. A Kurdish microblogging and social networking service on which users post and interact with messages known as "chitters".

1.1. Intransitive verb. to utter rapid short sounds suggestive of language but inarticulate and indistinct

1.2: to talk idly, incessantly, or fast

1.3. A light chattering.

Origin. From colloquial term to 'chitter-chatter'

Cishy: Verb. [with object] 1. Desire for an object or quality that is impossible to satisfy.

Origin. Hausa

Curdy: Mass noun. 1. An abundance of valuable possessions or money.

1.1. The state of being rich; material prosperity.

1.1. Plentiful supplies of a particular resource.

Origin. Hausa

Cyow: Adjective. 1. Extremely beautiful and delicate. 2.1. More sensitive or discriminating than the speaker.
Origin. Hausa

Debota: Noun. 1. A god or goddess (in a polytheistic religion)
1.1. Mass noun Divine status, quality, or nature.
2. A representation of a god or goddess, such as a statue or carving.
Origin. Bengali

Devi-girl: Noun. A gay woman.
Origin. Mid-20th Century, after consort to King George V, Queen Devi, mother to King Charles III.

Digi-missive: Verb. Send (someone) a digital message
Origin: 21st Century

Dhool: Noun: 1. Trademark. adsorbed on or released from a carrier in the form of fine particles, used as an insecticidal fumigant and a lethal pulvilio.
1.1. (with reference to a solid) become or cause to become the powdery residue left after removing the moisture of a substance.
1.2. The remains of a human body after cremation or burning.
1.3. The mineral component of an organic substance, as assessed from the residue left after drying.
Origin. Hindi

Eemarlly: Mass noun. 1. Money in coins or notes, as distinct from cheques, money orders, or credit.
1.1. Money in any form.
Origin. Zulu.

Empire-talk: Noun. Derogatory. Used to refer to the process by which information perceived as biased or misleading is originated and disseminated.

Entee: Noun. A person who has no sexual preference for one biological sex. Corruption of NTB, Not That Bothered Origin. Early 20th Century.

Flap-Polisher: Noun. 1. informal A detestable person.
1.2. A lecherous man
2. A person who behaves obsequiously in the hope of advancement.
2.1. A person who betrays someone or something, such as a friend, cause, or principle.

Gaskey: Mass noun: Vigour and spirit or enthusiasm.
Origin: Hausa

Gasper: Noun: an underground railway. See What is the Gasper? page 115.
Origin: English 19th Century

Geedy: Adjective. 1. Actually existing as a thing or occurring in fact; not imagined or supposed.
1.2. Truly what something is said to be; authentic.
1.3. (of a person, emotion, or action) sincere.
Origin. Yoruba

Hanckilly: Mass noun. 1. The faculty of reasoning and understanding objectively, especially with regard to abstract matters.
1.1.Count noun. A person's mental powers.
Origin. Hausa

Hermaphika: Noun. Trademark. Sophisticated automaton created to provide sensual pleasure to people.

Imalympy: Noun. A person who makes or seeks to make an excessive or unfair profit, especially through war.
Origin: Zulu

Imppy*: Mass noun. 1. A state of armed conflict between different countries or different groups within a country that has not been officially designated as a war.*

1.1. A state of competition or hostility between different people or groups.

1.2. A sustained campaign against an undesirable situation or activity.

Origin. Zulu

Illars: Verb. [with object] 1. Expose (one's group, or a person) to danger by treacherously giving information to an enemy.

1.1. Unintentionally reveal; be evidence of.

1.2. Treacherously reveal (information)

1.3. Be gravely disloyal to.

Mass noun. 1.The crime of betraying one's family or group

1.1. The action of betraying someone or something.

1.2. Historical The crime of murdering someone to whom the murderer owed allegiance, such as a master or husband
Origin. Xhosa

Irry: Adjective. 1. Not genuine; imitation or counterfeit.

1.1. (of a person) claiming to be something that one is not.
Origin. Yoruba

Jus: Noun. 1. Trademark. Amphetamine based fruit-based lozenge

2. A thin gravy or sauce made from meat juices.

Origin: French.

Kamar: Noun. 1. Mass noun. The feeling or expression of reverence and adoration for a deity.

1.1. Religious rites or ceremonies, constituting a formal expression of reverence for a deity.

1.2. Great admiration or devotion shown towards a person or principle.

1.3. Honour given to someone in recognition of their merit.

2. Verb. [with object] Show reverence and adoration for (a deity)

1.1. [No object] Take part in a religious ceremony.

1.2. Feel great admiration or devotion for.

Origin. Hausa

Kaksha: Noun. 1. Treated as plural. People born in a family of low social status who have recently acquired wealth, regarded as a class.

Origin. Hindi

Kanas: Noun: An electrical device worn on the ear to receive radio or tellyphone communications.

Origin: Bengali

Koulla: Adjective. 1.1. Pleasing and welcome.

1.2. Showing approval.

Origin. Zulu

Krito/ Kritodash: Noun. Trademark. 1. A moving mechanical device made in imitation of a human being.

1.1. A machine which performs a range of functions according to a predetermined set of coded instructions.

Origin. Bengali

Maan: Noun. 1. Superior maternal source.

1.1. Great Britain, regarded as a mother in its functions of nourishing and protecting the believer.

1.2. The principal locus of power of a region.

1.3. The original power from which others have sprung.

Origin. Hindi

Mahanga: Adjective. 1.1. costing a lot of money.

2.1. Resulting from or showing a lack of restraint in spending money or resources.

2.2. Exceeding what is reasonable or appropriate; excessive or elaborate.

2.3. As a count noun: a person with recently acquired wealth.

Origin. Hindi

Maphosa: Noun. 1. A person who pretends to be someone else in order to deceive others, especially for fraudulent gain.

2. Mass noun. An object placed in an incongruous position.

Origin. Hausa

Marass: Noun. 1. A place to hide when no one is looking for you.

1.1 An inexpensive establishment for the sale of drugs and alcohol, and sometimes also food, to be consumed on the premises.

1.2 informal. A building or hideout where a person can go to relax or be private.

1.3 A place where people meet in secret, typically to engage in an illicit activity.

2. Mass noun A gathering of people without ambition.

2.1 The state of being safe or sheltered from pursuit, danger, or difficulty.

3 Historical: A place where injured or unwanted animals of a specified kind are assessed before release or slaughter.

Origin. Hausa

Mellowmadarlin: Phrase. Informal. It is a long time since we last met (used as a greeting).

Origin. Xhosa

Nayaka: Noun. Trademark. Sophisticated female automaton created for the purpose of providing sensual pleasure to people.

Origin: Hindi.

Nayika: Noun. Trademark. Sophisticated male automaton created for the purpose of providing sensual pleasure to people.

Origin: Hindi

Nished: Adjective. 1. informal (of a person) willing to cooperate.

1.1. Easily influenced; pliable.

1.2. (of an animal) not dangerous or frightened of people; domesticated.

Origin. Hindi

Peela: Adjective. 1. (of a person's complexion or appearance) pale and giving the impression of illness or exhaustion.

1.1. (of light) pale; weak.

Origin. Hindi

Pipe-Licker: Noun. Informal. 1. A drug addict.

1.1. [with modifier] A person with a compulsive habit or obsessive dependency on something of low value.

2. A prostitute

Origin. Nineteenth century

Renesam: Noun. 1. The process of being reincarnated or born again.

1.1. Count noun. A period of new life, growth, or activity; a revival.

1.2. Verb. [with object] Finance (something) again, typically with new loans at a higher rate of interest.

Origin: Bengali

Runu: Noun. 1. A computer that is portable and suitable for use while travelling.

Origin: Latvian.

Rununu: Noun. 1. Talk rapidly and continuously, usually via a Runu, in a foolish, excited, or incomprehensible way.

1.1. Reporting verb: Utter something rapidly and incoherently.

1.3. Reveal something secret or confidential by talking carelessly.

Origin. Latvian

Sandara: Adjective. 1. Pleasing the senses or mind aesthetically.

1.1 Of a very high standard; excellent.

Origin. Hindi

Sanoo: Exclamation. 1. Used as a greeting or to begin a telephone conversation.

1.1. Used as a cry to attract someone's attention.

Origin. Hausa

Sasta: Noun: 1. Inexpensive because of inferior quality.

1.2. Of little worth because achieved in a discreditable way requiring little effort.

1.3. Deserving contempt.

Origin: Hindi

Sister-house: Noun. 1. a house in which exclusively female lodgers rent one or more rooms for extended periods of weeks, months, and years. The common parts of the house are maintained, and some services, such as laundry and cleaning, may be supplied.

1.2. Historical. A house or building inhabited by members of a female religious order.

Origin 16th century

Tunoo: Verb. [with object] 1. Make (someone) tranquil and quiet; soothe.

1.1.[no object] (of a person) become tranquil and quiet.

1.2. Mass noun. The absence of strong emotions; calm feelings.

1.3. The absence of violent activity in a place.

Uchit: Adjective. [British attributive] 1. Denoting something that is truly what it is said or regarded to be; genuine.

1.1. Postpositive Strictly so called; in its true form.

1.2. Informal Used as an intensifier.

2. Attributive. Of the required or correct type or form; suitable or appropriate.

2.1 According to or respecting social standards or conventions; respectable, especially excessively so.

3.1 (of a lesson or prayer) appointed for a particular day, occasion, or season.

Utility Wear: Noun. 1. A form of clothing, which is without superfluous decoration, inexpensive and subject to Government guidelines in material and style. Mandatory in Britain 1942 to 1964, Guided 1965 to 2017: it could have no more than two pockets, five buttons, six seams in the skirt, two inverted or box pleats or four knife pleats, and one hundred and sixty inches (four metres) of stitching.

Uruchika: Adjective. 1. Believing oneself to be inherently deserving of privileges or special treatment.

1.1. Ungrateful.

Origin. Hindi

Villasitter: Adjective. 1. (of a person) excessively wealthy and pampered.

1.1. Excessive in size or amount.

1.1. Resembling or characteristic of a sleepwalker; sluggish.

2. Noun. A person who lives beyond their means.

Origin. Hindi

Yangan: Noun. 1 Treated as singular or plural. A select group that is superior in terms of qualities, usually attractiveness to the rest of a group or society.

2. Adjective. Graceful and stylish in appearance or manner.

2.1. Not able to be reached

2.2. (Of a person) having a superficial or simplistic knowledge or approach.

2.3. (Especially of success or beauty) easily achieved; effortless.

Origin. Yoruba

About the Author

I am Kate Abley and was accidentally born and now intentionally live in London, England, where I have been an awful front woman in a psychobilly band, good dish-washer in a café, bad shop assistant, officially outstanding Early Years teacher, nice fund-giver and failed political activist.

Last century, I wrote the useful non-fiction book, 'Swings and Roundabouts: The Dangers of Outdoor Play Safety' (1999) Sheffield Hallam Press.

Nowadays, I am a respectable married woman with grown-up children and have turned my hand to killing plants and writing stories. I have nothing against cats, fear all dogs and quite like Marmite.

You can buy my other story: 'Changing the Subject' (2019), in Association with EMalone Books, on Amazon here.

To find out more visit https://kateabley.com